WINTER
OF THE
GODS

In her pack, she carried a golden bow forged by Hephaestus himself and a quiver of arrows sharp enough to kill. This was what she was born to do. *Peace on earth and goodwill toward men be damned,* she thought. As long as the Huntress roamed the streets of Manhattan, there'd be no peace for the wicked... and nothing but justice for the men stupid enough to get in her way.

By Jordanna Max Brodsky

Olympus Bound

The Immortals
Winter of the Gods

WINTER
OF THE
GODS

OLYMPUS BOUND: BOOK 2

JORDANNA MAX BRODSKY

www.orbitbooks.net

ORBIT

First published in Great Britain in 2017 by Orbit

1 3 5 7 9 10 8 6 4 2

Copyright © 2017 by Jordanna Max Brodsky

Illustration copyright © 2017 by Kirk Benshoff

Excerpt from *Chasing Embers* by James Bennett
Copyright © 2016 by James Bennett

The moral right of the author has been asserted.

A CIP catalogue record for this book
is available from the British Library.

ISBN 978-0-356-50727-9

Printed and bound in Great Britain by
Clays Ltd, St Ives plx

Papers used by Orbit are from well-managed forests
and other responsible sources.

MIX
Paper from
responsible sources
FSC
www.fsc.org   FSC® C104740

Orbit
An imprint of
Little, Brown Book Group
Carmelite House
50 Victoria Embankment
London EC4Y 0DZ

An Hachette UK Company
www.hachette.co.uk

www.orbitbooks.net

To Helen, my nine Muses in one

CONTENTS

THE GODS' FAMILY TREE

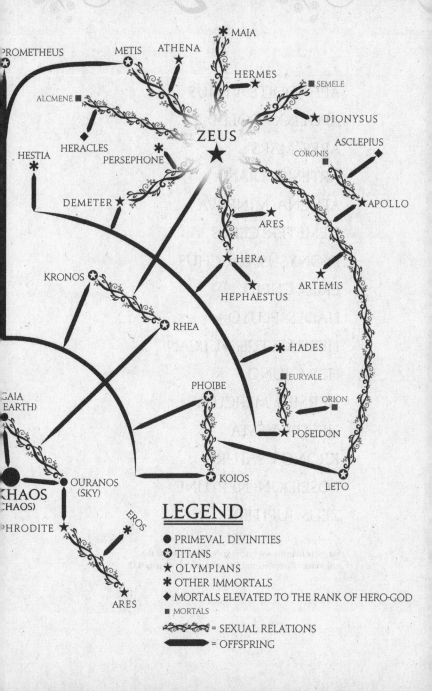

PROMETHEUS

METIS   ATHENA   MAIA

HERMES

ALCMENE   SEMELE

HERACLES   DIONYSUS

ASCLEPIUS

HESTIA   PERSEPHONE   CORONIS

ZEUS

APOLLO

DEMETER

ARES

HERA   ARTEMIS

KRONOS   HEPHAESTUS

RHEA

HADES

EURYALE

PHOIBE   ORION

GAIA (EARTH)

POSEIDON

KOIOS   LETO

KHAOS (CHAOS)

OURANOS (SKY)

APHRODITE   EROS

ARES

LEGEND

- ● PRIMEVAL DIVINITIES
- ✪ TITANS
- ★ OLYMPIANS
- ✳ OTHER IMMORTALS
- ◆ MORTALS ELEVATED TO THE RANK OF HERO-GOD
- ■ MORTALS

🌿🌿🌿 = SEXUAL RELATIONS

▬▬▬ = OFFSPRING

THE GODS' ROMAN NAMES

APHRODITE: VENUS

APOLLO: APOLLO

ARES: MARS

ARTEMIS: DIANA

ATHENA: MINERVA

DEMETER: CERES

DIONYSUS: BACCHUS

EROS: CUPID

HADES: PLUTO

HEPHAESTUS: VULCAN

HERA: JUNO

HERMES: MERCURY

HESTIA: VESTA

KRONOS: SATURN

POSEIDON: NEPTUNE

ZEUS: JUPITER

For more information on the gods, please consult the
Appendix: Olympians and Other Immortals on page 457.

And how many times, goddess,
did you test your bow?
    First at an elm
    Next you shot an oak
    And third some wild beast.

And fourth you shot not into a tree
but a city of unjust men, who betray
their guests and themselves with
many wicked deeds. On them
you press your fearsome wrath.

Callimachus, Hymn to Artemis,
CIRCA THIRD CENTURY BC

Chapter 1

THE FESTIVE MAIDEN

The Salvation Army Santa Claus narrowly escaped having his bell ripped from his hands and shoved down his throat. Lucky for him, the six-foot-tall, silver-eyed former goddess hoofing it down Broadway had recently decided to limit her less socially acceptable behaviors. But if the street had been a little less crowded and the streetlights a little less bright, Selene DiSilva might have made Christmas in New York just a little less annoying.

To avoid the jarring tinkle of Yuletide charity, she hopped lightly over an icy, pee-stained snowdrift and jaywalked across the street. But she couldn't escape the signs of the season. At the end of the block, a Christmas tree stand hogged the sidewalk, its wares bedecked with colored lights. She peered up from beneath the brim of her WNBA New York Liberty cap at the giant inflated angel wobbling atop the sales shed.

Tempting target, she mused, thinking of the bow and arrows in her backpack. *And much less morally abhorrent than taking out the Salvation Army guy.* She glanced up and down the street, then sighed. No way could she get away with it. Already the tree seller had taken note of her, blinking eagerly though the thin gap between his wool ski cap and striped scarf.

"Only eighty dollars for a ten-footer," he offered, his cheer apparent even through the muffling effects of his outerwear.

She should've ignored him, but the smell of cut pine assaulted her senses and demanded an answer.

"Only eighty dollars?" she marveled, stepping closer to bring all her superior height to bear. "What a bargain! I would've thought you'd charge a lot more for destroying our forests."

"It's a tree farm—" he began diffidently, but she cut him off.

"All these trees, cut down in their prime, and why? So rich New Yorkers can prop them up in a can of water, drape them with tinsel like some beribboned whore, then watch them lose their needles like mange until they toss them on the sidewalk, one more addition to the garbage heaps in the world. All to celebrate the supposed birthday of their supposed savior, but really just to wallow in a yearly tradition of gluttonous consumerism."

"The city chips them for mulch," the tree seller protested weakly, but Selene stopped listening as she headed off down the street. She heard only the outraged monologue that ran through her mind in an endless loop from sometime in late October to January second. Normally, she kept such ranting internal, but her recent association with a certain garrulous classics professor had taught her the cathartic effects of occasionally letting loose.

She turned down West Eighty-eighth Street, muttering angrily to herself about the gaudy twinkle lights her neighbors had strung across their brownstones. The building next door to hers had gone all out this year. Three-foot-long blue and white plastic icicles hung from every windowsill. Twinkling, flashing, *neon* icicles. As if Times Square had picked up its lurid horrors, dragged them forty blocks uptown, and plunked them down next door out of sheer pique.

Her own house remained blessedly barren. A narrow facade, half as wide as the others on the block, reaching up four stories. Only a single dim bulb illuminated the wrought iron grate shielding her front door. The building looked dark, uninviting, a little rundown. Just how she liked it.

She bounded up her stoop two stairs at a time, reaching into the pocket of her leather jacket for her keys.

"Selene!"

She froze and looked up.

Theodore Schultz, distinguished Columbia University professor of Ancient Greek and Latin and the cause of her recent loquacity, hung his head off the edge of her roof, his glasses slipping down his nose. A string of colored lights dangled from one hand while he waved eagerly to her with the other.

"Look what I found in your attic!"

Moments later, Selene had burst into her house, galloped up the stairwell, and launched herself through the trap door to the roof, moving just a little faster than any woman had a right to move. "You put a single one of those bulbs on my house and I'll strangle you with the whole damn cord."

Still lying prone on the snow, Theo rolled over and raised an eyebrow. "If you hate Christmas lights so much, why do you have them in your house?"

She thought about lying but decided she'd save the deception for the *really* bad things in her past. "I used them to strangle a pedophilic priest on Christmas morning in 1969."

Theo dropped the lights with a grimace. "And you *kept* the murder weapon?"

"Figured it might come in handy next time I needed to do some seasonal killing. Makes a statement."

Theo got to his feet and brushed the snow off the knees of his corduroys. "I'm assuming you don't mean a 'peace on earth and goodwill toward men' sort of statement."

"More like a 'screw this stupid holiday' and 'all men are assholes' statement."

"Ouch," he said mildly, coiling the string of lights with a

regretful sigh. "Why do I feel like the city gets jollier and you get crankier in direct proportion?"

"Cranky?"

"Poor choice of words. How about 'wrathful'? Is that more in keeping with your dignity?"

She glowered at his teasing grin but let him lead her to the western side of the roof.

They sat with their legs dangling over the edge. From here, she could see past the other houses on her block and the treetops in Riverside Park, all the way to the Hudson River. It glinted silver in the moonlight, while the illuminated windows of New Jersey formed yet another string of Christmas lights on the far shore. A bitterly cold night, but at least, for the first time in days, it wasn't snowing. Theo's arm felt warm as it snaked around her waist and tucked her close. She wanted to melt into his embrace and punch him all at the same time.

If my grandmother Phoibe, Goddess of the Night, could still look down from the moon, she'd be sick to her stomach, Selene thought. *Artemis, Goddess of the Wild, Protector of Virgins, the famous loner and misanthrope, snuggling in the arms of an extroverted mortal classicist who didn't even know I was real until three months ago.* Once, the thought would have sent her into spirals of self-doubt. But she'd learned to stop worrying about her relationship and just enjoy it. Mostly.

"You want to tell me what's going on?" Theo asked after a moment. "I've never seen you quite so angry for so little reason. Usually there's a woman being murdered or a god being dishonored or maybe a dog refusing to obey...but twinkle lights? They used to call you the Festive Maiden, remember? What happened?"

For their first weeks together, she'd simply ignored his demands of emotional openness. But Theo could be as relentless as the Relentless One herself. Better to just tell him.

"Everything about this loathsome holiday makes me mad.

The waste. The materialism. The false cheer. Worst of all, the Jesus carols, each one a little prayer offered up to the god who displaced us. They're like tiny knives in my brain, slicing out my sanity. The closer we get to Christmas, the more I want to throttle everyone around me. It's like my own little advent calendar from hell."

He laughed and refused to stop despite her angry scowl. " 'You're a mean one, Mr. Grinch,' " he started singing off-key.

"That string of lights is right over there," she threatened. "And you know I don't like pop culture references I barely understand."

"Fine," he said with a grin. "You're nothing like the Grinch. He mends his ways at the end of the movie. You're much too stubborn for that."

"Thanks."

"But at least admit that part of your Scrooge-iocity comes from the fact that everyone else in the city is spending the holidays with friends and family, while you've always spent them alone."

"I *like* being alone. In fact, I'm starting to regret giving you a key. Do you realize you've been singing nonstop for the past two weeks? Even though I specifically told you I hate Christmas carols?" He'd avoided the most religiously offensive of them, but still. Even "Jingle Bells" rubbed her the wrong way.

Theo ignored her. "How about we have people over for the holidays? We can call it a Saturnalia party. Invite your twin, maybe a few half siblings, some friends of mine."

She stared at him. "Can you see your friend Gabriela making small talk with *Dash*?"

"Yeah, actually, Gabi would love Hermes. She likes fast-talkers and has no respect for the law. The God of Liars and Thieves is exactly her type."

"Well, forget it. It's bad enough *you* know about the Athana-toi. You start having everyone over for cocktails, and your friends are bound to wonder who all your super-tall, super-attractive, suspiciously talented new acquaintances are."

"They'd never imagine the truth. Athanatoi? 'Those Who Do Not Die'? Hah! What self-respecting thanatos would believe they existed? And I'd never tell. I can be very discreet."

She snorted.

"What?" he protested. "*You're* the one whose emotions are written all over your face. Like right now. I call this one 'Disdainful Incredulity.'"

"Exactly. Because you can't keep your mouth shut, and you know it."

"I just don't see what the big deal is."

"Besides the fact that you're one of the few mortals in the world who knows that large portions of the ancient Greek pantheon are alive and well and living in Manhattan? And that if word got out to the rest of the world, we'd either be put in an insane asylum or locked in a secret lab?"

He rolled his eyes. "Hyperbole much? *I'm* the one they'd lock up as a crazy person for believing in Greek gods in the first place. But all right, maybe we don't invite my friends. How about an intimate dinner gathering for your immediate family instead? We could work on your whole 'antisocial and estranged' problem."

"I went to Paul's *concert* last month, didn't I?" she demanded. She and her twin brother Apollo, God of Music and Light, currently known as indie rocker Paul Solson, had been on the outs for millennia until they'd joined forces three months earlier to take down a homicidal cult terrorizing Manhattan. When their mother died that same week, the twins had begun a cautious reconciliation. Theo'd insisted Paul's music was quite good; Selene stood in the crush of sweaty bodies with her hands over her ears and her eyes closed until the torture ceased. It'd been a week before her head stopped ringing.

"Besides your twin," Theo pressed. "I thought you were turning over a new leaf, remember? But you haven't had anything to do with Hermes or Dionysus or Hephaestus since they showed up in September to help fight the cult."

She twisted to look Theo square in the eye. He glanced away, but not before she caught a flash of guilt. She poked him hard on the arm. "Gotcha."

"What?" He was all innocence.

"You just want me to reunite with my family because *you're* curious about the other Olympians. Admit it, you're using me."

He gave an exasperated groan. "Of *course* I'm using you! For God's sake, Selene, I'm a *classicist!* You expect me *not* to want to meet Zeus and Athena?"

"I told you not to use their real names if you don't have to. It can draw their attention to you. And why do you always bring *her* up?"

"She's my favorite goddess! I mean *was* my favorite goddess until I met you, obviously. Now I know Artemis would kick her ass."

"You're treading on very thin ice, Theodore. You shouldn't mess with me at Christmastime. I'm not in the mood."

He just laughed. "Christmas trees, candles, feasting... they're all just pagan anyway. Why not embrace it? The early Christians probably chose December twenty-fifth because the Romans already honored it as the birthday of Sol Invictus, the sun god. And it came with ready-made revelry: They always celebrated the Saturnalia festival the week before."

She curled her lip in disgust. "I didn't like *those* holidays either. Too many drunk thanatoi reeling around paying homage to trumped-up gods with nothing to do with me."

"Okay, but what about your association with Christianity?"

"My *what*?"

"Ready for a little pedantic explication?" He kept going before she could say no. "Remember how some Romans worshiped you as a threefold goddess? They thought Artemis—or Diana, I should say, if we're being strictly accurate—encompassed the

Huntress, the Moon, and Hecate, the goddess of dark magic. Some of that iconography might have influenced the Christian trinity."

She shrugged, growing more uncomfortable by the second. But once Theo embarked on one of his cerebral peregrinations, it would take more than her body language to stop him.

"I keep walking by these nativity scenes around the city," he went on, "and it reminds me that, in a way, the Romans never stopped worshiping Diana. The Christians see Jesus's mother as a Holy Virgin who's the Protector of the Innocent. Sound familiar? She's just an incarnation of *you*. Maybe you've been enjoying the benefits of that association all this time. Everyone's saying their Hail Marys, but really they're paying homage to Artemis. What do you think?" He offered up his scholarly insights like a Christmas gift, expecting her to rip open the paper and exclaim in delight. But this was one package Selene had no desire to unwrap.

"To assume Mary's worship, I'd have to assume her characteristics as well." She pulled away from him. "Is that what you want? To have me weak and mild? Impregnated by a shaft of heavenly light? Conforming to a cult of motherhood so all-encompassing that even *virgins* have to give birth? No thank you. I'd rather stick to hunting and punishing and leave the holy baby making to someone else."

Theo raised his hands in mock surrender. "Okay! I didn't realize it works that way. I don't want anyone having incandescent coitus with you except me, I swear."

She shot to her feet, feeling her cheeks burn despite the cold.

"Come on," he pleaded as she headed toward the trapdoor. "I know we aren't *having* sex, but can't we even joke about it? Where are you going?"

"Inside. It's cold."

"You barely feel the cold!"

"Barely's not the same as don't." Ignoring the ladder, Selene hopped through the opening in the roof. Her dog, Hippolyta, waited beneath; she jumped to her feet and proceeded to lick Selene's hand.

"Yeah, yeah, you can tell I'm in a bad mood," she said, giving the dog a cursory pat. "All this slobber isn't helping, Hippo." But it was, a little. She understood her dog's love, and she knew what Hippo expected in return—a safe place to sleep, plenty of exercise, and hefty portions of meat to maintain her prodigious girth. But Theo was still a mystery. As a goddess, she'd had only one responsibility to her worshipers: to protect them. Theo, however, wanted her heart, her mind...and her body. *Yet another trinity that I'm not about to give mankind any control over.* She stomped loudly down the stairs toward the kitchen, hoping Theo heard the fury in every footstep.

———◦———

Theo didn't follow Selene inside. *I should know better than to mention motherhood, much less sex,* he thought. *It's like waving a red flag in front of a bull and hoping it just sits down and compliments you on your dance routine.* Sometimes Selene seemed so relaxed and reasonable that he started treating her like a normal girlfriend—or as normal as a woman with the eyes of a hawk, the nose of a bloodhound, and over three thousand years of emotional baggage could be—then *whoosh!* She turned into a goddess, liable to pull out her golden arrows at any moment and make him beg forgiveness for provoking her wrath. When they'd first met, he'd found her tempestuousness exhilarating—three months later, he found it exhausting.

He stared out over the rooftops, trying not to let Selene's mood ruin his own holiday cheer. The Christmas lights on the nearby buildings glittered merrily, and he even caught a whiff of woodsmoke from some apartment lucky enough to have a not-just-decorative fireplace. Winters in New York could be vile—even the most magical of snowfalls took only moments to devolve into a morass of gray slush when trampled by the boots of nine million residents. But Theo'd always found that December held more than enough wonders to make up for the weather. The Handel's *Messiah* sing-along at Lincoln Center, ice skating in Rockefeller Plaza, the ornate window displays on Fifth Avenue, the menorahs and Christmas trees glowing in every apartment lobby—he almost broke into "Deck the Halls" just thinking about it all. Then his thoughts turned to the woman currently prowling the house below him, and his internal song ground to a halt. Christmas cheer was only one of the things he and Selene could never share.

But then he remembered the way his heart raced every time he saw her, every time he thought of how her courage and passion inspired his own. He remembered the way her sleek black hair framed the curve of her jaw, its one streak of white a constant reminder of her vulnerability, while the sculpted muscles of her long limbs promised a strength he could never match. He couldn't help smiling. *Who said dating a goddess was supposed to be easy?*

———◇———

Selene sat at her small kitchen table devouring the last portion of Canada goose from the fridge. She'd have to go hunting again soon: Taking down a pigeon or squirrel in Central Park might lessen some of her current desire to shoot her boyfriend. She knew full well he hadn't meant to anger her, but it took some particularly violent tearing of gooseflesh before she could regain any semblance of calm. In recent decades, a single goose would last her a few days, but now she could eat an entire bird in one sitting if she didn't pace herself. Her voracity was a rather inconvenient by-product of a recent uptick in her divine powers.

Theo appeared in the kitchen doorway. "You sure you don't want some salad with that? Something, I don't know . . . green?"

She knew from his smile that he had no desire to continue

their earlier quarrel. She made a face at him. "Have you ever heard of anyone *hunting* for lettuce? No? There's a reason."

"If it can't cower in fear, you won't eat it. You know you don't have to take your Huntress epithet quite so literally. Nothing's stopping you from becoming She Who Occasionally Eats a Balanced Meal."

An old argument. Theo constantly nudged her to move beyond the boundaries of her traditional attributes. But she found millennia-old habits hard to break. She tried not to dwell on what other epithets Theo wanted the Chaste One to abandon.

"Maybe not," she agreed. "But I spent enough time being what mankind imagined I was. Now *I* choose which of my attributes to keep and which to discard."

"All right." He nodded solemnly. They were talking about more than hunting, and they both knew it. "As long as I don't have to watch you butcher the goose next time." He'd dealt well with her shooting down the bird in the first place, but when it came to slitting its stomach and pulling out the still-steaming entrails, he'd blanched and left the room. She'd given up on any dreams of teaching him to hunt.

He yawned cavernously.

"It's two in the morning," she said. "You should go to sleep." As the erstwhile Goddess of the Moon, she normally stuck to a nearly nocturnal schedule. Theo might be a night owl, but he was, after all, still mortal.

"Yeah, I'm exhausted from all the end-of-semester craziness. Exam period starts tomorrow, so I'm looking forward to sleeping in."

She'd forgotten all about his academic calendar. *I'm just as ignorant of his life as he is of mine,* she thought with a sinking heart.

"Wake me if you get a call, okay?" he asked through another yawn.

"Sure, but don't get your hopes up." Her cell phone had remained depressingly silent for a week. In her role as an unlicensed private investigator, she'd always relied on word of mouth to bring her clients. She had a reputation as someone who'd do anything, no matter how illegal, to protect women from the men who abused them. In the past, she'd hunted down rapists, maimed wife beaters, even castrated a child molester or two. Now she was itching to bring down her renewed divine wrath on anyone who looked at her wrong.

"Don't worry," Theo said. "Business will pick up. It's the holidays—plenty of stressed-out couples arguing over budgets and in-laws."

"So you admit Christmas is a pain in the ass?"

"Not a chance." He bent to kiss her good night, the blond stubble on his chin scratching her cheek. "I'm off to dream of sugarplum fairies." He whistled a tune from *The Nutcracker* as he headed back up the stairs to the bedroom.

Just before dawn, Selene finally joined him. A month ago, he'd insisted on replacing her twin mattress so he could actually be comfortable when he slept over. He'd wanted a queen size, but Selene told him a double was more than enough change for one decade.

She lifted the covers and slipped into the cocoon of his heat. Theo immediately rolled over and slid an arm around her. His eyelids cracked open, and a flash of wonder crossed his face, as if even now he couldn't believe there was a goddess in his bed. He stroked the side of her arm sleepily, his eyes fluttering shut. But she knew from experience that he'd wake in a heartbeat if she gave him a reason.

She lay quietly, staring at the familiar slope of his pointed nose, the fall of fair hair over his forehead, and remembered their first night in this room together. Theo had only just learned her true identity. She'd been sure, in that moment, that she would give this new lover all of herself. She'd let him into her house, the first man to have that honor in the forty years she'd owned it. He'd been so consumed with her that he didn't even gawk at the fact that she owned an entire brownstone for just herself and her dog. Instead, they'd fallen onto her narrow bed in a flurry of kisses and laughter. It was easy, glorious fun. He'd pulled off his shirt, and she'd traced the lines of taut, lean muscle, accusing him of secretly lifting weights amid the library stacks. He insisted his brawn resulted purely from intellectual exercises. Then he reached to slip her shirt from her shoulders—and she'd balked.

So many millennia of virginity—how could she surrender it to a man she'd known for only a week? She might tell Theo she could choose which traits to keep, but she wasn't actually sure that was true. She'd long believed that the Athanatoi preserved their power in part by maintaining their defining attributes. Could the Chaste One take such a risk with the precious remnants of strength that she'd so recently regained?

So that first night, they'd lain in each other's arms, talking, laughing, kissing…and not much else. Since then, Theo had shown nothing but patience. Over time, she allowed him a little more access, relaxed a little more into his arms. But there were limits—strict limits.

Curled beside him in bed, watching him sink deeper into sleep, Selene couldn't resist placing a hand on Theo's chest, tracing the whorl of hair across his sternum. His eyes popped open, and a crooked smile brought a dimple to one cheek. She placed her finger in the matching dent on his chin, turning his face toward her, and kissed him lazily.

Ten minutes later, they'd both reached the very edge of her proscribed limits when Theo's phone rang.

"Ignore it," she panted in his ear, grabbing his wrist to stop him from pulling his hand away.

"We're not all on the lunar cycle, you know," he remonstrated. "Normal people don't call at five in the morning unless there's an emergency."

"I'm the PI. What sort of emergency could *you* have? Some

student doesn't know the difference between an *omicron* and an *omega*?"

"Let me just see—" He craned his neck over her shoulder, peering at his phone on the bedside table.

She growled low in her throat, unhappy to be disobeyed, but he pulled away anyway once he caught sight of his screen.

"Gabi?" he said into the phone, too loudly, near Selene's ear.

Theo's best friend, Gabriela Jimenez, worked as a curator in the anthropology department at the American Museum of Natural History. When she wasn't monopolizing Theo's time with overdramatic tales of the vicissitudes of life among the Native American dioramas, she was shooting highly suspicious glances in Selene's direction. Somehow, it wasn't surprising that she was the one to ruin Selene's night. It wouldn't be the first time.

"Don't worry, we'll be right there." Theo sat up in bed and gave Selene a pointed glance. "Yes, she's coming, too," he said into the phone before hanging up and reaching for his clothes.

"What? She needs you to come help with some recalcitrant Navajo mannequin?"

Theo ignored the jab. "She needs us."

"Us? You sure she didn't just want you?"

"Seems a woman just showed up at her door covered in bruises and refuses to go to the cops. In that situation, who would you want? The classicist or the vigilante avenger?" He tossed Selene's cargo pants at her head. "Gabi's not dumb. She only called me because she thought you wouldn't pick up if you saw her number."

Selene couldn't dispute that one.

Moments later, they headed out the door, with Hippo pulling excitedly at her leash. Theo's usually smiling face had hardened to an intense mask, his stride swift and determined. She marveled at the change in his demeanor. *Mild-mannered classicist becomes crime-fighting, mystery-solving, death-defying hero.* Selene could barely contain the smile that tugged at her lips.

In her pack, she carried a golden bow forged by Hephaestus himself and a quiver of arrows sharp enough to kill. This was what she was born to do. *Peace on earth and goodwill toward men be damned,* she thought. As long as the Huntress roamed the streets of Manhattan, there'd be no peace for the wicked...and nothing but justice for the men stupid enough to get in her way.

Chapter 2

SHE OF GOOD REPUTE

The hall outside Gabriela's apartment, as usual, smelled like chiles and chocolate. Theo noticed Selene's nose wrinkle as they waited by the door. "It's not a Christmas thing," he whispered quickly. "It's a Mexican one. Spiced hot cocoa. She drinks it all winter."

"Sounds highly unpleasant."

"Or amazing." The smell conjured memories of long nights filled with laughter and arguments and the occasional board game. *It's been too long,* he realized. This was the first winter in nearly a decade that he and Gabi hadn't spent any real time together.

The door finally opened. Gabi looked terrible, her warm skin ashen, her black curls even more out of control than usual. He'd forgotten how short she really was—she nearly always wore heeled clogs. In her fur-lined slippers, she stood barely five feet, and the distraught look on her face, so different from her usual wry smile, added to her appearance of vulnerability. He immediately folded her into his arms. "I'm sorry I finally come visit and it's because of this." She nodded wordlessly into his chest, then poked him hard in the kidney.

"What was that for?"

"For being an asshole and ignoring me all month. Also, for making me feel all safe and loved just now, which just makes me want to cry because Minh's *not* safe and *not* loved, and I don't know what to do about it." He pulled away, thinking she was done, but she grabbed him by his parka and kept going. "And because you're a *man*, and right now I *hate* you for it, even though you *know* I love you, and it's not your fault your whole damn gender are *dicks*." She finally released him and led them into the apartment. "Oh," she called over her shoulder, "and did I mention I'm *really* glad I'm a lesbian?"

"No, but it was implied."

"You know," Selene said quietly as she followed behind him, "it's too bad she hates me, because right now I kind of love her."

"She doesn't hate—" Theo began, but he fell silent when he saw the woman sitting at Gabi's kitchen table. She held a mug of cocoa, untouched, in her hands. After a glance at Theo and Selene, she quickly turned her head away. But not before Theo saw the massive bruise along her jaw.

"This is Minh Loi," Gabi said. "She works in . . . is it okay to tell them?"

The woman nodded without looking up.

"She works over in Earth and Space. You know I usually leave that wing of Natural History to its own torturously boring devices, but we've been working together on a special exhibit on Mayan astronomy. She's even proposing a show at the Hayden Planetarium to go with it, because she's that awesome. Minh's an astronomy rock star. Like a Chinese version of that chick from Fleetwood Mac."

At that, Minh gave a short laugh that sounded more like a choke. Theo knew Gabi's flattery was meant to lift the woman's spirits, but Minh did look a little like a middle-aged Asian Stevie Nicks. Long salt-and-pepper hair cut in bangs across her forehead. Delicate nose and high cheekbones, currently upstaged by her puffy, red-rimmed eyes.

Theo moved to sit at the table, but Gabi stopped him with a quick shake of her head. "Why don't you wait in the living room while Selene and I talk to Minh?" She batted her eyelids at him for emphasis. Theo tried not to look surprised by the dismissal— it made sense that the victim wouldn't want to speak in front of a man. But he was getting tired of every woman in his life lumping him together with his entire sex and all its multifarious faults.

He left the kitchen and sat in the notoriously uncomfortable wicker armchair in Gabi's living room. In an apartment this small, he could still hear the women talking in the kitchen. He told himself eavesdropping was unavoidable—what was he supposed to do, hang out in the lobby?—and then shamelessly scooted the chair a little closer to the door so he could hear more clearly.

"Tell me everything. From the beginning," Selene said. Her voice held little sympathy, but at least it wasn't tight with rage. She sounded calm and professional.

"I'm so stupid," Minh began. Selene, Theo noticed, didn't contradict her. "I finally went online a few months back. It's been two years since my divorce, and everyone kept pushing me to do it. I had a couple of dates, nothing too horrible, but nothing worth repeating." She paused, and Theo heard her take a sip of cocoa for the first time. When she remained silent, it was Gabi who pushed her to keep talking. Selene, for all her habitual impatience, had centuries of experience listening to women relate their suffering—she knew when to wait for the story.

"Lars was exactly what I was looking for. A scientist and educator, like me, and completely committed to his work. He's a keeper at the Central Park Zoo. Cute, right? And a single dad with two young kids, and I don't have children of my own, so I was excited about that. Not to mention he's six-four and Norwegian and age appropriate." Another sip of cocoa. "I spend most of my time in a darkened planetarium, so I found the whole outdoorsy daredevil thing irresistible. He goes into the grizzly enclosure and *plays* with the bears, safety precautions be damned. By our third date, I was ready for more. Then, in the middle, he asked me to…" She paused for a long moment before saying, "Do things I wasn't comfortable with. I said no, but he didn't listen. We'd shared two bottles of wine…"

"What exactly did that *hijo de puta* do?" prompted Gabi.

Minh's voice sank to a whisper. Theo couldn't hear her words, but Gabi's horrified gasp was unmistakable. "Is that when he punched you in the face?" she demanded.

"No, nothing like that. He sort of…slammed my head into the bedpost. It was just an accident."

Gabi snorted.

"Before we go any further"—Selene's voice was carefully controlled, almost monotone—"I have to tell you that your best option is to go to the police and have this man arrested for rape."

"It wasn't rape. It was consensual…at first."

"Like I said. Have this man arrested for rape."

"I couldn't do that. Even if I thought that's what happened, it's too murky. I said yes…then I might've said no…but I can't really remember, and I should've been smart enough not to get myself into that situation in the first place. And his kids…they adore him. He's a great dad. I'd never want to see him taken away from them."

A chair scraped back from the table. "Then why are you wasting my time?"

Theo glanced at his watch. It had taken Selene all of ten minutes before she'd said something insensitive and inappropriate. *She's improving.* During their last private investigation case, a month before, Selene had gotten so angry at the victim for saying she still loved her child-abusing husband that she'd brought the woman to the point of a hysterical breakdown five minutes after walking in the door. Eventually, Theo'd convinced the woman to call the police—a task made easier by threatening her with the only other option: having to work with Selene.

Minh's voice took on a new fierceness as she answered Selene's question. "I told Gabriela to call you because whatever happened...I never want him to do it to anyone else again."

"So you're looking for a castration?" Selene asked matter-of-factly.

"No! My God..."

"Selene's just kidding," Gabi put in.

No, she's not, Theo thought, not without pride. There was something refreshing about Selene's brand of ancient justice, even if it did make him unconsciously cross his legs.

"I just want someone to talk to Lars. Not take him from his kids or anything. Just warn him to stop what he's doing."

"Why don't you do it yourself?"

"Because I'm scared, all right? I don't like to admit that. I'm a forty-three-year-old woman, and I'm scared of this big man who could...who *has*...hurt me. Gabriela said you sometimes pose as a police officer, so I was thinking you could pretend to be a cop and give him an official visit."

"That would be illegal." But Selene didn't refuse. "And Gabriela shouldn't be talking about something she knows nothing about."

"Knows nothing?" Gabi spluttered. "I saw you with a fake badge when you were investigating that cult!"

Theo winced at the memory. *No wonder she doesn't trust Selene, having seen her at work.* But Selene didn't seem fazed. She spoke to Minh with a chilly calm that only highlighted the ruthlessness of her words.

"If you want my help, I'll proceed as I see fit. The only guarantee I can give you is that this man will never bother you—or any other woman—again."

A long pause. Then a barely audible sound of agreement.

"Good. Now tell me more about this Lars. Where can we find him without his kids around?"

"He's at the zoo four days a week."

As Minh continued, Gabi rejoined Theo in the living room. "Knowing Selene's methods, I don't think I should hear any more," she whispered. "Plausible deniability and all that." She gestured him to follow her into the bedroom and closed the door. They sat companionably on the neatly made bed.

"You know that dead giant squid that used to be in the glass case in the lobby?" she asked with her usual disdain for exposition.

"At Natural History? Yeah..."

"You know how no one's ever captured a living specimen? It's this massive deep-sea monster, forty feet long, eyes the size of dinner plates, and it's so wily, so rare, that the closest we come is the occasional dead body washed up onshore?"

"Where are you going with this?"

"Well, that squid in the case reminds me of your girlfriend."

"Are you saying Selene looks like a slowly decomposing cephalopod? That's a bit unfair, even for you."

"Are you kidding me? She's maybe the most beautiful woman I've ever seen. Those legs! That face! It's just that I get the same feeling when I'm with her that I get when I'm looking at the squid. Like I'm seeing something that's so deep and dark that it should never see the light of day. Like it's a secret we aren't meant to uncover."

Theo shivered. For all Gabriela's bluster, she was one of the most intuitive people he knew, and she'd hit shockingly close to the mark. He lay back on the bed, suddenly wishing he'd gotten more than three hours of sleep. "You're only saying that because she's so tall."

Gabriela sighed. "Maybe you're right, *chico.* You know I can't deal with women over five-eight. I feel like I'm staring at their breasts the whole time I'm talking to them, and it's completely dehumanizing for us both."

"I thought you liked staring at women's breasts."

"Please. I'm a lesbian, not a man. And Selene's breasts, sorry to say, are her one less-than-impressive feature. Way too small for my taste. It's just that watching her with Minh, she had the most bizarre look on her face. Any other woman would've been sympathetic. Or maybe scared. I, for one, was angry. But Selene was all ice. Is she some sort of sociopath?"

"Overdramatic, are we?"

"She does *not* have normal human emotions, that's all I'm saying. Then again, next time I go for a walk through the park in the dead of night, remind me to keep her number on speed dial. Girl is fierce."

Theo laughed. "As if you'd be dumb enough to walk through the park in the dead of . . . wait . . . *why would you do that?*"

"Oh, calm down. I'm trying to get in shape." She looked down despairingly at the curve of her belly. "I'm too busy at the museum to exercise during the day."

"So *when* have you been going into *what* park?"

She screwed up her face at him. "Morningside Park. Like two or three."

"*A.M.?* Are you carrying mace or something?"

"I don't believe in mace. It's a tool of the elite. It's something white women carry because they're scared of big black men. No thank you."

"This isn't about politics, Gabi. It's safety. Promise me you'll go join a twenty-four-hour gym or something instead. Or, Christ, do some Richard Simmons in your living room at two in the morning!"

"I *like* the park at night!"

"Then *carry mace*. Or a gun!"

"What are you, some NRA member!" She recoiled in horror. "What is that woman doing to you? Didn't you say she *hunts* for fun? I'm telling you, she's deranged. Or at least a Republican." She shuddered.

A knock on the door. Theo suppressed a groan. "You know she just heard all that, right?" he said, keeping his voice to a totally futile whisper. Selene had ears like a bat.

"So? She knows I don't like her," Gabi replied, not bothering to lower her voice. "Come on in!" she called sweetly.

Selene stood in the doorway. She didn't even look at Gabi. "I've got all the info I need. Let's go."

"What should I do with Minh?" Gabi asked.

"How would I know? I'm a sociopath, remember?" Selene stalked away.

"You're amazing," Theo said to his friend. "You're deliberately sabotaging my relationship."

"False!" she pouted. "I just want you to be happy."

"I *am* happy. Or at least I was before you insulted the woman I love."

"You *what*?"

"I haven't told *her* that yet...but...I don't know what else you call it when someone enters your life and remakes the whole damn thing. I see differently now, I *feel* differently. If she left, I'd be like Dorothy returning to black-and-white Kansas after seeing the Technicolor glory of Oz."

That shut Gabi up. If only for a moment. "I'm sorry, Theo-dear. I was being a bitch, you're right. Maybe I'm just jealous." She let out a long sigh. "But...be careful, okay? I don't want you getting your heart broken."

"Only if you promise not to get your heart *stabbed*. Will you think about the mace?"

She gave him one of her usual wry smiles. "Fine. Pepper spray. For you." She patted her sternum. "I'll keep it right here between my breasts for easy access. And I'll think of you every time it accidentally goes off in my face while I'm jogging."

Chapter 3

BEAR PAWS FOR HANDS

"Hey, *Arktios*, you sure this is a good idea?" Theo's voice over Selene's archaic flip phone was an urgent whisper.

"Do you have a better plan?" she hissed back as she prepared to break into the Central Park Zoo the evening after they'd met Minh.

"Catch Lars *after* he leaves work? Or is that too easy for the *Potnia Theron*?" He'd been using her epithets all night. *Arktios*: Ursine. *Potnia Theron*: Mistress of Beasts.

"Too late for second-guessing, Theo. I've worked it all out. I'm about to climb over the wall."

"You sure that's wise, you being the *Arktokheir* and all?"

She Who Has Bear Paws for Hands. Even Selene didn't remember that one. For all she knew, Theo had just made it up. *Having three hundred epithets gives him* way *too much ammunition,* she thought, not for the first time. "Are you ready for your part, or not?"

"My part's easy. I just wish I could be there with you."

"The plan needs a pay phone, or else the cops can trace the call back to you. So you're going to have to stay where you are."

"Fine, but as soon as I'm done, I'm running back to the park.

This is possibly the most dangerous thing you've ever done, and that includes venturing into the Underworld and confronting the Lord of the Dead."

She didn't bother replying; she didn't want him to hear her trepidation.

"I still think we should test this out before you—"

"Too late." She snapped her phone shut. Theo might be right, but once she'd put a plan into motion, she didn't like to back down. *He should be grateful I even* have *a plan*. Her usual course of action involved leaping into the fray with arrows flying and worrying about strategy later.

She stood on the narrow sidewalk beside the busy Sixty-sixth Street transverse that passed through Central Park. It was five thirty—still rush hour—and a stream of cars and taxis blazed by her, creating far too many witnesses and blinding her night vision with their headlights. She waited for the stoplight on Central Park West to create a brief break in the traffic, then scaled the stone wall that separated the street from the park.

She fought her way through overgrown shrubbery until she reached a chain-link fence topped with concertina wire. An obstacle, but not an insurmountable one. Clearly the zoo officials didn't expect anyone to break into the exhibits from this direction—especially when the animals inside could cause far worse injuries than the razor wire.

Selene had considered bringing a pair of bolt cutters to slice through the wire, or even a carpet fragment to protect herself from cuts while she climbed over it. In the end, she'd decided to simply circumvent the wire entirely. She found a sturdy tree close to the fence line. The maple's lowest branch was still thirteen feet off the ground, impossible to reach for even the tallest climber—but the tallest climber hadn't spent millennia communing with trees. Selene shimmied easily up the trunk using only the strength of her arms and legs.

From her perch, she could see over the fence and into the zoo itself. Feeling confident, she scooted along a branch that reached toward the chain-link—only to find herself still six feet shy of the fence. Her self-satisfaction evaporated. She considered her options. *I could shoot an arrow with a rope attached, hope to gain purchase on a zoo building, and then zip-line over the fence—likely drawing the attention of every worker in the place. I could give up on the tree, cover the razor wire with my leather jacket, and get it—and myself— torn to shreds crawling over. Or, as Theo would no doubt suggest, I could give up on the plan entirely and find a different way to catch our zookeeper that didn't involve risking my life.* Then, with a shrug, she discarded all three options—and jumped.

She nearly made it.

One heavy leather boot caught in the razor wire, and she found herself hanging upside down, her chest pressed to the inside of the fence, and her head dangling four feet off the ground. Grasping the chain-link with both hands, she wiggled her foot free. The boot came loose with a metallic rattle, shaking snow onto her face and up her nose. Then the weight of her legs dragged her inexorably off the fence; she flipped forward like an accident-prone gymnast and landed on a snowy ledge above the bear enclosure. Various shrubs poked perilously close to her most sensitive areas. *Deeply undignified for any burglar,* she thought, heaving herself to her knees, *much less a goddess supposedly endowed with preternatural grace.*

She reached back to brush the snow and twigs off her pants. Trying to make up for her cacophonous entrance, she crawled slowly and silently toward the front of the ledge.

Betty and Veronica were waiting for her.

The pair of six-hundred-pound grizzlies, each standing on her hind legs, snuffled curiously at the intruder as if waiting for a treat to descend from above. Selene scooted backward in alarm, then reminded herself that the faux-rock walls stood at least twelve feet high and sloped slightly inward so that no mammal could climb up without a grappling hook—or at least an opposable thumb.

Veronica, the darker of the two bears, sniffed loudly, her squat snout twitching dexterously in the snowy air. Betty, the blonde, dropped back onto all fours with a thud and turned to the side, showing Selene her size. Both clacked their teeth and made popping sounds with their breath as they worked over Selene's scent. Betty even reached out a paw to swipe at the air before her. Neither charged. Not yet.

Once, as the Mistress of Beasts, Selene had possessed the power to speak with nearly all denizens of the wild. She still maintained a special connection to her closest companion—the hound. As for her other sacred animal... well, she was about to find out.

"Hello, *arktuloi*," Selene said softly, knowing full well that creatures born in the Rockies wouldn't know the Ancient Greek for "little bears," but hoping the words might help nonetheless. These bears were larger than those she'd played with in her Mediterranean youth. Their curved, four-inch claws stood out from their dark paws like piano keys—if piano keys could kill you.

For her plan to work, she needed to enter the enclosure itself and approach the animals. For most people, that would mean getting bitten, mauled, or even killed. But not for the Mistress of Beasts. Or so Selene hoped.

She glanced at Betty's beady eyes, then away, not wanting to rile her. Bears were solitary creatures, not pack animals. They didn't respond to dominance the way a hound would. Yet even in that brief instant of eye contact, Selene felt a flash of recognition, as if she'd met a sister again after a lifetime apart. They'd both changed over the years, but an unquenchable spark of kinship remained.

"You and me, we're the same, it turns out," she said, keeping her voice low and unthreatening. "We're both trapped in a world far from our home, amid creatures who don't understand who we are or where we came from. Finding solace in whatever tiny patch of wilderness is left to us." She found herself slipping into an old cadence, not a goddess commanding her worshipers, but a deity communing with her acolytes.

"We see with different eyes than they do, we hear with different ears." She lifted her own nose to sniff the air. "I smell the snow and the smog. I smell your curiosity. I smell how healthy you are—so well fed you don't bother to hibernate, though winter's hard upon us. Your keepers give you peanut butter on branches and sweet potatoes beneath cairns to keep you from going mad." She hadn't prepared this speech—hadn't even expected to talk to the bears in the human tongue at all. But seeing them there, so strong and powerful, yet utterly helpless, the words welled out of her in a torrent. Her own bitterness surprised her. "I, too, have found distractions here, enough to make me forget who I really am. I fight for women, I prowl the streets, sometimes I even shoot prey with my arrows like in days of old. I have a house and a dog and…a boyfriend." She laughed shortly, and Veronica snuffed in acknowledgment. "What does that make me? A caged animal. Just like you."

Veronica sat down on her rump, and Betty simply flopped all the way to the ground with a sigh. Signs of submission and relaxation.

"I'm jumping down now," she warned them. "Don't get pissed."

She dropped off the ledge and into the exhibit, landing hard and slipping slightly on the gravel beneath the snow. Now she stood only a half-dozen paces from the bears. She glanced past them to the glass-enclosed viewing areas and the rest of the zoo beyond. Empty. It had closed a half hour earlier. Most of the keepers would be tidying up and moving their charges indoors for the night. But Minh reported that Lars liked to give the bears a little extra time outside, especially in winter.

From her pocket, Selene pulled a flexible plastic collar with a small container affixed to one end. "Who wants to wear this and do She Who Has Bear Paws for Hands a huge favor?"

Veronica walked slowly forward, nose still dancing curiously.

This close, the bear's head hung nearly level with Selene's. Her heavy breath puffed white like a steam engine, and Selene could taste the dark musk on her tongue. The bear paused, and her ears swiveled backward. Selene forced herself not to tense up at the sight of the sudden aggressive gesture. Instead, she bleated—the sound a mother bear makes to summon her young—and Veronica's ears swung forward once more, listening. Selene bleated again, then took a step forward to demonstrate her own lack of fear.

"Easy there, my *arktulos.*" She reached around the bear's massive neck, her hands disappearing in the thick fur, and secured the collar. Then she scratched Veronica behind one swiveling ear and placed her head against the bear's. Veronica warbled a high-pitched, pulsing thrum, a cub's response to its mother's attentions. The bear took one last look at her, then lumbered toward the gate that led to the climate-controlled enclosure and indoor swimming pool. Every evening, she'd been trained to go to the door, wait for it to open, and enter her chamber, where a fishy treat awaited.

Selene could've just left then, message delivered. Lars would eventually find the container, read the note enclosed, and hopefully be impressed enough by its method of delivery to obey. Selene could no longer send men dreams or spy upon them from her chariot as she rode the moon through the sky, but she'd learned to get the same effect through trickery. Lars would have no idea who could've managed to plant the message on the bear without leaving a severed limb behind. He was a scientist—but somewhere deep in the primal portion of his brain he might secretly wonder if something supernatural had been at work, and that suspicion would likely get him to obey the message's command.

But that would be too easy. And too merciful. He needed to be more than astonished—he needed to be terrified.

Betty followed Veronica toward the door, her massive haunches jiggling with winter fat as she went. Selene stepped in front of her and drew a folded T-shirt from the capacious pocket of her cargo pants. Lars had left it in Minh's apartment the night of the assault. Selene lifted the fabric to her own nose and sniffed loudly, then held it out so Betty could do the same.

"You know this man," she said. "He brings you food. You like him. But he must be taught a lesson about how to treat females." The bear would not understand her words, of course. She'd long lost that kind of supernatural power. But that didn't mean she couldn't communicate her needs. She put the fabric in her own mouth and bared her teeth. She huffed and clacked her jaws, then threw the scrap to the ground. Then, with another quick scan of the viewing area, she pulled down her pants and pissed on Lars's T-shirt. She hadn't told Theo about that part of the plan—he'd *never* let her live it down. But bears communicated largely through odor, and a sure way to convey her rage was to have them smell it in her urine.

Betty stared at her, ears flat and anxious. Selene smiled. Now all she had to do was get Lars inside the enclosure. That was where Theo came in.

With a scraping of gears, the metal door behind the security gate slid open. A man's deep voice, with the barest hint of a Scandinavian accent, floated toward her. "How did you get this number? No, I'm not going to go into the bear den—it's prohibited. What I *am* going to do is call the cops and tell them someone is threatening me. Then I'm going to alert my superiors."

But he wasn't. He was coming to look inside the bear exhibit, just as Selene knew he would when he heard what the stranger on the phone had to say. Once Theo mentioned Minh's name, Lars would be too skittish to involve anyone else. He knew what he'd done was wrong.

"I haven't seen that woman in days," he lied. "She was fine. I don't know what you're talking about."

Selene ducked behind a rocky outcropping as Lars appeared behind the gate. He was less attractive than she'd imagined him from Minh's description. Tall and muscular, yes, his lush blond hair gone gray at the temples. But his face was hard, his pale eyes nearly hidden beneath a protruding brow. A Viking marauder. He stood behind the grate, cursed roundly into the phone, then hung up on Theo.

He stared for a moment at his bears. Veronica snorted and raised a claw to scratch at the plastic collar around her neck. Just in case Lars hadn't noticed it. He cursed again.

"How'd someone get that on you?" he demanded of the bear. She gazed at him impassively. "You come inside, I'll get the tranquilizer gun, and we'll get that off." He disappeared, probably entering a secure observation area. After a moment, the gate swung open. Veronica took a step forward, following her usual routine.

But that wasn't part of Selene's plan. From her hiding place, she made a high whining sound, the closest she could come to a bear's warning signal. Veronica swung her head to look at her curiously. Selene whined again. The bear sat back down, obeying the command. Then the three females waited patiently.

Eventually, the safety gate swung shut and Lars reappeared behind it, this time holding a large silver fish by its tail. "Come on, girls, come inside and have a little dessert." But the bears didn't move. He repeated the performance three times: tempting the bears, disappearing into the safety enclosure, opening the gate, and then closing it once more when they refused to budge. Finally, as Selene knew he would, he appeared behind the bars and muttered, "Fine, if that's what it takes." He pushed a button and the gate swung open. In his right hand, he held a tranquilizer pistol. In his left, a box cutter.

He walked slowly toward Veronica, murmuring calming words to her the whole way. He looked cautious but not nearly as terrified as he should've—clearly he'd done this before. If his boss found out, he'd be immediately fired. *Minh called him a daredevil. I call him an arrogant, reckless asshole,* Selene decided.

The bear lay down and rolled to her side, then cocked her head in a show of submission.

"You gonna make it easy on me, huh?" Lars asked. "No dart gun needed?" He came within two feet of her, then dared to put the gun aside and lift the box cutter to the collar around her neck. The bear's heavy panting lifted the wisps of hair from his forehead as he slit the plastic. The message container dropped into his hand.

Quickly, he backed out of Veronica's reach. He should've immediately retreated to the observation area, but his curiosity got the better of him. He pried open the plastic cylinder and drew out the roll of paper.

" 'Lars, if you ever touch another woman again,' " he read aloud, " 'we are coming after you.' " Lars looked to Veronica, as if she could answer the obvious question. "Who's *we*?"

That's when Betty bit off his hand.

Chapter 4

THE FURIES

From his post on the busy road beneath the zoo walls, Theo heard the screams. For a moment, he thought they were Selene's and that her ridiculous plan to talk to the bears had gone just as badly as he'd feared. Then he realized that even if she had an entire *pack* of slavering grizzlies on her heels, she'd never make a sound that high-pitched. When he caught a few Norwegian curse words through the screaming, he knew Lars was the one shrieking like a woman.

Theo stared at the helix of razor wire above him, hoping to see Selene climbing to safety. Five minutes passed. He didn't dare call her cell—he didn't want to give away her position. Finally, just as he was about to attempt an ill-conceived scaling of the fence, Selene appeared at the eastern end of the transverse, running full tilt toward him.

She waved him ahead of her. "Go!"

He didn't ask questions, but sprinted down the sidewalk. He could hear her gaining on him—not surprising considering she was the Swiftly Bounding One, but still mildly humiliating for a man who considered himself in decent physical shape. Moments later, she'd passed him. Now he could see the torn leg of her pants and the blood dripping into her boot. Her hair lay flat and wet, frost already forming at the tips.

"What the hell happened?"

She ignored his question. She sprinted across the road and then up and over the rock wall and into Central Park. A moment later she reached down to help him up behind her. They dashed down a pathway that curved beneath an arching bridge. There, in the shadows, they finally paused.

Theo leaned against the brickwork, panting heavily, hands on his knees. Even Selene was heaving. "You're injured," Theo managed. "And wet."

She glanced down at her leg. "The bears got a little crazy once Betty bit off Lars's hand. Veronica turned on me—the whole Mistress of Beasts thing wasn't quite enough to stop her from taking a swipe. Then it turned out it was harder to get out of the exhibit than into it—especially with a grizzly chasing me in circles—and I had to scale a cliff, drop down into the harbor seal pool, get over a glass wall, and then run out the main entrance."

"Rewind. *Bit off Lars's hand?* What happened to telling the bear to just bluff-charge him so he'd wet his pants with fear but live to tell the tale?"

"I *did* tell her that. She just didn't listen. Or maybe she listened too well—bears are smart, you know; she probably intuited my true desires." She spoke casually, ripping off the rest of her pant cuff at the same time and fashioning it into a makeshift bandage around her calf. "Although if it was up to me, she would've bit off his cock instead."

"And now we're being chased by the police?"

"No, I don't think anyone saw me. The other keepers were too busy running toward the screams. I just wanted to get out of the area—you know, in case."

Theo slid down the wall and sat heavily on the asphalt. She sat beside him and threaded her fingers through his. Her sudden smile gleamed white in the shadows. *I haven't seen her this happy in weeks,* Theo realized. Personally, he had little stomach for such bloody punishment, but he'd decided that sometimes the world needed an avenging goddess.

"So I can pry my heart out of my throat?" he asked, finally catching his breath. "And Lars isn't going to bleed to death? And you're not going to get rabies from bear claws?"

"Let me answer in ascending order of importance," she said. Theo raised an eyebrow at her uncharacteristic levity, but let her go on. "Lars, unfortunately, is not going to die. He's also never going to look at another woman again without thinking of six hundred pounds of bear flesh ripping off an extremity. Second, the bear claws are nothing I can't handle, so don't worry about it. And third, I like your heart right where it is." She placed a hand on his chest, and he felt an answering flutter somewhere considerably farther down his torso. She lowered her voice and leaned toward him, her smile grown small and lopsided and meant just for him. "Not a bad night's work, partner."

Theo reflected that his role in the affair had involved frequenting one of the city's few remaining pay phones, standing like an idiot waiting for Selene to show up, then running for his life for no apparent reason. But even with his misgivings about the extremity of her justice, he found Selene's exuberance infectious. He loved seeing her in her element. He let himself fall into her kiss and tried to ignore the little voice in the back of his head warning that next time he found himself in a lovers' spat, he should guard his limbs from any passing bears.

Back in Selene's kitchen that night, Theo forced himself to sit down and finish writing the final exam for his Intro to Mythology class.

"What do you think?" he asked Selene as he flipped desultorily through the class syllabus, looking for inspiration. "What if I ask my students to explain why Greek mythology still holds such a fascination for modern society? And then, when none of them say 'because Selene DiSilva is a fox,' they all get F's."

Selene laughed shortly. "A wolf, maybe. A fox, never. Too timid." She sat beside him at the table, rolling up her pants to check the wound on her leg. "Why don't you ask them to imagine what sort of Underworld punishment the gods would devise for the department's four dead professors? Personally, I'd have the Furies tie them up while the shades of the women they murdered slowly skinned them alive to the sound of one of their own ritualistic drums. But that's just me."

Theo couldn't quite join Selene in her revenge fantasies. The professors she referred to had been his colleagues, after all—Columbia classicists drawn into the revival of an ancient Mystery Cult practicing virgin sacrifices. He'd met Selene while tracking them down three months earlier. The cult's leader, the handsome Everett Halloran, had promised the rite would give the professors immortality. The press dubbed the killers the "Classicist Cult," and a department usually ignored by anyone without a deep and abiding interest in Homeric Hymns had led newscasts across the country for a few days that autumn.

By the time the cult's ritual reached its climax, Theo had learned that Everett was in fact the mythological hero Orion, Artemis's onetime hunting companion and the great love of her life. Eventually, Selene's divine brothers showed up in the final shootout and helped kill the professors. Theo couldn't regret their deaths—it had been a matter of self-defense. But as much as he hated what they'd become, he still mourned the men they'd once been.

"Honestly," he said with a sigh, "I might travel to the Underworld myself if it meant I could bring one of them back to help me run the damn department." With the faculty roster decimated, Theo'd taken on the role of temporary chairman. Once, he might've jumped at the chance, but now he resented all the extra work. He wanted to spend his time with Selene, and when he wasn't obsessing over her, he wanted to continue delving into everything she'd taught him. She'd upended his entire understanding of the field he thought he'd mastered years before. *How does one talk of the gods as if they're legends, knowing that they're real?* So far, he hadn't come up with an answer. *Should I tell my students that Artemis still has her bow and lives on the Upper West Side and can control bears? Well—until they go crazy and try to kill her, that is.*

Selene unwound a roll of clean gauze to bind her leg. She was right; the wound wasn't bad. Either the bear's claws had only grazed her, or she'd already begun to heal. *Should I mention that she's sort of, kind of, almost, sometimes immortal? But most of her relatives are fading into oblivion? And she herself might lose what powers remain to her at any moment?*

The Athanatoi, he'd learned, retained their strength in correlation to how much they—or their attributes—were still revered in the modern world. So a god like Dionysus, the Wine Giver, still possessed much of his power—there were plenty of alcoholics to pay him homage, even if they didn't do it directly. But Artemis presided over virginity and hunting—two things considered thoroughly outmoded by much of the population. Thus, before he'd met Selene, she'd faded almost entirely into mortality, unable to heal quickly, barely competent with her own bow. The Classicist Cult had restored some of her power through their bloody rites, and even after their demise, she'd retained that newfound strength. But when Orion offered to return her to complete omnipotence by sacrificing Theo, she'd turned him down. Theo had no idea how long Selene had left before her fading began again in earnest. *One more thing I can't investigate with my students, much less make the focus of my next scholarly treatise.*

He took off his wire-rimmed glasses and rubbed his eyes. He'd made little progress on his questions—either the ones tormenting his brain or those written on the test pages. He glanced at his watch. Somehow, it was already three in the morning, although Selene still looked wide awake as she riffled through the fridge for yet another carnivorous snack. *I may just have to give up and use last year's test,* Theo relented, pushing the papers aside and resting his head on the table. The night's adventure had taken more out of him than he'd realized.

He'd fallen asleep when the cell phone in his pocket jolted him upright. Selene appeared at his side in an instant. "Maybe it's Gabriela with another client," she said, her silver eyes bright.

"I'm not sure how I feel about the fact that you *want* Gabi's friends to be assaulted just so you can have the pleasure of exacting vengeance on their behalf."

Selene shot him her usual scowl, somehow grinning all the while.

Then Theo read the caller ID on his phone and sat up straighter, completely awake. "It's Detective Freeman."

The smile dropped from Selene's face. Freeman had been one of the detectives on the Classicist Cult case. Theo had earned a rather peculiar reputation among the police as an expert consultant on crimes of a classical nature—crimes that, needless to say, hadn't recurred since the destruction of Orion's cult. But if the detective had called him, there could be only one reason.

He picked up and listened as Freeman gave him a brief rundown of a new case facing the NYPD. He hadn't spoken to the detective all fall, but he'd expected the call. Selene had warned him that other gods might learn of Orion's methods and try to create new cults in their own honor. More sacrifices, more innocent women dead, all for the benefit of gods who couldn't gain power any other way. Selene had vowed she wouldn't let that happen, and Theo had sworn to help. A knot of trepidation formed somewhere beneath his lower ribs as he realized it was time to keep that promise.

In retrospect, the oath had probably been a terrible idea. He'd barely survived his last run-in with a cult—technically, he *hadn't* survived. After his classicist comrades had made him their final sacrifice, it had taken a supernatural resurrection by Artemis and her brother Apollo to get him back on his feet.

He tried to focus on what Freeman was saying. "You should come down to the scene right away before they clear all the evidence away," she insisted. "You might see something we've missed."

Selene grabbed his arm as he ended the call. "It's happened, hasn't it? Another dead virgin."

"No. An old homeless man killed down near Wall Street."

Selene visibly relaxed. "Then why call us?"

"Freeman said the body's surrounded by a variety of ritualistic symbols. Not the same thing as last time . . . but definitely cultic."

Selene stood up from the kitchen table, her fury instantly reignited.

"Don't jump to conclusions," he said quickly. "This could just be some copycats intrigued by the press coverage from last time. Not some grand plot by an Athanatos." But his optimism sounded forced even to his own ears.

"Let's get down there and find out," she said, already moving toward the hallway.

This would be no romp through the park, bringing justice to the foolish mortals who dared ignite the Huntress's fury. Theo grabbed his parka from the back of a chair.

If Selene's suspicions are correct, he knew, *this will be a battle between gods. One fought over the right to immortality itself.* He couldn't repress a choked laugh. *And I thought* bears *were scary.*

Chapter 5

ANGEL OF DEATH

At four in the morning, Trinity Church stood like a ghostly apparition from another time, a tiny eighteenth-century island amid the soaring skyscrapers that crowded Wall Street. As Selene and Theo made their way from the Rector Street subway station, the church stood just before them, its tall, snow-capped spire illuminated by floodlights. A small cemetery kept the rest of the Financial District at bay. Through the wrought iron fence, Selene could see the gravestones, made from the same mica schist that formed the island's famous bedrock and allowed its skyscrapers to soar to such vertiginous heights. Two hundred years of wind, rain, and pollution had worn even the hardest stone to sharp flakes and erased the identities of the dead. She felt a shudder of foreboding at the thought, knowing that her own name remained barely legible on the collective memory of mankind, ready to be washed away completely by the next hard storm.

They turned down Broadway. To the south, the great boulevard that traversed Manhattan finally ended with a glimpse of the sky above New York Harbor, a flat, steely gray from the light pollution bouncing off the clouds. Despite the towering buildings, the colonial outlines still constrained the city: Broadway itself narrowed to a mere two lanes, and the side streets wriggled between the skyscrapers like cowpaths. Later in the day, buses, tourists, and investment bankers would throng the street. But in the predawn hush, only a few bleary-eyed stockbrokers walked by. The buildings around them stood mostly dark, although even now, with the New York Stock Exchange closed for the night, some windows remained bright; after all, in today's interconnected world, the sun never set on the global markets. If Tokyo traded, so did New York.

Selene glanced at Theo. He looked like a hyperventilating athlete, his breath coming in great white puffs. "Stop looking so guilty," she chided him.

"I can't help it. Every time I talk to Detective Freeman and Captain Hansen, I feel like they know exactly what happened that night."

"That we killed Orion? A man they think is no more than a constellation? Then burned his body in Central Park to hide the evidence? Unlikely." Still, Theo was right. The story they'd told the detectives was riddled with holes. The cops believed Professor Everett Halloran was still on the loose after fleeing the grisly sacrifice of three women and the murder of his four classicist acolytes. Theo had testified truthfully that the cult's rites honored Orion the Hunter, but the complete story—that Everett *was* Orion—would never occur to the hardboiled cops of the NYPD. Sometimes, Selene was grateful mortals didn't believe in gods anymore. It made them much easier to dupe.

But at the moment, she didn't care about their last run-in with the police. She was more concerned with this one. If the latest murder was the work of mortals copying the Classicist Cult for their own sick purposes, then she'd welcome police assistance in solving the crime. But if, as she feared, an immortal had started a cult in his own honor to restore his strength as Orion had, she didn't want the cops involved in a battle between Olympians.

"Did Freeman say exactly what she wanted from us?" she asked Theo as they approached the police barricade.

"She said she wanted my expertise."

"*Your* expertise?"

"Would you like to tell her you're an eyewitness to everything I've only read in books?"

Selene just scowled. The thrill she'd felt at bringing Lars to justice now felt hollow and petty. A real fight lay before her—one she wasn't sure she could win. If one of her kin had revived Orion's cult, she'd need all her cunning to defeat him—a real challenge for a goddess more accustomed to rage than calculation. The responsibility weighed heavily. The towering buildings around her only seemed to add to her sudden sense of oppressive dread.

"As if a killer cult on the loose wasn't bad enough," she grumbled, "you know how I feel about Wall Street."

"Probably about how everyone else in America does."

"Worse." She remembered the street from when she'd first come to New Amsterdam as Phoebe Hautman in the 1600s, when its name referred to the wall meant to separate the tiny Dutch settlement from the wilderness of Mana-hatta. She'd spent most of her time north of that wall, living with the Indians or alone in the forests. Every time she visited the town, it had grown a little bigger. The British replaced the Dutch. Ponds and streams disappeared beneath cobblestones. Ships crowded the harbor, a forest of masts dwarfing the island's ever-dwindling supply of trees. Eventually, the settlement overflowed its walls, razed the hills, and claimed part of the harbor itself, filling it with dirt to expand the island's outline. By the 1920s, the biggest, richest companies in the world built the ornate skyscrapers that still lined the street before her. The area became a temple to greed and wealth: two forces now worshiped with far more passion than she'd ever inspired, even at the height of her power.

The police barricade stood at the intersection of Exchange Place and Broadway. Before them, swirling lights illuminated the street in flashing blue and red: a sick parody of twinkling Christmas cheer. The crime scene seemed to stretch on forever.

At the chirping siren of an ambulance, Selene and Theo ducked out of the way. A policeman moved the barricade aside, and the ambulance sped off down the street.

"They don't move that fast to collect a dead body, do they?" Theo asked.

"No. Someone's hurt down there." Selene shivered, her sense of unease growing.

Captain Geraldine Hansen of the Counterterrorism Division, who'd worked with them on the investigation into the last cult, met Selene and Theo at the police barricade and waved them through. She wore a heavy, shapeless wool coat but no hat. Her short gray hair tossed in the wind, and her nose glowed red with cold. She looked older than when Selene had seen her last, the circles under her eyes a little more pronounced. Her breath smelled of cigarettes, and Selene wondered if the stress of the last case had driven the captain back to the habit.

"Detective Freeman told me she called you, Professor," Hansen said, shaking Theo's hand. She offered Selene a curt nod. "I hoped he'd bring you along."

Selene got chills every time the woman looked at her with such familiarity. During the last investigation, Selene had claimed to be the daughter of Police Officer Cynthia Forrester, Hansen's old comrade from the 1970s. Supposedly, Cynthia had died after leaving the NYPD in disgrace. Selene couldn't very well admit that she *was* Cynthia, barely aged in the forty years since she'd mentored rookie cop Gerry Hansen.

Detective Maggie Freeman joined them, a young, cherubic-faced black woman in a puffy parka and sensible fleece hat. She'd been the junior detective on the last case and had since earned a promotion to Counterterrorism, working as Hansen's aide.

"What's up with the ambulance?" Theo asked.

Freeman blew out a frustrated breath. "Really bad timing. Just after we arrive, a guy crawls out on a ledge on the building next to the crime scene and threatens to jump. Turns out he'd just made some really bad trade on the Tokyo exchange—lost millions in seconds. Then he looks out the window, sees the dead body beneath him, and decides that's the way to go."

Theo craned his head to see over Freeman's shoulder. "Shitballs. Did he make it?"

"We talked him down," she answered. "But it still feels a little like the Angel of Death passed over Wall Street tonight."

"Don't get overdramatic, Detective." The captain frowned at her young aide. "It isn't the first time men have tried to kill themselves over money, and it won't be the last."

Theo looked taken aback by her callousness, but Selene knew Geraldine was right. When the Depression had struck, she'd seen men jump from the windows of these same buildings, plummeting just as fast as the nation's fortunes. She'd never forgiven them for wreaking such destruction on her city, and had been both infuriated and unsurprised when it happened again a few years back. Now, less than a decade after the recession, Wall Street was at it again, playing with other people's money without regard for other people's lives. Before long, Selene knew, they'd bring the whole system crashing down again. Some things never changed.

"Obviously the suicide attempt and the murder aren't directly related," the captain went on. "But the crime scene made our jumper uneasy for a reason. Come take a look." She led the way past a veritable fleet of police cars, fire trucks, and ambulances. In the center of a circle of floodlights stood the massive bronze statue that symbolized Wall Street itself. Normally, the *Charging Bull* served as a photo-op for tourists and a goad for underperforming investment bankers. Tonight it was an altar.

A corpse lay facedown on the bull's back, its arms and legs draped over the statue's sides: an old man, by his long gray hair and the bulging veins on his hands. He wore a floppy black knit hat, a ragged army jacket, and dirty parachute pants last popular in the late eighties. A homeless man, probably, maybe even a veteran, a lost soul forgotten by the country he'd served. Selene had no special feelings for such victims—innocent women were her realm, not old men. But this was *her* city, and she was its Protector. If a new cult was killing mortals in her home, she was going to stop it.

"Tell me who the victim was."

Freeman raised an eyebrow at Selene's imperious tone but answered all the same. "No ID yet. Medical examiner's on his way. Until then, no one moves the body, so we haven't even seen his face." She had a quiet voice that some might mistake for meekness but that Selene suspected was mainly a strategy to make her seem less threatening in a profession dominated by white males. She understood the impulse, but preferred Hansen's unapologetic bossiness.

Freeman went on, describing the victim with calm detachment. "From the look of his hands, he seems to be in his seventies. A vagrant, probably. No visible wound, so it must be on the anterior torso." Selene could see the rusty rivulets of dried blood striping the bull's sides. Wherever the wound was, it was big.

"Victim likely died of exsanguination," the cop continued. "There're probably four quarts of blood on the ground around the statue."

"Sounds like a blood libation," Theo said. "And it looks like they threw in some burnt offerings for good measure." He gestured to the circle of charred brush around the bull, still wet and smoldering from the fire hoses. "Definitely ritualistic, and the choice of the bull as the central emblem points to Greek or Cretan influence."

The captain grunted. "That's what we're afraid of. But we're going to need more specifics."

"Different gods require different forms of sacrifice." Theo slipped into his lecturing mode. His voice rose; he gestured animatedly. "Celestial gods receive offerings from the fire's rising smoke." He raised his hands in waves above his head. "Chthonic ones, those associated with the Underworld, receive them through libations poured into the ground." He pointed downward. "Not many gods would require both types like this, so that might help us pinpoint the worshiped deity. If we find out what sort of cult they're reviving, we might understand who these guys are or what their next move might be."

Gods of the Earth, not just the Underworld, also receive libations, Selene amended silently. *Since fleeing Olympus, all Athanatoi consider themselves both celestial and earthbound. So the method of sacrifice doesn't narrow it down at all.*

"Whoever they're worshiping," interjected Hansen, "they're pulling out all the old pagan cult tricks." She pointed to a dead snake lying on the ground.

Theo groaned. "Not again." Snakes had featured prominently in the Classicist Cult's ritual.

Freeman motioned them to follow her around the statue's base. "There's more." She pointed to a black bird, a slit in its throat gaping crimson, blood caking the feathers of its breast. Then a large black dog, its chest opened to display a glistening red and white tangle of innards. Selene felt her skin prickle. She found the similarities between Orion's cult and this one deeply disconcerting. He had sacrificed a number of dogs as part of his ritual, all in homage to Artemis, Lady of Hounds.

Hansen's steely gaze moved from the dog to Selene to Theo. "Looks like Everett Halloran is back. And we need to stop him before he strikes again." Her voice was only a hair less commanding than Selene's.

The captain was wrong, of course, but Selene couldn't tell Hansen that. Then again, she didn't want the cops wasting time chasing a phantom culprit. *Leading them in the right direction without telling them the whole truth will take a fair amount of conversational finesse,* Selene realized. *Which is why I intend to let Theo do it.*

He seemed to have the same idea, jumping in with, "Halloran thought his Mystery Cult gave him power—power that came from reenacting the ancient rituals as accurately as possible. So, if he is back, we should think about December ceremonies. In the Greek calendar, that means mainly Dionysian festivals."

The captain grimaced. "Great. Dionysus is the God of Wine, right? Does that mean a bunch of drunken murderers roaming the streets?"

"That and sex-crazed maenads."

"There'd be ivy," Selene declared. "That's the main symbol of Dionysus, more than even the grape vine. Did you find any?"

"No plants this time," Freeman interjected quietly. "Except for the wood and brush for the fire."

"Honestly, nothing so far screams out any particular ritual to me," Theo said, rubbing the dimple on his chin. "But I'm not a walking encyclopedia." Freeman gave him a slanted smile that said she might disagree, but Theo just pointed to the statue of the bull, seemingly oblivious to everything except the mystery at hand. "*That's* clearly the main symbolic element. Might point to Zeus, the Sky God. He was known to disguise himself as a bull and have his way with unsuspecting maidens."

Freeman made a face. "He'd be brought up on charges for *that*."

"It was a different age," Selene said sharply. *But yeah, you're right.* If she hadn't loved her father quite so much, and if he hadn't been the King of the Gods, she would've put an arrow through him for more than one of his exploits. But she didn't really believe Zeus was behind this new cult—he'd been holed up in a cave in Crete for years, going slowly insane. "The bull's not just the Sky God's symbol," she corrected Theo. "It was a common sacrificial animal for all the Olympians."

Hansen and Freeman looked at the professor for confirmation, much to Selene's irritation.

"Selene's right," he nodded sagely.

That condescension better just be for show, she thought. As he continued to pontificate on the iconography of various Greek gods, she gave up trying to explain her own family to a bunch of thanatoi and paced the perimeter of the crime scene instead.

She squatted down to examine the dead bird. Black feathers and legs. Thick, straight beak. A crow.

Next, she moved to the dead snake. Its head lay at an odd angle—it had died from a broken neck, not a knife wound. She couldn't be sure about its species—she was no herpetologist, and snakes had always lain outside her realm—but its diamond-shaped head proved it a viper. Definitely not native to New York.

Finally, she moved to the dead dog, her anger mounting. *Bad enough to pollute our sacred rites with human sacrifice, but to target the animal I'm sworn to protect?* She wondered if the men behind this new cult—and she hoped they *were* men, not Athanatoi—knew they were enraging a very dangerous goddess with very good aim.

The dog was massive—probably a hundred pounds, with thick limbs, short black hair, and a jowly face. It would've taken a very strong man or a very foolhardy one to hold the animal down and kill him without getting a hand bitten off. *Or maybe the killer did get mauled . . . it'd serve him right,* Selene thought. The dog's guts lay revealed. The winding beige path of his intestines, the vaguely obscene knob of his heart, the wet red wings of lung. It took her a moment to realize what was missing. The liver. She eventually found the dark brown lobes a few paces away.

All the sacrifices lay just outside the ring of charred branches and scrub. Most of the wood looked to be the kind easily available from any local park—oak branches, pine boughs, the occasional linden twig. But on the east side of the circle, she noticed a burnt bundle of reeds still bound together with a plastic band. She found a similar object on the west side.

She stepped over the ring of still-smoldering brush and approached the victim sprawled across the bull. She desperately wanted to turn his body over. She needed to see how they'd killed him, but she knew the entire First Precinct would rush to stop her the second she tried. She'd have to leave it to the Medical Examiner's Office to do the autopsy and content herself with examining the rest of the crime scene instead.

She squatted to peer beneath the bronze belly of the bull. Decades of tittering tourists had rubbed its large dangling testicles to a golden sheen.

"Don't tell me you're about to take a selfie with the bull balls." Theo crouched just beyond the circle of brush. Hansen and Freeman had moved out of hearing range, convening with a cluster of uniformed cops and forensic investigators.

Selene relayed her findings in a low voice. "Someone performed haruspicy on the dog."

"Yeah, that's what I told Freeman, what with the entrails pulled out. Which means we're definitely looking at something Greco-Roman. Did you read anything in the liver?"

"Do I look like a haruspex? I used to send mankind omens; that doesn't mean I know how to interpret them."

He gave her a vaguely disappointed look. When he'd discovered Selene's true identity, Theo had instantly demanded answers to every question classicists had debated for centuries. He'd been more than a little frustrated that Selene's own memories of her godhood were often as patchy and confused as the remnants of texts in which men had recorded her deeds. She'd tried explaining it to him: Just as Theo couldn't tell if his childhood memories were merely confabulations inspired by his parents' stories, she couldn't trust that her knowledge of the past had not been altered by the poets' retellings.

"I'm not seeing much of a pattern yet," Theo admitted, still scanning the crime scene. "There are lots of references that *could* mean something, but nothing cohesive. The timing makes sense for Saturnalia or Dionysia, but they were both primarily harvest festivals, and there's no bread here. No wine, no food at all. Did you find anything?"

"The remains of two reed torches buried in the wood."

"Huh. Could indicate a reference to a god or goddess who

lights the way to the Underworld. Persephone, Demeter—maybe even you in your incarnation as Hecate."

"Another aspect of myself I never enjoyed." That much, at least, she remembered. She only ever thought of her realm as forests and mountains, not the caverns of death. "What did Hansen say about video footage?"

"Nothing useful. Our perps pulled up a ConEd vehicle to block the site, the kind with a tent on the back to cover manholes. Then, if that weren't enough, they managed to disable the security cameras on the surrounding buildings."

"So these guys aren't amateurs. They may even have someone inside the utility company." She took a step back, noting the orientation of the three animal sacrifices. The dog lay due north of the bull statue, the crow due east, and the viper due west. Most New Yorkers judged directions by the street grid: North would mean pointing directly uptown. But whoever organized this murder had oriented the sacrifices according to the geographic poles. Selene didn't need a compass to tell her their accuracy—her status as Goddess of the Moon gave her a flawless sense of direction. But why lay sacrifices at three of the cardinal points and not the fourth? Unless…

She circled back to the southern side. There, just under a large burnt branch, she spotted a black glimmer.

"Tell me if anyone's watching," she murmured to Theo.

"Why are we sneaking around?" he hissed. "I thought we were *helping* the cops this time."

"Not until we know for sure that there's not a god behind this." She pulled a pen from her pocket and used it to move aside the brush and reveal the small black creature.

A scorpion.

Staring over her shoulder, Theo let out a low whistle.

Selene let the branches fall back into place, a prickle of fear creeping across her spine. In some versions of the Artemis and Orion myth, she'd sent a giant scorpion to hunt down her lover as punishment for his misdeeds, later placing the constellation Scorpius in the heavens to chase Orion for eternity. In reality, the first time he'd died, she'd shot him herself after her twin brother Apollo accused him of raping one of her nymphs. But humans—and many Athanatoi, for that matter—didn't know the full story. They'd know the version repeated by poets instead—and they'd immediately associate the scorpion with Orion.

"Orion's dead and he's not coming back," she said aloud, partly to reassure herself. "So why put a reference to him in the ritual?"

"If this is just a bunch of copycats, then they probably put in some Orion stuff because they read that the last cult was dedicated to him."

"For what purpose? Who are they trying to worship?"

Theo shrugged. "Maybe no one in particular. Maybe they're just sick bastards who wanted to kill a homeless person, and they thought this was a creepy way to do it. Or they're neopagans tampering with rituals they think are purely symbolic. Honestly, I don't think this is the work of an Athanatos. It's just too scattershot. Besides, since when does a god need to search for omens in an animal's liver? That's a mortal's job." His eyes lit, clearly inspired by his own theory. "Since a haruspex looks for signs of whether his sacrifice has been accepted and whether he needs to appease any additional deities, maybe this new cult doesn't even have a specific deity in mind yet. Maybe they're looking for a message in the liver to tell them which god they should even be talking to." He finally paused for breath. "You don't look convinced."

"I want you to be right. I want this to be some mortal assholes. And I want to help Hansen and Freeman bring them to justice. But I just don't—"

A collective cry rose from the assembled crowd, pulling Selene's attention upward to the figure of a woman standing on a ledge twenty stories above their heads.

Captain Hansen immediately started shouting orders, and a mass of officers ran toward the building entrance. Before they even reached the door, the body fell forward, limp and thin like a child's toy, growing ever larger as it plummeted toward them. Selene heard Theo's strangled gasp beside her.

She wished she still had a chariot pulled by wide-antlered stags, so she might ride through the air to pluck the woman from her fall. Instead, she could only stand in silence and watch the street around her grow yet darker with blood.

Chapter 6

LORD OF THE DEAD

Theo's enthusiasm for crime solving had dissolved around the time the stockbroker's body landed a few yards away from him, her blood spattering the toes of his winter boots. Another trade gone horribly wrong, they said. Another master of the financial markets, seemingly invulnerable, brought to utter despair as millions of dollars disappeared into the electronic ether. She too, her coworkers reported, had seen the victim on the bull beneath her window and felt drawn to join him in oblivion. Theo hadn't seen her die: He'd screwed his eyes shut the second he saw her jump, unwilling to witness the crude carnage of her death.

Yet here I go, he thought as he approached the Medical Examiner's Office, *walking voluntarily into a charnel house. One dead body was too much. But dozens? Why not.*

Theo had never visited the morgue before. Few New Yorkers had. If, in some rare circumstance, they needed to identify a body, the police would show them a photograph. Civilians didn't get the dubious privilege of viewing the corpse in the flesh. But Selene had managed to convince Detective Freeman that she and Theo should get a crack at the body of the homeless victim. How else could they identify any further clues that would help them understand this new cult?

As Theo walked into the autopsy room, an overwhelming stench of rotten meat nearly knocked him flat. Beside him, Selene clapped a hand over her nose and mouth, her face green. Freeman gagged audibly. A slight, bearded medical examiner rushed over and handed them surgical masks that dampened the worst of the smell.

"What in the world, Janz?" the young detective demanded with none of her usual diffidence.

"I know! There must be something wrong with the refrigeration system because the corpses looked fine when I rolled them out, and then a few minutes ago, *bam!* It was like they'd all been sitting in the heat for days!" He turned to an assistant, panicked. "Let's get them all back into the drawers!" The coroners rushed about, rolling corpses in various stages of decomposition past Theo like the world's worst dim sum offerings. Finally, only one body remained in the room, covered modestly with a sheet. Janz came back to them, a sheen of sweat on his brow.

"Sorry about that, Detective. But I've got your John Doe ready for you. And let me tell you, he's as much a mystery as our broken cooling system."

"Maybe our visitors can help you out," Freeman said, gesturing to Theo and Selene. "They're specialists in human sacrifice."

"Well," Theo began, "that makes it sound a bit grim. I'm a classicist. Human sacrifice is sort of a sideline." That, he realized, sounded even worse.

"Oh, you're the folks who tracked down the Classicist Cult this fall?" The examiner reached for Selene's hand, but she just stared at him coldly.

"That's us." Theo proffered his own hand, then fought the urge to wipe it on his trousers to dislodge any corpse cooties.

"Good, because I'm stumped." Janz looked relieved. "It's not the cause of death that's the problem, because that's pretty clear:

His heart has been completely removed." He spoke as if this shocking fact were all in a day's work. "But the body itself is a complete anomaly."

"Why's that?" Freeman asked.

"First of all, he's not really a homeless man." The medical examiner pulled back the sheet. Theo noticed Selene stiffen beside him. She stared down at the body as if she'd never seen a dead man before. Strange, since she'd seen thousands—not a few of whom she'd killed herself.

Theo forced himself not to look away from the gaping hole in the man's chest. Other than that disfigurement, he seemed like a typical corpse. Sunken cheeks, deathly pale skin. Unlike the other bodies, however, he was relatively well preserved. No blackened flesh, no odor of putrefaction. He was well over six feet tall, his body an amalgamation of bony limbs and loose skin, like a man who'd only recently lost a great deal of muscle mass. A large beaked nose, thinning gray hair to his shoulders. His hands were overlarge, each knuckle protruding like a skeleton's. They'd removed his ragged clothing, and Theo turned his eyes away from the darker nest of hair between the man's thighs.

Janz lifted the victim's ring finger with his own gloved hand. "His fingernails were perfectly manicured and coated with clear polish, like some celebrity or tycoon. And there's not a spec of sebungual dirt."

Freeman whipped out a notepad and started writing. "So they dressed him up in rags and smeared his face with dirt to make him *look* homeless?"

Janz nodded. "Under his clothes, his body was perfectly clean."

The detective pointed toward the bloody well in his chest. "What could've done *that*?"

The examiner raised his eyebrows behind his glasses. "I was hoping you could tell me. Some sharp object with a serrated blade. Went in through his chest and sliced the ribs before severing the arteries to remove the heart. He would've been alive when it happened. Is that common practice among cultic sacrifices, Professor?"

"Um. I don't actually know," Theo admitted. "Human sacrifice was exceedingly rare in the classical world. But I can tell you that *animal* sacrifices certainly weren't tortured. They were supposed to go willingly to their deaths; otherwise the sacrifice wasn't auspicious." He drew his finger across his throat. "One clean slit. You might see an organ removed for haruspicy—examining the animal's entrails for omens—but usually the liver, not the heart. Amazing that classical civilization flourished as long as it did while basing all kinds of monumental decisions on the shape of organ meat, but there you have it." He looked to Selene, knowing he'd get an angry glare for implying the gods' signs were anything but authentic. But she continued staring down at the victim, her face creased with distress, ignoring Theo entirely.

Freeman didn't pay much attention to his history lesson either. "Any more progress on the ID?" she asked the examiner.

"No. We ran fingerprints, but no matches. But since he's no vagrant, it's likely we'll get a hit when someone reports him missing." Janz pointed to an indentation in the flesh of the man's finger. "Signs of a wedding ring, even though none was found. So maybe we'll hear from the spouse. But there are other anomalies. Johnny Doe *looks* like he's in his seventies, but—"

Selene spoke for the first time, interrupting the examiner with a growl. "Don't call him that."

Janz blinked behind his glasses. "What?"

"Don't act like his name's already been erased."

Freeman jumped in before Theo could. "Ms. DiSilva, it may sound harsh, but that's just standard procedure until we identify him."

Theo glanced down at Selene's clenched fists. "Do you want to step outside for a minute?" he asked. "Take a break from the dead bodies?"

"We're done here," Selene said, already walking away.

"Don't you want to hear the rest of the autopsy report?"

"We don't need to."

Theo stayed behind for a few minutes, apologizing to Freeman and Janz for Selene's rudeness, then exited the building. A small concrete courtyard lay before him. Bare trees, a single bench. Selene paced in a tight circle through the snow, talking on her antiquated phone.

"You don't understand." She threaded a hand through the white streak in her black hair, tugging with uncharacteristic agitation. "We need to talk right away. Someone blabbed, Paul. And it better not be you. Don't hang up on me. I don't *care* about your concert." She barely paused for a response before barking, "Sure, I'll be *careful*, Paul, don't worry." She snapped her phone shut and sat down heavily on the bench, not bothering to brush away the snow.

"What's going on?" Theo asked, trying not to sound as frustrated as he felt. "And what the hell was that back there? We were about to learn something, and you rushed out like Cerberus hearing a dog whistle with all three heads."

She ignored the jibe. "The examiner made it all sound like some vast mystery, when really it's very simple."

"Oh yeah?"

"He was about to tell us that the evidence so far showed that the victim wasn't an old man after all. That his body was wrinkled and weak, but he showed few other signs of normal aging: no bone loss, no worn teeth."

"Oh." Theo started to understand. His mind spun, trying to reorganize everything he'd observed so far. He sat beside Selene on the bench, searching her face for some sign of grief over the death of one of her kin. She just stared up at the pale blue sky, her face emotionless. He had the sudden impression she sought something—or someone—among the wisps of cloud.

"Is that your father in there?" Theo asked, taking her hand in his. Selene had never told him where Zeus currently resided. She rarely even spoke of him, but he'd always gotten the impression she loved him deeply. After losing her mother so recently, he wasn't sure how Selene would react to losing her father as well.

But she only shook her head. "The stockbrokers losing their money, the corpses suddenly putrefying...Sometimes, when a god dies, his death has ripple effects on the parts of the world he once controlled. A last little gasp of homage from a place that has otherwise forgotten him."

Only one god would affect both corpses and bankers. "Hades. Lord of the Dead. God of Wealth," Theo said, a shiver crossing his flesh. Of all the Athanatoi, Hades was the only one he'd never wanted to meet.

Selene nodded solemnly. "It happened when my mother died. The babies in the hospital cried, mourning the loss of the Goddess of Motherhood. But she faded away naturally—she was ready to go. The death of a god like Hades, murdered while still strong, might cause a much greater reaction."

"If he's so strong, then why did he look so frail?"

"In his own realm, he was almost invincible—you know how men still worship wealth. But our powers are funny things. They work differently for all of us. An old proscription from my father meant that when Hades emerged aboveground, he lost his strength. An Athanatos would know that."

"So you're saying a god did this—one who knew the secrets of Orion's rites. But your brothers who took down the last cult with us promised not to perform rituals of their own."

"They can't be trusted. I've been trying to explain that to you. Why do you think I don't talk to them? Because I *like* being lonely? It's because they're all insane. The lure of unlimited power—it's just too strong for them to resist, no matter the consequences."

"I don't buy it," Theo insisted. "How could this be a cult in their honor if it's got none of their attributes? No ivy for the Wine Giver, no laurel or sun emblems for the Bright One, and nothing that would indicate the Smith or the Messenger either."

She huffed in exasperation. "Then one of my brothers told *another* god about the cult, and *that* immortal is behind this. Either way, one broke his promise."

"You don't know that. There are humans out there who know about the gods, right? Humans like *me*. So maybe Hades let the secret of his strength slip to some trusted mortal drinking buddy, and that mortal turned against him. Because, let's face it, having the Lord of the Dead drop by all the time for trivia night is about as socially awkward as you can get. So eventually this mortal buddy decides that a cult ritual is the perfect way to kill off a god while showing him some respect at the same time."

"That's ridiculous."

"Any more ridiculous than one of your brothers murdering his own uncle? And doing it in a ritual with none of his own attributes—so it can't give him any strength? Why would they bother?"

"Whoever this is—mortal or immortal—they knew where to find Hades." Her voice tightened in anger. "That means they might know where to find *me*. I'm in real danger. *All* the gods are in danger. I *think* I'd heal from anything but a divine weapon—but a wound like that? So much blood? I'd have to test it to know."

"Jesus. How about we not try that particular experiment." In theory, he was well aware that Selene's immortality was incomplete at best. But in practice, he'd gotten so used to seeing her perform preternatural feats and heal with uncanny speed that it was easy to forget just how vulnerable she truly was.

"Don't worry. So far, my theory's been 'avoid massive chest wounds whenever possible, no matter the weapon.'"

"Glad to hear it." But he wasn't reassured. Any thought of Selene as a superheroine and him as her faithful, sleuthing sidekick was banished by the sudden image of her bleeding to death on a bronze bull, her power gone, her eyes dim.

She must have felt his change of heart, because all hint of lightness left her voice when she said, "I've never seen a god killed before." She didn't need to say she was scared. He saw it in the sudden tension of her jaw. "My mother died peacefully, fading into mortality. Orion—he wasn't really a god to begin with. But Hades...*Styx*," she cursed, blinking away tears before they could fall. Theo knew her appearance of divine frigidity was largely a facade—her emotions were as fluid as any human's—but seeing her so afraid shook him to his core. He wished, not for the first time, that he was an old-fashioned hero. Someone like Perseus, wielding a magic shield to protect the woman he loved from monsters real and imagined.

"You're using Hades' real name," he noted quietly. Usually, Selene only called the gods by their epithets.

"Now that he's gone, the name doesn't have any power. It's just part of a myth. Like Hades himself."

Theo felt her shudder beneath his touch and held her hand a little tighter. "You're safe," he said, wrapping her in his embrace. "We didn't let the last cult hurt you. This one won't either. You're strong, Selene. And you're not alone, remember? You've got me. You've got Paul."

"Paul?" She spoke Apollo's mortal moniker like a curse. "Don't you see? Now we *know* someone revealed the secrets of the last cult. Someone who knew that the only sacrifice more potent than a human was a *god*. I called my twin just now—he denied it, of course, but he wasn't even *listening* to me. And don't tell me to give him the benefit of the doubt," she went on before Theo could protest. "He's playing a concert at the Bowery Ballroom, and he's in the middle of a *sound check* or something. He sounded completely distracted and said we'd talk later."

"You told the Bright One someone murdered an Athanatos and he didn't care? Wow. Your twin really *does* think the sun rises and sets with him." He'd hoped the pun would help calm her down, but she only shook her head.

"Either he's part of this plot or something is deeply wrong with him—and I have no idea what that could be."

That's the second time she's admitted her ignorance, Theo realized. Usually, when she didn't understand something, Selene remained stonily silent. Now all her worries streamed out, dragging Theo into their wake and sending him reeling alongside.

There was a catch in her voice as she admitted, "I thought that since Paul and I aren't fighting anymore, it'd be just like old times. We used to be two halves of the same whole. But it's not like that at all. Too much time has passed. All I know is that he won't be so calm once he realizes that even the strongest of us is a single blow away from death. From becoming exactly what men already think we are: figments of their imagination."

Theo placed a finger on her chin and gently turned her face toward his. "Selene, you're right here. You're not going anywhere." He kissed her, hard, on the mouth. A reminder that when she foundered, he would be her rock, just as she so often was for him. She took a deep breath, and he saw her visibly steady herself. He smiled. "And you *better* exist outside of my imagination, or *damn*, I'm even more of a loser than I thought."

Chapter 7

INTERMISSIO:
THE HYAENA

Six months earlier

The others called her the Hyaena, but the title fit poorly: In the precincts of the Templo, she never laughed.

The patient who lay before her in the hospital bed knew the name bothered her—he called her daughter instead.

She called him the Praenuntius. The Harbinger. She'd never asked whether he preferred his real name. It didn't matter if he did: She wasn't allowed to use it. And the Hyaena always followed the rules.

The patient stared up at her with eyes the color of new-turned soil. Eyes that had long ago forgotten how to cry.

"Time for your test," the Hyaena told him, moving around the windowless chamber with practiced efficiency.

He didn't respond. It wouldn't have done him any good.

She powered up the computer and folded the thin blanket back from the bottom of the bed. His feet were overlarge and tangled in an old man's knobbly veins, but the soles were smooth as a baby's. She tightened the straps around his ankles, then winched the restraints around his wrists. She bent down to retrieve a final strap that dragged off the side of the bed—then froze at the feel of his fingertips brushing against her hair.

She remained crouched beneath his touch, her breath shallow. *Will he kill me?* she wondered, not for the first time. *Will he tear free of his bonds and rip my head from my body?* But his fingers, constrained by the bindings around his wrists, only stirred the errant wisps of her hair.

She took a careful step out of reach, then stood swiftly, hands on hips. "That's not allowed."

His mouth opened with a gummy pop, and he spoke in a hoarse whisper. "Your hair feels like the antennae of butterflies."

On the way to her monthly appointment with the patient, she'd noticed the first butterfly of summer fluttering above a rosebush on Fifth Avenue. She'd had no time to appreciate its beauty, much less imagine the touch of its antennae on her palm, but she raised an unconscious hand to her hair, wondering if the Praenuntius was right. At her gesture, the patient's chapped lips pulled back from yellowed teeth. It took her a moment to recognize the unfamiliar expression as a smile.

"How do you remember what butterflies feel like?" she asked, for surely he hadn't been near one for a very long time.

"Time passes strangely for me. I've forgotten much, yet some things I remember still." His eyes fluttered closed as if to better conjure the memory. "I lay against stone. I had a single visitor. She looked like a moth, pale gray and plain. But when she lifted into the air, she danced like a bright copper coin." His eyes snapped open. "You remind me of that butterfly, daughter."

In that moment, the Hyaena remembered her real father. He, too, had lain in a hospital bed for longer than anyone could endure. Poked and prodded by those who believed they did what was best, but who only prolonged his agony. Even at the end, her father had seen something in her that no other man had—something bright and precious and strong. She'd tried to be worthy, tried to bring him solace in the end. She had no such words of comfort for the Praenuntius. What does one say to an old man who should know better than to love you?

The Hyaena gathered her instruments from the cabinet and arranged them neatly on a metal rolling tray, then picked up one of the digital stopwatches. Next, she adjusted her surveillance earpiece so it nestled more firmly against her skull; her superiors rarely spoke during the tests, but it was her duty to be prepared.

The patient looked away from her preparations and stared straight up at the bare white ceiling. His pupils contracted in the cold glare of the fluorescent bulb. "I wish I could see the sun again," he said.

Then, at the beep of the stopwatch, his entire body tensed.

She plunged a scalpel into his heart.

His body seized, each limb straining against the straps that bit into his flesh. His head flew backward, exposing the loose, wrinkled skin of his neck. She waited patiently until sixty seconds had passed, then yanked the scalpel free of his rib cage. Blood pulsed across his chest in a red, rhythmic tide. It pooled in the hollow of his belly, then streamed onto the rubber sheets. He gasped. His gnarled hands clutched into fists. Then his eyes rolled back in his head, and the tide ceased to flow. He lay motionless.

The Hyaena checked for his pulse and felt nothing but inert flesh. She clicked off one stopwatch and started another before placing both back on her tray. She reached for the sponges and bucket.

The first twenty times she'd killed the Praenuntius, she'd vomited in the pail, yellow bile swirling with bloody water. Now she felt no more than a mild twinge of pity. She wiped the blood from his body, revealing the thin lines of white, pink, and red that covered his chest like cuneiform. The wound from last month's test remained crusted with brown. The one from the month before was livid red. Infected perhaps. She made a note of it on the computer.

In her life, the Hyaena had seen suffering of all kinds. Children abandoned, men maimed, women defiled, whole neighborhoods drowning in sorrow. But nothing like the agony this man suffered at her hands. Slow torture without end, trapped in a room with no hope of release. Yet she had no choice. This was the role she'd been assigned.

She finished mopping the sheets, squeezed a bloody waterfall into the bucket, then washed her hands in the utility sink. She picked up the stopwatch. Five minutes since death. Her thumb hovered over the button. *Any second now . . .*

But nothing happened. The Praenuntius still hadn't breathed. His skin, always pale from his centuries without sun, had taken on a grayish cast. Worse than she'd ever seen it. For the first time in years, she started to worry.

Then, as if a silent windstorm had ripped through the room, everything before her eyes suddenly blurred. She sat back heavily on her stool, pressing a palm against the sudden emptiness in her chest and wondering if she was having a heart attack. It felt as if a great hand had reached into her gut and hollowed her out, yet somehow, bizarrely, she couldn't find the will to panic.

She saw her reflection in the polished tray before her. Her face calm, detached. Bored, almost. She watched the image dispassionately as all color fled her cheeks. As her veins turned cold and her limbs refused to move. *This is what it feels like to have my soul removed,* she decided. She looked at the Praenuntius. *Have I truly killed him this time? Has his death caused this?*

Then the sensation of apathy fled, the world stopped spinning, and her body was her own again. She gasped aloud with the sudden return to feeling. She had no time to wonder what had happened—a voice in her earpiece rasped to life, demanded attention: *"Do not let him go."* She recognized the voice instantly. Old and feeble, almost as weak as the Praenuntius's, yet the words echoed in her brain like those of her own conscience. He was another father to her. Not the man who'd given her life and died years before, nor the one who now lay dead at her hand, but the Pater Patrum, the Father of Fathers.

She leaped into action, tossing down the stopwatch and grabbing the suture needle from her tray. She'd never done this before, but pressure didn't scare her, it steadied her. After she'd closed the wound and attached the IV for the blood transfusion, she removed the defibrillator paddles mounted on the wall. She spun the charging dial, one eye on the motionless patient. Somehow, she still expected him to take a sudden, harsh breath as he had a hundred—a thousand—times before without any help from her.

But his face was the color of silt. His chest as still as marble.

She pressed one paddle against the sunken flesh of his left breast and the other on the laddered rungs of his right rib cage. His entire body jerked with the electric shock, then flopped back with a thud.

Wait for another charge. Repeat. The voice in her ear did not speak again. It didn't have to. But she could hear the Pater's breathing. Heavy. Panicked.

One more time. Charge. Shock. Pray. Wait.

Charge. Shock. Pray.

Breath.

The Praenuntius coughed back into the world, his chest heaving with effort. When the coughing subsided, the sobs began.

She'd never seen him weep.

"Good work, Hyaena," said the Pater in her ear. Rare praise to be treasured, but she barely heard it.

She couldn't help herself: She broke the rules and released the straps around the patient's wrists so he might hide his tears beneath his fingers.

Another woman might have thought he wept because after a thousand years of trying, his captors had finally killed him.

She knew he wept because they hadn't.

"Why?" he gasped between his sobs. "I'm the Praenuntius. *The Harbinger.* Surely now I've delivered my final message. Why not let me die?"

Her earpiece hissed. *"There is much we learned from his death,"* the Pater said in her skull. *"There is even more we can learn from his life."* She started to say as much to the Praenuntius, but when he lifted his hands from his face and stared at her with red-rimmed eyes, her words drained away. She'd never seen such desperation.

"I will give you what you need." His voice was rough with tears. "But only if you promise to kill me again. And leave me dead."

Before she could respond, the Pater spoke. *"I will come to him myself. Leave now, Hyaena."* The hum in her earpiece fell abruptly silent. The man who ruled her life didn't wait to see if she obeyed his order. He simply knew she would.

"What do you mean...you'll give me what I need?" she asked the patient.

The Praenuntius raised a hand toward her. She took a quick breath—but didn't pull away. He placed his palm against her cheek. It was warmer than she'd imagined it.

"Promise me first." His forefinger rested on her temple, his thumb on her jaw. "Promise to let me die."

It was not her place to do so. She was only the Hyaena. But this man had called her daughter.

She let him draw her closer until their foreheads met. His eyes were pools of liquid darkness. She heard the Pater's footsteps in the hall.

"I promise," she whispered.

His smile quavered, infinite relief warring with infinite regret. "Then tell your Pater," he said, releasing her, "that my death will be only the first of many."

———◇———

In the monitoring room, the Hyaena hit Pause on the video, the Praenuntius's words still echoing in her brain. The images from the hospital bed were nearly six months old now—six months she and the rest of the Host had spent preparing and training for the most important mission in the history of the world.

They'd taken the first step a week ago, when, for the first time since the Praenuntius had come into their power centuries before, they'd captured another Deathless One—she wouldn't call Hades a god, for he was only a Pretender. He'd fought with the strength of ten men until they'd hauled him aboveground. Then they'd watched as he aged forty years in forty seconds. His skin grew slack, his muscles atrophied, his black hair streaked with gray. No one could explain why.

When they'd brought him to the bull's back a few days later, she'd turned away at the last minute. Even then, she couldn't escape the carnage—the sacrificial flames turned the new-fallen snow the color of blood. When she looked back, the man was Deathless no longer.

The door to the monitoring room swung open. She came to attention as the Heliodromus Primus entered, his features sharp as an axe. He wore a well-tailored dark suit today, not his ceremonial robes. Without his customary mask, his expression was easy to read. Arrogance, disdain, suspicion. *He worries that my success with the Praenuntius will raise me in the Pater's regard and threaten his own standing,* the Hyaena knew. As the second-in-command, the Heliodromus served as the Pater's enforcer, always testing the Host's other initiates to make sure of their loyalty. Recently, he'd applied special scrutiny to the Hyaena.

He looked over her shoulder at the frozen image on the monitor. "You're watching that video again," he said coldly. "Are you having second thoughts?"

"No," she snapped, swallowing a more pointed rebuttal that she knew would only fan his ire. "I am proud of how far we've come."

"Yet you care for the Praenuntius, and he for you. Don't try to deny it—I've seen the video, too."

She followed his gaze to one of the monitors, where a live image of the windowless room showed the old man asleep, his chest moving with irregular breaths, his body now a wasted shell, his skin chalky white. He looked more skeleton than man.

As he watched the Praenuntius on the screen, the Heliodromus's lips twitched—the closest he ever came to mirth—then he spared a glance for the Hyaena. "You want to keep your promise to him. You don't like the way we use him, do you?"

Because I'm not a sadist, you sick fuck, she thought, *no matter how hard you try to make me one.* But she said only, "We are *all* instruments in the Pater's hands, our only purpose to craft a better world." *That means you too, Heliodromus, despite your delusions of grandeur.*

He nodded, and put his hands on his hips, casually moving aside the hem of his suit jacket. She knew the move was deliberate; he wanted her to see the curve of the long leather whip he wore looped over his shoulder. The sign of his rank. A silent threat. She'd seen the stripes it could draw upon an initiate's back.

"We are instruments indeed." His fingers strayed to the whip's narrow tip, rolling it like rosary beads. The Hyaena wondered what she would do if he actually drew the whip and raised it against her. Would she submit as she was sworn to do? Or grab that nasty little tip and loop it back over his neck?

The Heliodromus lowered his chin, staring at her as if he knew the treasonous thoughts in her mind. "The battle has begun," he warned her. "The *true* battle."

She knew he spoke not of the silent war they waged for the Pater's favor, but of the greater conflict they'd both dedicated their lives to. The Hyaena's anger drained away. *He is right to remind me.*

She didn't try to stop him as he stepped to the computer console. "The arsenal is being assembled, even as we speak," he said as he deleted the video file from the hard drive.

"Yes, Heliodromus," she said, bowing her head.

"The Pater demands you look forward, Hyaena, not back." His words were as sharp as his whip and just as effective. He no longer toyed with her, and she respected him more for his bluntness.

With his hand on the door, he stopped to glance once more at the live feed from the old man's room. "The Praenuntius and his kind are obsolete." His eyes flicked toward her. A final warning. "See that you don't become the same."

Chapter 8

THE BARE-FISTED

That night, deep in the heart of Central Park, Selene stared upward into the light haloing a lamppost. Snowflakes tumbled toward her like slow-motion stars falling from heaven, coming to rest on her eyelashes and cheeks. Around her, the park glowed blue as moonlight reflected off the snow that limned the trees and muffled the sounds of the city beyond. The tracks of an intrepid midnight cross-country skier lay like ribbons across the ground, the lines already blurring beneath the ceaseless fall of flurries. She carried her bow in her backpack, but she'd have little chance to use it. The squirrels were hidden in their nests, the birds had flown south, the humans were tucked warm and snug in their apartments.

Theo lay asleep in her bed, no doubt dreaming about the evidence surrounding Hades' murder, trying to find some angle that didn't implicate the other Athanatoi. But Selene wasn't interested in Theo's scholarly take. She felt, deep in her gut, that one of her brothers had tattled about the cult.

It was foolhardy to venture into the park alone tonight, knowing an Athanatos might be hunting her. Theo would've tried to stop her if he'd been awake. But the wilderness was her realm, and she wore a leather quiver of golden arrows at her waist just in case a divine enemy showed up. *If they mean to come for me next,* she decided, *at least they'll have to do it on my turf.*

She looked to the sky, where once Zeus had ruled, his mighty thunderbolt promising to wreak vengeance on anyone—thanatos or Athanatos alike—who dared threaten his family.

"Your brother Hades is dead," she whispered, wishing her father could hear her. "A Son of Kronos has fallen."

She'd last seen her uncle three months before when she journeyed into his home in an abandoned subway station to confront him about Orion's cult. She learned that he and his wife, Persephone, had nothing to do with Orion's murders—but they were still dangerous. In their descent toward madness, they'd tried to force Selene to live for eternity as their involuntary party guest. She'd had to fight her way free—not an easy task when dealing with a god as powerful as Hades, especially when he donned his Helm of Invisibility.

Whoever kidnapped him probably took the helmet, she realized. She could only hope the magic item wouldn't function for anyone but the Lord of the Dead himself.

Did his killers know what effect Hades' death would have on the mortals nearby? she wondered, thinking of the stockbroker's broken body. Most Athanatoi wouldn't have cared, even if they had known. But Selene had given up drawing strict lines between mortals and immortals when she'd allowed Theo into her life. That woman on the ledge might have stood for all the materialism and greed she despised, but she was still an innocent, still someone Selene had sworn to protect.

She needed to stop her whirling brain. *I'm a goddess of action, not reflection,* she thought, hitching her backpack higher on her shoulders and breaking into a jog. *I might be slowly growing more like the mortals, but I refuse to take on their neuroses.*

She sprinted past the reservoir, its surface clouded with ice. Past the empty picnic tables on the Great Hill, up into the North

Woods, where no lampposts lit the way. Her boots squeaked on the snow, and the flakes whirled faster as the wind picked up, stinging her cheeks like sand. Another storm in a winter full of them. The city nearly groaned with the accumulated weight of weeks of ice and snow, its denizens growing more downtrodden with each successive inch of slush. But tonight Selene refused to let the weather depress her. She opened her mouth, and the flakes fell upon her tongue, tasting faintly of pollution and moonlight.

At the top of the hill stood a roofless one-room building with walls of the same rough-hewn mica schist that marked the city's dead. The American flag hanging from a pole in the interior clapped sharply with every gust of wind, its colors muted gray in the faint light. On the northern side, the ground dropped off in a steep cliff, providing an unobstructed view of Harlem in the distance. A small plaque explained that New York had constructed this blockhouse to defend against a possible British invasion during the War of 1812, a conflict most modern Americans barely acknowledged. But a silver-eyed, six-foot-tall woman named Dianne Delia had witnessed it all. She'd seen how the city had lived in perpetual fear that a flotilla flying the Union Jack would sail into the harbor, cannons blazing, and destroy their nascent experiment in democracy.

Only once since then had the Huntress felt such fear pervade her home: a day in September, not so long ago, when she watched two planes strike terror in the city's heart. Selene had not shared in their panic—at the time, she was too removed from the concerns of thanatoi to mourn another few thousand dead.

But today, staring at the wound in Hades' chest, Selene had felt as if those planes had struck once again, and this time, they'd knocked away her foundations and left her teetering and hollow, ready to collapse.

Once, she would've dreaded showing that vulnerability to anyone, much less a mortal man. But Theo had seen her at her weakest, her strongest, and everywhere in between. She still found it hard to share her feelings with him...but it was getting easier all the time. *Maybe that's love,* she thought, daring to think the word that neither of them had ever said aloud. *Knowing that he sees me not as the goddess the poets sang of, nor as the mortal others take me for, but as something at once less and more than both.*

She shrugged off her backpack and pulled out the two limbs of her golden bow. She screwed them together, making a single curving length that reached from her knees to her shoulders, then strung it. She ran a finger over the fletching of the golden arrows in her quiver. She'd brought them for target practice—they flew differently than wooden shafts, and she needed to be at the top of her game if an Athanatos showed up to challenge her. Only a divine arrow would take down divine prey.

She peered around at the trees, making sure she was alone. While entering the park after closing time would probably earn her a citation from the police, using a projectile weapon would more likely land her in jail.

With no one in sight, she chose three trees nearly a hundred yards away at the base of the cliff. Hitting them wouldn't be a challenge—ever since she'd partially regained her strength from Orion's ritual sacrifices, her aim had returned to nearly supernatural levels. To make things harder, she slipped three arrows between the knuckles of her right hand. She tried to picture three of her brothers in place of the trees. Dionysus the Wine Giver, perhaps? Drunk and stoned, surrounded by empty pizza boxes. Hermes the Messenger, with his sly grins and his perennial teasing? Her twin, Apollo? No, despite her suspicions, she couldn't even *pretend* to kill her kin—not until she knew they were guilty.

I'm getting soft, she thought ruefully, nocking the first arrow to her bowstring and picturing three wild boar instead. She let the arrow fly, then shifted her fingers and moved the second into place, then the third. They thunked into each tree in quick succession. Satisfied, she unscrewed her bow and put it back in her bag, then skated down the snowy cliff on the soles of her boots to retrieve the arrows; she only owned six golden shafts, after all.

On the way back up the cliff, she pulled herself hand over hand like a swimmer racing for shore, enjoying the pounding of blood in her heart. She lowered herself to the steps of the blockhouse, panting only slightly, and leaned back against the weathered iron gate barring the building's only entrance. Once, the citizens of New York thought such fortifications would protect them. Now, they trusted in cops like Geraldine Hansen and Maggie Freeman to man much less obvious defenses: surveillance and data gathering and other counterterrorism measures meant to thwart any potential threat. Selene almost laughed aloud at the thought. *What use is any of that against an Athanatos with the Helm of Invisibility?*

A sudden whiff of scent brushed her nostrils. Sweat and fear and a hint of cologne. A man. Close by. With her Huntress's senses, she peered around the clearing. Yet the scent vanished, lost in a gust of wind. She tensed, silently daring the man to show himself, and inched a hand toward her pack. *If he's a cop, he would've already approached,* she decided. *But if he's one of my brothers—*

Large gloved hands snaked around her throat and dragged her backward against the iron bars. She gasped, but only a choking clack emerged. She clawed at her attacker's hands, but couldn't get a good grip on his fingers through his puffy gloves. So she lurched forward with all her strength instead, dragging her attacker's arms through the grate until his torso slammed against the bars. He grunted in pain, but hung on, his fingers digging deeper into her throat. She relaxed for an instant, letting him yank her back, then jerked forward again. His head smacked against iron with a clang and his grip finally loosened.

Tearing free, Selene spun around, catching only a glimpse of her attacker before he disappeared behind the wall of the blockhouse. A man in a dark parka, too short and slight to be one of her brothers. Yet he couldn't be a random mugger—he'd planted himself inside the blockhouse to attack her without risk to himself, so he must've known she was a dangerous foe. She picked up her backpack and jangled the gate, but the lock held firm.

"You think you can hide?" she shouted, her voice rough from her near-strangulation. "You think you're safe in there?"

The only other way into or out of the roofless building was over the wall. The crumbling stone slabs didn't provide much of a handhold, but that didn't stop her. In moments, she'd crested the top. She could see her attacker now, climbing slowly up the opposite side to make his escape. As the man frantically reached for the next handhold, Selene calmly stalked along the narrow top of the wall and squatted above him.

When he looked up, she saw his face. He was young, and his hands on the stone wall shook from fear. Olive skin, a flattened nose, a bulging wool cap spherical enough to hold a pile of dreadlocks. Not an Athanatos—she would have recognized him. He had an earring in his right ear, the hint of a tattoo crawling up his throat.

Maybe he is an ordinary criminal after all, she pondered, *committing what he thought was an ordinary crime.*

As he reached for another slab in the wall, she rested her wrists on her knees and stared down at him curiously. "Where do you think you're going?"

He didn't speak, just let go of the wall, falling backward into the snow. He waded through the drifts to the opposite side of the chamber and started to climb again.

Selene stepped unhurriedly along the building's perimeter like a gymnast on a beam, reaching the other side before he was even halfway up the wall. She squatted above him once more, balancing easily. He looked up at her, gave a short grunt of surprise, then dropped down again. He went for the barred entrance this time, shaking it futilely. Then he turned back to her, his expression desperate, and drew a small knife from his parka. "Stay back," he warned.

Selene merely snorted. "Are you going to throw it at me? Is your aim that good?" With exaggerated slowness, she reached into her quiver and pulled out a shining arrow, rolling it between her fingers so the shaft glinted in the moonlight. He raised one hand to shield his face; his knife trembled in the other. Selene paused, some of her anger dissipating in the face of his obvious weakness.

"Something tells me I won't need this," she said, her voice dripping with careful condescension. She replaced it in the quiver and drew a simple wooden shaft from her backpack instead. No need to waste a divine arrow on a clearly mortal man. "Do you always prey on women in the park?"

He shook his head vigorously. "I was just desperate. I'm out of cash, and I thought if I could rob you—"

"Or strangle me."

"Just until you passed out. Then I'd climb over the wall, steal your pretty gold arrows, and leave you alone. I swear to Christ."

She laughed shortly. "You're not helping your case."

"Come on, lady, I just wanted to buy some presents for my kids." He looked up imploringly, the large knit hat wobbling comically on his head. "It's almost Christmas! What would Jesus do?"

With a hiss, she reached into her pack for her bow. Her fingers closed around the cold metal. She could see the man's tattoo more clearly now: a large black cross emblazoned between his collarbones, its longer limb disappearing beneath his jacket. She could almost feel the bite of the bowstring on her fingertips, hear the thrum of the arrow as it flew through the night, a burst of light to cleanse her realm of this man and his god. Then she paused. Did he really deserve death? Theo would say no. Killing him would merely make her feel better, knowing there were some adversaries she could easily defeat.

She let go of the bow. If she wasn't going to kill him, at least she'd make sure he didn't get her into too much trouble with the police. *But just a little trouble . . .* she thought with a smile . . . *sometimes that can't be helped.*

Arrow clutched in her hand, she dropped down into the building, sinking two feet deep into a drift. He was weak, scared, a rabbit cowering before the Huntress. She didn't need to shoot him from above. In fact, she was looking forward to getting her hands a little dirty. *They called me Bare-Fisted for a reason,* she thought, leaping through the snow like a stag.

He jerked his knife left and right, as if to ward her off, and reached for her quiver with his other hand. She knocked his forearm aside with her own, pinning it to the stone wall. "Still want my pretty gold arrows, huh? Should've gone for my wallet. I might've forgiven that."

She slammed her shoulder into his chest and held the arrowhead to his throat. A bead of blood appeared just below his Adam's apple. She pressed a little harder, and the red ran in a thin stream down the shaft and over her knuckles. She leaned against his forearm until the sharp stones dug into his tendons, and he dropped the knife with a gasp. Then she grabbed the front of his coat and pushed him before her toward the flagpole in the center of the clearing.

Keeping her arrow at his jugular, she unwrapped the flag's halyard from its cleat and let the Stars and Stripes tumble down the pole. She unlatched the flag, dropping it unceremoniously to the ground, then secured the halyard's hooks to her attacker's belt loops instead. Finally, she stepped back, holding the halyard with both hands, and hauled the young man up the pole.

"You don't want to do this," he protested, his voice edging toward panic. "It wasn't supposed to happen this way."

"I'm sure it wasn't," she replied calmly, leaning backward and using all her weight to hoist him another three feet into the air.

"I'm warning you! Don't make me come after you. I shouldn't, but I will."

"From up there?" She laughed. "Go ahead. You unlatch the rope and you'll fall twenty feet. Broken leg at least. But be my guest. Otherwise, just enjoy the view, and in a few hours, when I know your testicles are about to freeze off and you'll have sworn to your Jesus that you'll never try to mug a woman again, I'll call the police and report an anonymous citizen's arrest, complete with patriotic asshole-raising up the flagpole. I'm sure they'll take you down before you're dangerously hypothermic." She smiled at him cheerfully, her spirits finally restored.

Then he pulled the bulging wool hat off his head.

Two graceful wings unfurled from either side of a round golden cap, each metallic feather shimmering in the moonlight. He unhooked himself from the halyard—and began to fly.

Chapter 9

GODDESS OF GOLDEN SHAFTS

Selene stood dumbfounded as the man in the winged cap swooped toward her. She twisted aside as he barreled forward, but he managed to wrench the quiver of golden arrows from her belt and then launch back into the air before she could stop him.

Furious, she reached for a large stone and hefted it as if it weighed no more than a snowball. "Come back down here, thanatos! And tell me who sent you!" She hurled the stone at his head, but he dodged easily out of the way.

Even though he clearly had the advantage over her, he suddenly looked absolutely terrified. He clutched her quiver to his chest like a talisman.

"The Pater warned me not to use the cap," he said, his voice trembling. "I was supposed to just get the arrows and disappear. Sorry, Diana. This wasn't part of the plan." He reached into the pocket of his coat and pulled out a gun.

Selene dove around the corner of the blockhouse for cover as the first two bullets kicked up snow at her feet. She half fell, half skied down the cliff side, then took off through the thickest part of the forest, hoping to obscure his aerial view. Then, with all the speed she still possessed, she took an absurdly circuitous route home, ducking into subway stations and back out, entering a drugstore through one entrance and leaving through another, all in the hopes of losing her pursuer.

When she no longer saw the glint of gold overhead, she resolved to get home as quickly as possible. Her attacker clearly knew she frequented the park—she could only hope he didn't know her address as well.

Picking up speed, she moved so fast that her boot soles barely touched the ground. Sweat streamed down her face; she dashed it from her eyes and kept on running. Down Broadway. Right on Eighty-eighth Street. She jumped up her front stoop in a single leap, key at the ready, and slammed the door behind her.

Quickly, she threw all three of her deadbolts, grateful that she hadn't removed a single one when gentrification pushed the pimps and the drug dealers out of the neighborhood.

Panting, she glanced at the parlor-level windows—their iron gratings would stop only a ground-floor incursion, not an attacker who could fly. She sprinted up the stairs even as Hippo appeared on the landing, her tail wagging in wary agitation.

"Move!" Selene shouted, pushing the huge dog out of the way. She ran to the unused back bedroom on the second floor, empty but for a large wardrobe and a few storage chests. She grabbed the wardrobe in her arms and tried to move it. *Why don't I just own a modern particleboard piece of crap?* she wondered. *Instead I went for three hundred pounds of solid walnut.*

"Redecorating at four in the morning? Really?" Theo yawned from the doorway, wearing only his boxer shorts.

"Help me!"

One look at her face and he was instantly alert, rushing forward to grab the other side of the cabinet. "What's going on? Tell me!"

"Hopefully nothing. But we'll know soon enough." With a mighty heave, they slid the wardrobe a few inches.

Theo glanced out the window, just as a grim face in a winged golden cap appeared hovering above the sill. "That's not nothing!"

Hippo lunged, barking frantically. "Get back!" Selene shouted at her dog. "He's got a gun!"

Face ashen with fear, Theo put his back against the wardrobe and, nearly shouting with the effort, helped her slide it across the window.

"How many more wardrobes do you have?" he asked a little desperately.

"Not enough." She rushed up the stairs to her bedroom on the third floor, ignoring the front-facing rooms. Her attacker would stick to the back of the building, where there was less chance of being seen by her neighbors. "There're too many windows," she called over her shoulder while locking the casement. "Styx! He's going to get in eventually, even if he has to break the glass and let the neighbors alert the police."

"Alerting the police sounds like a great idea!" She could hear Theo on the fourth floor, slamming the shutters closed.

"And tell them there's a god in Hermes' winged hat trying to assassinate me?" She threw open her closet as Theo returned to the third floor to join her in the bedroom. She shoved a handful of wooden arrows into her backpack. "He must've followed me here—or he knew where I lived. Either way, you've got two minutes to gather anything you want, then we're leaving. And we're not coming back."

Theo cursed, fumbled his glasses onto his face, grabbed a large satchel, then tossed in his laptop and a seemingly haphazard collection of clothing, books, and papers.

"Shoes, Theo! Don't forget shoes!"

Nodding frantically, he dove under the bed and emerged with a pair of sneakers that he shoved onto his feet.

Broken glass clattered on the floor above, followed by a crack of wood. Hippo skittered toward the sound, teeth bared. Selene loosed an ear-splitting howl, stopping the dog in her tracks. The house fell silent, as if the intruder, too, had frozen at Selene's command. Hippo tucked her tail between her legs and slunk back to her mistress. Selene grabbed her by the chin and snarled at the dog. *Stay quiet, do exactly as I say, and guard Theo,* she communicated. Sometimes it paid to be the Lady of Hounds.

Then footsteps on the stairs above. Slow and cautious.

Selene slung her bag onto her back and nocked a wooden arrow to her bow. She stepped out into the hallway, motioning curtly for Theo and Hippo to fall in behind her. *Go now,* she mouthed. *I'll meet you in the basement.*

Theo looked like he was about to protest, but she bared her teeth at him, too.

Be careful, he mouthed back at her, before heading down the stairs with his satchel, dragging Hippo by her collar.

Selene kept her eyes locked on the landing above. As she knew it would, the sound of Theo's descent brought the attacker darting into sight. Her fingers released the arrow the instant before he appeared—he jumped right into its path. It sliced into his shoulder, but not before he fired his gun.

She felt as if she'd been slammed in the head by a crowbar. Everything went black as she staggered toward the railing and tumbled down the steep, narrow staircase, smacking her head against the wall on the landing below. One hand to her bloody skull, she managed to crack her eyes open; the world spun around her, a blur of colors and light with no up or down. Half falling, half crawling, her bow clanging loudly against the banister, she turned the corner and made it down the next set of stairs, dimly aware of a shadow sprinting toward her from below. Another attacker.

Panic gripped her chest. She reached for an arrow, but the fletching slipped through her blood-slick fingers. Her eyes couldn't focus anyway. She'd never make it through another attack. Then Theo was pulling her into his arms and heaving all six feet of her over his shoulder with a strength she didn't know he possessed. He headed straight for the front door.

"No," she gasped. "He'll just come after us. He's wounded but…" She could hear her attacker moving awkwardly on the floor above. "He's still conscious. The basement."

Theo spun around and flung open the low door under the stairs. He pushed Hippo through with a kick, then ducked to pass through with Selene still lying over his shoulder. She bit back a gasp of pain as her head knocked into the lintel on the way through.

Theo scrambled down the rickety stairs, laid Selene gently on the concrete floor, then dashed back up to close the door behind them, thrusting them into darkness.

"No, don't turn on the light," she insisted. "There's a bolt on this side. You can feel it—" She heard the lock slam into place, then Theo was at her side once more, cradling her head in his hands.

"You're shot," he said. "There's… there's blood everywhere."

"It's my head. That's why I fell," she managed. "Anything else and I would've been okay."

"Oh, Jesus."

"Shh. He's right upstairs," she whispered. "We've got to get out of here before he breaks down the door."

"I've got to get you to a doctor. This is *not* the time to try that invulnerability experiment!"

"I'm not going to die, Theo. There are no divine handguns out there. I should be fine. As long as…"

"As long as *what*?"

She felt gingerly for her forehead, hoping the bullet hadn't lodged itself in her brain. She might not die, but that didn't mean she couldn't be paralyzed. Then she began to laugh quietly.

"Please tell me what's so funny," Theo begged.

"It's a graze. That's all. Bleeding a lot because it's a head wound, and it must've given me a bit of a concussion, but there's nothing—" It was all she could do not to yelp as Theo fumbled in the dark for her face and kissed her soundly.

The basement door rattled on its hinges. With Theo's help, Selene struggled to her feet. Her head cleared enough for her to discern the sliver of moonlight leaking through the basement's one tiny window. It provided just enough light for her night vision to function. She grabbed Theo's hand and led him toward the back corner of the basement. There, a small round grate covered a drainage hole. She lifted the grate and flipped a hidden trigger that loosened a larger square of cement in the floor. She lifted it aside—anything was lighter than the wardrobe.

"There's a ladder," she whispered in Theo's ear. As he clambered down, Selene grabbed Hippo by her hindquarters and dragged her toward the hole in the floor. The dog whimpered, her claws scrabbling on the concrete. The rattling on the door got louder.

"I know you're in there, Diana!" came her attacker's muffled cry. Then a loud slam as he kicked the lock.

Selene shoved the dog's backside in the hole, growling at Hippo to be quiet. But for once, her power over hounds didn't work: The terrified dog wouldn't stop whimpering. *Sorry, girl.* She punched her beloved dog on the side of the head. Unconscious, Hippo was much easier to handle. She passed the animal down to Theo, who caught her with a surprised grunt. Then Selene slipped through the hole.

Another angry cry from the floor above, a slam, and the lock on the basement door splintered. Footsteps pounded down the stairs just as she pulled the cement block over the hole and dropped down the ladder to stand beside Theo.

In the blue light of his phone, his eyes were wide with bewildered fear. She put a finger to her lips, then covered his phone with her hand to block the light. Above them, she could hear her attacker stalking through the basement, tossing aside her possessions as he looked for their hiding place. A trunk scraped across the concrete. The lid of an old trashcan clattered against metal shelves. A paint can rolled across the floor with a sound like a snare drum.

Then, for a moment, silence.

"Please, don't tell the Pater, but I'm at her house." Her attacker's voice was a terrified whimper as he spoke into his phone. "I got the arrows, but she got away . . . I know, but I thought . . . Yes, right away. It won't happen again."

Selene heard him retreat back up the stairs. She held her breath, her hearing tuned for his tread. He entered the foyer, then she heard him go out the front door and onto the sidewalk. "He's gone," she whispered to Theo.

"Can we go back up now?"

She could hear his teeth chattering. "It's not safe. If he knows where I live, we can never go back."

"Never?"

"Not until we've taken care of him. And anyone else who knows to call me Diana. From the sound of that phone call, there's a whole organized group behind this. Clearly the same guys who killed my uncle."

"So until we solve Hades' murder, I'm going to live in the sewers like some mole person?"

"This isn't a sewer. It's a bootlegger's tunnel—part of why I bought this building in the first place. During Prohibition they used it to smuggle crates of liquor from the Hudson to the speakeasies. Now it leads down to the Amtrak tunnels. Come on, help me with Hippo. I'll feel better the farther we are from the basement."

She reached for Hippo's front legs, Theo took the back, and they carried the dog's limp body a few hundred yards down a low corridor. As they went, she grew increasingly light-headed from the blood loss and the probable concussion, and she felt her already diminished strength threaten to give out entirely.

Just in time, Hippo cracked open her eyes. They put the dog down, letting her stumble about a little until she regained her balance. Selene knelt and pressed a kiss to the dog's nose. "Forgive me for knocking you out, Hippolyta, but you're the least stealthy animal in the world."

When she stood, the light from Theo's phone fell on her bloody face. He gave a yelp of dismay and dug through his satchel. He emerged with a Columbia Classics Department T-shirt, which he quickly ripped into three long strips.

"You don't have to do that," she assured him. "My head will heal on its own faster than you'd think."

"Not fast enough." He wrapped the makeshift bandages tightly around her forehead. "You're looking even paler than usual. And between moving that wardrobe, slinging you around, and hauling Hippo's fat ass, my back's about broken. Sorry to ruin the chivalrous hero routine, but I don't want you passing out, especially if it means more lugging for me."

Only when he was done did he extricate a pair of pants from his bag. Shivering with cold, he pulled them on, then dug a little further, clearly looking for a second shirt among his hastily packed possessions. He came up empty. He cast a wistful gaze at the torn T-shirt strips on Selene's head.

"Regretting the Clara Barton move?" she asked.

"Nice attempt at a pop culture reference, but nineteenth-century celebrities don't count." He gave up looking for a shirt and donned a bulky sweatshirt with a broken zipper instead. "Now, how about you tell me who the hell was just shooting at us."

"Who do you think? One of the Messenger's followers, obviously. That cap's one-of-a-kind."

"But it wasn't Hermes himself? I didn't get a good look at his face."

"I did. He didn't even look like a god. Until he started to fly, that is."

"So your brother gave one of his few remaining divine objects to some mortal acolyte?"

"Except divine objects shouldn't even *work* for mortals."

"Wait. You're telling me I couldn't use your bow?"

"You probably couldn't even bend it."

"I'm not *that* much weaker than you," he said with a hint of wounded pride.

"It's not a matter of strength. Despite all my fading, the bow has always retained some of its divinity, so it can only be effectively used by a god. Some of the more supernatural items—like the Earth Shaker's trident—just ceased working entirely after the Diaspora, even for the god they belonged to."

"But the winged hat guy—"

"Wasn't a god. I'd have recognized him. There just aren't that many of us left. Which means someone, somehow, has figured out how to give their mortal acolytes the power to use divine weapons. I told you. My relatives *cannot* be trusted. Dash Mercer may seem completely harmless," she said, using Hermes' latest mortal pseudonym. "He may even help me out from time to time with new identities, or come to my aid like he did when we fought Orion, but he's not just the Messenger. He's the Trickster too, remember? And now he's given his cap to some mortal and sent him to kill me."

"You don't know that! Why would Dash want to hurt you? Maybe somebody stole his cap to frame him."

"Stole it from the God of Thieves himself? Does that seem likely?" She wasn't sure whether the piercing pain in her temple was from the bullet graze, the concussion, or her exasperation.

"Then I think it's time you gave up on the whole recluse thing. Your twin did promise to help if anyone tried to revive the sacrifices."

Selene shook her head. "Absolutely not. Paul could be in on this, too."

"Why in the world would you think that? I thought you guys were reconciled!"

"Think of the dead crow at the crime scene. It could be a reference to my twin."

"Because of the Coronis myth? That's a stretch."

"No, it's not. Coronis was my twin's lover, the mother of his son, Asclepius." Her own memories of Coronis's story were shaky, but she remembered enough to know it had actually happened—and she wasn't proud of her part in it.

She'd been with Apollo at his temple at Delphi when his sacred bird, the crow, came flying across the valley on white wings. The bird landed on the god's outstretched arm and told him that Coronis, one of his mortal lovers, had been seen in the arms of a human warrior. Apollo raged and cried, and Artemis swore she would exact revenge on her twin's behalf.

She raced forth in her stag-drawn chariot and found Coronis, eight months pregnant with Apollo's child, playing amid the gardens of Thessaly. She sent a single golden arrow through the woman's creamy white throat. She didn't dwell on Coronis's last gurgling cries, on the way her hands clutched at her swollen womb, on how her eyes had silently begged She of Good Repute for mercy. In that ancient time, Artemis didn't struggle with the contradictions of her godhood. She was the Goddess of Childbirth, who eased women's pain in labor, yet she thought nothing of murdering an unborn babe or his mother. She was the Protector of the Innocent, who defended women from the abuses of men, but she turned her back on those who needed protection from her own twin.

If only I could still close my heart so easily, thought Selene, looking to Theo. *Despite all my responsibilities as a goddess, it was a simpler time.* Given the chance, she wouldn't go back—she'd made that decision when Orion offered to revive her immortality, and she would stick to it. But that didn't mean she didn't long for a little merciless, omnipotent godhood every once in a while.

Apollo, as the lover of countless humans and the father of many half-divine hemitheoi, had always been more vulnerable to mortal emotions. When Coronis lay on her funeral pyre, and the flames licked up her saffron robes toward her rounded belly, Apollo relented. He ripped his infant son Asclepius from

Coronis's womb, pulling him through the fire to safety. The child grew to become the hero-god of medicine and healing, one of the most powerful and important hemitheoi in the ancient world. Men saw the myth as a reminder of Artemis's heartlessness and Apollo's mercy. But the Huntress knew better. If Apollo had truly repented his actions, he would've assumed responsibility for them. Instead, he decided he was not to blame. "If the crow had not told me of Coronis's treachery," he explained to his sister, "she would still be alive. So you see, the bird is at fault, not I." As punishment, he smeared the bird's white wings with the ashes of Coronis's pyre. The crow had been black ever since.

Thinking of the slaughtered bird lying beside the *Charging Bull* statue reminded Selene that her twin could convince himself of anything. Even, perhaps, that reviving a human sacrifice cult was a good idea.

"Selene, you've got to trust *someone*, sometime," Theo insisted.

"I trust you. Isn't that enough?"

"I'd be lying to myself and to you if I said it was. I'm damn good at research and problem solving, and you know I'd do anything to protect you, but when it comes to taking down some dude who can *fly*? I think someone who's got a little more combat experience is in order."

He was right. Theo'd proven himself more than once in a fist fight, but once the swords and spears came out... "No. Not yet. Someone's messing with the mortals in *my* city. And someone's killing *my* family. It's up to me to stop them."

Theo cleared his throat. "You mean *us*."

"What?"

"It's up to *us* to stop them. You've got a partner, remember? One besides Hippo! And not just for hunting down rapists, but for anything, no matter how terrifying. And that's true whether you like it or not."

"You do slobber less than Hippo at least, I'll give you that," Selene admitted, allowing the hint of a smile.

"And most of the time, I smell better, too," Theo said. "Although I clearly possess the personal hygiene of a college freshman, because this sweatshirt reeks. But speaking of Hippo, we can't keep her with us."

The smile fled Selene's face. "Why not?"

"Now that our flying attacker got a look at her, Hippo's a target. And together, you guys make an unmistakable pair. We, at least, can wear disguises if we have to." He eyed the massive mutt skeptically. "Hippo wouldn't make a particularly convincing dachshund. A bear, maybe, but that would present its own difficulties. Besides, we can't bring her on the subway."

"The subway? Where are we going exactly?"

"To find your twin." Before she could protest, he barreled on. "We need *help*, Selene! You're wounded, homeless, and being chased by a dude with wings on his head! This is *exactly* why people have families—to protect them from crap like that."

"Yes, but *my* family—"

"I know, I know, it may be composed of homicidal lunatics. And *sure*, there's a slim chance that Paul may be part of this plot. But last time you misjudged your twin, remember? At least give him a chance. And if I'm wrong, and he pulls out his silver bow in the middle of his rock concert, then—god or not—I'll kill him with my own two hands."

"I'd like to see you try."

"Okay, let me rephrase that. I'll *attempt* to kill him with my own two hands, and while I'm distracting your nearly immortal brother with my feeble mortal attempts, you'll swoop in and take him down with a well-placed arrow to the throat."

"Sounds more like it."

Theo laughed shortly. Selene did not.

Chapter 10

LADY OF HOUNDS

After walking fifty blocks through the Amtrak tunnel that paralleled the Hudson River, Theo and Selene emerged at Penn Station and made their way aboveground.

Theo cast an eye to the night sky. No sign of aerial pursuit. At least not yet. Maybe even evil cult initiates had to sleep sometime. Still, they hurried along the sidewalk toward their rendezvous, eager to avoid exposure for long.

They stopped at an all-night bodega to pick up a knit hat to cover the rough bandages on Selene's head, then met Ruth Willever beneath the wide awning for the Thirty-fourth Street movie theater, where they hoped any airborne attacker wouldn't see them.

Ruth and Theo had been friends for the past two years. They'd met when Theo was dating Helen Emerson, Ruth's roommate. The ensuing difficulties—first Helen dumping Theo, then getting murdered by Orion's cult—had only brought them closer together.

Ruth stood with her hands tucked under her elbows for warmth, her already narrow shoulders hunched even further with the cold. Feathers poked from the seams of her down coat. The brown hair falling from beneath the earflaps of her flannel hat was more rat's nest than ponytail, and the bags under her eyes proved Theo's desperate phone call had woken her from a deep sleep. But she grinned when she saw him.

She got down on one knee in front of Hippo, took off a woolen mitten, and let the dog sniff her fingers before clasping her in a hug. Theo raised a brow to Selene. *See? Hippo's going to be in good hands.*

Ruth stood, her eyes moving to the woman at Theo's side, and her smile vanished. The knit hat had ridden up, revealing a sliver of bloody bandage across Selene's forehead. She yanked the hat lower, her steady gaze daring Ruth to comment.

Ruth looked at Theo next, taking in his unzipped sweatshirt and bare chest with widening eyes. "What happened?"

"Water main break at Selene's house. And some roofing problems with all the snow and ice. Just general falling apart, really. Place is so dangerous we had to run off before I could grab a coat."

"Here—" Ruth began, shrugging out of her parka.

"No, no! I'm fine," he assured her. "We've got contractors looking at it. Predawn contractors. And my apartment's getting fumigated, so we're spending the night at a hotel." He was too tired to lie convincingly.

He could tell Ruth wasn't buying it—as a research scientist, she knew contradictory evidence when she saw it—but she was too polite to pry. "Sure." She looked questioningly at Selene, clearly wondering just how rich Theo's new brownstone-owning girlfriend really was.

One more reason to be grateful Gabriela's not here, Theo thought. *She'd never let me get away with this. A hotel? With lodging prices astronomical for the Christmas holiday and a dozen friends in the city who would put us up for free? Jesus.*

"And, Ruth?" he pressed. "You won't mention to anyone that you saw us, will you? Just in case, you know, someone asks?"

"I don't suppose you can tell me why all the secrecy?" she asked, with a curious smile at them both.

Selene didn't smile back. "'Fraid not. Hence the secrecy part."

"We're having a little romantic getaway," Theo interposed. "And it'd be better if no one comes to bug us."

"Um. Okay." She looked at Selene again, obviously confused by the "romantic" part, since Theo's girlfriend had dropped his hand, crossed her arms, and turned to glare at him.

"But you're doing us a huge favor by taking Hippo," Theo went on breezily. "I would've called Gabriela, but she's as distrustful of dogs as she is allergic to them. So, thank you." Theo nudged Selene in the ribs.

"Yes. Thanks." She didn't sound the least bit grateful.

"Is there anything I should know?" Ruth asked. "Like medications? Or the vet's number? Or what kind of dog food she likes?"

Selene looked like she might choke.

"Hippo eats meat, not dog food," Theo said quickly. "Beef, pork, anything. Right, Selene?"

Selene nodded stonily.

"And don't worry, this won't be for long. Just until we can get back into the house. Go on, Selene," Theo urged. "Give Ruth the leash."

Selene breathed deeply, narrowed her eyes, and spoke with the voice of a goddess commanding a mortal. As far as Theo knew, the voice didn't really work, but that didn't stop her from trying. "You will protect this dog with your life," she intoned, still holding on to the leash. Hippo's ears perked up, and she looked at her mistress as if she understood every word. Ruth just looked alarmed. "She is my companion. She must not be harmed."

The Lady of Hounds got down on one knee before her friend and took her muzzle in her hands. She didn't speak to Hippo, but just looked into her eyes. Theo had no doubt that some deep understanding passed between them. She couldn't speak telepathically to dogs, but through a combination of posture, eye contact, and the occasional growl, she had an uncanny way of expressing her will to them. And if they knew what was good for them, they listened. Hippo held her stare. Then licked her under the chin.

Ruth chuckled, but shut up when Selene raised steely eyes to her. Not bothering to wipe away the dog drool, Selene stood, handed the leash to Ruth, and walked toward the downtown subway entrance without another word. Hippo made the smallest of movements as if to follow, then froze as she remembered her mistress's unspoken command. She gave a faint whimper, tucked her tail between her legs, and began to pant in agitation.

———◇———

Selene paused at the top of the subway stairs, just out of Theo's sight. *Eavesdropping's not polite,* she thought, *but is it my fault if I have preternatural hearing? I'm just standing here waiting.* She crept back up a stair and peered through the railing so she could see him.

He smiled ruefully at his friend. "Sorry about that. Selene's had a rough night. *We've* had a rough night."

"You know, don't you," Ruth said hesitantly, "that I'd do anything to help? If you're in trouble. Or something." Clearly, Theo's halfhearted fabrications hadn't fooled her for a second.

"Me? In trouble?" Theo raised his arms in a muscle man pose. "You think someone's gonna mess with these photon torpedoes?"

Ruth laughed, louder and longer than Selene would've thought her capable. She'd always seemed mousy, but her smile lit up her face with a sweet charm.

Theo grinned back at her—looking more at ease than he had all night. He liked making people happy. Liked being *liked.* *Someone like Ruth would make him feel good about himself all the time,* Selene thought with a heavy heart. *She even understands whatever arcane pop culture reference he just made.*

Ruth took a step closer to him. "But seriously, if you need me . . ."

Selene tensed. Theo might be oblivious, but she'd known since the first time she'd met Ruth that the woman was a little bit in love with him. She was staring up at him with big doe eyes, but he just gave her a quick hug and patted her soundly on the back. *Like a friend,* Selene decided.

"Thanks," he said. "You're amazing. Really. I don't know what I'd do without you." He let her go. Selene wondered if he noticed the red flush on Ruth's cheeks. "I promise I'll make this up to you. I'll fish-sit for you on your next vacation."

Ruth laughed again, her cheeks turning even brighter. Selene decided enough was enough. She padded down the stairs, fishing in her jacket pocket for her MetroCard. On the platform, she leaned against a steel pillar, impatient for Theo to arrive before they missed the next train. *Whatever challenges lie ahead in our relationship,* she thought grimly, *are nothing compared to what I'm about to face when I meet my twin.*

Selene and Theo had three months of relationship angst to navigate.

Artemis and Apollo had three millennia.

Chapter 11

LEADER OF THE MUSES

"She's his *sister*," Theo explained to the bouncer at the Bowery Ballroom stage door for the third time. "Just tell him we're here, and he'll let us in."

The dour man with a pencil-thin beard crossed his melon-thick arms. "Mr. Solson is performing. Onstage. Right now. What do you not understand? Either you're on the backstage pass list, or you're not. Do you want me to interrupt him in the middle of a song to ask him if he wants me to let in a bleeding chick and a half-dressed man?"

Theo noticed Selene's balled hands and knew it wouldn't be long before she knocked the bouncer senseless. But he also knew the man had a point. Their trek through the train tunnels had left them coated in a thin layer of soot, and the combination of his own coatless state and the blood-soaked bandages peeking from beneath Selene's hat made them look more like half-crazed disaster refugees than the long-lost relatives of one of the city's most popular indie rock stars.

"Let me handle this," Theo said softly.

"Selene?" A young woman peered past the bouncer, her eyes

round. "You're Paul's sister, right? Dickie, let her in! My goodness, you poor thing!"

And just like that they were past the ropes, following a wisp of a woman into the club's cramped back hallway. She waved down a passing roadie and asked him to bring a first aid kit, then turned back to Selene, nearly shouting to be heard over the acoustic folk rock blasting through the walls. "I'm Sophie. I don't know if you remember me. I'm Paul's girlfriend."

"I need to speak to my brother immediately."

"He's in the middle of—"

Before Sophie could finish, Selene was striding down the hallway toward the stage entrance.

Theo held up a placating hand to Sophie. "I'll get her, don't worry. It's been a rough night." *And it's about to be very a rough day.* Dawn had just begun to lighten the sky. In keeping with his God of the Sun persona, Paul's concerts coincided with the sunrise. His rabid fan base didn't seem to mind. Theo, on the other hand, could barely stand upright.

When he caught up to Selene, she was standing in the wings with her hands over her ears, ignoring the stage manager's angry threats. To Theo's relief, Sophie appeared shortly afterward to pull the man away, assuring him Selene posed no danger to the musicians onstage.

I wouldn't be so sure about that, Theo thought, noticing the fury in her eyes. He had a nagging suspicion she might leap onstage and drag her brother off in the middle of the chorus.

Sophie tapped Selene on the arm and stood on her tiptoes to yell into her ear, "Two more songs and then a set break." Theo felt like he could blow the young woman over with a well-aimed sneeze. With her shabby chic clothes, stick-thin arms, and heavily made-up eyes, she looked like a Victorian urchin. Selene just nodded curtly, not even deigning to make eye contact with her.

Paul Solson, the God of Music, Poetry, Prophecy, Plague, Healing, and the Sun, stood in a spotlight playing a gleaming acoustic guitar, singing his face off to a crowd of adoring fans. As always, he wore his golden curls long, just brushing his shoulders. He'd dyed the white streak in his hair that mirrored the one in Selene's—now there was nothing about him to indicate he was any older than his mid-twenties.

He'd gathered the front of his curls into a topknot. To the audience, it probably seemed a perfectly practical, if somewhat eccentric, hairdo for a sweaty, hardworking hipster, but Theo recognized it as a style worn by Roman maidens and often used in statues of Apollo to represent the god's indeterminate sexuality.

Even without the hair, there was something almost womanly about him. He stood as tall as Selene, but while her flesh was marble and her lean muscles perennially taut, a certain softness overlay Paul's frame. His skin was tawny honey, his movements as languorous, and Theo could almost taste the sweetness of the God of Music's voice on his own tongue. The rest of the band panted, their faces unnaturally flushed, but Paul performed effortlessly. Theo had the distinct impression his voice would reach the back of the club even without the microphone, every note tugging at the heartstrings of his fans, who listened raptly as if to the revelation of a god.

"How long's the set been?" he asked Sophie.

"Two hours straight," she replied. "The rest of the band's about to drop, but Paul never gets tired." She sighed with adoration. "There's no one like him."

So either he's still supernatural, or he's high on cocaine.

The song ended to a roar of approval from the crowd. Selene lowered her hands from her ears, ready to spring forward.

As if sensing her distress, Paul suddenly glanced toward the wings. His eyes grew wide; the instantaneous communication between the twins hummed. Even Theo's mortal senses perceived it. *If this is what it looks like when they don't know each other anymore, what must it have been like before their estrangement?* he wondered. For a moment, he could picture them, side by side in white tunics, gleaming bows drawn, hunting their enemies across the hills of Attica.

Paul turned back to the crowd. "One more before we take a break. This one's dedicated to the first girl I ever loved."

At that, Selene grunted and put her hands over her ears once more. Sophie turned a distinct shade of pink and wandered over to the edge of the proscenium so she could be as close to her boyfriend as possible. Theo wondered what lies Paul had told her. Could she really believe she was the first woman he'd given his heart to? Even if she didn't know he was a god—and a famously promiscuous one at that—he *was* a rock musician.

Selene didn't take her eyes off the singer either. But her gaze was filled with anger, not love.

"Your twin's really good," Theo said quietly, knowing she could hear him even over the din. She shot him an annoyed look. He was, after all, stating the obvious. Very gently, he reached for her wrists and urged her to lower her hands. She snarled, but complied.

The drumbeats had slowed to a mournful march, the keyboardist picked out a syncopated roundelay, and Paul strummed his guitar in counterpoint. His voice soared over the room, teasing octave after octave.

Sweet, sweet-voiced Muses,
Sweet-voiced Muses,
Tell me of the long-winged Moon.
She climbs through the sky
With an all-seeing eye,
And the mountains shake,
The forests quake
At her bold, bold heart.
Her bold, bold heart.

Theo threaded his hand through Selene's. He recognized a few of the lyrics—some came from the Homeric hymn to Artemis and others from the hymn to Selene the Moon. But Paul had put a spin on it all his own. He launched into the second verse, clearly an ode to himself borrowed from the hymn to Helios, the Sun.

Sweet, sweet-voiced Muses,
Sweet-voiced Muses,
Tell me of the tireless Sun.
His bright rays beam,
His bright locks stream,
And his stallions rear
When his chariot draws near
To his bold, bold love.
His bold, bold love.

On the chorus, the whole audience joined in, a great wall of sound.

Sun and Moon,
Midnight or noon,
Never together.
Never together.

Apollo, called Phoebus, "Bright One," was earning his epithet: Paul's skin seemed to glow as if he were the Sun once more. His eyes shone a luminescent golden-brown while his sister's glowed faintly silver. Then the band dropped out, the audience fell into a reverent silence, and Paul sang the coda a cappella.

But never say never.
When the mountains shake
And the forests quake,
They'll dance together.
Their love's forever.
Their love's forrrrrrrrr . . . eeeeeeeev . . . UUUCHK!

A gasp from the audience.

Face horror-stricken, Paul raised a hand to his neck as if to throttle his cracked voice. There was a long moment of terrible silence. Finally, wary applause, growing into a halfhearted ovation.

"Bring down the lights," Sophie hissed to the stage manager. "Get him out of there."

The other band members stumbled offstage toward the dressing rooms, looking like they might pass out at any moment. Paul walked toward the wings like a man in a dream, his gaze unfocused. Up close, Theo realized Paul's divine visage was a facade. His golden eyes were veined with red, and sweat had turned his topknot into a limp, wet wad. He handed his guitar to the stage manager as if thrusting away a dangerous animal.

Sophie rushed toward him. He held her tightly, his chest visibly heaving. After a long moment, his gaze met Selene's. He left Sophie with a reassuring kiss and crossed to his sister, falling into her arms. Selene stiffened and didn't return the hug, but she didn't push him away either. Sophie watched them with a hand pressed against her chest, obviously moved by the touching reunion.

As usual, Selene seemed to have no idea how to console those in distress. She patted Paul's back awkwardly.

Over her shoulder, Paul saw Theo and stood upright. He wiped a sweaty lock of hair from his face. "Hey," he said casually, as if he hadn't just cracked in front of six hundred fans. "What's up, Theo?"

"Great show," he replied without thinking. *What else does one say backstage to a rock star?*

"Thanks, man," Paul said, massaging his throat as if to rub away the strain. "You know what I always say about the power of music—under the spell of pulsing notes, the eagle sleeps on the scepter of Zeus, relaxing his swift wings."

You *always say?* Theo thought. *You mean the Pindarian odes always say.* Mentioning Paul's plagiarism, however, seemed about as tactless as pointing out his cracked voice. Selene, of course, didn't see it that way.

"No eagle could sleep to that racket," she said with a single raised brow. "You sounded like shit out there."

Paul's attention snapped back to his sister. "Well, you *look* like shit." He spoke with all the vitriol only a twin sibling was capable of, but the finger he reached toward the bloody cloths on her forehead was gentle. "What happened to you?"

She dodged his hand, her eyes darting to Sophie and the bustling roadies crowding the wings. "Let's not discuss this in front of your entourage."

Paul nodded, his face suddenly gone vague. "Yes, yes…it's coming…" he murmured, before heading off down the hallway without another word of explanation.

"What the hell is he talking about?" Selene asked, staring after her brother.

Theo could only shrug. He was far too tired to understand much of anything anymore. "He's the God of Prophecy, right? The oracles are supposed to be cryptic."

◇

Selene followed her brother into a small dressing room that reeked of cigarettes, sweat, and whiskey. Her nose wrinkled, but the room was warm and dry and a far sight better than roaming dank underground tunnels in the middle of the night. Theo slumped into a patched armchair.

Her twin went straight for a row of bottled water on the counter. After downing one without taking a breath, he started on another.

Selene couldn't believe it. "Aren't you even going to ask about Hades?"

"Hades?" Paul looked completely bewildered.

"He's dead! Weren't you listening on the phone yesterday?"

"Oh shit." He rubbed his face. "Yeah, of course I remember. I just..." His eyes looked glazed. "I thought maybe it was a dream."

"A *dream*? What are you *on*? Coke? Speed?" Selene demanded, ready to slap the sense back into him.

Theo leaned wearily forward in his chair, chin propped in his hand as if he couldn't hold up his own head. "I *wish* tonight were just a dream. But I'm afraid the man with a gun who chased us out of Selene's house was very real. Normally he wouldn't have been a problem for the Huntress, of course—except for the whole *he could fly* thing."

"He wore Dash's cap," Selene said, her voice tight. "Which means the Messenger sent someone to kill me."

"No, no." Paul shook his head as if trying to clear it.

Maybe he's drunk, Selene thought. *Or just whacked out from centuries of hanging with musicians—isn't that how rock stars' stories always end?*

Paul crushed the empty water bottle in his hand. "This can't be Dash's fault...but something's coming."

"What do you mean, 'something's coming'?"

Paul closed his eyes for a moment. "I've been having..."

"Prophetic visions?" Theo asked, sounding hopeful.

But Paul shook his head. "My prophecies were of the future... these are visions of my past. I'm not sure how to explain it except..." His voice slowed, as if dragging forth long-forgotten memories. "I am an ouroboros, a snake eating my own tail, forced to move always in circles, never forward. Yet something stands ready to break the cycle. A release from pain, a destination as stygian as death itself."

Selene wondered if his break onstage had caused his overwrought melancholy—or vice versa. Either way, she needed him lucid to help defeat the new cult, not meandering through poetic flights of fancy. "You've always been overdramatic. Comes from being the Leader of the Muses. Get over yourself—you're just having the Christmas blues."

"Yeah, maybe." He moved to a sink in the corner and splashed water on his face. He cupped his hands, took another long drink, and smoothed the hair from his forehead. When he turned back to them, his eyes were clear gold once more, as if he'd pushed away his despondency by sheer force of will.

With a tentative knock on the door, Sophie appeared with a first aid kit. She put it on the scarred coffee table and then went to her boyfriend. She ran a hand through his damp hair, her eyes glued on his. "You all right?" she murmured.

He kissed her in answer, hugging her so hard that her feet came off the floor. She wrapped her legs around his hips and he placed both hands on her ass. Selene winced but couldn't look away. Finally, Paul put the woman down and whispered something in her ear. Sophie cast a glance at Theo and Selene. "Okay, pookums, whatever you need." Then she kissed his cheek one more time and left the room, closing the door softly behind her.

Theo, seemingly unfazed by the public display of affection, popped open the first aid kit and removed a few adhesive bandages and some antiseptic. "Okay, Selene, you might heal a little faster than a mortal, but I'm not sure you're immune to infection." He reached for the bloody T-shirt strips on her forehead, but she raised a hand to stop him.

"No complaints," he insisted. "The Rambo look is very 1982. And not in a good way."

As he worked, Selene peered around his arm to look at her brother. He'd picked up an electric guitar and begun to pluck out a melody. Without amplification, the sound thunked flat and muffled, but she recognized the tune: an old dancing song, once played by the light of a midnight pyre as she and her nymphs spun in joyous circles beneath the stars. *I grabbed Apollo by the hand,* she remembered suddenly, *and he threw down the lyre to join us. We didn't need the music anymore—it rang in our bones.* But right now, she had no time for such memories.

"Would you put that down and listen to me?"

He didn't look up. "I can play and listen at the same time. I haven't grown *that* weak."

"You said Dash wasn't involved in the attack. How do you know?"

The melody altered—a simple shepherd's tune, like the kind Hermes once coaxed from a bundle of reeds.

"How could you think our little brother would want to kill you?" He looked up, his eyes sad. "Do you trust us all so little?"

"He's the Dissembler," she insisted.

Paul shrugged an acknowledgment. "He stole my cattle once, do you remember?"

"Vaguely."

"He was just a kid. I found him lying on a cow's back, grinning and totally unrepentant. He offered to give me the pipes he'd carved from reeds and a lyre made from a turtle's shell in return for my golden cattle. A good trade."

"Your point?"

"Dash might lie or cheat or steal, but he's always been the Giver of Good Things."

Selene couldn't help picturing Hermes as he'd been—hair a wild black halo, bright eyes always filled with laughter. He hadn't changed that much over the centuries. Whenever she'd needed a new identity, a new job, a new place to live, he leaped to her aid. When they'd confronted Orion, Dash had made sure she had a new bow to replace the one that had broken, and then he'd shown up himself to fight at her side. *I don't actually want him to be guilty,* she admitted to herself. But out loud, she scoffed. "He's also the God of Eloquence. And you've fallen for his rhetoric. How about I hold an arrow to his throat, and then we see what tale he tells?"

The door to the dressing room burst open. Dash Mercer himself stood framed in the doorway, a flannel fedora tilted rakishly over one eye. "Did someone say 'telling tales'?" he asked nonchalantly. "Because I've got a good one. Did I ever tell you all—"

Before he finished the sentence, Selene had launched herself at her younger brother, one hand reaching for his throat—the other gripping the shaft of an arrow.

Chapter 12

MESSENGER OF THE GODS

With a speed that rivaled Selene's, Dash leapt nimbly out of her path and onto the makeup counter, pulling two pistols from beneath his coat as he went. He stood above her, bouncing on his toes, both guns pointed straight at her.

"So much for the happy family reunion," he said without losing his smile.

From the corner of her eye, Selene saw Theo leap to his feet and grab a pair of wooden drumsticks off an end table, wielding them like the least effective nunchucks ever.

She growled low in her throat. *If I throw an arrow at Dash, he'll just dodge it,* she reasoned, *and his bullets are too fast for me. But if I tackle him, I can use my superior strength to wrench away his weapon. I just have to be fast enough—*

"Moonshine!" Paul cried. "What are you doing?"

"Getting some answers," she replied, her eyes still fixed on Dash. "About why our brother sent a man to *kill* me and then tracked me to this club."

"Track you?" Dash spluttered. "Paul *invited* me."

"You did *what*?" Selene demanded, sparing her twin a glance over her shoulder.

"I've been a little out of it, okay? But it's true—when I got your message about Hades, I called Dash for help. He knew our uncle better than the rest of us. And if there's an Athanatos reviving a cult, he's the only one who knows where everyone lives."

"I didn't tell you to do that!"

"You needed *help*. We all promised to stop another sacrifice cult. What did you expect me to do?"

Before she could retort, Theo interrupted, "How about we all put down the weapons and talk calmly?" He twirled one of the drumsticks awkwardly. "Before I'm forced to knock you both out Ringo Starr style."

Dash spun his pistols around his index fingers with far more grace and gave an insouciant grin. "Just as soon as your girl-friend puts away that arrow."

Selene scowled at his choice of words. "I'll put it away once you explain why the man who shot me flew into my house wearing a winged cap."

Dash stared at her, uncomprehending, before spluttering, "*My* cap? Round gold thing, little dent in the side, pretty metal wings?" He looked genuinely shocked. "No, no, no. It stopped working soon after the Diaspora, the same time my winged san-dals stopped flying and the rest of our more conspicuous powers went kaput. Turned into nothing more than a very silly hat. Last time I dusted it off was for a particularly fetching Carnival cos-tume in eighteenth-century Venice. I dimly remember falling off a gondola after one too many proseccos, the hat went into the Grand Canal, and I haven't seen it since."

Selene kept the arrow pointed at her younger brother. "So you *didn't* have anything to do with Hades' murder?"

"I wasn't even here!" he protested. "Tell her, Paul. Hades was kidnapped three days ago. I was still in L.A., at a movie premiere! I swear it—you can check my Twitter."

She glanced at Theo, thinking, *What the hell is a Twitter?* He'd already pulled out his phone and swiped to something or other.

"Dash is telling the truth." Theo turned his phone to show her a photo of her brother standing on a red carpet with a blank-eyed woman on his arm.

Selene still wasn't convinced. Dash wouldn't know the "truth" if it were wearing a name tag and shouting hello. "If you were in Los Angeles, how do you know when Hades was kidnapped?"

"Because his wife told me."

"What?" Her head was splitting trying to follow Dash's story. There was a reason he was called the Many-Turning One. "When did you talk to *her*?"

"I called her as soon as I heard about Hades, of course!" he said, looking mildly surprised. "Didn't you? Didn't you wonder if she was okay?"

Selene lowered her arrow and sat heavily on a rickety wooden chair, a bit ashamed, a bit relieved, but mostly just tired. "I guess I assumed she made it out, otherwise we would've heard." In truth, she hadn't bothered to think about Persephone at all.

"Well, you're right about that much at least," Hermes said, holstering his pistols and hopping easily off the counter. "She fled to Peru, completely hysterical, of course, but she'll be in good hands with her mom."

Selene sighed in exasperation. "I thought she *hated* her mother."

"She might hate her, but she loves her too." He pulled off his fedora and gave her a winking bow. "That's what family's for."

Selene could feel Theo's "I told you so" from across the room.

"Fine. So she's safe in the Southern Hemisphere, but *we're* still targets. And we don't even know who's after us."

"We know one thing," Theo said. "The man who attacked Selene called her Diana, not Artemis. And when he spoke about his superior on the phone, he referred to him using the Greek and Latin word for 'father,' but he said *PA*-ter, not pa-*TEER*."

"Pater…" repeated Paul. "That's the Latin pronunciation."

"Exactly. So what Athanatos would use Latin instead of Greek?" Theo looked at Selene, suddenly alarmed. "Don't tell me there are Roman versions of you running around. Am I going to bump into some woman named Diana who looks just like you?"

"No," she said with a sigh. "When the Romans incorporated us into their pantheon, most of us just…expanded a little. It's hard to explain."

"You could say that again."

"Diana's just a part of me—or at least she was. When I don't just think of myself as a New Yorker, I think of myself as fundamentally Greek. But some Athanatoi gained so much power in the Imperial Age that they embraced the Roman incarnation of themselves above all others."

"Good, that should narrow the search," Theo said, clapping his hands. "What about Helios? The Romans worshiped him as Sol Invictus, the personification of the Invincible Sun."

Dash buzzed him like a game show host. "*Eaahhh.* Helios kicked the bucket sometime in the sixteenth century. No real worship after the fall of the Roman Empire. Sorry, Makarites."

Few mortals in history had ever been dubbed Makaritai, or "Blessed Ones," and most of them bore names like Heracles and Perseus. In more recent millennia, a select few artists and scholars—like Theo—had earned the title for their extraordinary insight into the gods. But the honor clearly wasn't helping the professor now.

"Okay," he said, turning from one god to the other, clearly exasperated. "Then who did *you* all have in mind?"

"Don't bother reasoning this one through, Theo," Selene snapped. "Someone in this room already knows the answer." She turned her withering glare on Paul. "Because one of my supposedly loyal brothers must've told someone about Orion's cult. Maybe not on purpose, but they did. Even though they *promised* not to."

Her twin held up his hands. "I swear on the dropping water of the Styx, I had nothing to do with this."

She wasn't sure she believed him. In the past, he'd freely admitted to a fear of fading, and with the way he was acting, she doubted he'd even remember what he had or hadn't said to someone. But that song...she couldn't believe he'd attack her.

"And don't look at me," Dash insisted. "Trust me, darling, if I still had that cap, *I'd* be wearing it, not giving it to some mortal to dick around in. Private jets aren't half so fun."

Theo yawned and rubbed the bridge of his nose. "Okay, so if it wasn't either of you, and you still insist there's definitely an Athanatos behind this, then you think the God of Wine tattled? In one of his drunken stupors?"

Selene shook her head. "He's usually so high that he'll tell anyone anything, but he's too isolated."

"And Hephaestus the Smith?" pressed Theo. "He looked pretty grizzled when we saw him this fall. Maybe he couldn't resist giving himself a little extra power."

Dash chuckled. "The Smith with a band of mortal acolytes? Running—or should I say limping—around the Financial District? No way. Too social. Too public. Not to mention, too desperate. If he wants to make himself more powerful, he just devises some clever gadget to do it for him. He resigned himself to fading years ago, and now he never talks to any of the other Athanatoi unless he's got no other options—a little like you, Selene," he added with a wink. "Trust me, when the Smith showed up *in person* to help you take down Orion, I wondered if he'd been sniffing too many volcanic fumaroles."

"Well, whoever it is," Paul interrupted, "if they have your cap, they're going to be *very* hard to defend against. I don't know about you guys, but I lost my flying chariot a long time ago."

"The man stole my gold arrows," said Selene. "The cult probably took Hades' helm as well when they kidnapped him. And I know from experience that it still works—at least underground."

"Great," Dash said with a dramatic sigh. "There's probably some invisible murderer sitting in this room right now." Paul gasped, and spun to look behind him.

Dash flipped his fedora up his arm like Charlie Chaplin. "Kidding! I'm sure our Huntress here would sniff him out." He paused, his grin fading. "Right?"

Selene just glared at his antics and tried to pretend he hadn't completely freaked her out. Paul was on his feet now, his fingers twitching anxiously. "All we've got for divine defense are our bows and a few of my silver arrows." He swung to his sister. "What happened to Orion's sword after we killed him?"

"I hid it in my house," Selene answered. "But we shouldn't go back there. And besides, what good would it do us? I've never used a sword, and surely any magic talent it might've once bestowed on its holder doesn't work anymore."

Dash tutted. "Then pour some wine on your heads and bare your necks, because we're the next sacrifices—unless we can find some more divine weapons."

"All right, so maybe we *should* go after the Smith," Theo proposed. "He could give us weapons, right?" Selene shot him a wary glance. Something told her Theo imagined himself carrying a golden spear and shield like the heroes of old. Once, she would've wanted him that way. Now, she rather liked him with his laptops and books. He was quite enough of a hero already.

"Theo's right," Dash concurred. "Flint is fading pretty badly these days, but I try not to underestimate He of Many Arts and Skills. So, let's just call him and see what he's got for us." A moment later, cell phone pressed to his ear, he crowed, "Flint, dude! How is my broadest, brawniest, stepbrother doing? . . . No, never! . . . I have a teensy weensy question if I could . . ." He pulled the phone away from his ear and stared at it. "That did not go well."

Selene grimaced. "Dude? You call him dude?"

"What else am I supposed to call him?" Dash asked helplessly. "He's a little hard to communicate with, okay? He doesn't like being bothered, so you've gotta play it cool."

"And how did that go?"

"He said he was in the middle of an experiment out in the woods and how dare I interrupt and that he wouldn't be home until tonight and...well, then there were some expletives that I don't think are necessary to repeat. Like I said, he doesn't like to be bothered."

"Great." Selene slapped her hands on her knees and then rose to her feet. "Well, I'm not waiting around. I'm going after him. If he isn't our culprit, at least he can make me some new gold arrows to take down whoever is."

"Wait," Paul interjected. "Remember, I've had this feeling that something bad was coming. If the Smith *is* behind this..."

The glazed look of despair that she'd noticed when he first came offstage was back. Selene knew she should be worried about him, but impatience overwhelmed her concern. "If I can't defend myself against the Lame One, then I'm really in trouble," she scoffed. "Can you tell me his address, Dash? Or are you going to be as cagey and unhelpful as usual?"

Dash looked deeply offended. "*Me?* Unhelpful? Have you *ever* gotten a job in this city without my help? Or a new ID card? I demand an apology, most ungrateful of sisters."

"Your help entails having to deal with *you*, so it *seems* unhelpful...even if it isn't," she grumbled. "How's that for an apology?"

"Execrable. But considering it's you, I've heard worse. So, I usually don't hand out addresses, but the Smith has always had a soft spot for you, so I'll make an exception. He's up in the Catskills—about a three-hour drive. I can give you directions."

"Then we rent a car, and we go *now*," Selene decided.

Theo got unsteadily to his feet. "I'm right behind you, I swear...but *you* don't have a driver's license, and if you make *me* drive to the Catskills right now, I'm going to crash us right into the nearest deer." He yawned. "And once I kill one of your sacred animals, you'll have to kill me as punishment. And then it all gets very Greek tragedy very fast."

"You can rest here for a few hours before you set out," Paul offered. "I'll see if I can rustle up a shirt and coat for you in the meantime."

Dash looked dubiously around the musty room. "And I'll secure some less pungent accommodations for when you get back. If I have to spend another minute here, I'm never going to get the percussionist funk out of my suit."

Theo's eyes had already fallen shut. *He must be truly exhausted if he can sleep at a time like this,* Selene thought. She wasn't doing much better herself; she was used to sleeping with the sunrise. If she wanted to be awake for their confrontation with the Smith, she'd need to get some rest, too. But right now, she was too riled up. There were simply too many questions and too few answers. She couldn't shake the feeling that if they delayed one more night, this new cult might strike again. She followed her twin out into the hall.

"I don't like all this waiting," she said.

"Seems to me you don't have a choice," Paul replied. "Dash said Flint won't be reachable until tonight, and he's the only lead we've got at the moment. But hey...if you want me to come with you to his place..." He didn't sound very sure of his offer. He still looked rattled from his crack onstage, and Selene had the sudden feeling his bizarre visions were worse than he was letting on.

"Don't you have a second set to get ready for?"

He nodded. "I'm just worried about you."

"*You're* worried about *me*? You're the one with the morbid hallucinations, Sunbeam."

To her surprise, he seemed at a loss for words. The God of Poetry usually knew exactly what to say.

"How's it going—with Theo?" he ventured finally.

The reason for his reticence became clear. For millennia, she never would've permitted him to ask about her love life. Paul had a tendency to guard his sister's honor a little *too* jealously. She settled for a terse, "Fine."

"Have you . . . you know?"

"Are you going to put an arrow through him if we have?"

"Not at all—"

"What's happening with *Sophie*?"

"I'm enjoying every moment."

"That's clear," she huffed.

"The connection I have with her, the intimacy—it's the only point to existing anymore. She may not know my true name, but I try to give her every part of myself. Body and soul." He emphasized the word "body" with a raised brow. When she just stared at him stonily, he went on. "Love is where my music comes from. Love for her. Love for you. It's the only thing putting me back together after these visions rip me apart. You could have that with Theo, you know."

"I'll think about it," she growled.

"Don't wait too long, Selene."

"We've been together for *three* months."

"Look, I spent the better part of three thousand years trying to be the only man in your life. And when you first started seeing Theo, all my old jealousies came right back. But I *like* him, Selene. And I like who you are when you're with him. But time passes swiftly for mortals—you have to seize the moment. Theo's what, in his thirties? He's going to be an old man soon enough, and you're still going to look pretty much the same. What sort of nursemaid will you make? No offense, but probably a piss poor one. And what happens when Selene DiSilva gets too well known and has to become some other woman in some other part of town?"

"I'm not a celebrity like you. This name will last at least another few decades."

Paul raised his eyebrows. "A few decades? Theo will still be alive. You're going to make him change his identity too? Trust me, it won't work."

"Then why should I bother in the first place?" she snapped. "Why not just walk away right now?"

Paul just shook his head sadly. "At some point, you'll have to do just that. But when you do, you want to leave with no regrets, Moonshine."

Selene laughed shortly. "Sometimes I feel like my whole life has been nothing but regrets."

He gave her a pained smile. "That's exactly what I'm afraid of."

Chapter 13

DEERLIKE

"I guess we walk from here," Theo said, pulling into the empty parking lot of Grossinger's Golf Course. "Hopefully, the Smith's hideout isn't too far away." Before he'd even shut off the engine, Selene had fled the car. In the rearview mirror, he saw her shake off the journey with all the vigor of a disgruntled hound, then reach into the trunk to retrieve her bow and wooden arrows, not bothering to hide them in her backpack.

Theo sat watching her for a moment, struck by her alienness. She'd seemed distant the whole car ride through the Catskills, even more than usual. Seeing her here, amid the rolling mountains, she seemed like an entirely different person from the one he knew. The wilderness was her realm, of course, but he'd only ever seen her in city parks. *Is this a different Selene?* he wondered. *She has so many names, so many lives—how can I ever know them all?*

He climbed out of the car and buttoned Paul's drummer's winter coat a little higher under his chin. Gray wool with a shearling lining, military epaulets, and pewter buttons down the sides—*Les Misérables* meets U2. He felt positively hip. Not to mention warm. Finally.

He laid a hand on Selene's shoulder. She turned toward him,

curious, and he quickly kissed her on the lips. She pulled back and stared at him for a moment, then kissed him back, harder. He no longer felt the cold.

"The resort was abandoned in the 1980s," he said when they pulled apart. "And a lot of it's falling down and dangerous. We might want to—"

She headed off confidently toward a cluster of buildings just visible through the woods.

"Okay, then." Theo trotted gamely after her, trying to keep his balance on the icy ground.

Before them lay a narrow stream rushing silently beneath a layer of frozen crystal. Struck by the wild beauty of the place, Theo pulled out his phone for a photo.

Selene slammed her boot heel into the creek's surface, cracking through the ice. She pulled the bandages from her forehead, revealing a thick red scab from the bullet's graze. Theo watched silently as she knelt and cupped a hand into the current. She took a drink, then lifted the water to her forehead, dribbling it across the wound. A moment later, the scab fell into the stream and tumbled away. The skin beneath gleamed alabaster smooth. Theo knew that, as the Goddess of the Wild, she could gain strength from natural running water, but he'd never actually witnessed its healing powers before. It was fascinating and unsettling all at the same time.

Selene turned her face toward the skeletal trees around her. Suddenly, her mouth trembled into a smile. Theo followed her gaze.

A doe. Ears swiveled forward, neck sweeping gracefully skyward. Liquid eyes fixed on the Deerlike Goddess.

Theo swung his phone toward the animal, realizing he was already in video mode.

Very slowly, Selene got to her feet. For a heartbeat, Theo wondered if she'd unsling her bow. She was, after all, the Shooter of Stags as well as their protector. But she simply stood there, as motionless as the deer. Finally, the doe broke the connection, pawing at the snow to unearth a few blades of grass.

Selene murmured something under her breath, then turned and headed toward the cluster of buildings.

"What did you say to her?" Theo asked, surreptitiously switching off his phone with a guilty pang. It felt wrong to let twenty-first-century technology intrude on such a sacred moment.

Selene didn't respond at first. When she did, it was with a quiet reverence. "I told her it was good to see her again."

Only then did Theo realize what the encounter must have meant for Selene. As far as he knew, she hadn't left Manhattan in years, maybe decades. Which meant the woman who'd once ridden a chariot drawn by stags, and who counted deer among the most sacred of her animals, hadn't seen one in all that time. No wonder she didn't want to shoot it.

As they crested a low rise, the main hotel appeared before them, a lumbering 1950s behemoth of boxy yellow concrete and graffiti-covered glass. Theo whistled softly. "Looks pretty deserted. What if the Smith's not here?"

She pointed to the ground. "See?"

"I see ice and pine needles."

"I see footprints. Big, crooked footprints, one deeper than the other, and the imprint of a crutch on either side."

"You're making that up," he said, staring harder at the solid ice.

"Why would I?" she asked, genuinely bewildered.

"To show off."

Without a word, she unslung her bow and sent an arrow flying into the gloaming. A distressed squeal emerged from beneath a snowbank. Selene retrieved her prey, holding aloft a dead rabbit by its long brown ears. "*That's* showing off," she said with a smile.

Theo grimaced. "When you didn't shoot the deer, I thought you'd given up on the killing-innocent-animals thing."

"Deer are sacred—I'd never hunt one without ceremony. But

rabbits are vermin. *Delicious* vermin." She slung the limp body from her belt. "The Smith will love it."

"That's the worst host gift I've ever heard of," he grumbled, following her up to the main entrance of the hotel.

In the 1950s and '60s, Grossinger's had entertained up to 150,000 people a year as one of the premier resorts of the Borscht Belt, the string of Catskills destinations catering to Jewish families desperate to escape the steaming streets of New York but unwelcome in the swankier hotels of New England. Mothers would tote their Baby Boom's worth of children, park themselves beside the swimming pool or shuffleboard court, and wait for their husbands to arrive on regular weekend visits. Dances, talent shows, comedy acts, buffets—a middle-class paradise. Then, with the rise of air travel and the decline of anti-Semitism, the resort's devotees sought summer vacations farther afield, leaving Grossinger's to die an inglorious death. Now the grand main lobby, a hangar-size expanse with a huge stone fireplace and a double-wide staircase, lay abandoned and decrepit. A sea of icy mold covered the carpet; midwinter darkness shrouded the ceiling high above.

This was not how Theo'd imagined his first out-of-town trip with Selene. He'd thought they'd jet off to Paris or Rome or even just Cape Cod. *I was hoping the Catskills would've maintained at least a little of the* Dirty Dancing *vibe,* he thought, stepping gingerly around a torn armchair covered in bird shit. He looked uneasily through the shattered windows at the low sun. "Once night falls, it's going to be pitch black in here."

"Don't worry," Selene said, striding forward. "I'll have found Flint by then. Dash said once we got here, we should just 'follow the signs.' How hard can that be?"

"And then? What if the Smith really is the Pater? I can't help remembering all those stories about his famous rage."

"We all have stories about our famous rage. The Smith is the least of your problems."

"He does have that hammer."

"He's also on crutches, remember? And he's really quite reasonable. I wouldn't worry about him."

Theo didn't push her further, but he mentally reviewed what he remembered about Hephaestus, God of the Forge. It wouldn't hurt to be prepared. Stories of his birth varied, as did most myths, but the usual version held that his mother Hera, Queen of the Gods, became pregnant without the help of man's seed. Probably a way to get back at Zeus, her famously philandering husband. When Hephaestus was born, Zeus—furious at his wife's hubris—hurled him off Olympus. The fall left the Smith permanently crippled. Among a pantheon of stunning beauty, he was the only Olympian renowned for his ugliness. His bad luck didn't end there. His marriage to Aphrodite, most gorgeous of goddesses, ended in heartbreak and betrayal when she left him for his brother Ares. Hence the rage.

"You know the story of Harmonia?" Theo asked Selene.

"Should I?" As with most of the lesser-known myths, if it had nothing to do with Artemis, Selene hadn't retained the memory.

"Aphrodite and Ares have a daughter, Harmonia, and the Smith is so pissed off that he makes her a cursed necklace as a wedding present. She's tortured by bad luck for the rest of her days. And not just her. *Four* generations of offspring. Does that sound reasonable to you?"

Selene stopped and turned around. "Are you scared to come?"

"What? No."

"That story's just a story. Or maybe it's not. It's not my myth, so I'm not sure either way. But you of all people should know that the gods aren't always what the legends make us out to be. Harmonia's descendants are long dead. The Smith is Flint now. He could be a completely different person."

Theo raised a hand in submission. "Fine. I'm just trying to get my facts straight, that's all."

She snorted. "You shouldn't come any farther."

"What?"

"Flint spent most of his life holed up in a volcano. He's always been antisocial and a little surly. That's what I like about him. I've decided he'll be easier to talk to if it's just me."

"*You've* decided. I see. And you couldn't have thought of that before I left the warm, electrified, *safe* rental car and wandered onto the set of the zombie apocalypse?"

"I just think it's better if I do this alone."

"I'm not letting you risk your life—"

"*Letting* me? I'm telling you I can handle this. We're just going to talk."

"All the more reason I should be there. Your conversational sparring has a bad habit of turning into *actual* sparring very quickly." She bristled, but he pressed on. "Look, I'm not trying to pretend like I know more about the gods than you do—"

"Good. Because you don't. You may be a 'Makarites'"— her voice dripped with disdain—"but you're still just a mortal, Theo."

He stopped in his tracks. "What's that supposed to mean?" When she refused to even reply, he felt an unaccustomed anger flush his cheeks. "You sound like Orion. A mortal will never be able to understand your glory, so you should just go live happily ever after with some immortal lover. Is that it?"

"Don't be ridiculous."

"Then don't talk down to me."

Her eyes flared, but she stalked away without another word. Still, the message was clear: *I'm a goddess. I talk down to you by definition.*

Theo watched her go, fighting the urge to shout something cutting, and wondering when he'd become a guy who took cheap shots at his girlfriend. He tromped off toward the parking lot. Did he really want to wander Grossinger's asbestos-filled halls, fighting off the ghosts of angry Jewish grandmothers swinging their beach bags at the goyish intruder, only to wind up facing the Sooty God swinging his massive hammer instead? Better to get back in the car, turn on the heat, and write some exam questions while waiting for his supernatural girlfriend to finish her little chat with her quasi-divine relative. Just the weekend in the country he'd been hoping for.

———◇———

Pushing aside her frustration with Theo, Selene headed down a long, windowless passageway, determined to find her step-brother. With no light to see by, she turned to her other senses. Smell was no good: The scent of mold and decay overpowered everything else. But she could feel an almost intangible wave of heat emanating from somewhere ahead of her. Surely that was one of the "signs" Dash had told her to follow.

She opened a door to an apartment; the dim sunlight leaking through its dirt-smeared windows provided just enough illumination for her night vision, so she could avoid the tumbled furniture and ripped-up carpet in the hallway. She followed the sensation of warmth down a series of long corridors, opening doors on either side for light.

She peeked into one of the rooms. Once, sunburned children would've crowded the Murphy beds, dreaming of swimming and hot dogs and endless summers. Now only rat-bitten mattresses remained beneath graffitied walls proclaiming, "Turn back now!" and "I fucked on this bed!" *This* was the place the Smith called home?

Finally, she found the source of the warmth: a large double door with "Natatorium" written in faded paint across the lintel. A swimming pool. A thick metal chain looped through the door handles: Someone didn't want visitors. She tapped lightly on the door but got no response. She leaned her ear against the wood, hoping to pick up the slightest noise. Nothing. Impatient, she rattled the door and yanked on the chain, but to no avail.

She looked around for another way in and found a rusted

sign reading, "Handicapped Entrance." But the arrow on the sign pointed only to a bare wall. She scanned the hallway for any reference to her stepbrother's attributes—hammer, tongs, donkey—but found nothing that might lead her to some secret way of unlocking the door.

"Hey!" she finally just shouted. "It's the Huntress! Let me in!"

After a final loud pounding on the door, she turned and went back the way she'd come. A swimming pool would certainly have exterior windows; maybe she could see through from outside.

By the time she made it back outdoors, the sun had set. Only the moon illuminated the snow ahead of her. She traipsed around the building until she came to a large, intact structure with walls of paned glass: She could see the pool inside, but no sign of the Smith. Only the deep end still contained water—a black stagnant puddle filled with trash and the floating remains of metal chaise lounges, their legs jutting from the water like the skeletons of pre-historic sea creatures.

She turned to walk away, deciding she must have been mistaken. Then she noticed the lack of snow around the building: a wide bare ring surrounded by melting slush. The chill winter air blew away most of the heat, but when she pressed her hand against the glass wall, it felt warm. *Hot* even.

She scrounged in her jacket pocket for a scrap of paper and a pencil stub. *Selene DiSilva,* she wrote. *Open up.* Then she pulled a shoelace out of her boot and used it to tie the paper to the shaft of an arrow. She broke off the arrowhead—no use trying to gain the Smith's trust if she wounded him in the process—then took a few steps back from the glass wall. She aimed high, toward the unlit starburst chandelier suspended above the pool.

Even without the tip, the force of her golden bow sent the arrow easily through the glass. She hadn't quite planned on it shattering an entire large pane, but physics had never been her strong suit. She winced at the deafening clatter, hoping the Smith hadn't booby-trapped the place. She stepped back, just in case.

As soon as the glass fell away, a bright orange glow burst from the hole in the wall, along with a massive cloud of white steam as superheated air met the winter's chill. And the *noise*. A resounding thrumming of machinery, the clang of a hammer on an anvil, and underscoring it all, the indecipherable yowling of some heavy metal "singer."

Before she could ponder her stepbrother's musical tastes any further, an invisible door in the side of the wall swung open, and the Smith himself stood before her, looking as if he'd emerged from another dimension. Around the door frame, the image of the dark, abandoned pool remained intact, but over Flint's shoulder she could see a brightly lit room full of machinery. He was shirtless, sweat pouring down his hairy barrel chest. Soot and grease streaked his craggy face. Rather than using his traditional crutches, he wore complicated titanium braces on each of his shriveled legs. In one hand, he held her arrow. In the other, the scrap of paper.

He clenched the note in his massive fist, crumpling it into a small ball, and squinted into the darkness.

"Huntress?" he asked, his voice a low, fierce rumble. Something in his tone made Selene pause. *Maybe Theo was right. Maybe he* is *dangerous.*

Cautiously, she stepped into the light.

Then, before she could stop him, he lunged forward, surprisingly fast on his withered legs, and grabbed her by the forearms. Despite his aging, his grip remained as hard as iron, and his eyes burned with a fiery intensity that raised the hair on the back of her neck. She reacted instantly, twisting her arms free and stepping backward to deliver a roundhouse kick to his sternum. The Smith stumbled, his braces squealing in protest. Then his legs crumpled beneath him, and he lay on the ice like a felled beast, his eyes on the ground, his back heaving.

"Why did you attack me?" she demanded, careful not to get too close.

"I didn't ... *attack* you," he panted. Finally, he turned his face up to hers. The intensity was gone. Only a deep, weary sadness remained.

She finally understood: He'd been excited to see her. Not exactly the reaction of a man who'd sent someone to kill her.

He turned his face to the ground and started the laborious task of raising himself up. She started forward to help, then thought better of it. All gods, even those who had declined to the state of a thanatos, had their pride.

Once he was back on his feet, he pressed a few buttons on the side of his braces. They released a faint hydraulic hiss, and he could stand straight once more. His expression hardened into a stern mask. "I wasn't expecting visitors," he said. "I'm not usually so ... demonstrative." He rubbed at his chest, where the imprint of her boot sole branded his flesh.

"Here," she said, pulling the rabbit from her belt and thrusting it at him with a belated attempt at courtesy. He accepted it slowly, his small eyes narrowing further.

"I guess you know it's too hard to catch the buggers with my legs." He gave her a thin, bitter smile, more accusation than gratitude, then turned back to the open door. "Come."

Score another one for Theo, she decided. *A terrible gift. Next time, just bring a box of chocolates.* She hesitated in the doorway to the forge. The Smith might not be dangerous, but he was damn hard to predict, and the last thing she needed was another moody man in her life. *Guess I don't have a choice,* she thought, following him inside with a sigh. *If I want any more divine weapons, looks like I'll have to put up with the man who made them all in the first place.*

Chapter 14

THE SOOTY GOD

When the door closed behind her, Selene immediately felt sweat popping on her brow. Normally, she was as impervious to heat as to cold, but this was worse than a hundred degrees in August trapped in an un-air-conditioned subway car. This was *volcanic*. The heat issued forth from the dozens of machines pounding away in the depth of the empty swimming pool. Most were steam-driven, great turbines and pistons flailing like the limbs of epileptic spiders, jetting steam toward the ceiling high above. But along the perimeter of the room, large banks of computers and electronics covered the lower half of the walls. Heavy-duty acoustical paneling covered the upper half.

She pointed to the crisscross of blue laser beams shooting out from the computers. They reminded her of something from one of the science fiction movies Theo was always making her watch. "Is that what keeps the illusion going?" She had to shout to be heard over the heavy metal cacophony.

Flint nodded. "Works well, except when an uninvited guest shoots out one of my panes of special holographic glass." With a gait only slightly stilted by the braces on his legs, he grabbed a massive sheet of steel in one hand, a welding machine in the other, and walked to a large metal plate sitting atop a contraption of gears and accordioned struts. He rolled the welder onto it, yanked a series of levers, spun a few wheels, and was soon zooming upward on an elevated platform. When it reached its apex, the Smith hovered a mere four feet below the ceiling. Six segmented steel legs emerged from the mechanism's base. It started crawling across the ground with the steady tread of a praying mantis. As if in appreciation of Flint's invention, a guitar screamed its way through a frenetic riff; Selene finally began to appreciate Paul's brand of folk rock.

Flint arrived at the broken pane in the wall, donned a welding helmet, and flipped on his machine. It hissed like a steady wind, and a lightning-bright spark appeared between his torch and the sheet metal he placed over the gap.

Selene shut her eyes to the glare and shouted up, "Won't that look suspicious from the outside?"

"Better than having light gush out," he called down to her as he worked, his voice muffled from the helmet. "Google Earth could pick it up. Then I'd have *more* annoyances pounding down my door."

Annoyances? It took all her self-control not to burst out with: *If you want annoying, I'll start by ripping out your sound system and shoving it down your hairy throat.* But she was here to enlist the Smith's help, not antagonize him. She took a steadying breath and shouted up, "Speaking of pounding on the door, I tried that. You didn't answer. You might consider turning down the music so you can hear a little better."

He didn't take the hint. He finished his welding job, took off his helmet, and lowered the lift back to the floor as the song reached its screeching climax and then came to an abrupt halt. "You have to ring the bell," he said into the sudden silence.

"What bell?"

He gave her a black look. "Didn't Dash tell you to follow the signs?"

"I followed the heat. Is that what you mean?" she asked testily. Between the stifling temperature, the pounding of machinery, and the opening riffs of the next metal anthem, Selene's stomach had twisted itself inside out.

"Not the heat. The *signs*. The one that says, 'Handicapped Entrance.' If you follow the arrow—"

"I tried that."

"You see an alarm handle that says, 'Pull in Case of Fire.' That's the doorbell."

Of course. Hephaestus the Lame One, God of Fire and Forge. She felt like a moron, and from Flint's expression, he wholeheartedly agreed.

Theo would've probably figured out the reference, she realized, *but my method worked, too. It was just slightly more destructive.* At the moment, she was actually glad she'd resorted to wrecking the Smith's little hideaway—he deserved it for his condescension.

"I can't hear myself think in here," she said through gritted teeth. "Turn off that music—if that's what you call it. And while you're at it, shut down all these infernal machines."

"No." He didn't elaborate.

"Then I guess I should just leave without telling you my incredibly vital news."

"News you couldn't just leave on my phone, like I've told everyone to do *repeatedly*?" he asked, drawing an oversized device out of his pocket. Rather than the usual static screen of colored icons, the Smith's phone was in constant motion. He saw her looking and held it up for her. "I still prefer to make things with my own hands, but if I didn't use other people's inventions too, I'd be a fool."

"Or a purist," she replied archly. "I don't bother with the Digital Age if I can help it." *And it makes me feel all of my three thousand years when I can't figure out how to even open the damn "apps," or whatever they're called.*

Flint raised a grizzled eyebrow. "You must find life in the

twenty-first century tough without a little help from gadgets like this. We may not be omniscient anymore, but the Internet's almost as good." He swiped his finger across the screen, bringing up a graph covered in scores of jiggling colored lines. "It's monitoring all my systems here in real time, not to mention tapping into the volcanic seismographs around the world. It's like I've got eyes everywhere."

"Sounds amazing," she said dryly. "But I prefer the eyes in my own head. They're better at telling me when someone is trying to kill me."

He shot her a sharp look. "Why would someone—"

"Hades is dead. Dragged out of his own lair and left in a ritual sacrifice in the middle of the Financial District."

The Smith stared at her for a long moment, expressionless. Then he disappeared into the warren of machinery. The song cut off abruptly in the middle of a head-splitting drum solo. The pounding steam engines slowed their rhythm, then ground to a hissing halt. He returned, his face even darker with soot than before.

"You sure?"

"I saw the body myself. Then, the next day, they came for me."

The sudden intensity of his stare raised her hackles, and she took an involuntary step backward. She tried to read his emotions in the tightening of his lips but couldn't decide if he was angry, afraid, or merely annoyed at being dragged into the situation.

He turned to the rabbit on the workbench, chose a small saw off one rack and a metal basin from another, and began to gut her host gift with a speed and skill that rivaled her own. A minute later, he'd speared the carcass with an aluminum rod and placed it into a nearby low-burning furnace to cook. He slammed the door shut and turned back to her. *Is he actually hungry,* she wondered, *or is he just taking out his frustration on my rabbit?*

"At first, my attacker just wanted my gold arrows—the ones you brought to me this fall," she offered when it became clear

Flint had no intention of speaking. "Stole the whole quiver and then flew off in Dash's winged cap before I could snatch it back. He was mortal, but he could use a divine item—an item Dash himself said stopped working long ago. How is that possible?"

Flint's thick beard shifted with the clenching of his massive jaw. "I don't know."

"Aren't you the expert? Didn't you make the cap in the first place?"

"That was millennia ago. I haven't invented a new divine weapon since the Diaspora."

"Because you can't? Is that one of the powers that's been lost to you?"

"Because I can't. Because I choose not to. Is there a difference?" The Smith reached into his pocket and handed her the bootlace she'd used to secure her note to the arrow shaft. Then, as if that marked the end of their meeting, he turned his back on her and opened a drawer in his workbench. He grabbed a fistful of metal wire seemingly at random and started angrily bending each thread with a small pair of pliers. He didn't even look at his hands as he worked, much less at Selene. He just stared at the wall, as if his brain whirred so fast that it shot off into space like a propeller blade loosed from its hub.

I've got little patience for my own bitter musings, Selene thought, resisting the urge to shake him. *I've got even less for those of my stepbrother, or my cousin, or whatever I'm supposed to call my father's sister-wife's parthenogenically birthed son.*

The Smith fit a series of small aluminum plates onto his wire mesh, creating a nearly spherical container. She had no idea what it was for, but it clearly wasn't going to help her figure out more about her mysterious attacker, and it certainly wasn't any kind of useful divine weapon.

She stepped close to the workbench so he couldn't ignore her. "I could use some more arrows if I'm going to hunt down my attacker and his friends."

The Smith grunted disdainfully. "I don't sit around all day making gold arrows just in case you run out, you know." Yet he put down the wire contraption and stomped off into the bowels of his forge, returning moments later with three gleaming shafts. "These are all I've got." He thrust them toward her.

Selene nodded her thanks. Flint went back to his wires, ignoring her. *At least the trip wasn't a complete waste,* she thought, tucking the arrows into her belt and preparing to leave. Theo would be waiting, probably still angry at her for dismissing him earlier. *He's right—my conversational skills leave a lot to be desired.* Predictably, she'd managed to alienate both him and the Smith in a single hour.

"Any other ideas about that cap?" she asked her stepbrother, giving diplomacy one more shot.

Surprisingly, he actually answered. "Think of Perseus using Athena's shield. If a god chooses to loan a mortal his divine attributes, then the mortal can use them." He shrugged his heavy shoulders. "Or it could be a man elevated to immortality. Maybe."

"Well, Dash says he didn't even know the cap still existed— he certainly didn't gift it to a thanatos. And it can't be a mortal newly elevated, because after the Trojan War, Zeus declared the Age of Heroes over, remember? No more handing out immortality right and left."

"You think the old rules still apply?" He snorted. "Don't you know that the one constant in this world is inconsistency?"

"Great. Now I know even less than before. Maybe Theo's first instinct was right, and there's no god associated with this at all."

"Theo." Flint's hands froze. "Your friend."

"He's waiting in the car." One look at the Smith's white-knuckled grip on his wire sphere and Selene was suddenly sure she'd made the right decision in sending Theo away. "He's assisting. And trust me, we need all the help we can get. We're being targeted, and if I'm right and Hades' murderer is a fellow Athanatos, then we need to be extremely cautious. We've got some evidence that points to someone with a penchant for the Roman Era."

She started describing the crime scene and the attack in the park. The more she told him, the faster his hands worked. By the time she described the flying man calling his leader "Pater," the Smith had finished his basketball-sized sphere. He grabbed a pencil-width rod of aluminum from a cubby and bent it into the shape of a small arrow. Before she could finish her story, Flint stuck the metal rod onto the top of his orb and held it up for her. The entire structure now formed a circle with an arrow on top. She stared uncomprehending for a moment before its import finally sank in: the universal sign for "male." More important, the astronomical symbol for the planet named for the bloodthirstiest and most untrustworthy god in the entire pantheon: Mars.

"Oh." She felt a sudden tingling of dread as the clues coalesced. Mars, the God of War, was arrogant enough to conduct a sacrifice outdoors in the middle of Wall Street; he'd slain the dog with all the sadistic brutality he was best known for; and one of his attributes was a poisonous serpent. The god she'd known first as Ares—before he'd adopted his Latin name amid the slavish devotion of the Roman legions—had no loyalty, no honor. Hephaestus was his brother, yet he'd stolen Aphrodite from him without a shred of compunction.

Selene could still remember the look of agonized betrayal on the Smith's face as he watched his wife and her lover struggling to escape the golden net he'd fashioned to trap them in their illicit union. Aphrodite had buried her face in her hands, humiliation flushing her naked skin a brilliant red. But Ares roared his defiance. The sculpted muscles of his body strained in vain against threads of gold as thin as spider's silk and stronger than iron. His parents, mighty Zeus and terrible Hera, stared down at him with disgust. But Ares merely cursed his brother, his father, even his mother, for not giving him what he wanted. How dare they let the most beautiful goddess in the universe marry a cripple, when he, boldest and bravest of the gods, deserved her more? *"I'll kill you all if I get the chance,"* he'd cried, reaching through the net for his spear. With an angry gesture from Hephaestus, the threads of gold tightened around Ares' bulging forearm, threatening to slice it from his body. Ares screamed, his voice like the blaring of war horns. *"I'm the Man-Slayer, but I could be the God-Slayer if I wished!"* Madness filled his rolling eyes, and even Aphrodite looked away in fear.

While the other Olympians cowered, Artemis, the Virgin Huntress, had laughed. *"I'd put a golden arrow through your heart the moment you tried."*

She no longer felt so confident. Mars, she suspected, maintained much of his divine strength. War was the one constant in mankind's existence—and the conflicts of the modern age had grown only larger and bloodier. He would grow stronger right alongside.

"Are you sure it's him?" she asked Flint, desperately hoping he was wrong.

Without warning, the Smith hurled the ball across the room with a grunt; it bounced off a bank of computers and rolled back toward him. Then he grabbed a large pipe wrench off the workbench and raised it over his head. Selene covered her head with her hands as he slammed the tool into the ground, opening a great hole in the floor. She dared not raise a hand to stop him— he might have faded, but his legendary strength still matched her own. She backed up, looking toward the exit.

Then, as suddenly as it began, Flint's wrath subsided. He fell awkwardly against the side of his workbench and dropped the wrench. His cheeks burned above the thicket of his beard.

"Mars isn't here, you know," she said. "Who the hell are you so angry at?"

His voice was a low rumble of anger. "Myself."

"*You* told your brother about the power of sacrificing a god?"

He glared at her. "Of course not. My *wife* did." He spat out the word as if it were too bitter to swallow.

"And who told *her*?" Selene demanded. Aphrodite, the Goddess of Erotic Love, ranked high on her very short list of reasons to be thankful for the Diaspora. The thought of her throaty chuckle and creamy skin made Selene nauseous all over again.

Flint pulled a metal crate down from a shelf and started filling it with various tools and electronics—most of which she couldn't begin to identify. Some looked purely utilitarian; others were covered in intricate Bronze Age engraving, shaped into graceful art deco curves, or crafted from delicate Victorian clockwork. "I didn't *tell* her. But she's…" He tossed dozens of neat coils of wire and tubing into his crate.

"She's what? Irresistible? Is that what you were going to say?"

"She gets what she wants," he said shortly.

Selene wanted to scream at him about the frailties of men. To punish him for betraying her trust. But something about the ferocity of his scowl made her think he was already punishing himself enough. She picked up her bow and slung it over her shoulder, turning to go.

"I'm not done packing," Flint rumbled, loading his overflowing crate into a larger trunk.

"Don't bother," she said shortly.

"The Man-Slayer is Hera's son," the Smith went on, pulling down a second crate. "He inherited all her worst qualities: jealousy, fury, arrogance, capriciousness. To confront him, you'll need me."

Selene bristled. *Yet another man in my life telling me that I need him,* she thought. *Great.* But could she face the Man-Slayer alone? It would be foolish not to accept any help the Smith was willing to give. So she said nothing, merely watched him add a series of smaller boxes to his crate. Then, with what seemed an unnecessary amount of force, he unfastened his space-age titanium leg braces, lashed them to the trunk, and picked up a pair of simple aluminum crutches.

He's the "Lame One," she remembered. *Just as I cling to virginity, he must remain crippled to hang on to some semblance of his divinity.*

But at least I got to pick my own attributes—he had no choice at all. Yet now, she realized, they were both hobbled by the very traits that defined them.

The Smith walked haltingly across the room to retrieve the wire orb he'd made. With a single calm gesture, he bent the "male" arrow straight, then folded it into a carrying handle. Now, instead of a Mars symbol, it was just a basket. "I don't know where my brother is now, and neither will Dash," he said, his voice dark. "But I know who does."

He tossed a last roll of copper tubing into his trunk more violently than was strictly necessary. *He's going to call Aphrodite,* Selene thought with a barely stifled groan. Hard enough dealing with the gods in her life. The goddesses were even more complex. "Do what you have to," she said with a sigh.

Flint looked up, surprised. "I always do."

He opened the furnace door and pulled out the rabbit, its skin perfectly crisped. Selene nearly drooled at the odor of sizzling fat. Flint placed the rabbit in the spherical wire basket and handed it to her.

"For the road," he said.

Then, for the first time since she'd entered his domain, the hint of a smile cracked his grizzled beard. And Selene, to her surprise, found herself smiling back.

—◇—

Introduction to Classical Mythology. Final Exam Question 1: *Choose two of the four works we've studied this semester:* The Iliad, Theogony, Oedipus Rex, *or Ovid's* Metamorphoses. *How does the work define "humanness"? How does it define "divinity"? Make sure to address systems of obligation, homage, and protection, while also considering issues of gender and—*

Theo's laptop battery finally died, thrusting him into darkness. He glanced at the gas gauge on the car. He couldn't keep running the engine indefinitely, but he was pretty sure his own impatient anger wouldn't be enough to keep the car warm without the heat on.

He realized he'd written an impossible assignment anyway. "Every student who gets handed this test is going to burst into tears," he said aloud. "How would *I* even answer it? How about: A human is the one with the obligation to wait in the car, while the divinity offers protection by doing all the cool things without him. And as for issues of gender…"

The roar of an engine interrupted him. A single blinding headlamp barreled toward the car, then came to a squealing halt in the adjacent parking space. A souped-up Harley dragging a large cargo trailer, Hephaestus the Smith at the handlebars. Theo's excitement at the chance to interact with another Olympian was immediately tempered by the sight of Artemis the Huntress sitting behind her stepbrother, clasping his broad, leather-clad chest. In her own leather jacket, she fit right into the tableau—a biker's girlfriend, enjoying the roar of power between her thighs. The Smith lent her an unnecessary hand to dismount. Even in the dark, Theo could see the way his touch lingered on hers. He shook the image from his head, put aside his useless laptop, and tried to look as manly as possible despite his visible shivering.

New answer, he decided. *Being human means knowing you'll never be as strong, as cool, or as competent as a god. Being divine means loving the human anyway. I hope.*

Chapter 15

LAUGHTER-LOVING

Selene awoke to a light rap on the door of the hotel suite. She squinted at the silk-padded walls and panoramic windows that surrounded her. When they'd gotten in from the Catskills around dawn, she'd been so weary she'd barely noticed the absurd opulence of Dash's chosen hideaway: the Four Seasons. Too exhausted by her many brothers' many absurdities to argue, she'd fallen asleep on one of several plush couches.

Theo, she suspected, hadn't slept at all. He'd disappeared into the bedroom to work on the final exam he was due to administer later that day. He must've already gone up to Columbia and back, because she could hear the shower running in the marble bathroom.

Still prone on the couch, she peered blearily out the window at the glittering skyline before giving up on telling time by the moon and checking the digital clock on the cable box. Five in the evening. She'd slept for nearly ten hours. Another tap on the door, slightly more insistent. Then a warm coo like a dove's trill, at once sensuous and playful.

Selene sat up with a curse. She remembered that sound. Laughter-Loving Aphrodite must be standing in the hall. She rubbed the sleep from her eyes and ran a hand over her tousled hair, wishing she'd woken up early enough to follow Theo's example and wash some of the soot and sweat from her body. She'd never cared what her brothers and uncles thought of her appearance, but she couldn't stand seeing the ever-glamorous, ever-youthful Aphrodite gloat at her decline. As another warm chuckle floated through the door, Selene picked up the phone on the end table and rang Flint's room down the hall. "She's here," she said. "Don't you dare leave me alone to deal with her." She didn't wait for his response.

She opened the door to a young man with bleached blond hair staring at his cell phone, chuckling at something on his screen. On the ground beside him sat a massive Louis Vuitton suitcase. He looked up after a moment, caught her staring, and gave her a frank grin. "Don't feel bad, Huntress," he said, his accent faintly French. "No one recognizes me without the . . ." He gestured to his conspicuously wingless shoulder blades with his thumb, then held out his hand to her. "Call me Philippe."

Last time she'd seen Aphrodite's son, Eros, he'd been a winged child, carrying around a tiny bow and shooting love-arrows at anyone who looked at him wrong. This tall, slender young man looked no older than sixteen and exuded a coy sensuality far more delicate than Aphrodite's blatant eroticism. But he had his mother's soft pink cheeks and—of course—a cupid's bow mouth. If he'd inherited anything from his father, Mars, it was the gleam in his gray eyes—not violent or brutal, but piercing nonetheless. Defying the winter weather, he wore sky blue pegged trousers and a tailored jacket over a pinstriped shirt of pink and yellow. In the hall behind him, a large window looked out onto Park Avenue's sparkling wreaths and twinkling trees, making Philippe look like an Easter pixie who'd stumbled into a Christmas diorama. His only concession to the season was a voluminous cashmere scarf looped multiple times around his neck.

Selene wondered what had happened to his feathered rainbow-hued wings. None of the possibilities were pleasant. She ushered him inside the suite just as Flint appeared from the room next door, hobbling on a single crutch. He saw Philippe's large suitcase, lifted it in one massive fist, and followed them inside without a word.

She found herself standing awkwardly between Aphrodite's bastard son and her oft-cuckolded husband. Flint dropped the suitcase unceremoniously. She took one look at his lowering gaze and steeled herself for some sort of volcanic outburst. Instead, he opened his arms; Philippe brushed right past her and into his stepfather's embrace.

"Bonjour, Papa," he murmured. Flint returned the hug with a brief, fierce squeeze. Philippe laughed and broke away. "I get it! You're still strong!"

"Don't you forget it." Flint clapped Philippe so soundly on the back that the slight youth stumbled forward a step.

"And where is the rest of the family?" he asked. "You promised me *une grande réunion!*"

"Who can keep track of Dash?" Flint asked grumpily. "I think he's flitting around with some movie bigwigs."

"And Paul has some all-important recording session with his band," Selene said, trying to reconcile this new, affectionate Flint with the surly stepbrother she'd returned with from the Catskills. "But we can get started without them."

Philippe sprawled across a sofa like a sheik in a seraglio. "How about we get started on some snacks first? The flight from Paris was unbearably long and the food in first class gets worse every decade, have you noticed?" He paused as if actually waiting for an answer.

"No," Selene said finally. "I hadn't."

"Really?" he asked earnestly. "What are you flying?"

"I'm not flying anything. I don't travel much," she replied stiffly.

Philippe made a face and pulled a pack of cigarettes from his breast pocket. "Don't you get bored after centuries in the same city?"

"My city's never boring." She felt her customary scowl grow even deeper.

"Oho!" he exclaimed around the cigarette clenched in his lips. "You're saying Paris is?"

"I wouldn't know."

"Ah! You must come visit." He lit up, inhaled. "The cafés, the art—"

"I've got plenty of cafés and art. I'm the patron goddess of *New York*." She'd never actually called herself that before. In fact, she often felt that the city itself was the deity and she just one more lowly worshiper among many. Yet since she'd defeated Orion's cult, she'd seen it as her duty to protect the inhabitants of New York from the supernatural forces that threatened it. Her neighbors might not pay her homage, but that didn't make her role as their protector any less real.

Philippe just laughed his mother's trilling laugh. "You can love two cities at once, you know!" He spread his arms expansively, smoke trailing from his cigarette as if to underline his point. "Love is infinite, whether it be for cities, or people, or—"

"Enough," Flint grunted. "We know how you feel about it, Phil." But the Smith seemed more amused than annoyed, and Selene had the distinct impression he'd only stifled his stepson for her sake.

"But Selene doesn't." Philippe pulled out his phone and waved it merrily. "Does she even know about my website?"

"Phil works at a dating site," Flint said, sounding deeply unimpressed.

Philippe pouted prettily. "I *own* the *best* dating site in the world. So trust me when I say I know about love." At that, he turned his attention to his phone and became as instantly absorbed as any other teenager.

Selene glared at Flint. They'd wasted a whole day waiting for someone who could lead them to Mars. She had little faith that this flighty kid would be any use at all in taking down his mighty father. He didn't look strong enough to lift his own luggage.

Theo emerged from the bathroom, a towel around his waist and his chest still glistening with water. "Oh. I didn't know we had company," he said, glancing warily from the young man on the couch to Selene. "And isn't this a nonsmoking room?"

Philippe craned his neck to peer over the back of the sofa. When he saw Theo, he instantly sat up. Selene didn't like the way he stared at Theo's bare torso. She could just imagine the God of Love's lascivious thoughts. Philippe cocked an eyebrow, looked from Theo to Selene and back, and said, "I don't live by the rules. And nice to meet you too . . . *Makarites*."

Theo blushed, the color traveling down his throat. "How did you know what I am?"

"I don't always understand mortals—none of us do—but I understand *l'amour*. And my lovely aunt here"—he glanced at Selene—"if that's what you want to call our rather confused genealogical relationship—would never reveal her divinity to anyone unworthy. You must be . . ." He circled his cigarette as if searching for the right word in English, although Selene suspected his occasional French was purely for effect. His eyes moved back to Theo's torso before he finally came up with, *"Exceptionnel."*

Theo only blushed harder and tucked his towel more firmly around his waist before holding out his hand.

"Theodore Schultz."

"Theodore means 'Beloved of God.' So appropriate." The corner of his lips curled slowly. Selene wasn't sure whether he referred to her feelings for Theo or his own. Either way, she wanted to fling the smug smile off his face with a well-placed fist. *This,* she decided, *is going to be a very long night.*

◄◦►

You wanted to meet other gods, remember? Theo chided himself as he retreated to the bedroom to get dressed. He yanked on a pair of corduroys and a buttery-soft pine green cashmere sweater that he'd found hanging in the closet. Compliments, no doubt, of Dash Mercer.

He wasn't used to seeing Selene surrounded by so many men—immortal or otherwise. *Of course I want her to reach out to her family, but do they all have to be so damn attractive and charismatic and powerful?* Paul could woo an entire audience with a single guitar chord. Flint, who had a frustrating habit of pretending Theo didn't exist, looked like he could break a man in half just by staring at him. Dash preferred to treat him like a mannequin. *Although he does have amazing taste in clothes,* Theo thought, catching sight of himself in the mirror. And Philippe . . . *well, there's one god who's paying attention to me,* Theo admitted. *And I sort of wish he wouldn't.*

Stop being an asshole, he told his reflection sternly. *If you're weirded out by them, how do you think Selene feels? She doesn't like any men, much less the ones she's related to. If you leave her out there with Philippe any longer, Mars will have one fewer Athanatos to kill.* The least he could do was get back in there and help her deal with them. *What else am I good for?* he wondered. Having learned from Flint that the God of War was likely their culprit, they knew the cult wasn't just the work of mortals. And Selene had been correct that one of her kin had spilled the secret about Orion's ritual. So far, in fact, Theo had been right about pretty much . . . nothing.

When he rejoined the group in the suite's living room, Selene was sitting across from Philippe, describing Hades' murder in gruesome detail.

The young man looked grave despite the smear of grease on his chin from the bacon-wrapped scallops room service had delivered moments before. "And you think whoever killed Hades is now after the rest of us?" He looked to his stepfather, who sat staring moodily at the half-empty plate of hors d'oeuvres and said nothing.

Theo perched on the arm of Selene's sofa and laid a hand lightly on her shoulder. He knew she loathed public displays of affection, but she didn't pull away. Perhaps she felt the need for solidarity as much as he did.

"The cult already came after Selene," Theo offered. "You're all in danger."

Flint finally spoke. "Phil's not in any danger. Not from his own father."

"My *father*?" Philippe rose to his feet. "Oh no, Papa, when you said you needed my help, you didn't say anything about Martin!"

"Is that Mars's alias now?" Theo couldn't help asking. He knew gods used names that related to their original roles, but "Martin" sounded more like the God of Javascript than the God of Bloodlust.

Flint ignored Theo's comment, picked up a scallop, and squished it in his fist as if the foam-born goddess were riding atop it. "It's my fault," he rumbled before confessing that his wife had somehow wheedled the information out of him about Orion's cult. "I told her that gods could get more powerful through—" He paused to look at Selene for permission.

She just sighed. "Go ahead. The secret's out anyway, and Philippe doesn't look like the human-sacrifice type."

When Flint had finished describing the cult's practices, Philippe stubbed out his cigarette angrily. "I'd hoped my father had changed his ways. But this sounds like Martin. Rampaging through the world with no thought for who lies bleeding in his wake."

Theo's curiosity was piqued—what kind of filial affection could a God of War and a God of Love possibly maintain? Not much of one, it seemed.

Selene leaned forward, her silver eyes cold. "Are you going to help us find him, then?"

Philippe lifted his head. "Mama wouldn't want me to," he said quickly. He flicked a glance toward his stepfather. "She still loves Martin, despite everything he stands for."

Selene's lip curled. "Or *because* of everything he stands for. Passionate rage and passionate love—are they so different?"

Philippe laughed shortly. "Maybe not. Theirs is the one

relationship I've never understood." He lit another smoke and took a deep draw, his expression brooding. "Let me propose a compromise," he said finally. "I'll take you to my father. But—" He held up a hand to halt Selene's wolfish grin. "We don't hurt him until we know for sure he's the culprit. I owe my mother that, at least. But if Martin *is* trying to kill Athanatoi, then go ahead and do whatever you want to him. With my blessing."

Flint looked at his stepson, a fierce smile slashing his beard. "That's my boy."

Selene immediately headed into the bedroom and returned with her backpack in one hand and her new golden arrows in the other. "Cults like this don't wait around. Let's go."

The Smith shook his head. "We can't just rush in there without a plan."

Selene lifted her arrows. "*This* is my plan. You bring your hammer. We'll be fine."

At the thought of Selene confronting Mars with her usual recklessness, Theo nearly choked. "We have to at least wait for Paul and Dash."

"Your mortal is right," Flint said with a sagacious nod. "We should wait for the others."

I have a name of my own, Theo thought. He was liking Flint less and less.

"We shouldn't underestimate Martin," the Smith went on. "Trust me. I know my half brother."

"He's my half brother, too," Selene said testily.

"You share a father. So what?" said Philippe. "Almost everyone shares the same father. It's the mothers who count. Thank Kronos. Or should I say, thank Rhea?" He leaned across the coffee table toward Theo. Despite his chain-smoking, his breath smelled of chestnut trees in bloom, musky and rich, and just a little like semen. "If I took after my father, I'd be sticking my spear into everything that moved. And I *wish* I meant that in a sexual way."

Flint ignored the interruption. "If we show up unannounced, he may let one of us in, but once he's accused of murdering Hades, who knows what he'll do? We should have as big a force as possible if we're going to confront him directly."

"What about the Wine Giver?" Philippe asked, popping a final scallop in his mouth. "Isn't he around?"

"No," Selene and Theo said at the same time.

"We're better off without him," Theo explained quickly. "Unless you want to spend the next week in a drunken coma. Trust me."

Philippe shrugged. "Too bad. He and I always worked well together. He always loosens things up." As he moved toward his luggage, he slid a glance at Selene. "Don't you think?" He pulled out a pair of silk lounge pants. "A little loosening sounds like just the thing." He moved a step closer to her, his smile coy. "You look like someone who could use a drop of the Wine Giver's gift right now. So tense!" With his fingertip, he brushed her cheek, her neck, and her wrist in quick succession.

Theo jumped to his feet. He wasn't sure whether he should save Selene from Philippe or vice versa, but he knew something very bad was about to happen. He held out a hand to draw her away, but she ignored him.

"Why am I not surprised that you're trying to ply me with alcohol, Philippe?" Selene snapped. She looked angry and flustered and defiant all at the same time. "Is that what you do to all the girls? Is that why you're such an *expert* on love? You give a woman enough of the Wine Giver's miraculous potion so that she's about to pass out, and then you can do whatever you want to her. She wakes up drunk and alone, not even remembering her violator's face." She glared down at the shorter man. "So *muhr-cee*, Philippe," she said, pronouncing the French with an exaggeratedly terrible American accent. "But I don't need any wine. And I don't need any of you."

Silence.

"Okay!" Theo clapped his hands. "Everyone's probably very

tired." False, he knew. Selene, at least, had slept all day. But considering the situation, platitudes seemed safest. "Why don't we all turn in, and we'll regroup in the morning once Dash and Paul grace us with their presence."

Selene disappeared into the adjoining bedroom without another word and slammed the door behind her.

Flint just shook his head at Philippe, clearly disappointed, then hobbled silently into the hallway.

Philippe sighed, looking genuinely chastened. "I am the original *enfant terrible*, aren't I? I didn't mean to be so rude, but sometimes my nature gets the better of me. She is very easy to piss off, no?" He put a hand on Theo's arm and gestured toward the adjoining room. "You sleeping with her tonight?"

Theo nodded, wondering if Philippe knew Selene could hear everything they said.

"The Goddess of Virgins?" He air-kissed his own fingers appreciatively.

"I'm sleeping with her. I'm not...uh...*sleeping* with her. At least not, you know, completely." He wasn't sure why he'd just revealed the details of his stilted sex life to a teenager he'd just met, but sometimes the gods were a bit hard to resist.

Philippe raised his eyebrows in surprise, but Theo couldn't help feeling he was just being polite. Of *course* Selene wouldn't lose her virginity to a *mortal* after she'd held on to it for three thousand years.

"Must be...hard," Philippe went on with a sly smile, brushing Theo's wrist lightly with the tip of his finger. Theo was a little taken aback by the crass double entendre. He was even more unsettled by the response in his own body. Philippe's smile only widened, as if he knew exactly what was happening inside Theo's pants. The God of Love took another step toward him so his face hovered an inch away. "I'm not sure how she resists," he whispered in Theo's ear. "A handsome Makarites like you, I'd have you in my bed in a heartbeat." He kissed Theo lightly on the cheek, bid him a cheery, *"Bonne chance!"* and headed into the suite's other bedroom. Slightly dazed, Theo got a much-needed glass of water from the bathroom. He was on his way to join Selene when Philippe stuck his head back into the living room. He was shirtless now, his narrow bare chest as smooth as a child's. "You know where I am if you need anything."

<o>

Selene lay propped up in the oversoft king-size bed, angrily tossing gratuitous satin throw pillows across the room, and listening to everything happening in the sitting room.

Theo opened the door, shut it behind him, and locked it for good measure before turning to her with a look of stunned bewilderment. "You heard?"

"Of course I did. And Philippe knows it. Deliberate provocation."

"It's not *that* bad. If I don't mind when a man hits on me, why should you?" he asked.

"His gender isn't the issue," she snapped. "But it's the *worst* sort of disrespect for him to steal you from me."

Theo laughed lightly and sat beside her on the bed. "He's not stealing me. He's just trying and failing. I don't even think he was serious."

"But you're attracted to him. I can smell it on you," she said, not bothering to hide the accusation in her voice.

"I'm attracted to *you*. I'm *always* attracted to you, remember?" He sounded more exasperated than appreciative. "But you're right that Philippe does have a knack for guiding my mind right into the gutter. Wait a sec..." He narrowed his eyes as Selene felt a rare heat flush her cheeks. "You feel the same way! That's why you're in such a bad mood."

"He's been smoking the whole time, but the whole damn suite smells like sex instead of cigarettes," she muttered angrily. "If only he were fading as much as the rest of us, his effect wouldn't be so potent. But we live in a world where everyone's either dreaming of finding their one true love or dreaming of sleeping with someone they can *pretend* is their one true love. The little shit will live forever. But that doesn't entitle him to take other people's lovers."

"Oh, is that what I am?" Theo asked the question lightly, but one look at the glow in his green eyes and she knew he meant it. She opened her mouth as if to respond, then closed it again. *Of course you are,* she thought. *You sleep at my side more nights than not. You feel my body, kiss my skin, touch me in places no one has dared for millennia.* But she knew that wasn't his question.

Theo smiled at her silence and ran a finger along the edge of her jaw. Tonight she could smell his arousal, could feel the waves of heat pouring off his skin. Her own body tightened in antici-pation as his lips brushed hers. He backed up just far enough to pull off his sweater; it caught on his glasses, but he finally suc-ceeded in freeing himself from both with a yank. She sat up on her knees, suddenly unwilling to let him go far, and placed her palms on the planes of his chest, feeling his heart gallop beneath her touch. Shocked by her own boldness, she kissed the sweat from his collarbone, then ran her tongue down his sternum. Theo's breath came deep and ragged as he buried his hands in her hair. Before long, she'd ripped off his pants and her own, desperate to feel more of his flesh against hers. He clasped her tight as they rolled back onto the bed. If she moved her hips another inch, if she invited him in, she'd be a virgin no longer. Paul had urged her to do just that.

For so long, she'd resisted. If she gave up her most precious attribute, would she lose more of her powers? Possibly. Flint used his crutches to maintain his identity, yet other gods had assured her that she had more freedom than she thought. She'd clung to her virginity for so long because it had allowed her indepen-dence from the demands of men and family. But now, when sex didn't equate to motherhood and men didn't have to mean oppression, could she find a way to lose her virginity without losing her self? With Theo's mouth hot on her neck, his touch blazing a trail of agonizing bliss across her skin, she was ready, finally, to take that risk.

"Go ahead," she breathed in his ear, wrapping her legs around his narrow hips.

He clutched her tighter and whispered back, "You sure?"

She nodded.

He pulled back, brushed a lock of sweaty fair hair from his eyes, and met her gaze. "You have to say it again."

"You're going to make me think twice."

"If you're going to think twice, do it now. Not sure my ego could take it if you want to stop in the middle."

"I want you. I want all of you. Now." She spoke with the authority of a goddess, but this was one command she knew he followed of his own free will.

He grinned and rolled off her.

"Where are you going!"

He dashed over to his bag in the corner and started riffling through it. "You don't want to have any godlings running around in nine months, do you?" He grabbed a foil-wrapped condom out of a pocket. "Sorry, I would've done this all much more romantically if I'd known, but—"

A sudden trill of laughter from the living room interrupted him. Philippe. Selene put her hands over her ears, but she could still hear it. Then she remembered the way he'd brushed her cheek, her neck. *Damn that little conniving asshole. He doesn't need arrows anymore.* Now his mere touch could inspire lust.

The realization brought rage, her old companion, burning through her body. Her desire collapsed like a mound of ash.

Selene leaped out of the bed and started pounding on the wall. "Stop it!" she screamed. "You're *manipulating* me, you pimp!"

"Selene!" Theo hissed, grabbing her arm. "He's probably just getting a drink of water from the kitchen!" She shook him off.

"No, you don't understand." She was still shouting. "I almost let you have me not because I *wanted* you, but because he made me *think* I did. And Paul too, with his little digs about *love*. All these damn *men*. They're corrupting me, confusing me, can't you see? This isn't *me*. It isn't *real!*"

Theo looked as if he'd been slapped in the face, but she refused to take back the words. "It was real to me," he said slowly. "I know how I feel about you. Or at least I did—right now I'm not so sure. You're playing with me. It's unkind. It's childish."

"*Childish!* I'm three thousand years—"

"Which makes it all the sadder."

"Don't give me that look, like I've offended you. You're the one who's offended *me*. All you want is sex! You're no better than the *zookeeper*."

He stood there, breathing deep, his face a frozen mask far more terrifying than any expression of anger. He grabbed his glasses, sweater, and pants off the floor and dressed without another word.

"Wait—" she began, instantly regretting her words. He picked up his satchel and slung it over his shoulder. "I didn't mean that last part. Where are you going? We're supposed to be attacking Martin tomorrow."

He paused. "Call if you need me." Then, when he was already out the door, she heard the rest. "But you won't."

Chapter 16

THE WINGED GOD

Theo was alternately tying his shoes and jabbing the elevator button when Philippe appeared in the hallway.

"Where're you going, Makarites?" he asked, sounding mildly alarmed. He wore only his silk lounge pants.

"Somewhere not here." Theo hadn't gotten any further than that. His own apartment wasn't safe—not if the flying man had identified him. He had no money for a different hotel—his wallet was lying somewhere on the floor of Selene's house, victim of his rushed packing job.

"You're welcome to spend the night in my room." Surprisingly, Philippe's offer sounded more earnest than flirtatious.

"No thanks. You've done enough already."

He looked stricken. "What did I do?"

Theo sighed. "Nothing. Sorry. She heard you laughing and decided you'd worked some love potion…" It all sounded too ridiculous to even repeat. "I just need some time away." The elevator still wasn't coming. *They charge four thousand dollars a night—you'd think I'd at least get a goddamn private elevator.*

He heard Philippe sigh a little wistfully.

"What?"

"You really love her." It was a statement, not a question. "I was the God of Love, I know it when I see it."

"Really? Is that why I'm running away from her?" Theo said, more sharply than he'd intended. The elevator finally arrived. To his dismay, Philippe accompanied him inside.

"I was in love with a mortal once," he said with a pained smile.

"Only once?" Theo couldn't help noting. "You've been around a long time."

"Oh, I've *been* with all sorts of people." Philippe leaned against the side of the elevator, staring intently at Theo, who kept his own eyes on the digital display, willing the floors to count down more quickly. "Men, women, immortal and mortal," Philippe went on. "Mama deals exclusively with the heterosexual stuff—but I've been coaxing all sorts of people to love each other, in every possible permutation, for thousands of years. My website's got a higher rate of weddings—straight, gay, and otherwise—than any of my competitors. But as for myself… I've only considered myself married once."

"Selene and I aren't talking about getting married." *Right now, I pretty much never want to speak to her again. But even before, we never discussed it. Is that weird?* he wondered for the first time. Most people his age, when they finally met the right person, wanted to settle down. Yet another sign that maybe their relationship had been doomed from the start. *We've never even said "I love you" to each other.* He looked up at the elevator display again, hoping it might stop so another guest would get on and put a halt to their conversation. Clearly in no hurry, Philippe propped one bare foot against the wall and cocked his head at Theo.

"You know my story, I assume," he said. "Cupid and Psyche."

"Sure." An old myth made famous by the Romans and memorialized in paintings, sculpture, and poetry for nearly two thousand years.

Philippe raised a narrow brow skeptically. "But do you know the *true* story?"

Normally, Theo would've jumped at the chance to hear a myth retold from the perspective of the god who'd lived it, but tonight he found it hard to muster much enthusiasm for a love story. He'd barely slept after they got back from Flint's lair, and he'd spent the day trying to care about his students and their final exams while he yearned to be with Selene instead. He spent *every* day yearning to be with Selene. And yet she'd pushed him away as if he were no different from all the abusive men she'd punished over the millennia. He was tired, angry, and more than a little heartbroken.

Philippe followed him blithely out of the elevator and into the lobby, ignored the receptionist's pointed stare at his bare chest, and plopped himself down in an armchair, clearly expecting to be listened to. Theo let himself sink into an adjacent divan. He didn't, after all, have anywhere else to go.

"You know that Psyche was a mortal princess of unparalleled beauty," Philippe began, "worshiped by some misguided fools as the new incarnation of Venus herself."

"Yeah." Theo stifled a yawn, wondering just how much trouble he'd get in for lying down on the lobby floor and going to sleep.

Philippe went on, oblivious to his audience's exhaustion. "Mama didn't take too kindly to Psyche's hubris—as you can imagine—so she sent me to punish the girl. I'd been around a long time, of course, but I spent most of that time as an infant, with an infant's impulse control. By now, I was a youth. I probably looked about thirteen, just starting to realize I could make love, not just make *others* love, and Psyche wasn't much older than that. And once I saw her, my heart just *seized*, I don't know how else to describe it. I couldn't look away."

Theo remembered the first time he'd met Selene. Her silver eyes, her perfect pale features, the way she strode across a small stretch of parkland as if she ruled the whole city. She'd tormented his dreams from that moment on.

"Psyche's father went to an oracle, who told him she was destined to love a hideous monster. They led her to a rocky crag and abandoned her to her fate. I saw her there, so scared, so beautiful, and I sent Zephyrus to lift her into the air and bear her to a splendid palace deep in a secret grove. That night, with the curtains drawn against the Moon's eye, I went to her bed, the gentlest of lovers. I told her we would be happy together—as long as she never looked upon my face."

Theo couldn't help a disgruntled snort. "That's the part that never made sense. Why not just tell her who you were? It all sounds a little perverted and manipulative to me." *Maybe Selene's right and manipulation does run in the family,* he mused. *And she's the worst culprit of all.*

At that, the receptionist finally appeared at Philippe's side. "I'm sorry, sir," she said with a polite, frozen smile. "Shirts and shoes are required in the lobby."

Philippe looked up, surprised. "Of course, *ma chérie*, let me just see if I have something..." he exclaimed, his French accent growing markedly more pronounced. He reached into the pocket of his pants as if to retrieve the world's smallest pair of footwear, then withdrew a tiny dart about the size of a man's thumb instead.

"Ouch!" The woman leapt backward as he stabbed her swiftly in the thigh. "Sir, I must ask you to..." Her gaze suddenly went soft, the outrage melting from her face. Her eyes drifted over his spiky hair, his smooth chest, his bare feet. Not with lust, but with adoration. A small smile pulled at her lips, then she simply returned to her desk. Every few seconds, she snuck a dreamy gaze in Philippe's direction.

"See. Perverted and manipulative," Theo said with a raised eyebrow.

"Oh, I know. I'm very bad. Do you think I should get her to bring me a smoke, as well? Too much? *Oui, bien sûr.*"

"So Selene was right... you still have your powers."

"Not much supernatural about this." He brandished the dart before slipping it back in his pocket. "It's mostly a chemical aphrodisiac."

"Mostly?"

Philippe just winked and then continued with his story. "Every night, I returned to Psyche's bed. They were the happiest days of my life, living in anticipation of her touch. Her laughter was like the flutter of butterfly wings—unexpected and rare and utterly beautiful. But I guess I wasn't enough." He gave a casual shrug, although his eyes were suddenly somber. "Psyche was lonely. She begged me to allow her sisters to visit, and I gave in. The other women were jealous, of course, and they told her she must have a monster for her lover. Why else would I have kept my identity hidden? So one night, while I slept in post-lovemaking bliss, she carried over a lantern, saw my face, and *voilà!* She was *very* impressed." Philippe didn't smile despite the lightness of his words. "She stood there so dumbfounded that her lamp slid from her hand and spilled hot oil all over my naked body. I was... shocked. I'd never been hurt like that before." Theo couldn't tell if Philippe meant physically or emotionally. Likely both. "Idiot that I was," he went on, "I ran to my mother for help." He shook his head. "Stupid. Stupid. I'd never seen Mama so livid. I'd refused to punish Psyche, fallen in love with her instead, and kept our affair hidden. You know the next part... Psyche wandered through the wilderness, where my mother set her a series of impossible tasks—all of which she accomplished anyway—and then when my lover finally reached the end of her strength, I took her to Olympus to become my true bride."

"And you both lived happily ever after." Theo took up the familiar tale. "Jupiter grants Psyche immortality and makes her the Goddess of the Soul. It's all very allegorical. Our hearts and our psyches—united at last by true love and commitment."

"You've been with Selene for *how* long, and you still think our lives are just allegories?" Philippe didn't seem offended, just surprised.

"Sorry, I just—"

"The poets got the ending wrong, *mon ami*. I took Psyche to Olympus, I told the King of the Gods that I already considered her my wife. I asked him to make her immortal...and he said no."

"Why?"

"I'd never shown Psyche my face because I didn't want her to love me for my appearance. I *didn't* strike her with a dart. I didn't tell her any of my names. *Cupidos* means 'desire.' *Eros* means 'love.' How could a mortal resist that? So instead, I let her believe I was hideous. And I knew that if she still fell in love with me, that love would be real."

"And she did. So what was the problem?"

"The King of the Gods didn't believe it. He said Psyche didn't trust me—that's why she brought in the lamp despite my explicit instructions. Only once she saw my face was she able to overcome all the obstacles Mama put in her way to win me back. If she still thought me a monster, would she have bothered? I didn't want to listen, but I finally decided that he was right."

"How about just giving her the benefit of the doubt? Seems a bit ungenerous."

"*Cupidity.* They made that word from my name. Not 'desire,' but 'greed.' And I've always been avaricious when it comes to love. People think I'm just a hedonist because I want it everywhere and always, no matter its shape or size. But real love, *true* love—I want it to be perfect. I want it to be *idéal*. And if Psyche couldn't give that to me...then maybe she didn't deserve to live an eternity at my side."

"I haven't asked for immortality," Theo said stiffly, fairly sure that such a thing was impossible anyway. "So are you saying I don't deserve Selene?"

Philippe stared at him intently. "I'm saying you don't deserve *each other*. See, the poets say Psyche and I were married on Olympus at a feast with all the gods in attendance. The story's so often repeated that if you ask Selene, she might even remember it that way. But the true memory is one I've clung to—the only one I know is my own." The muscles of his chest clenched as he fisted his hands. "Psyche left Mount Olympus. She aged—she grew sick and feeble. I flew above her on my rainbow wings and watched, trying to harden my heart to her suffering. Finally, when she'd withered into an old woman, I decided I had to know the truth. I came to earth as an elderly version of myself, my body sagging and my face lined. She cried when she saw me. I lied and said I'd given up my immortality for her, but that I knew she could no longer love me, as old and gray as I was. And she laughed, and it was no longer like the flutter of butterfly wings. It was a harsh caw, full of bitterness and sorrow. 'Do you think I care about your appearance?' she asked. 'I love you more today than ever I have before.' And then I knew I'd been wrong. The King of the Gods had been wrong. I let her leave Olympus, and she never even looked back, because she thought I wouldn't listen to the truth." Philippe leaned forward. "So that's what I'm trying to tell you. The mortals don't understand the gods. And the gods don't understand mortals. Their love cannot last."

"Thanks for the vote of confidence, Philippe." Theo stood and hefted his satchel. "But how about you all mind your own business for once in a millennium?"

"She died there in my arms." Philippe slumped back in his chair. He turned his face away. "I cut off my wings in mourning. They never grew back."

Theo felt his stomach constrict in horror. Those rainbow wings reduced to bloody stumps. *Is that what love between a mortal and a god looks like?*

Philippe slapped the arms of his chair, suddenly all business, and stood up. "Nice chat, Theo. Sorry if it was a bit of a downer. Just thought you should know what you're getting into."

When he walked away, Theo saw his naked back for the first time. Two thick, ropy scars ran down his shoulder blades.

As Theo buzzed Apartment 4E one more time, his head drooped forward with exhaustion. He nearly knocked himself out as his forehead smacked against the directory listing. Finally, a weary voice answered with a cautious, "Hello?"

"Remember how you said if I needed anything..."

"Theo!" The buzzer sounded in his ear, jerking him upright.

Moments later he stood in Ruth's small living room. She'd moved in recently. A small stack of boxes stood in a corner, and the walls remained bare, but a comfortable couch with a warm fluffy afghan was all he needed. He sprawled across it, eyes closed, only to be immediately licked into near drowning by Hippo.

"I know, girl," he said through closed lips, unwilling to allow the dog's saliva into any more orifices than he already had. "I missed you, too." The dog took to snuffling loudly at his clothes, his bag, his coat, no doubt searching for Selene's scent.

He wiped the drool from his face and cracked open his eyes to peer at Ruth. She wore a pair of flannel pajama pants and a thin T-shirt. *No bra,* he noticed, before quickly removing his gaze from her chest. Her face was swollen with sleep, her hair even more of a tousled wreck than usual.

She perched on the wicker footstool beside the couch, squinting at him through glasses so thick they made her eyes look even bigger than usual. *Did I even realize she's been wearing contacts all this time?* he wondered, ashamed. Had he even known what color her eyes were? If pressed, he would have said...not brown. They were a patchwork of gray and blue, he saw now. Gold ringed the pupil, like a secret treasure for those who bothered to look closely.

"Um..." she started.

"Yes," he agreed.

She looked startled. "Yes to what?"

"This *is* the second night this week that I've gotten you out of bed at an inhuman hour of the morning." *In-human. Hah. More like im-mortal.* He wanted to laugh, but he was too tired.

"It's not a problem. I'm just—"

"Tired? Annoyed? Worried about me?" He managed a smile. "Sorry about the former. As to the latter, I'm perfectly safe, I promise. I just need a place to crash for a night or two, if that's okay. Another homeless puppy in your life."

"Of course! Where's…"

"The Relentless One is at the Four Seasons, relentlessly pursuing her own agenda at the moment." *How convenient to have a girlfriend with ready-made epithets. It makes snarky comments so much easier.*

"Wow. You said a hotel. But the Four Seasons…"

"Is very nice, turns out. In case you were wondering how the other half lives, the answer is: with super soft beds and excellent room service. Really. Any thought I had of finding it offensively decadent pretty much disappeared the minute I ate that chocolate mint off my pillow. I'm considering hiring someone just to leave goodies lying on my bed at home. Imagine—I come back from a long day of lecturing, stagger toward my bed, and *boom!* There's a chocolate chip cookie, still warm, wrapped in a cute little paper bag. What do you think?"

He knew he was rambling, but he didn't care. Ruth was chuckling at him, Hippo was staring up at him adoringly, and all, for once, seemed right with the world.

Ruth went to get him a pillow and linens. He rolled off the couch to paw through the meager possessions in his satchel. He wasn't sure when it'd feel safe enough to go back to his own apartment. Probably only after this new cult had been eliminated. Until then, his association with Selene made him a tempting target. He searched fruitlessly for a clean pair of boxer shorts to sleep in, realizing belatedly that he'd thrown Selene's dirty shirt in his satchel instead. The bracing, piney scent of her had filled his bag with memories. He held it to his nose, unable to stop his body's Pavlovian response. *You're supposed to be angry at her,* he reminded himself. *Hence the whole sleeping on Ruth's couch thing.* He allowed himself a moment more to imagine her as she'd been only an hour before, naked and willing in his arms.

He held the shirt away, wondering what to do with it. That's when he noticed the bloodstains from when the bullet grazed her temple. For all her strength, she was still vulnerable. Could he really stand by and do nothing tomorrow while she strode into danger? *Will she let me do anything else?*

He shoved the shirt back in the bag, kicked off his shoes, removed his pants and cashmere sweater, and lay back on the couch in his old underwear. Then, unable to resist, he reached for his phone. No messages from Selene. He found himself staring at a still image from the video of Selene by the creek in the Catskills. Wild and beautiful and mysterious. He swiped past, unwilling to linger on her face, and clicked on the photos Freeman had sent them of the *Charging Bull* crime scene instead. The crow, the snake, the statue itself…he felt like there was a pattern there he'd never identified. With a start, he realized he'd never even bothered to do his own research into the symbolism. Between working on his classes and the unexpected visitation from the flying man, he'd never found the time. He swiped to the next photo: a close-up of the eviscerated dog's liver. Another question he'd never answered.

He tossed the phone back into his satchel and forced himself to wipe the gruesome images from his mind. *If Selene's right about Mars,* he decided, *then she'll get all the answers soon enough.*

He was almost asleep by the time Ruth returned from rustling up a pillow. She reached to tuck the fuzzy blanket more firmly around him, a surprisingly motherly gesture. Her chest hung over his face, and he caught a whiff of her scent. Sweet and warm. He'd forgotten that's how normal women smelled in the middle of the night.

Impulsively, he reached for her hand as she pulled away.

"Thank you," he mumbled sleepily. "Really. I didn't know where else to go."

She nodded and didn't pull away. Finally, he released her hand and closed his eyes. Dimly, he realized Ruth still stood there, staring at him. But that didn't stop him from drifting toward much-needed oblivion.

Chapter 17

THE HARUSPEX

The next morning, Theo rapped lightly on the open door to Ruth's molecular biology lab in Columbia's Fairchild Center. "Excuse me, is this where they keep the vials of apocalyptic zombie plague?"

Ruth swiveled toward him on her stool. "Theo!" Even her exclamations of surprise were soft and a little breathless. "You're up! Did you find the cereal I left for you on the counter?"

"Yes, and the strawberries and banana, too. You shouldn't have."

She shrugged and hitched her red cardigan sweater a little higher on her shoulders. "I was up early to walk Hippo and just swung by the grocery store. No big deal." But it was a big deal, at least to Theo. He wasn't used to anyone taking care of him that way. "Come in! This is such a pleasure. You never visit me here."

"'Never' is a strong word."

"Well, not since ... you know. You started seeing Selene." A flush crept up Ruth's neck. She wasn't the sort to complain.

"I'm here now, and I come bearing gifts to thank you for putting up with my unwanted incursion last night." The scent of melting chocolate filled the room as he pulled out the bag of still-warm cookies from Levain Bakery; he thought Ruth might pass out from shock at the gesture. He knew then and there that he'd been a terrible friend.

She reached for the bag, weighing it in her hand with a scientist's puzzled frown. "This feels like a pound of cookies. All for me?"

"It's just two. Two enormous cookies. When I hire the goodie depositor for my nighttime ritual, these are going to be the kind I request. I wanted you to partake in the dream."

A single chocolate chip cookie filled her entire hand. She took a tentative bite, the chocolate smearing across her chin, and her eyes widened. Today, Theo noticed, her red cardigan turned her pupils a warm shade of olive green. "Oh my God," she gasped. "This is...like...I don't..."

"Like you've arrived in the Elysian Fields?" Theo asked. "Like Saturn himself is there to welcome you to a world without pain or work or suffering? That's what I felt the first time I tried one."

She could only nod. "Not sure what you mean. But it sounds about right."

"Here." He pulled a circle of filter paper from the box on her worktable and dabbed the chocolate from her chin. Ruth turned a brighter shade of pink, and she wiped furiously at her face.

"You're fine!" he assured her, laughing. "It's physically impossible to eat a Levain cookie and not be drenched in chocolate. It's a scientific law—so really you should already know it."

Ruth giggled, and her face returned to its normal color. Theo forgot how much he liked spending time with someone who always laughed at his jokes—someone whose emotions he could not only predict but, to some extent, influence. When Ruth was sad, he could cheer her up. When she was happy, he knew why.

"Speaking of scientific laws," he went on, pulling his cell phone from his pocket. He'd spent the morning trying to remember his pledge to let Selene solve her own problems. But his first good sleep in days had assuaged some of his anger and resentment, and he'd found himself staring at the crime scene photos again. Whatever issues they were having with their own relationship, the lives of all the gods hung in the balance. If Theo could help discover the truth behind Hades' killing, he had to try.

"I have yet *another* favor to ask you." He flashed Ruth his most charming smile. "I know I've already worn out my welcome in about a million ways—"

Ruth paused with the cookie halfway to her mouth. "Anything."

Theo was a little taken aback by her alacrity. He was used to bargaining, cajoling, convincing. It felt odd to have someone so willing to help. He opened a photo on his phone and handed it to Ruth. "I need you to do a little anatomical analysis for me."

Ruth put down the cookie. "Is that a *liver*?"

"See? Brilliant already. It's from the dead dog found beside the *Charging Bull* statue. There was also a crow, a snake, and a scorpion."

He swiped the picture of the animal's innards aside and called up a website featuring the image of a bronze, liver-shaped artifact covered in inscriptions. "*This* is the Piacenza liver, a tool from the second century BC. Think of it as an instructional diagram for ancient Roman haruspices."

"Haruspices?"

"Literally 'gut-starers.' Priests who used animal livers for divination."

Ruth's eyebrows rose. "You think a dog's liver is going to tell you the future?"

"Nope. I haven't turned into a pagan believer quite yet," he lied. If Mars was indeed the Pater of the cult, then perhaps he could still send omens to his followers. Such a supernatural ability was unlikely—considering how far most Olympians had fallen—but not impossible. He'd given up on impossible somewhere around the time he'd found out Selene remembered hanging out with Amazons. "But I do think the *cult members* might think a dog's liver will tell them the future. Why pull it out and examine it otherwise?"

"How can *I* help? You're the one who can read... whatever that is." She peered skeptically at the writing on the bronze liver.

"Etruscan. The language of the indigenous people of Italy before the Latins took over. For centuries, the Roman emperors hired Etruscans to act as their haruspices, divining the will of the gods from animal entrails, lightning patterns, bird flight— you name it. I can't actually read Etruscan, but I don't have to. Scholars translated the Piacenza liver a long time ago. See how it's divided into different regions?" He traced the grid lines along the artifact's bronze surface. "Each is labeled with the name of a different Etruscan god, most of whom are variations on the Greco-Roman pantheon. The haruspex would look for anomalies in the liver—swellings, striations, that sort of thing—and then associate their location with the labeled deity." He looked hopefully at Ruth.

She raised her hands helplessly. "Theo, I dissect fish to extract enzymes from kidneys that regulate blood pH. I want to help, but..."

"You can! You understand livers."

"As much as any biologist, I guess."

"That's a hell of a lot more than me. I don't even know what a *normal* animal liver looks like, so I've got no idea where the abnormalities lie. And the Piacenza diagram is of a *sheep's* liver, because that's what the Etruscans usually used for divination. I've got to translate the diagram onto a dog's liver, and since you might recall that I've recently taken over the entire Classics department and am teaching twice as much as usual, I don't have time to take a veterinary class."

From the pursing of her lips, Theo could tell Ruth thought he might be mildly insane. But it didn't take long before she moved the vials on her counter aside and pulled an animal anatomy book down from the shelf above her head.

"All right. But promise not to tell any of my colleagues about my dabbling in the occult. I'd get laughed out of the university."

"Don't worry, I've had plenty of experience with people who think I'm a lunatic. I'll show you the ropes."

The more Theo stared at the various highly detailed photos of dissected dog and sheep livers, the more he regretted eating an entire Levain cookie two hours before. He much preferred the stylized anatomical drawings, but Ruth claimed nothing compared to the real thing. She pointed to a series of small striations along a lobe of the sheep's liver. "See all these markings? They're subsidiary ducts that carry gall to the hepatic portal. No two livers have the same pattern."

"So different omens every time. Makes sense. Otherwise, the haruspex would just say, 'Another brown, icky liver. Guess the omens are . . . status quo.'"

"Exactly," Ruth said with a grin, turning back to the photos. She consulted the Piacenza diagram. "So this big bronze pyramid sticking out is supposed to represent the *processus pyramidalis*, which is part of the caudate lobe, right? And the hemisphere beside it is the papillary process."

"Um-hm," Theo agreed, as if he had any idea what she was talking about.

"Here're the same two organs on the dog's liver." She traced two wet lobes on the photo. "Normally, like in the sheep, the pyramidalis should be significantly bigger, but on the dog at the crime scene, the papillary is abnormally large."

"So a reversal . . ." Theo consulted the online text of *Studies in the History of Religion*. "It indicates an overturning of the natural order. Could mean a son is going to overthrow his father, or a servant becomes the master. Interesting. Anything else?"

"Well, if you're looking for asymmetries, the hepatic portal is longer on one side than the other."

Theo nodded, getting excited. "Which side?"

"The right."

"Ha! The Romans saw the right side as a favorable sign, the left as bad. So a deformation like that is a good omen." He consulted the text again. "Usually it would predict victory in battle. What about all those striations?"

She rattled off a few locations, pointing out their corresponding placement on the bronze diagram.

"Markings in those sections indicate a reference to Maris, Satre, and Tin." Theo cross-referenced the Etruscan names with the Roman pantheon. "Mars, Saturn, Jupiter."

"So this is an astronomy thing?"

Theo laughed. "You're a scientist through and through, aren't you? They meant the gods, not the planets."

"How do you know?" Ruth asked, looking more hurt than defensive.

Theo felt bad for laughing at her. "I just assume, since the purpose of the divination was to know which gods to sacrifice to." He wasn't surprised by the Mars reference—it fit perfectly with Selene and Flint's current theory. But he was unsure what to make of the indications that the cult might also worship Jupiter and Saturn. Then again, the ancient art of divination was inexact to say the least. Ruth might have a point: Modern scholars weren't completely sure what exactly the inscriptions referred to.

After a moment, Ruth swiveled her monitor toward Theo and read aloud. "'Some scholars think the Piacenza liver was a planisphere—an ancient starfinder and calendar—rather than purely a tool for divination.'"

"Shit. Why don't I ever listen to you?" He scooted a little closer to the screen, his arm brushing Ruth's.

She moved self-consciously aside and turned back to the crime scene photos on Theo's phone. "I hate to rub it in," she said after a moment, "but I think I'm right." She showed him one of the photos—an overview of the entire scene with the dog, snake, and crow surrounding the bull statue.

"I bow to your brilliance, of course, but you want to explain how?"

"Didn't you say there was a scorpion too?"

"Yeah, on the other side of the bull."

She shrugged. "I wouldn't have thought of it if we hadn't just seen how animals, or animal organs, could represent both gods and celestial bodies at the same time, but the way all the sacrifices are arranged in a circle reminds me of an orbit. And they're all constellations. Taurus the Bull, Canis the Dog, Hydra the Snake, Corvus the Crow, and Scorpius the Scorpion."

Theo just stared at her.

"What?"

"I never thought of that."

"What did *you* think they were?"

"Attributes of a god. Selene thinks it's a Mars cult, and once she brought it up, it made sense: Poisonous animals like asps and scorpions are common Mars references, and the Roman legions used big dogs like that one to attack their enemies."

"And the crow?"

"Well... that's more of an Apollo symbol. I figured it meant— Uh, to tell the truth, I never bothered to come up with a theory. Selene was so convinced about Mars that I just let the inconsistencies slide. But if you're right..." His voice trailed off as his mind spun through the possibilities. *If this is about astronomy, then Mars the god may not be involved at all—only Mars the planet. Which means Selene is chasing down the wrong god, and the* real *Pater is still on the loose.* Still, he had no real evidence yet, only a sinking suspicion that he'd accepted Selene and Flint's ideas far too easily. Ruth was a scientist—she examined evidence for a living. As a scholar, he needed to do the same. Until all the pieces fit, he knew the mystery wasn't solved.

"What do those constellations even have in common?" Ruth mused. "And do they connect to Mars or Saturn or Jupiter?"

"Despite my love of *Star Trek*, I can only answer that question mythologically. All the constellations are examples of catasterism—the 'placings of the stars' by the gods. So, for example, the crow is put in the heavens by Artemis as punishment for upsetting her brother Apollo. She puts the scorpion there after it hunts down her disloyal companion, Orion. And she turns Canis the Dog into a constellation because he's Orion's pet."

Ruth whistled. "Artemis sounds like a very hard woman."

Theo winced. "They called her the Long-Cloaked Marshal of the Stars because she sent so many people and animals to the heavens. I like to think it's a reminder of her mercy—she punishes wrongdoers, but she gives them a semblance of immortality as well. She wants them to be remembered."

"Yeah, to teach us all a lesson, you mean."

"Maybe."

"And what about Hydra?"

"Nine-headed water serpent killed by Heracles as one of his great labors. Later put in the sky by the goddess Hera, Queen of the Heavens. Taurus was another of Heracles' conquests. He's the bull sent by Poseidon so the queen of Crete would have sex with it and give birth to the Minotaur."

Ruth wrinkled her nose. "Your area of study is surprisingly icky, you know."

"You're the one dissecting fish all day."

She laughed. "Then let me dissect this whole astronomy thing for you. Maybe the myths behind the constellations don't matter. Maybe we should check out the *science* behind the stars instead. The ancients Romans were pretty good astronomers, right?"

"Sure. They learned from the Greeks and Babylonians. They measured the size of the sun correctly, identified the stars of the zodiac, knew how to predict eclipses. Granted, they thought the sun revolved around the earth, not the other way around, but hey, nobody's perfect."

"Then a cult based on ancient Roman practice could be incorporating some pretty sophisticated calculations."

Theo sighed. "Yeah. We're going to need an astronomer. And I know just the woman."

"Then why do you look so worried?"

He remembered Lars's screams from the zoo as the bear bit off his hand. With all the distraction of Hades' murder, they'd never found out how Minh had taken the news of her ex-boyfriend's amputation. "Let's just say Ursa Major isn't the only bear we'll have to discuss."

Chapter 18

SHE WHO BRINGS UP THE REAR

Selene was convinced that Dash was making up for his lack of a winged cap by driving his newly purchased speedboat across New York Harbor at a brain-jiggling sixty knots. After a morning and much of the afternoon spent arguing over the best way to confront Mars, they'd decided to approach after sunset, when they were less likely to be spotted by the God of Bloodlust or any of his acolytes. Now, they were racing through the darkness toward Mars's hideout, the boat's hull pounding against the chop like a slow but unstoppable jackhammer. She'd nearly vomited three times already—the only thing holding her back was the sight of Philippe, perched on the bow like an elegant figurehead, looking perfectly at ease with a cigarette clenched between his teeth and his long cashmere scarf streaming behind him. *I guess that's what happens when your mother was birthed from sea foam.*

No one had commented on Theo's absence. Paul had given her a brief, knowing look, filled with sadness. Dash seemed mildly disappointed that he'd lost a plaything. The others barely seemed to notice he was missing. It only made her realize how little mortals—even useful ones—mattered to the gods. She doubted Theo would forget the Athanatoi so easily. She'd picked up her phone a dozen times to call him then put it down again. Despite his anger, she knew he'd join them if she asked him to. But why drag him into such danger? Just so she could have the pleasure of his company? *That would just be using him again,* she decided, leaving the phone in her pocket. Another jolt of the hull drew her attention back to the challenge ahead.

Even in the depths of winter, ships still plied the harbor. Despite the darkness, it was only five thirty in the evening: rush hour for the boxy orange Staten Island Ferry lumbering its way to and from Manhattan. Cargo ships heaved toward the Hudson. Tugboats plowed the waves. *But only reckless Athanatoi would chose to cross the harbor in an open top speedboat with no running lights in the middle of December.* She didn't protest when Paul scooted closer to her, his natural warmth a blessing amid the icy salt spray.

Flint sat across from them, immersed in pawing through his large duffel bag to check his hoard of mechanical and electronic instruments. When Paul and Dash had joined them at the hotel, the Smith had retreated inside his shell of surliness, and all sign of the affectionate stepfather disappeared. He'd barely spoken a word in the last few hours. Occasionally, one of his screens flashed a red warning signal, illuminating his face with an eerily volcanic glow. His crutches rested on the floor of the boat. Selene had been surprised he'd chosen them over his titanium leg braces for today's foray, but he'd grunted something about knowing what he was doing, and she'd left him alone.

On the bow, Philippe listened attentively as Dash nattered away from the cockpit. The young Athanatos had made no mention of her outburst last night, nor had Selene bothered repeating her accusations to him this morning. They sounded absurd now—of course he no longer possessed the ability to inspire lust with the touch of his hand. She tried not to dwell on the injustice of her comments to Theo. They'd already kept her up all night, and she couldn't risk losing focus now. She'd need all her wits about her if she came face to face with Mars.

She'd fought alongside the Man-Slayer in the Trojan War, yet she'd kept her distance. *Battle-Insatiate* they'd called him, leading his troops with a bellow as great as that of ten thousand war-mad men. At his cry, warriors on both sides leapt into the fray, their armor clashing with swords, with lances, with darts. Spears plunged into flesh, and Mars drank his fill of blood. Beside him ran his sister Discordia, Goddess of Strife, her head and shoulders blood-splattered, her laughter peeling forth in maddened glee. Mars shouted in response, stirring courage in the Trojans and panic in the Greeks, whose reeling squadrons shook at the sound.

Despite Mars's fearsome reputation, Dash and Philippe chatted on, apparently unconcerned about the confrontation to come. Over the roar of the engine and the rush of the wind, even Selene's keen hearing couldn't pick up their conversation.

"They look pretty confident," she shouted in her twin's ear. She herself had a knot in her stomach born of equal parts fear and seasickness.

"They've got a decent plan." But Paul didn't look any more at ease than she. In fact, his perennial tan couldn't disguise the gray cast to his skin.

"You don't have to be the one to confront Martin, you know. I could go instead."

Paul laughed. "No offense, Moonshine, but you'd piss off Martin so fast he'd have you impaled on that spear of his before you even mentioned Hades' name."

"I don't like sitting back and watching you take the risk."

"You don't have to lead every fight. Remember they called you She Who Brings Up the Rear."

"Huh. One of my stupider epithets."

"No, I like it. It reminds me you've got my back."

"Philippe should go in. Martin's *his* father. Or Dash—he can run away faster."

"Except that Martin hates his son, remember? And you know how distractible Dash is—he's liable to completely lose track of what he's supposed to be grilling Martin about. I'm the God of Poetry—I'll know how to get him to admit to his role in Hades' murder, and then I'll demand that he stop targeting other gods. And if he refuses—well, then I'm glad I've got you in my corner."

His words were confident, but Selene noticed the sheen on his brow.

"I don't like it." She rested her hand on her twin's. His obvious shock at her affection made her ashamed. "You don't seem yourself. You're still having those visions?"

For once, he was the one who pulled away. "I'm fine," he assured her. But he wouldn't meet her eyes.

With all the bouncing around, Selene felt like she'd been tortured for days, but they'd only been at sea for five minutes when the Governors Island dock came into view.

A former Coast Guard installation abandoned in the 1990s, the island now served as a park and historic monument. In the summer, ferries dropped off passengers from Brooklyn and Manhattan. The desperate city dwellers could escape the heat and overcrowding on one of the small island's famous hammocks or wander through its diversity of avant-garde (and often inscrutable) art installations. But this close to Christmas, Selene and her companions would have the island to themselves—except, of course, for the bloodthirsty god hidden somewhere on its shores.

They bypassed the main dock and headed for the less populated eastern side of the island. Dash throttled down the engine, and Philippe threw the anchor overboard. Quietly, so as not to alert any sentries, they clambered out of the boat and waded onto the shore. Selene heaved a few breaths of the cold, salty air to settle her roiling stomach.

Dash, as the God of Travelers, took point. He led them up a

small rise and into an open quadrangle surrounded by stately brick buildings in the federal style, part of the old Coast Guard facilities.

"Now we're going to need to stay together, and out of the castle's line of sight, all right, everyone?" he said. "Like little ducks in a row. Otherwise, our dear Man-Slayer might wonder why half the pantheon's coming to visit. Not known for his hospitality, after all. We need a secret approach that will hide someone as impressively broad as our sweet Smith here." He turned to Flint. "Map, please?"

Flint's thick brows lowered at Dash's teasing, but he pulled out his enormous tablet smartphone and brought up a bird's-eye view of the island. On its northeastern tip stood Castle Williams, a large, circular brick fort constructed in the early 1800s. Over the years it had served as a barracks, a prison, and eventually, a community center for the Coast Guard. Now it was just a tourist attraction—a curious relic from a time when New York City thought itself vulnerable to attack from the sea. But according to Philippe, it just so happened to have a double life as the God of War's winter pied-à-terre.

"Between us and the castle are a slew of military buildings," Flint rumbled. "Most are laid out along a pretty wide road in the castle's direct line of sight. But there's also this—" He pointed to a moat surrounding a large star-shaped building in the middle of the island. "Fort Jay. That's our way across."

"If my father's sentries are stationed on the walls of the fort, we'll be seen," Philippe observed.

"How many sentries does he usually have?" Selene asked.

Philippe shrugged. "No idea. I don't visit much. And he isn't usually running a cult. So your guess is as good as mine."

His calm only increased Selene's unease. "You're sending my twin into danger because *you're* too chicken to face your own father. You should at least know what he's up against!"

Dash chuckled. "There she goes—turning supernova over nothing."

"*Nothing?* I'm trusting Paul's life to a plan *you* came up with. I'm beginning to think that was a terrible idea."

Paul, his face pale, offered a weak, "It's fine—" but Flint interrupted him.

"The Huntress is right to be cautious." He turned disapproving eyes on Dash. "We've all seen you lie, cheat, steal, and trick your way through the centuries." Dash gave an indignant huff, but the Smith's attention had already turned to Selene. He held her gaze, his dark eyes serious. "Paul's the best choice for this. And the plan *will* work. I'll make sure of it."

Selene wasn't sure why, but she trusted Flint. As an Athanatos with few preternatural powers left, he would avoid unnecessary risks. But it was more than that. He exuded a gravity that tempered Dash's insouciance. A strength that allayed her worries about Paul's emotional vulnerability. He might be weak in the face of his wife's wiles, but since he'd joined their mission, he'd shown a tenacious determination to make things right.

She gave him a solemn nod. "Fine. But from here on out, we go armed."

She withdrew the pieces of her golden bow and screwed the limbs together. Flint watched her appreciatively; he had, after all, made the weapon for her. She braced the bottom limb between her legs and bent the metal easily to attach the string. The bow looked both graceful and deadly, like Selene herself. She'd lost her quiver to the flying man, but she slipped her three new gold arrows and a few wooden ones through her belt.

Flint, his hands occupied with his tablet and crutches, left his hammer slung across his back, its massive cylindrical head resting against his shoulder blades. Paul readied his own silver bow. Dash patted the sides of his coat, clearly checking his pistols. Flint glanced up at his stepson. "Come on, you too. You never know when it could come in handy."

Philippe glared at him. "It's so *gauche*."

Flint raised a single bushy brow. Philippe sighed and reached into his own stylish shoulder bag. Out came the most absurd bow Selene had ever seen. Only a foot and a half long, made of myrtle wood carved with doves. A child's toy. She couldn't help a barely stifled chortle, enjoying the deepening flush on Philippe's cheeks.

"Flint, surely you could've made your stepson something a little less... laughable."

He shot her a warning look. "I don't make new divine weapons, I told you. Only copies. Repairs. That's the bow he had when he was on Olympus, so that's what he's got now. Another bow wouldn't have the same power."

"*Power?* That thing couldn't send an arrow more than ten feet!"

Philippe scowled at her and withdrew his matching quiver of diminutive darts. "It works just fine, thank you."

Dash clapped him on the back. "Don't let big bad Selene scare you, boy. For all her posing as a feminist, to her it's still all a competition about shaft size."

Before Selene could retort, her twin silenced them all with a curt wave of his hand. "Please! I'll feel much better about all of this if you stop bitching at each other."

Chastened, Selene tilted her head at Dash. "Let's do this."

In return, Dash gestured grandly for Flint to take the lead. "Go on, big man. You take us in."

Selene assigned herself the task of sweeping the rear in case of a surprise attack. They headed through the complex of buildings, then tramped up a low rise to the edge of the moat surrounding Fort Jay. Flint limped down a set of snowy stairs on his crutches and the others followed him into the empty moat without a word. Selene jumped off the moat's lip, twisted in midair to land a foot against the opposite wall, and hopped lightly to the ground twelve feet below. Philippe smirked at her acrobatics.

"I'm not showing off," she insisted in an angry whisper. "Just stretching my legs a little after that boat ride."

"Ah."

With Paul's admonition in mind, she tried to sound conciliatory. "So is there *anything* you can tell me about your father?"

He gave a shrug. "Haven't seen him in a very long time." He slowed his pace to fall behind the others and spoke in a conspiratorial whisper. "But last time I did… well, he was perfectly willing to give me a slap or two if I didn't agree with everything he said. He knows Papa wouldn't let him get away with more than that. I mean, fucking my mother—*that* Papa will allow. But hurting me? That's where he draws the line."

"You call Flint 'Papa.'"

"*Oui.*"

"But he's not… I mean… I thought he hated his wife's bastard children."

"He used to. That story about my sister Harmonia and the cursed necklace—I hope it's not true but… well, the memory's a bit fuzzy. But ever since the Diaspora, he's treated me with more love and care than my real father ever did. His own kids are gone—weak hemitheoi long forgotten. And his assistants—remember the Cyclops, the metal Automatones? All dead. He adopted me in their stead."

"You don't seem to have a lot in common," she observed.

He shot her a hurt glance. "You mean because he's brawny and plain and *très* straight and I'm slender and pretty and a bit fey?"

"Well…" She was admittedly surprised that Flint liked anyone at all.

"He likes to think I need his protection."

"But you don't."

"No. He's the one growing old and gray, weaker year by year. I'm feeling magnificent. But I like having Papa watch my back. Besides, he's about the only one of us who doesn't judge people entirely on their outward appearances."

"I don't judge people—"

He gave a short laugh. "True! You've already decided about

people before you see them—no real judging needed. If he's a man, he's an enemy. If she's a woman, she either needs your help or deserves your disdain. Isn't that about right?"

"Now who's judging? You don't know me at all."

"But I know people. *You* know how to hunt them. *I* know how to love them." He looked at her pointedly, his challenge clear. "You think choosing to be alone makes you so strong. But I see a woman shaped by men's perceptions of her, whether she realizes it or not."

"Is this your way of saying I should be nicer to Theo?" she bristled.

"No, I'm saying you should be nicer to Papa. You could learn a lot from him about making choices for yourself."

Selene opened her mouth for an angry protest, but ahead of them, Flint raised a warning hand for silence.

She followed the others out of the moat and down the hill. They crouched in the snow behind a dilapidated wooden library. Just across the road loomed Castle Williams.

Paul's usually expressive face had frozen into a careful mask. "I'm ready," he said with a smile that Selene immediately saw through. Something was bothering her twin—something beyond the obvious danger of walking into the Man-Slayer's den unarmed. She handed him a small metal dog whistle. It would emit a shrill note beyond the edge of human hearing—but not hers. "Use it the second you think you're in danger," she said sternly.

"Martin usually has transmission scanners set up at the entrances of his forts," Flint warned. "So we can't put a camera on Paul. But this will at least let us see something." From his bag, he withdrew a three-inch-long metal sculpture in the shape of a sea serpent. Its tail narrowed to a small antenna. A black glass lens covered its single bulbous eye. Perfect tiny scales lined the cylindrical sides. "If we can get this over the wall of the castle, we'll be able to see the courtyard. Once Paul enters the fort itself, however, he's on his own."

He held out a hand to Selene. "Arrow." She passed him a wooden shaft. Flint pressed a button on the serpent-camera's back and a row of tiny legs emerged to grasp on to the arrow. Then he turned his tablet phone toward Selene to show her a photo of her target: the three-story circular castle of mottled brownstone. Two beefy soldiers in white and gray winter camouflage guarded the massive double door banded with ornate iron hinges.

"Not too bad, see?" Dash observed. "I could take them down with my guns alone."

Selene peered closer, looking for weapons. She couldn't see any, but they probably carried concealed guns. "We still need to be careful. I'm sure the flying man's around somewhere."

Flint pointed to one of the narrow brick towers on either side of the circular building. "This is where the arrow should land. You've got to shoot just far enough to make it over the outer wall and up to the roof. There's a cupola on the tower, so you've only got about two feet to stick the arrow, otherwise it'll smack off the side and fall into the courtyard. That'll blow our whole plan. You think you can do that without looking?"

In response, she took the arrow back and raised her bow, barely hesitating before sending the shaft through the air, a black blur against a sky pewter with light pollution.

After a moment, Flint pulled up a new window on his tablet phone. With a few taps, he brought the video feed into view. He gave her a brief glance of approval then turned it to show everyone. They had a perfect view of the castle's interior: a snowy circular courtyard surrounded by three stories of cement and cloudy glass. Two more guards stood before the inner doors that gave entrance to the building itself.

Flint gave Paul a curt nod. Time for action.

Paul handed his bow and quiver to Selene. "Keep these safe until I get back, okay?"

"This doesn't feel right, Sunbeam." She stared at the gleaming silver in her hands. He hadn't let her hold his weapon since they were children. "You should be armed."

"You fight, I talk. Two halves of the same whole." He kissed her lightly on the cheek. She let him. Then he patted the pocket of his coat to check for the whistle and headed toward the castle.

Flint strung a second camera on a flexible rod around the corner of the building. He split the screen on his phone so they could watch Paul walk toward the front entrance of the fort.

The older guard took a step forward. "Sorry, sir, the island's closed to visitors today. I'm not sure how you got here, but—"

"Tell Martin that Phoebus is here."

The guard gave him a skeptical frown.

"Trust me, he'll let me in," Paul insisted. "Go ahead. Ask him." The older guard looked at his companion, who raised his coat cuff to his mouth and spoke into a concealed microphone. After a moment, they unbolted the doors and waved Paul through into the fort's shadowed entrance corridor.

"So far, so good," Philippe observed.

On the feed from Selene's arrow, they watched Paul enter the courtyard. The second set of guards had already opened the interior door for him.

Flint nodded, satisfied. "Now we wait." He sounded confident. But as Selene watched Paul enter the fort and disappear from view, she couldn't help wondering if he'd ever make it back out.

Chapter 19

LONG-CLOAKED MARSHAL OF THE STARS

The modern Rose Earth and Space Center loomed beside the nineteenth-century American Museum of Natural History like an alien spaceship sent back in time. From his position on West Eighty-first Street, Theo could see straight through the six-story glass cube to the glowing white sphere of the planetarium. The entire building served as an orrery, a representation of the solar system. The planetarium's sphere represented the sun, and models of the other planets hung in orbit around it. As he and Ruth drew closer, he could make out families streaming through the building, lining up for the last planetarium show of the day, and tromping down the Cosmic Pathway that spiraled from the sun to the ground, tracing the evolution of the universe from Big Bang to the present along the way.

Theo and Ruth entered the museum at the Earth and Space Center's lower level. The museum was about to close, and most of the researchers had already gone home for the day, but Minh Loi stood waiting for them with arms crossed. She looked neat and professional, her long gray-streaked hair pulled back in a loose chignon. The welts on her face had faded to a light yellow, and her eyes snapped clear and sharp. Yet she seemed a woman suffering beneath a great weight that no one else could see. *Selene and I were supposed to lift that burden from her,* Theo thought. *Instead, it looks like we made it all the heavier.*

"I don't know whether to thank you or report you," Minh said without a hint of humor.

"How about I say 'you're welcome' and 'I'm sorry' so you don't have to decide?" Theo offered. "If it makes you feel better, the plan was never...amputation. It just sort of turned out that way." He could feel Ruth's eyes on him and prayed she would focus on one mystery at a time. Selene's vigilantism was not something Ruth would understand.

Minh just stared at him a moment longer before saying, "I should never have asked Selene DiSilva for help."

"Her methods can be"—he thought of the constellation myths—"punitive. But I'm not here on behalf of Selene. I'm helping the cops solve the mystery of the *Charging Bull* murder."

She didn't believe him at first, but with a little cajoling and a lot of begging, she finally agreed to answer their questions.

To Theo's disappointment, the walls of Minh's office contained no elegant star charts or brilliant photos of colorful nebulae. Nothing to satisfy the science fiction nerd in him, only spreadsheets of numbers and a whiteboard covered in equations. The only thing he found interesting was a picture of the Mayan zodiac that she must have gotten from Gabi as part of their joint astronomy project.

Ruth had transferred Theo's photos of the crime scene to her own phone, along with a summary of their haruspicy findings. She handed the phone to Minh. "We think the liver might be a star chart, and the animals at the murder site represent five constellations. But we don't know why."

Minh leaned back in her chair, swiping through the phone

with a look of intense concentration. After a long moment, she peered up at them. Her cheeks had regained some of their color, as if the workings of her brain had distracted her from the ache in her heart. Theo knew the feeling.

"I'm thinking this is an archeoastronomy reference," she said. "Your whole crime scene—not just the liver—could be a star chart." She handed the phone back to Ruth and turned her attention to her computer.

Ruth leaned toward Theo and whispered, "What's archeo-astronomy?"

"You look at ancient astronomical observations," he replied, "and from that, you can date texts and artifacts." He hoped she didn't press him further because he'd just disclosed the full extent of his knowledge.

"The night sky has changed over the millennia as the position of the earth varies," Minh explained without looking up from her computer. "So, if we know *what* someone sees in the stars, we know *when* they saw it."

Theo quirked a smile at Ruth. "What she said."

Minh flipped her monitor around so they could see it and pulled up a map of the night sky. "The bull is the central image of your crime scene, so we should start with the constellation Taurus." She pointed to a V of stars. "We don't think of it as anything special, not anymore, but the folks in the Age of Taurus would've thought differently."

Ruth gave a skeptical frown. "Age of Taurus sounds like astrology, not astronomy."

"It's both. Astrology is just incomplete astronomy—with a bunch of other junk thrown in. The Age of Taurus is what astrologers *and* astronomers call the roughly two thousand years when the spring equinox lay in Taurus."

Theo hadn't felt so undereducated in years. "You're going to have to explain that. I like science fiction for the fiction more than the science, I'm afraid."

Minh stood, wiped a section of her whiteboard clean, and grabbed a red marker. "Okay, this is the sun," she said, drawing a large ball. "Here's the earth's path around the sun." She drew an ellipse around the ball. "In order to explain why we see the sun move, you have to understand the earth's rotation and orbit."

"Stop there." Theo held up a hand. "The only thing I do know about astronomy is that the ancients didn't believe in a heliocentric universe. They thought the sun orbited an unmoving earth instead."

Minh stared at him. "But it doesn't. I'm not going to teach you erroneous astronomy."

"Please, let's go with the simple—if scientifically false—explanation."

She sighed, but erased her diagram. "Fine. Here's our vantage point on *earth*." She drew a flat line. "Here's the path of the sun as it rises and sets at the equinoxes." She drew an arc from east to west. "But in the northern hemisphere, the sun rises farther and farther to the south as the year progresses until it reaches its farthest point at the winter solstice on December twenty-first."

"Tomorrow," Theo said, suddenly sure they were on the right track.

"Very observant." She drew another series of arcs beside the first. "Then the sun's path travels backward until it rises at the farthest *northward* point six months later—at the summer solstice. Ancient astronomers kept track of the pattern by noting which constellation the sun rose in front of each day. They'd say 'the sun is in Scorpius,' for example. Over a whole year, the sun's position moves through twelve constellations: That's the zodiac."

"The Babylonians figured out the constellations first," Theo couldn't help adding, "but it was the Greeks who named it the *zodiakos kuklos*—the circle of little animals." He knew the interruption was pure pedantry—Gabi would've rolled her eyes. Selene would've been annoyed that he knew more about the ancient world than she did. But Ruth only nodded encouragingly and looked fascinated.

Minh drew a small horned circle—a stylized bull's head—on the central arc. "From about 4000 BC to 2000 BC, the sun rose in front of the constellation Taurus at the spring equinox." She tapped the symbol. "Hence the Age of Taurus."

"Wait, what happened in 2000 BC?" asked Theo.

"The simple version?"

"Please."

"Just like a spinning top, the earth wobbles on its axis very slowly. That motion changes our perspective on the stars, and thus the equinoxes themselves are drifting across the constellations. So every 2,160 years or so, we move into a different 'age.' Ancient astronomers figured out that the equinoxes were moving—they knew that they had already shifted from the Age of Taurus into the Age of Aries—but their geocentric model of the universe couldn't explain why. It must've blown their minds."

Ruth's eyes lit up. "So is this where that hippie song comes from? *This is the dawning of the Age of Aquarius . . .*" she sang in a surprisingly sweet alto.

"Yup. Depending on where you measure the borders of the constellations, today we've either already moved from the Age of Pisces to the Age of Aquarius—or we will soon. Astrologers think the shift of ages will herald some great world cataclysm or future utopia. It's part of how the New Age movement got its name." She smiled indulgently. "But now you're beyond my area of expertise."

"Cataclysm, huh?" Theo couldn't share in her humor. "Societies that believe in a coming end times or apocalypse are usually perfect feeding grounds for cultic practice." He grabbed a notepad from his satchel and started scribbling furiously. "What about the other symbols at the crime scene?"

"That's where things get really interesting. In each different age, as the equinoxes shift, the celestial equator moves through the constellations as well."

He stopped writing. "The celestial what now?"

Minh turned back to the whiteboard and drew a round ball in blue. "Here's the earth. According to the ancients, the planets and stars existed on hollow 'celestial spheres' that surrounded it. Imagine the stars as holes poked through an eggshell, and the earth as the yolk floating inside." She drew a large circle around the earth in black. "They thought the celestial sphere with the stars rotated, causing the constellations to move across the heavens. And it had an equator that mirrored the one on earth." She drew the earth's equator in blue, then a parallel arc onto the outer shell in black. She added a red ellipse that intersected the celestial equator in two places. "This is the circle of the zodiac constellations that trace the sun's movement. Where the celestial equator and the zodiac intersect, you get the sun's position at the equinoxes. And it just so happens that when the spring equinox is here in Taurus"—she drew the bull symbol on one intersection point—"the autumn one is here. In Scorpius." She tapped her marker on the other intersection point. Around the curve of the celestial equator, she added three dots. "And the celestial equator also passes through..." She tapped each dot in turn. "Corvus, Hydra, and Canis Minor. Bird, snake, dog."

Ruth clapped her hands. "Fantastic! There you go, Theo, it all fits together."

Theo couldn't celebrate; he was too busy trying to consider all the repercussions. "Okay, so the crime scene represents a star chart from somewhere between 4000 and 2000 BC."

"Approximately. Again, it depends how you measure."

He shook his head. "But that's *way* before the Roman Empire! It's before the Golden Age of Athens! We're talking Neolithic or early Bronze Age here."

"So?" Ruth looked at him quizzically. "What's the problem with that?"

"First off, there are no written records describing cults that old, so we'll be completely in the dark. And it doesn't explain why the cult calls their leader 'Pater.' Why use Latin if it's not a Roman cult?"

"How do you know what they called their leader?" asked Ruth. "Was it written somewhere at the crime scene?"

Actually, I overheard it from a man in supernatural headgear as he flew toward me with a gun, Theo thought. He couldn't tell his friend the truth, but he was damn tired of lying. He settled for, "Selene and I had a few extracurricular adventures. I'll explain later, I promise."

Ruth let the matter drop, and Theo hoped her habitual circumspection would save him from ever having to make good on his vow.

An hour later, they left the museum, replete with more astronomical information than Theo ever imagined he'd need. As they reached the street, he reached compulsively for his phone, then let his hand drop. He wanted to call Selene and warn her that she might be on the wrong track, but what would he say? That the cult was re-creating some incomprehensible ritual from six thousand years ago? How was that helpful?

Beside him, Ruth suddenly stopped walking, hummed softly as if searching for the right words, and said, "What are you not telling me?"

So many things, Theo thought, *that I don't know where to start.*

"You know I hate to pry, and you don't have to tell me if you don't want to," she continued in a rush. "I just don't know how to help if I don't know the whole story."

"You're helping just by wanting to help," Theo assured her. "It's nice to have someone on my side for once."

"Selene's not on your side?"

"She's . . . well, sides are sometimes irrelevant when you're on a whole different plane of existence." He gave her a wry smile and tried to keep walking, but she put a hand on his arm. And left it there.

"I think I know what you mean." Her expression made him

suddenly uncomfortable. She wasn't nagging, or curious, or even worried. She was terrified. For him. "I didn't mean to look, but the video got transferred over to my phone along with the liver photos."

"What video—"

She held up her screen to him. Selene amid the twilit trees in the Catskills, the wound on her forehead miraculously healing with the touch of creek water. "Am I seeing what I think I'm seeing?"

"That my girlfriend is disturbingly unconcerned about drinking water that's likely contaminated with giardia parasites?" He tried to sound completely nonchalant.

Ruth just looked at him steadily. "Is she holding something over you? Are you keeping her secrets? Is that why you can't tell me the truth?" Her grip on his arm tightened and she took a hesitant step closer to him.

"I don't know what you think you saw—that video's so dark she could have bat wings and I wouldn't be able to tell. Really, Ruth, you're overreacting." He tried to sound good-natured, but from his friend's reaction, he knew she took it as a criticism. She released him immediately, nodding to herself as if disappointed— but unsurprised—by his evasions. He instinctively put his hands to her face so she would meet his eyes once more.

"Hey. Without you, I never would've figured out the truth behind this cult, and then I really *would* be in danger. Now at least I have a hint of what I'm dealing with." She looked at him with too bright eyes, and he wondered for the first time if her feelings for him went beyond the platonic. He dropped his hands, suddenly realizing that he might be unintentionally leading her on. *What am I doing caressing her face like an asshole?*

He tried to sound casual. "I'm going to stop by my office and see what I can dig up on cults from the Bronze Age, okay? And would you delete that video and the photos from your phone? Selene's a pretty private person, and the cops wouldn't want me sharing the official crime scene pictures."

Ruth gave him a noncommittal hum that would have to do.

"Thanks. I'll stop by your apartment later and get my stuff."

"You don't need to stay tonight?" Her voice had grown so soft he could barely hear her. He resisted the urge to joke with her, to hug her, to remind her how much he cared. He didn't want to do any more damage than he already had.

"Nope, Selene's house is probably habitable again," he lied. "And I need to see her tonight." That part was the truth. "Thanks again," he said, chucking his friend on the shoulder and feeling like a jerk. "I owe you one."

He hailed a passing cab and sank back in the seat with an audible groan. If he had inadvertently played with Ruth's heart, how could he blame Selene for playing with his? Did he really expect a relationship with a woman who'd clung to her virginity for three thousand years to be *easy*? Here he was trying to help her, and instead he'd nearly spilled the secret she'd spent millennia trying to protect. He didn't know where she was or what dangers she faced. He didn't know how his new information would help. But he couldn't bear the idea that she might think he didn't care. He looked over his shoulder, to where Ruth stood by the subway entrance, staring after him. Then he pulled out his phone and texted Selene. He'd let down one woman he cared about already today. He refused to do it to another.

Chapter 20

INTERMISSIO: THE HYAENA

Twelve hours earlier

Winter clung to the bronze helm. When the Hyaena touched it, the skin of her fingertips froze to the dark metal for a painful instant before ripping free, leaving a single layer of skin behind.

"It is cold because of where it is from," the Praenuntius said, answering her unspoken question. "The Underworld is a place of unending night."

She nodded, though she didn't fully understand—one more thing to add to the list of mysteries that seemed to grow longer by the day. "No wings on this one," she said, laying the dark helm on the Praenuntius's bed. "But they say it's even more powerful."

The old man nodded slowly, staring at the helmet warily. *The more power the item holds, the more it saps from him,* she thought, noticing the wine-dark bruises beneath his eyes. The Host had worked him hard—and the battle had just begun.

The bolts on the door slid open with a pneumatic hiss. The sharp-faced Heliodromus strode into the room, wearing his red robes. At his waist hung his traditional coiled leather whip—a fitting weapon for a man who considered himself the master of everyone around him. The Hyaena dreaded what he would do with more power than he already had. But it was not her place to question the Pater's decrees.

The Heliodromus didn't greet her, didn't even look at her—if it were up to him, she wouldn't even be present, but the Praenuntius would obey only her. The thought gave her little comfort.

As the Heliodromus stared down his beaked nose at the Praenuntius, his jaw jutted forward defiantly. She wondered if he felt afraid. Or whether he simply couldn't bear to have a Pretender in his sight without sending him to his death.

She released the straps around the Praenuntius's wrists. The Heliodromus took a wary step backward, his hands straying to the handle of his whip, and the Hyaena repressed a smirk. For all his arrogance, he still feared the old man.

The Praenuntius made no move to attack. He'd long ago resigned himself to fulfilling his side of the bargain. He merely circled his wrists and danced his long fingers in a slow pattern, as if sculpting the air. The first time she'd seen the motions, the Hyaena had thought he only sought to stretch his hands. Now she wondered if he reenacted some ancient ritual. He believed, after all, that he had sculpted mankind in the dawn of time. *Does he wish he'd left us in the riverbank?* she wondered. *Unmolded clay, unable to wreak destruction upon his kind?*

His hands fluttered back to the blanket, and he looked at the Hyaena with mournful eyes. He knew what had happened with the last item she'd brought him. She'd told him how the young Corvus Secundo had ignored the Pater's instructions to keep the winged hat hidden and pursued Diana on his own.

"Hubris," the Praenuntius had said when she finished the tale. "No mortal can take down the Huntress without help, no matter what he wears." Yet now he was about to add another weapon to the Host's arsenal. How long could Diana—or any of the Pretenders—survive against an enemy so well armed?

"Go on," the Hyaena urged her charge, not ungently. "You know this is the only way."

"Remember your promise," he said, his voice strained.

"Only if you remember yours. You said all the Pretenders would fall. So far, we've captured only one."

He held her gaze a moment longer, as if he had a thousand things to tell her and none he wanted to say. Then he relaxed completely, closed his eyes, and inhaled. When he let out the breath, it sounded like wind on a winter's day...then it rose to the keening cry of a father mourning his child. And it didn't stop.

His eyes snapped open, and his hands streaked through the air to grab the Heliodromus's wrists. He dragged the man forward so that both their hands rested on the frigid crown of the helm.

Frost gathered on the Heliodromus's thumb and forefinger where they touched the dark bronze, yet sweat poured down his high forehead. His eyes watered as the Praenuntius's breath stung his face like hail; his body spasmed with the power of the gift he received. His knees crumpled, his head lolled, but the Praenuntius wouldn't release him. He merely took another deep breath and continued the storm. The Hyaena wondered if he made it hurt on purpose. A tiny revenge for centuries of torture.

She checked her stopwatch. It had been one minute so far. It would take a hundred more before the Praenuntius's breath would allow the Heliodromus to wield the helm. A hundred minutes of violent, paralyzing torment. He wouldn't be able to walk for hours. She'd watched it happen to the Corvus. Yet when he donned the winged cap, he'd flown.

She would give anything to endure that pain.

When it was over, the Heliodromus sat slumped on the ground beside the bed. The Hyaena wrapped the dark helm in a cloth. She retied the old man's restraints. He made no move to resist.

"Thank you," she said softly. He turned his head to the wall, as if he couldn't bear to see what he'd done.

The helm clutched against her breast, she left the patient's room and walked to the vault deep within the Templo. She unwrapped the helm and placed it on the shelf beside the Host's other treasures. A bronze hand mirror, its back intricately ornamented. A leather quiver of six golden arrows. A sickle, its handle plain wood but its curving blade serrated with teeth so fine they sparkled like diamond chips. A staff twined with gilded serpents, their eyes uncut rubies. A wreath of unripe poppies, each a waxy green bulb leaking dream-milk. A whalebone trident, the shaft inlaid with branching corals in hues of orange and red. A gold cap, the sweeping wings at each temple shining with silver, copper, and bronze, fluttering in the air like the softest down.

The helm seemed almost to suck the light from the brighter objects around it, a hulking, evil thing, crouched in a pool of shadow. For a moment, the Hyaena wondered if that's what she'd become—a destructive darkness, erasing the beauty from the world. Then she brushed aside the thought. *I do only what has been fated.*

The Pretenders must die. Will *die. Then, and only then, can we restore the one true God to the world.*

Chapter 21

DEATHLESS ONES

Selene's patience wore thin five minutes after Paul disappeared into Castle Williams. She couldn't just hide behind a building doing nothing while her twin ventured into danger.

"I'll keep watch on our flanks," she told the others. Then, with the gold and silver bows slung across her back, Paul's quiver on one hip, and her own three divine arrows on the other, she sprinted silently back to the higher ground surrounding Fort Jay. Crawling on her elbows to a low hummock, she could see not only the small library that concealed Flint and the others but also Castle Williams, the surrounding buildings, and the harbor itself.

She was supposed to be looking for additional patrols, but she found herself staring at her fellow Athanatoi instead. She could've seen them even without her night vision—the screens of their devices illuminated their faces with an eerie blue glow. They were a motley bunch—the hunched Smith, his face bent over his tablet; the Messenger bouncing on his toes in impatience, trying to peer over his stepbrother's shoulder; the God of Love crouching in the shelter of the wall with an unlit cigarette between his teeth, immersed in his cell phone. She wasn't sure she liked any of them—but she was starting to respect them. *We were never truly omnipotent—not like the Hebrew version of God,* she thought. *Each of us only presided over our little slice of the world—is it any surprise that we're stronger together?*

These last few days had represented the closest thing to a Gathering of the Gods that had occurred since her father, Zeus, summoned them all to Mount Olympus to announce the Diaspora. The day was a clear memory, a true memory—untold and unclouded by the poets—but one she rarely relived. Yet as she looked down on her kin, a vision of the past suddenly rushed upon her.

Dust coats my sandaled feet and the musk of boar still clings to my tunic as I climb the slopes of Olympus. I don't want to leave the hunt, but I must obey the Sky God's summons.

Selene shook her head as if to knock the memory away. This was no time for daydreams. Yet the motion only rooted the vision more firmly in her mind. A great weight constricted her chest, black shadows clouded her eyes, and she felt herself drawn inexorably into the past. For a fleeting moment, while she was still Selene, she wondered if this was how mortals had felt when a deity sent them a vision in days of old. Like a woman drowning in the mind of a god. And then she stopped fighting—and was Artemis one more.

At the pronaos of the feast hall stands Hephaestus, one sooty hand on a crutch, the other resting on a towering column of porphyry. I think he won't speak to me—he rarely does—but he raises his eyes at my approach.

"Zeus commands I make certain the hall will stand for the Gathering," he says, tracing a wide, branching fissure down the column's flute with his thick finger.

"And?" I am more comfortable outdoors than in buildings, especially ones that are about to collapse.

"A few days more. Then all is dust." His thick beard hides whatever grimace or frown might touch his lips, but his eyes are liquid brown and full of pain. He limps heavily into the hall, and I have no choice but to follow.

Inside, my gaze traces a long gash in the gilded concrete up to the oculus in the center of the domed roof. No longer does a thick column of smoke pour forth from the brazier in the middle of the chamber as men on earth burn offerings of bulls and blood, grain and wine to honor the Athanatoi. Now only the merest trickle of smoke curls from the fire.

Hestia, the Hearth Goddess, sits on her low wooden stool, tending the coals with vacant eyes, veil pulled tight. The paucity of offerings, which has left all the gods weakened, has hit her the hardest. I can't bear to look at her. Yet Hephaestus lays a hand briefly on her shoulder.

I take my seat, and Hermes skips over to sit beside me. He's shaved his beard, and the slanting line of his narrow jaw mirrors the sweep of the wings on his cap. I wonder if it still works. I suspect it doesn't. He holds his snake-twined caduceus loose in his hand, slapping it distractedly against his leg. "You see who comes among us?" he asks slyly.

"Everyone." Wise Athena with her owl upon her wrist, beautiful Aphrodite and her son, Eros, Dionysus with curling vines twined in his hair and wine staining his lips, Mars the Man-Slayer gleaming in golden armor with a mighty spear. My father and his wife have yet to make an appearance, but all the rest of the Olympians, as well as most of the lesser gods, are present.

Hermes points his staff to the far corner. "And him."

To my surprise, my grandfather Kronos is here. He looks quite dignified with his curled white beard and midnight blue robes. The other Athanatoi ignore him, and he ignores them right back.

"Father allowed him to come?" I ask, surprised.

"Who dares keep him away? You know his strength remains, even as ours flees falcon-swift."

"You speak true? I pay little heed to such things." My mother bears my love, my father my respect, and my twin my fury. The other Athanatoi mean little to me.

"Have you not seen Saturn's glorious temple within the Forum of Rome?"

I remember the columned edifice dimly, but I rarely pass through Rome's city walls. "So? Kronos is not Saturn."

Hermes laughs, the sound jarring amid the tense murmurs in the hall. "So you are Diana and I Mercury, but our grandfather must content himself with one name alone? Have you always been so selfish, sister? The people of Rome joined their harvest god to our grandfather after his release from Tartarus. So Kronos is Saturn now, and he answers to that name only—as Ares now is Mars. The Romans honor him as a god like to Jupiter himself."

"You mean they used to honor him. Surely they forget him now. No one can escape that fate."

Hermes only nods, and for the first time, I notice the tension in his narrow shoulders. Even my most carefree brother is scared. He does not speak again.

Finally, my father arrives. Zeus's beard is still dark, his shoulders broad beneath his blue robe, but his eyes, usually as wide and clear as a summer sky, are stormy gray, the skin around them dark and slack. Hera strides next to him, her inky hair elaborately coiffed, her arms as white and round as always but her eyes swollen.

"Hark, Athanatoi, to my words," *Zeus begins.* "First came Gaia and Ouranos, Mother Earth and Father Sky, parents to us all." *The old recitation of lineage that begins all our gatherings. A reminder of the debt we all owe the Father of the Gods.* "From them sprang the Age of Titans, among them wily Kronos, who swallowed whole his children so he might rule unrivaled."

All eyes turn to Saturn, whose gaze remains on the oculus overhead. A faint smile hovers on his lips. My father continues his litany. "With my mighty fist, I split Kronos's gullet and freed my sisters and brothers to rule at my side. Thus began the Age of the Olympians. Until the fall of Troy, we lived in the Age of Heroes. Until today, for more than fifteen hundred years, the Age of Iron reigned, and mankind paid us homage still." *He pauses. I wish I were hunting, dancing, anywhere but listening to a story whose end I cannot bear to hear.* "Today we gather to determine what the next Age will be."

"There is no choice to make," *says blue-haired Poseidon, rising from his seat with his whalebone trident held high.* "The Age of Man. Already it draws nigh. Like wave upon stone, their indifference erodes our strength. Soon, we will be washed away entirely. No more does my trident shake the earth. Like a pitchfork it sleeps in my grasp, and all the roaring of my waves cannot awaken it!" A murmur of assent sweeps through the chamber.

My twin brother stands bare chested and beautiful, a laurel wreath upon his brows. Apollo's pose is confident, but he does not meet my eyes. Ours is an old fight—our wounds remain unhealed. Yet the others turn to him like flowers to the light. "Once I could drive the newborn Sun across the sky. With a touch I could heal the wounds of men. No longer."

A chill runs through me. My shot is still true, my feet still swift, but I too have lost much.

Aphrodite moans that men no longer allow her naked body to haunt their dreams. Her son Eros begins to cry and wail. Other gods join the chorus, reciting litanies of their diminishments, their voices growing louder and more desperate.

"I have no hearth to tend." With her whisper, Hestia silences us all.

I follow her gaze to the last puff of fragrant smoke as it drifts slowly toward the oculus. Then, with a collective gasp, we watch it dissolve completely in a breath of wind. The brazier has gone cold.

After a long moment, Father speaks again. "Isis, Serapis, Mithras, the Magna Mater. Always, such new gods twined their own worship with ours, strengthening the weave with colors bold and patterns intricate. Then, a man appeared in Jerusalem to rip that cloth to shreds. To tear us from the hearts and minds of all our followers." He took a deep breath, as if to prepare for his next words. Now, finally, we would come to the heart of the matter. "On this day, the Roman Emperor Theodosius outlaws all worship of the Olympians."

He holds up his hand for silence as a cry of despair fills our throats. There is worse yet to come.

"He will imprison those who tell our stories or send us their prayers. Without our worshipers, we diminish. No longer may I wield the thunderbolt. No longer may I set men into the stars. No longer may I be bull or swan or rain shower. This is my skin now." Even as he speaks, some of the radiance leaves his eyes.

I blink back tears. Others weep openly. Hestia, eyes dry and lifeless, rises from her stool. Carefully, she places her staff upon the brazier and walks slowly from the chamber. No one speaks. No one tries to stop her. No one thinks they will see her again.

"We shall do as Hestia does," my father pronounces when his sister's figure has disappeared beyond the boundaries of Olympus. "We shall leave behind this land that rejects us."

"Rome knows me still," Mars insists. He does not look distraught. Perhaps he is too obtuse to understand what's happening. "Its legions spread my name across the world. They forget me not!"

"No, son." Father's voice bristles with impatience. "You must not aid those who refuse to pay homage. Athens and Rome have abandoned us, and so we abandon them, never to return." With that, his strength leaves him. My mighty father can only whisper his last words. "Hope flees like an eagle on the wing. And so must we."

The roar of a boat's engine offshore finally wrenched Selene from the memory's grip. She allowed the snowy, moonlit buildings of Governors Island to replace the sun-drenched marble of Olympus's halls. Yet the dread, the despair, were harder to banish. She laid her fingertips on the fletching of her new gold arrows and looked down at her hands, noticing the faint lines that crisscrossed her skin as they never had when she'd been Artemis. *Why do I still pretend to be a goddess?* she wondered. She glanced down at her brothers, hiding behind the library. *Why do any of us?* Even Saturn, who'd seemed so confident at the Gathering, had disappeared long ago like so many others, remembered as little more than a name for a faraway planet more distant and unknowable than the god himself had ever been.

The boat's engine revved again, closer now, and she finally turned toward the sound, though part of her cared little for the dangers of her present existence.

Red and green running lights slowly materialized into a large motor yacht. It was still too far away to make out the driver—he was a silhouette in the darkness, nothing more. The engine stuttered to a stop. Suddenly, the wrongness of the image snapped her from her melancholy—no one took a pleasure ride in December. She felt her despair lift and wondered how she'd ever let a memory enervate her so. She slipped from her hiding place and rejoined the others behind the library.

"I hope you've got a telescope in that bag of yours, because we've got a visitor."

Flint grunted, handed off the video feed to Dash, and reached for his duffel. Seconds later, Dash yelped as he stared at the screen. "Ouranos's balls, what the hell happened to—"

Selene snatched the tablet phone for herself, and for a moment she couldn't make sense of what she saw. The feed from the front entrance of Castle Williams showed Mars's two guards slumped in place, livid welts snaking around their throats. "When did that—" Then movement at the other side of the screen caught her attention. In the interior courtyard, one of the soldiers reached for his throat, where an invisible rope circled his windpipe, indenting the skin and turning his face blue. As he collapsed, the other soldier rushed toward him. But before he'd taken more than a step, a bright gash appeared on his own neck, his flesh split open as if from the lash of a whip. He raised one hand to his throat and waved the other about, searching in vain for his opponent. Then he too fell to the ground, his lifeblood gushing onto the snow.

Selene took in a quick breath. "Hades' Helm of Invisibility."

"But why would my father kill his own men?" asked Philippe.

"He wouldn't. Someone's using the divine weapons against them—which means Mars isn't the Pater." She threw the tablet back to Flint and pulled a gold arrow from her belt. Just then, a piercing whistle that only she could hear almost brought her to her knees. "Paul!" she gasped.

As one, the Athanatoi raised their weapons and rushed toward the castle.

Then the earthquake began.

Chapter 22

EARTH SHAKER

Only Selene stayed on her feet. The others tumbled to their knees with a cry, gripping the ground as it trembled beneath them. She turned to look back at the large yacht offshore. Four figures emerged from the cabin and headed toward the stern. They threw a rubber raft overboard and clambered inside. She was just about to call out to her brothers to get ready for an attack when another figure emerged in the prow, holding aloft a staff of some sort. Its three prongs shone like ivory in the moonlight.

"Get up!" she hollered. "We've got to get Paul!"

Philippe bounced to his feet and hauled his stepfather up beside him.

Dash rose, feet spread like a surfer as the earth continued to shiver beneath him. "Look!" he cried, pointing toward the harbor.

"He's got Poseidon's trident, I know—"

"No, look!"

The water, flat and calm a moment before, now receded quickly from the shoreline, as if the Earth Shaker himself had pulled a plug in the middle of the harbor. Selene knew they had only a few minutes before the water reversed course and flooded the entire island.

A tsunami.

"They know we're here," Philippe moaned. "They'll either kill us with that wave or capture us with whatever other weapons they've got!"

Selene watched the rubber raft speed toward shore, even as the harbor began to swirl and heave. Three men leaped into the water and waded toward land. All wore black body armor and SWAT helmets with reflective face shields, but no insignia.

The armored men stopped for a moment onshore and looked directly at the gods' hiding place behind the library.

"They've seen us now," Philippe said, his voice a panicked whisper. "If they've got the trident, they could have anything! Zeus's thunderbolt!"

Selene gestured sharply for silence and raised her own weapon. From here, she couldn't tell if the men were Athanatoi or mortal, but she wasn't taking any chances. She nocked a gold arrow to her bowstring.

The armored men scrambled up a bank of loose boulders to reach the road. Behind them, the water swelled, climbing steadily up the shoreline. The men passed the two downed guards without a second look and entered Castle Williams.

"See," Selene said. "They're not coming for us at all. Paul's the one in danger. Now come on!" She stepped toward the castle just as the first massive swell of water reached the road like a ripple from a giant's skipping stone. She sent a futile prayer to Poseidon to make it stop, but it only came faster, a rushing, inexorable tide that swept her and all her family off their feet.

The wall of water never crested—it merely crushed her to the ground. The frigid December ocean chased the blood from her limbs and stiffened every muscle, driving away what little breath she had left. She tumbled in a swirling mass of splintered branches and broken lumber that sliced at her flesh. The wave ripped the arrow from her hand—the gold shaft spun in the water, just out of reach, then streaked off into the blackness.

Somehow, she managed to keep hold of her bow, slinging it over her body and leaving both her arms free to stroke for the surface. She gasped air, thinking the worst was over. But the water funneled her relentlessly down the road. She caught a brief glimpse of Philippe and Dash, both clinging to a lamppost, their faces wet and scared in the halo of light.

She tried swimming toward them, but she might as well have fought the flow of time itself. She flailed anyway, unwilling to surrender. Bobbing and spinning like a cork, she looked desperately for something to grab on to before the water swept her off the island entirely. The bodies of the two guards floated past like logs in a flume. The water grew ever deeper, the wave more swollen.

Now she floated well above the first floor of the solid brick buildings. Castle Williams itself, made to withstand the direct hit of a cannonball, also remained unmovable. But the wave ripped the derelict library off its foundations with a mighty crash of snapping wood and breaking glass. The building revolved, revealing Flint, his duffel bag over his shoulder, clutching at a windowsill with one hand and holding his crutches in the other. The building spun faster, and even his massive strength couldn't resist the tsunami's force. It threw his body like a discus into the churning water.

Just as Selene decided they'd both be washed all the way to Brooklyn, the tide stilled. She treaded water for a moment, catching her breath, knowing full well that another wave would follow the first.

A strangled gasp drew her attention to Flint, who flailed wildly, vainly attempting to hold his bag of electronics over his head. He sank beneath the black water for a moment, the bag with him, then came up spluttering.

Philippe let go of his lamppost and struck out toward his stepfather, moving with surprising swiftness. He grabbed Flint under the arms and dragged him back to the lamppost. Flint clutched the pole, his head resting against his hands as his chest heaved.

Selene knew they had only a few minutes of respite. "Dash, come with me to find Paul!"

He pulled out one of his pistols, his face stricken as water poured from its barrel.

"*Styx*," Selene snapped. "You can't help if you're not armed."

Philippe swam toward her instead, brandishing his small bow. Selene would rather have had Dash's speed, but she'd take whatever she could get.

They paddled as fast they could toward Castle Williams, Dash calling after them: "I'll get the boat so we can skedaddle out of here—I'll be waiting when you get back with Paul."

As they reached the wall of the castle, a second wave rushed forward. But this time the rising water worked in their favor; it carried them up until they floated just below the roof. Selene hauled herself up the rough brownstone walls, then crawled across to peer down into the courtyard.

Philippe came up behind her, his yellow hair plastered to his head but his eyes bright with determination. The courtyard had flooded to the second story.

She could see no movement through the castle's windows nor on to the taller roof that ringed the opposite side of the building. The rubber raft, tied to a drainpipe, sat empty.

"Do you think they all drowned in there?" Philippe asked, his voice shaking—whether from cold or fear she couldn't tell.

"Start a tsunami with no way to survive it? These guys seem more organized than that." She tried to sound confident, but her pulse raced. *I'd know if Apollo were dead,* she told herself. *Part of me would die with him.*

"We're going into the castle through the windows, then?"

Before she could reply, a low voice said, "Why not just wait for them to come out?" To her shock, Flint had clambered up behind them onto the roof.

"How did you get up here?" she asked.

He lifted one crutch so she could see the large silver balloon sprouting from the top. "Flotation device," he muttered. "Works great...except when it jams." He pressed a button on the side of the handle and the balloon quickly deflated, sucked back inside the hollow leg of the crutch like a chewing gum bubble.

Philippe grinned. "Bravo, Papa. Or you could learn how to swim."

Flint just grunted.

On the opposite side of the courtyard, a large third-floor window swung open. Selene raised her bow and pulled a silver arrow from Paul's quiver—at this point, she needed to save her last two gold shafts. Philippe nocked a dart to his own miniature bow.

"You going to make them all fall in love with you?" Selene asked, wishing again she had a more useful relative around.

A man in black body armor dropped through the window and into the waiting raft below. Selene didn't hesitate. Her shaft streaked like a comet across the yard. With unerring aim, the arrow struck the man in the head—and bounced harmlessly off the opaque faceplate of his helmet. It tumbled into the water below as if it were no more powerful than a wooden shaft. Whatever special properties Paul's divine arrows still possessed, they didn't work for her—and now her clumsy attempt had only alerted the men to their presence.

"Try aiming for the crack between helmet and neck guard," Philippe offered.

She grabbed a wooden arrow to do just that, but the man

drew his gun and fired two shots toward the roof, forcing her to lie flat as the bullets whizzed above their heads.

"How invulnerable are you?" Philippe asked her.

"Not enough to risk getting shot in the face."

He nodded. "Me neither. Not with this face anyway. What about you, Papa?"

"I heal no faster than a mortal." Flint said it matter-of-factly, but Selene knew what the words must have cost him.

"So there goes a frontal assault," Selene decided. She dared to lift herself up on her elbows, only to have another shot ring out, the sound echoing crazily in the round fortress. She flattened herself once more. "Good aim. These guys know how to fight, even if they aren't Martin's men."

The creak of an opening door ripped her attention away from the courtyard to the upper roof opposite her position. The door to the stairwell swung open, and a second armored man emerged, holding a rifle. From his higher vantage point, he had a clear view of the three Athanatoi. Selene reached desperately for an arrow as another bullet from the man in the courtyard sent concrete chips flying just inches from her hand.

The armored man on the roof pointed his rifle straight at Flint's broad chest. Before he could fire, Selene sent a wooden arrow into the chink between his shoulder and arm. She'd been aiming for his neck, but shooting a bow while lying prone was never easy, even for her. He dropped his rifle and clutched at his arm.

Selene slung her bow over her shoulder, where it clanged against Paul's. She clambered up a ladder to the upper roof. As she pounded toward her quarry, she could smell his streaming blood. He snatched up his rifle with his left hand, tearing off in the opposite direction.

Selene sprang like an antelope, floating in a silent, graceful arc for three heartbeats before tackling him to the ground and ripping the rifle from his hand. She turned it on him, pressing her foot against his chest to hold him still.

"*DON'T—*" cried Flint just as she shot the man point blank in the neck.

"*Merde*, Selene!" Philippe shouted as he ran up behind her. "We could've gotten information out of him."

"Before or after he shot you in the heart?" She ripped off the man's helmet. He was still alive, but barely. His bloody lips moved, but she could make out only a single gurgled word: "*Pater.*" Then he fell still. A middle-aged man, face lean and weathered but unremarkable. Noticing a black arrow tattooed on his inner right wrist, she pulled up his sleeve to see the entire design: the spear and shield "male" symbol of the planet Mars. She checked his other wrist: the stylized hand mirror of Venus, also the universal symbol for "female."

She had no time to look any further; a shot whizzed by her ear from the courtyard.

She threw herself to the ground, Philippe beside her. Flint, who'd only just managed to make it up the ladder, lay with his large duffel shielding his head.

"Come on, we've got to find cover!" she shouted.

Before her loomed a Civil War cannon that promised a bulletproof shelter. The massive iron weapon, its barrel fifteen feet long, pointed out over the water toward the lights of Manhattan. They crawled toward it and crouched behind its base. "Too bad we don't have some cannonballs to lob at this asshole," she complained. The shots fell like hail, ricocheting off the cannon with earsplitting pings. She peeked out between the iron struts, looking down into the courtyard.

"The rest of the men are coming out the window," she reported. "They're holding something shiny..."

"What?" Philippe couldn't see with his back pressed against the cannon.

"Paul's alive... but they've got him. And they've captured your father, too."

Two black-clad soldiers held a net that shimmered in the

moonlight like molten metal. The gleaming threads bent and twisted as the figures within it struggled to escape. Selene could make out Paul, stripped of his wool coat, his unbound hair tangled about his face. He writhed like a trapped cat, shouting curses at his captors. *It's going to be all right,* she told herself. *Mars is there, too—he'll break them out.* Yet the Man-Slayer lay curled in a ball, his hands over his face. Selene recognized him only by his build—nearly seven feet tall, with arms as muscled as a wrestler's and thighs that strained against the fabric of his military-issue fatigues. He crouched in the net's grip like a babe afraid of the dark.

"That's my golden net," Flint grumbled from beside her, peering over her shoulder.

"The one you made to trap my parents?" Philippe asked. "How'd the cult get their hands on that?"

"I have no idea. I buried it on Lemnos millennia ago. But if it still works, they'll never be able to break free."

"Why not?" Philippe sounded desperate. "My father's still strong."

Flint paused before replying, as if ashamed of his words. "I made it so that only someone who truly loved me could rip it open."

"Does Martin know that?" Selene demanded.

Flint shook his head.

"Then why isn't he trying to escape?" None of it made sense. Not the tattooed attackers. Not the cowering god. Not the fact that her twin had walked right into a trap and she'd let him do it.

The man holding the bottom of the net dropped into the boat, now floating halfway down the first story as the water receded. The other stood on the window ledge, holding the net steady. Selene rested a wooden arrow against her bowstring, took a deep breath, and leaned out from behind the cannon's protective bulk. The arrow struck the man standing in the window, lodging in the gap between shoulder and neck. He gave a strangled cry and retreated into the fort, dropping his side of the net: It crashed into the boat, falling open as it went.

Paul rolled free before the men could stop him, slipping over the side of the raft like a seal and disappearing into the black water. Mars merely raised his head, looking dazed. His features were much as Selene remembered: a sharp blade of a nose, regal forehead, brows that slanted upward like an eagle's wings. But his mouth, once a fierce, unsmiling line, now hung open like a bewildered child's. He made a weak clutching gesture with his right hand, as if he expected his spear to be there. Then the two men in the boat threw the net back over his head. Mars barely struggled.

The men turned their attention back to the water, their gun barrels twitching as they searched for sign of Paul.

The rubber raft rocked as if something had fallen into it, and another man materialized in the stern, pulling a dark Grecian helm with long cheek guards from his head. In his right hand he gripped a gleaming spear, nearly eight feet long. His widow's peak and sharp jaw reminded her of a hawk.

"Leave Apollo!" the man commanded. "We can't risk losing what we already have."

"He's holding Hades' helm and my brother's spear," rumbled Flint unnecessarily.

Selene barely heard him. She watched the water, desperate for any sign of her twin. Finally, she spotted him emerging onto the low rise of a hill over three hundred yards away—out of sight of the men in the courtyard. Paul crawled slowly from the water, but then turned and looked directly at her—their old connection still held. He gave her a weak wave.

She reached for another arrow to send toward the man with Mars's spear but paused when Flint grabbed her arm. "Look!"

The man she'd shot in the shoulder had reappeared in the window, his pistol pointed straight at her. He'd removed her arrow; now blood streamed down his chest plate. Without his black military helmet, she recognized his olive skin and squashed face—the same man who'd attacked her in the Central Park blockhouse.

He pulled Hermes' cap from the bag at his waist and flew toward them, the metal wings a bright slash against the dark sky. At the same time, the raft's motor roared to life, and the boat headed toward the castle's exit.

"You guys go after the raft. We can't let them take Martin," Selene said. "I'll deal with the flying guy."

"No," Flint insisted, reaching for the hammer on his back. "It's too dangerous. Let me—"

But Selene cut him off by stepping out from the cannon's shadow with her hands raised in the air.

"Hi again," she said calmly to the man flying toward her.

He hovered at roof level, his pistol aimed at her chest. Behind her, she was dimly aware of Philippe pulling Flint toward the stairwell entrance, but most of her attention remained glued to the gun wavering in her attacker's hand. She was honestly surprised he could hold it at all with the arrow wound in his shoulder.

"Don't move!" he shouted.

"Now, now, don't shoot. You need me alive, don't you? More victims for your special rites."

"I'll take you dead if need be." His voice trembled. "You'll *all* be dead before long anyway."

"Oh?" she asked innocently. "It seems to me that you're getting out of here with only Martin and me."

"We didn't expect so many of you or we would've brought reinforcements," he answered defensively. She was surprised—he spilled his secrets like a sieve. Young, indeed.

A longer shudder passed through his body and his arm twitched. As he reached to loosen his armor where it chafed at the wound, she saw the tattoo on his neck. When she'd seen it in the park, she'd thought it a cross. Now she recognized it as an upside-down symbol for the planet Mercury: a circle with an arc on one end and a cross on the other, representing the god's snake-twined caduceus.

While he struggled with his armor, she seized upon his momentary distraction and leaped off the roof like a bird of prey, catching him in midair. She landed a punch hard on his chin while grabbing his wounded shoulder with her other hand. He screamed in pain, eyes squinting shut, and dropped his gun from nerveless fingers into the last remaining feet of water. They jerked through the air like a kite on a gusty day as the cap strove to keep them both airborne.

As they careened over the ramparts of the castle, she punched her attacker in the face. She felt his cheekbone shatter under the impact, but he remained conscious. Teeth bared in anger, he raised both hands to her throat and squeezed. *This feels familiar,* she thought as she scrabbled with her free hand at his grip. Where moments before she'd felt like a raptor, now she was a mouse in a hawk's talons.

She struggled, raising a knee into his groin, but only managed to bruise herself painfully on his armored crotch. Just as the lack of oxygen dimmed her vision, a steel dart sprang from the man's chest, passing cleanly through his body armor. *The God of Love has unerring aim when he shoots for the heart,* she realized, grateful for once that Philippe still possessed some preternatural powers.

The man yelped, but the dart fell free with no sign of blood; its short tip must have barely pierced his flesh. He smirked at her, his confidence restored. "You think your weapons are any match for ours?" he asked, tightening his grip on her throat. She tried to croak out a response, but no air would come. *This is it,* she thought. *Death at the hands of a mortal man who's stolen our power for his own.* It seemed apt, somehow, in this Age of Man.

The man's face grew suddenly pale and sweat ran down his forehead. His eyes rolled desperately, and he gasped in pain. As he weakened, the cap's wings began to jerk and spasm in response. She glanced down and saw Dash's motorboat below her, the Messenger at the wheel, the Smith and the Bright One in the center, and the God of Love perched in front of the cockpit with his bow raised and a confident smile on his lips.

Her attacker released her. She plummeted through the air; the flying man—no longer flying—tumbled beside her, clutching at his chest as his heart finally succumbed to the God of Love and ceased beating.

She splashed into the water feet first, hitting the roadbed with a thud that nearly broke her ankles, then shooting back up through the frigid water like a cork. The tide had receded; she could nearly touch bottom, but not quite.

Her attacker's corpse floated out to sea, but the winged cap bobbed beside her. She grabbed it by the wings and paddled to the side of the motorboat. Flint reached out a hand to heave her onboard.

He didn't release her right away.

A ripple of fear passed across his features. "I saw you up there with his hands around your throat..." Before she could respond, he dropped her hand and turned away.

Selene lay the winged cap on a bench and went straight to her twin, who huddled in the bottom of the boat, clutching his knees to his chest. Thin red lines scored his face where the golden net had cut his flesh. She squatted before him. "They'll pay for this."

She unslung his silver bow and placed it in his hands.

"I don't want it," he said hoarsely.

"Don't be ridiculous." She wrapped his fingers around the grip. "You're safe now, and we're about to get these guys."

Paul hung his head and let his weapon clatter to the deck. She growled in exasperation. She'd deal with her brother's emotions later. Right now, they had another Athanatos to rescue.

Dash revved the engine and they took off, heading straight for the other yacht. There were only five men left aboard besides Mars. *Pretty good odds,* Selene decided. Then again, the cult members had a small arsenal of divine weapons. Poseidon's trident,

Hades' helm, Mars's spear, Hephaestus's net. Who knew what else they might have in the hold?

Flint tore open his duffel and started pawing through his sodden equipment. He pulled out a tiny capsule no bigger than a vitamin pill. "Can you get this into my brother?"

"Not without shooting an arrow shaft clear through him. What is it?"

"Tracking device. Just in case we lose them."

Selene set her mouth in a firm line. "We're not going to lose them."

Philippe raised a hand. "Give it to me, Papa. Sometimes a tiny bow comes in handy." He quickly affixed the capsule to the end of a dart and aimed for the glimmering net in the back of the hold. His bow released with a comical twang, the dart flying too fast for even immortal eyes to see. Selene didn't see it strike, but she glimpsed a slight twitch of the net. Mars's captors didn't react, so she could only hope the capsule had embedded in the target with them none the wiser.

They drew near, Dash's speedboat an easy match for the larger yacht. Hand over hand, Selene made her way across the bouncing boat, climbing over the cockpit and coming to perch on the bow. The man with the hawk face who'd appeared out of thin air turned at their approach. He still held Hades' helm in one hand and Mars's spear in the other. From beneath the hem of his coat peeked a loop of green, waxy bulbs.

The hawk-faced man met her eyes, then shifted his coat with a smug smile, as if to grant her a better view of the strange object. *A wreath of poppy bulbs,* she realized with a start. Suddenly the visions tormenting Paul made sense—they had been sent by someone using the crown of Morpheus, the God of Dreams. *This man is not an Athanatos I recognize,* she decided, *but if he can wield Morpheus's poppies, then he might be more than human.* Her heart full of icy rage, she sent one of her last golden arrows rocketing toward his chest.

At the same instant, the man donned Hades' Helm of Invisibility. And the boat vanished.

Selene roared her disappointment.

"Follow their wake!" Flint shouted, pointing to the frothing water that marked the yacht's movement. Selene leaned forward, eager to shoot at something, anything. Then the waves all around them turned to whitecaps. Their own motorboat rocked dangerously from side to side, threatening to dump them all overboard.

"They're using the trident again!" she cried, grabbing on to the rail while her feet slid out from under her. For a full five minutes, the boat tossed and pitched in the sudden whirlpool. When the sea subsided, all signs of the yacht or its wake had disappeared.

She threw her bow onto one of the benches and slumped down beside it. "Now what?"

"Use the tracking device, Papa," Philippe urged, his voice shaking.

But Flint didn't respond. He frantically jabbed at the screen of his tablet, trying to get it to turn on. Finally, he looked up and shook his head. "Waterlogged. Whole thing's busted."

Dash cut the engine. In the sudden silence, Selene felt all hope slide away. Then Paul raised an arm and pointed silently toward Manhattan. Selene spun around, hoping the yacht had reappeared. Instead, she saw the Staten Island Ferry lying on its side not far offshore, surrounded by helicopters and rescue boats. In the skittering circles of searchlights, hundreds of people floated in the icy water. From this far away, Selene couldn't hear their screams for help. But she could imagine them. "The tsunami," she breathed.

Paul rose to his knees to peer over the gunwale. "It looks like the buildings downtown are standing," he murmured.

"But flooded, no doubt," said Dash. "Like in Hurricane Sandy. The subways too."

He tuned the boat's radio to WNYC. Selene found herself

gripping her bow so hard the metal cut into her hands. The emergency response vehicles had surrounded the wrecked ferry like a herd protecting its young. Another boat would just get in the way. According to the news reports, the water had already receded from downtown. There would be massive property damage, but the flooding had only reached a few feet deep—no one there had drowned. But at least one child and one old person had been proclaimed dead at the ferry site.

"Is there anything we can do?" Flint asked quietly.

Selene let out a long, shuddering sigh. "I think we've already done enough." And then, for a long moment, the gods simply sat in silence, listening to the reports of the havoc a war between immortals could wreak on a city of men.

Chapter 23

PLAGUE BRINGER

As the gods bounced across the harbor toward nothing in particular, Flint shook his head. "Too much salt, too much water." He grabbed his tablet in both hands as if he would crack it in two. "Even if the tracking device is transmitting, I can't pick up the signal."

Selene was still reeling, unable to block the images of the flailing men and women in the harbor. She forced herself to pay attention to Flint's words, though she barely cared anymore about Mars's fate. What was one god's life compared to that of a hundred mortals? It was a calculus she undoubtedly saw differently than the others. But then she remembered how Hades' murder had caused the suicidal stockbrokers on Wall Street and the rotting corpses in the morgue. *If they kill blood-thirsty Mars,* she wondered, *what will happen?* Would the world mourn him with an end to violence—or an outpouring of it? The ferry accident might be only the beginning of the terror.

The Smith laid his device atop his soaked duffel bag. He stared at it, as if commanding it to repair itself. Perhaps once he'd had such magic powers, but no longer. Now he was just a weary and bedraggled man, hunched in the back of a boat with his weary and bedraggled family, with no idea where to go next.

A chirp issued from Selene's pocket. "Guess who's got the only working cell phone," she marveled. "It might not have Internet access, but it can withstand a little salt water." It was the first good news she'd had all day. "I've even got a text message." *Be careful!* it read. *Ruth and I think there's more to this cult than Mars worship. I don't know what it means yet, but there are factors at play we don't understand. Please be safe.*

"Well, that would've been nice to know about an hour ago." She snapped the phone shut, thinking, *Ruth, huh? I guess that's where you went.*

"What?" Philippe asked hopefully.

"Theo figured out it wasn't a Mars-worship cult about the same time we did."

"Then what is it? *Who* is it?"

"I have no idea. But we have to stop them from killing Martin." She tried to sound confident.

From the back of the boat, Paul gave a bitter laugh that sounded like her own. "How? They just summoned an earthquake, a tsunami, and a maelstrom. Even Poseidon himself doesn't have that kind of power anymore."

Selene had to admit the thought was disconcerting. She'd regained her own power over the tides briefly at the climax of the Classicist Cult's ritual, but her resurgence had been both fleeting and dangerous, brought about only by a week's worth of human sacrifices.

"This is the Age of Man." Flint didn't look up from the tablet in his hands, and the roar of the engine nearly drowned his muttered words. "They have more power in this world than we ever did in ours. They remake the earth itself every day...why not harness earthquakes? What're my volcanoes to their atomic bombs?"

"I thought you said only a man elevated to immortality could use our weapons!" Selene flared. "*Now* you tell me differently?"

He shrugged. "I told you what I thought was true. But what do any of us know anymore of the powers we once held? Maybe some priest granted them the ability to use our weapons—or maybe they simply seized the power for themselves. Who knows?"

Selene could barely restrain herself from yelling at him. Yelling at them all. Is this what they had become? Useless? Helpless?

"What about you?" she demanded of Dash. "Please tell me you're heading to Manhattan because you've got a feeling that's where they took Martin. Or have you also decided you have no idea what to do?"

Dash had pushed his thick-rimmed glasses onto his forehead so he could see more clearly in the ocean spray. The lack of his spectacles should've made him look younger. But new lines carved his mouth, and exhaustion hollowed his cheeks. His legendary cap lay on the dashboard beside him. When he replied to her, he didn't smile. "Sorry to disappoint. I'm just heading back so we can get warm, regroup, try to plan our next move."

Philippe rose to his feet. "You're giving up? You're just going to let them take my father? *Kill* my father?" His usually light tenor deepened to something black and fierce. For the first time since Selene had known him, he sounded like Mars's son.

Dash snapped back at him. "You want to wander in circles around all of Manhattan, New Jersey, and Staten Island, hoping we stumble upon an invisible boat? They could be *anywhere*. I'd rather go somewhere with room service and wait for Flint to fix the tracking device."

"Dash, you're the *Messenger*," Selene insisted, for once agreeing with Philippe. "You bring word to the gods no matter how far we roam. *Surely* you can locate Martin."

"I've got a cell phone," he said. "One that's currently shorted out and full of salt water. I've got no supernatural telepathy or magical homing beacons, if that's what you're asking. I keep track of you all because it's my job, not because I've got some magic ability for it." His eyes wandered to the golden cap, its wings of bronze and silver limp and dull. "Even the strongest of us has lost everything."

She suddenly knew that he'd tried it on while she'd been talking to Paul—and it hadn't worked. A thanatos could fly. A god was earthbound.

"Dash is right," Flint growled. "You all just need to give me some time."

Philippe tensed. "How do I know you don't want my father to die?" he demanded. "You hate him."

"So do you," Flint said with a strange, cold calm.

Philippe nodded. "But I always wanted a chance to love him."

Flint turned back to his electronics before he said, very low, "So did I."

Selene knew what they had to do. Dash's plan to return to their last hideout was absurd—if the cult had known how to find both Hades and Mars, they would no doubt be able to track the rest of them to the city's most glamorous hotel. And as much as she shared Philippe's sense of urgency, she also knew they probably had some time to spare. Hades had been kidnapped days before the cult murdered him. If they planned something half as elaborate as the *Charging Bull* scene for Mars's sacrifice, then they'd need time to set it up. Besides, they'd killed Hades in the dead of night, when there would be fewer witnesses to deal with. She checked the position of the moon—it was just past seven o'clock. The city would still be roiling with Christmas shoppers until much later. Even if the cult struck tonight, it wouldn't be for many hours yet.

"Take us up the East River, Dash," she said finally. "Remember your favorite hidey-hole from the 1920s? No one would ever think to look for us there; we can hide until Flint gets the tracking device working again."

"Aye aye, Huntress." Dash turned the wheel, angling away from Lower Manhattan.

Selene rejoined Paul, sitting down heavily beside him on the floor of the boat. Chilled to the bone in still-wet clothes, exhausted from the swimming and fighting, she inched a little closer to her twin. He might be growing weaker, but he still radiated a subtle heat that had already dried his own clothes and hair in a manner her own natural chill could never manage.

"Are you all right?" she asked him softly. He still looked pale and shaken. He didn't answer her, only laid an arm across her shoulders and pulled her close to his warmth. Suddenly, she was no longer taking care of him—he was taking care of her.

A few minutes later, the boat came to a sudden, bobbing halt. She extracted herself from Paul's embrace. Before her lay a thickly wooded island. In the distance, a few brick buildings poked above the treetops, their roofs caved in, their walls crumbling.

"Where are we?" asked Philippe.

"North Brother Island," she replied. "Not far from the Bronx. Used to be a quarantine hospital, but it's been a bird preserve for decades—mankind strictly prohibited. We wanted isolated, right?" She'd never bothered to visit before—she didn't have access to a boat and there were no ferries or bridges to the island. She knew about it only because she made it her business to keep track of the city's last remaining scraps of wilderness.

"Sadly, no dock," Dash said with a sigh. "So we'll have to get wet. Again."

Selene jumped off the boat and into the chest-high water.

There's something solemn about this place, she thought, as her feet sank into the soft sand of the riverbed. She trudged toward shore past the rotting remains of a pier. *I should revel in its return to wildness, but there is such decay here, such sorrow, I can barely breathe.*

Even more than Grossinger's in the Catskills, the island made plain the damage that time could wreak on gods and man alike. *Why are we drawn to these places?* she wondered, thinking of Mars in his abandoned fort, Hades in his defunct subway station, Hephaestus in his derelict resort. *To remind us of our own inevitable decline? Or to assure ourselves that mankind's work is ephemeral, while we're eternal?*

She had the sudden impression that this place was more than just a long-abandoned island. That she walked through a time far in the future, when men had perished entirely from the earth, and nature had reclaimed their vast cities. In the moonlight, she could see the vines overrunning the walls, the grass and bushes covering the streets. The very curbs had rotted into the soil, and wind and rain had washed the letters from the signs. She felt herself slipping once more into a waking dream when Philippe's voice snapped her back to the present. "How do you know where you're going?" he asked Dash, who strode confidently ahead through the darkness.

"Bootleggers used it in the twenties. Whole island of tuberculosis victims—perfect place to hide our contraband from curious eyes."

"I thought you were a cop in the twenties. You and Selene."

Dash grinned at the younger man. "Bootlegger. Cop. In the twenties, it was all the same."

Selene couldn't share in Dash's sudden return to confidence. Nor could she summon her usual indignation at the idea that while she'd been working to prevent crime in her city, her brother had been fomenting it. She was more concerned with her twin. He'd stopped in the middle of the path, his eyes unfocused. His hands, his beautiful long-fingered hands that could strum a lyre with such delicate grace, trembled at his sides like an old man's.

"Sunbeam?" she said, touching his elbow.

He jerked toward her as if startled from a dream. "Huh?"

"Were you having another vision?"

He swallowed, and when he spoke, his voice shook. "I feel like I'm drowning in the past. I fight against the memories, but they hold me down until something breaks me free."

Selene's skin prickled, remembering the memory of the Diaspora that had come upon her with the steady, crushing force of the tidal wave.

"They've got Morpheus's crown," she said. "That's how they're plaguing you. You've got to fight it, Paul. Just like you'd fight any other weapon."

"You say that like it's easy," he groaned. "I've always tried to move forward. This getting drawn into the past—it's killing me."

"What did you see?" She half expected him to echo her own vision of the last Great Gathering.

But Paul surprised her. "I saw myself, here, on this island. A century ago at least." He spoke hesitantly. "I didn't want to be the Plague Bringer, my arrows killing with disease. I tried to be the Healer instead, treating children in the typhus ward. I couldn't cure with a touch anymore, but I knew how to make a child feel better, to bring them hope. Yet when we stepped ashore just now, I didn't remember my patients safe in their beds—I saw a vision of children wandering the beach instead. Wet and scared and motherless, their hair singed and their cheeks smeared black." His eyes grew distant, as if seeing once more into the past. "The steamboat was only twenty yards offshore, a fireball still, listing to the side and about to disappear completely. We ran into the water, all of us, nurses and doctors, to try to save them. So many that couldn't swim. Over a thousand people in their Sunday best, headed to Long Island on a picnic."

Selene suddenly understood. The fire aboard the steamship *General Slocum*. The deadliest disaster in New York City history...until September eleventh. She'd lived far away in Greenwich Village at the time, unable to aid in the rescue. She'd never known her twin had seen it all.

Paul went on speaking as he walked slowly down the path. "The mothers screamed in German, 'Spare my child. Spare my child.' They put life preservers on their babies and tossed them overboard...and they sank like stones. The ship owner had stocked the boat with rotted life jackets. Rotted fire hoses. The pleasure yachts on the Manhattan shore wouldn't come help. The lumberyard at 139th Street wouldn't let them dock, for fear their wood would catch fire. And so the ship wound up here, with the winds down the channel fanning the flames."

Selene wanted to tell him to stop, but he chanted the story like a Greek chorus, bringing the images to life as only the God of Poetry could. "I saw a man jump overboard and get caught in the paddlewheel, blood flying. I saw a boy climb the flagpole on the bow and perch there as the flames got higher before letting go and plummeting into the inferno. And I saw the bodies. Hundreds of them. Mostly women and children, washed ashore right here. And I...a god...a healer...could do nothing to help." He came back to the present, his eyes bright with unshed tears. "My paltry efforts to help a few sick children—what did they matter in the face of such carnage? I was like a boy plugging a dam with a finger while the whole structure collapsed around me. So I left. I gave up my life in medicine. I became a musician instead. With no pretensions of healing the world. No pretensions of mattering at all."

"Don't say that." Selene struggled for something encouraging to say. In truth, she understood her brother's despair. "Your music *is* healing, Sunbeam. In its own way."

He snagged his lower lip between his teeth as if to stop its trembling. "My songs are passing fancies, just like gods. Remembered and worshiped for a month, a year, a decade even...then forgotten as if they never existed. Mortals' memories are weak—and so are ours. I'd forgotten the *Slocum* until today. Such horror, such pain...did any of it matter? Those people on the Staten Island Ferry...they'll be forgotten, too. And so will I."

"What about your great love? What about Sophie?" she asked, desperate to break through his sadness.

"Sophie." He said the word slowly, like an incantation. "Yes. A bright flame of beauty amid the fog." He seemed to hearten a little, but then a shadow crossed his face again. "Extinguished so soon. So soon..."

He walked faster, as if to escape from her concern. She let him go, unsure how to help, wishing she had Theo's gift of knowing what to say.

She hadn't realized how much she'd slowed her pace until she sensed Flint hobbling beside her. She could feel his eyes on her before she could wipe the expression of anguish from her face. She kept her gaze on Paul, who walked alone, his arms clutched across his chest. "I'm worried about him," she said in an undertone.

Flint's thick brows drew low above his dark eyes. "I'm worried about us all."

Dash led the Athanatoi straight to the Tuberculosis Pavilion. Leafless winter vines covered its brick facade—in summer, jungly growth would hide the entire building, but in the depth of winter, it lay revealed. A circular four-story tower stood in the center, its large windows mostly broken, but much of its art deco brickwork still intact.

Flint made a hasty torch from some fir branches and a jar of black goo he pulled from his duffel—none of the other gods shared Selene's gift for seeing in the dark.

Holding the torch, Dash took them through the front entrance, its wooden door long since rotted away, up a rickety staircase, and into a top-story room in the central tower. Paul took the one chair, sitting with his hands clasped in his lap. Flint settled down awkwardly on the ground, his gadgets, both electronic and mechanical, spread before him. Philippe paced in nervous circles, watching his stepfather work.

Dash stuck the base of the torch into a gap in the floorboards and sat cross-legged, clucking. "The Four Seasons it's not, but at least it's dry. Wouldn't mind a bigger fire, though." He looked at Flint reproachfully.

The Smith only glared at him. "Then don't just sit there. Get me some firewood."

Dash rose to his feet with a dramatic sigh. "You know the problem with this family? We like ordering people around too much. But whatever the Smith needs, the Smith gets." He gave Flint a gallant bow. "I, for one, am actually adaptable. I'm off for wood. Come with me, Philippe, before you wear a hole through the floor." Philippe just shook his head distractedly and continued pacing. "Seriously, Phil, my friend," Dash insisted. "This whole place is about to collapse. Come on."

Selene followed them out, determined to find dinner.

Little game roamed the island—she found the prints of a family of raccoons in the snow, the only mammals intrepid enough to swim the river. But birds aplenty nested there, even in the winter. Nuthatches and finches hopped through the trees around her, more curious than afraid of the strange giant intruding on their peaceful idyll. She looked for bigger prey. A moonshadow on the snow drew her gaze upward, where a bald eagle soared effortlessly overhead, only its white head visible in the darkness. Some of the island's decay felt suddenly less threatening. This was a place of wild things. Selene took a deep breath of the frozen air, letting it brush away the lingering unease from her conversation with Paul.

She paced toward the shore, following her own tracks in the snow. There she spotted a pair of hooded mergansers. A single arrow took the male duck in his dramatic black-and-white chest. The chestnut-colored female fell only a few seconds later. She wished Hippo were there to retrieve them for her, but then reckoned her boots were already soaked through. Another dousing would do her no harm.

On the way back to shore, she noticed a bank of tall reeds at the water's edge. She sliced a few with an arrowhead and bundled them under her arm beside the ducks.

When she returned to the hospital, Flint had started a fire. Dash asked him if he was going to set the whole building ablaze—the Smith just gave him an angry stare.

"Sorry!" Dash chuckled. "I shouldn't question the God of Fire."

Flint's face brightened when he saw Selene's ducks. She skinned and dressed the birds quickly with the edge of an arrowhead while he carved a spit from a branch, and soon their dinner crackled above the fire.

The Athanatoi gathered around, holding their damp clothes toward the flames. As sensation rushed back into her feet, Selene welcomed the sharp needles of pain. Duck fat dripped and sizzled in the fire, and the meat warmed them all. It wasn't enough food to sate five normal people, much less gods with supernatural appetites, but it dulled the keen edge of their hunger.

Selene handed the reeds to Dash. "I thought maybe..."

"Say no more!" His eyes lit up, and he immediately began to cut them into shorter lengths.

Flint sat with the pieces of his phone spread before him, working by firelight with the small tools he pulled from his duffel. Selene kept her eyes on her twin, who stared blankly into the flames.

"Will you tell us what happened when you saw my father?" Philippe asked Paul. "Why didn't he try to escape? I've never seen him like that."

Paul glanced up—not at Philippe, but at Selene. "What's happening to Martin," he began softly, "is happening to me." His eyes flicked to the others around the fire. "I went into the castle, and a guard took me down many stories below the part the tourists see. Martin was sitting on the floor, his back to the wall, holding his spear in his hands and just...staring at it. He looked horrified. When I came in, he looked up and that's when

I saw—" Paul stopped and swallowed hard before he continued. "He was crying. He thought I'd come to save him. Before I could even ask about Hades, he started talking about the visions he'd been having. Flashbacks to Marathon, Thermopylae, Actium. And to Troy. That was the worst of all, he said. He'd forgotten the horrors, for war to him had only been glory and bloodlust. But now he could not banish the memory of the night Odysseus led his men from the wooden horse to sack the city. Blood ran in torrents. All the earth lay drenched."

Paul slipped into the ancient rhythms, his words echoing the tale as poets had told it for millennia. "The Trojans wandered in wretched plight around their homes, and with groans unutterable crawled amid the corpses. And all about the city dolorous howls of dogs uprose, and every home rang with the cries of women, like to the screams of cranes, which see an eagle stooping on them from the sky and scream long terror-shrieks in dread of Zeus's bird."

Selene felt herself drawn back to that night of horrors, when all the gods of Olympus witnessed the gruesome consequences of their hubris. Around her, the others sat silently as Paul finished his tale. "The wine left in the mixing-bowls blended with blood. The fire-glow mounted upward to the sky, the red glare spread its wings over the firmament...and all the city sank down into hell."

Tears ran down Paul's cheeks. Selene felt the sting of grief in her own eyes. "You see," her brother said, coming back to himself. "For the first time in all his life, Mars saw war from the victims' eyes. He looked at his spear not as an instrument of strength, but as a symbol of his own savagery. And he no longer wanted to live. When the men in black armor burst into his fortress, Mars handed them his spear himself."

"But they were just visions forced on him by the cult," Selene said, explaining to the others about Morpheus's crown.

"Perhaps," Paul said with a weary nod. "But that didn't make them any less true."

Silence fell once more. Philippe's face was carved of stone, as if he dared not allow any emotion into his heart. Flint kept his focus on his tools, still tinkering with the tablet in his hands. And then, after a long moment, Dash began to play the reed pipe he'd fashioned. Not a simple shepherd's tune, but a melody Selene only dimly remembered. Only once Paul began to sing along did she recognize it. The *Hymn to Ares*.

Ares, chariot-rider, golden-helmed, shield-bearer, harnessed in bronze,
*   mighty with the spear,*
O defense of Olympus, sceptered King of manliness,
Who whirls your fiery sphere among the planets in their sevenfold
*   courses,*
Hear me, helper of men.

Paul's voice began softly, hesitantly, as if he barely remembered the words. But it grew in strength as the song drew to a close.

Shed down a kindly ray from above upon my life,
That I may drive away bitter cowardice from my head.

She knew the prayer came from his heart. And though Mars would never hear the words, they seemed to help. Paul dashed the tears from his eyes and looked imploringly at his sister. "We have to find him. Before it's too late."

He spoke with a sudden certainty—as if he were the God of Prophecy once more. She wondered suddenly if she'd been wrong—could the cult really kill Mars tonight? What would that do to his son? His brother? What would it do to her city?

She glanced out the window, where the moon had started its descent: It was already after ten. Just as she'd begun to worry that all hope was lost, a loud pulse issued from Flint's hands. A red flash shone on his suddenly grinning face. "I found him."

Philippe gave his stepfather a wan, relieved smile. "*Voilà!* Who needs supernatural telepathy or magical homing beacons when you've got the Smith and some good old-fashioned twenty-first-century technology?"

Chapter 24

GOD OF
BLOODLUST

The massive Rockefeller Center Christmas tree towered over the ice rink, where the last skaters of the night glided arm in arm in lazy circles as the clock ticked toward midnight. The tree had grown for nearly a hundred years before men cut it down. Now particolored lights obscured its majestic boughs, and a heavy crystal star augmented its natural ninety-foot height. Selene turned her back on it and stared instead at the plaza's iconic central skyscraper, its soaring sides illuminated by floodlights against the night sky.

Flint looked up from his tablet in confusion. "The tracking device says Martin's up there somewhere."

"But where?" Philippe begged. "Hurry, Papa. It's almost midnight. What better time to commit a ritual murder?"

"I bet I know where he is," Selene said, a cold knot of dread settling in her stomach. "The *Saturday Night Live* studios, where Orion's cult murdered that young actress on live TV. Check the eighth floor." If they'd already taken Martin to such a public location, then there was no time to waste. It had taken them too long to get off the island, too long to find a place to dock the boat on the East Side, too long to make their way to Rockefeller Center.

But Flint shook his head. "Martin sure as hell isn't that close." His eyes traveled upward, from the building's main entrance all the way to its roof, nearly seventy floors above. "What's at the top?"

"The Rainbow Room," Paul answered. "I've performed there. Super classy spot with an amazing view. Used mostly for private events."

"Sounds perfect." Selene's pulse quickened. "No one to disturb the ritual."

Dash hummed thoughtfully. "As a frequent invitee to the city's most exclusive soirees, I happen to know you can't get to the Rainbow Room without taking a special elevator that's only activated by an employee, and the place is crawling with guards. No way we're getting anywhere without taking a few of them down."

Selene grabbed him, not bothering to be gentle. "No more innocent mortals will die tonight, got that? These are my people, I will——"

She stopped talking when a woman's shriek cut the air. She spun toward the skating rink. A brawl had broken out in the center of the ice: One man lay on the ground, a silent bloody heap. Another stood above him, pinning his wrists to the ground with the blades of his skates while a woman screamed and tried to yank him backward. On the other side of the rink, two teenagers held an older man by the elbows while their friend threw punches at his face. Three small children lay on the ice in a scrum, their parents trying in vain to pull them apart while yelling threats at one another. Security guards rushed onto the rink, made clumsy by the ice. An attendant in skates glided across more easily, but he was too scrawny to stop the violence. Selene stood, momentarily frozen in confused horror, before an NBC cameraman nearly bowled her over as he rushed to the edge of the rink, a well-coiffed man with a microphone on his heels. She heard the distant wail of police sirens, growing louder every moment.

She turned back to the skyscraper, her heart pounding against her ribs. The sudden convulsion of violence could have only one cause.

Without a word, she ran toward the entrance, trusting that her brothers would follow her. As they pushed through the revolving doors, the security personnel rushed toward the brawl, leaving the express elevator momentarily unguarded. The Athanatoi crowded in together, staring in silence as the numbers of the floors flashed by. They knew they were too late to save Mars. They could only hope they'd arrive in time to bring his killers to justice.

Selene knew there'd be cameras in the elevator. She couldn't risk taking out her bow, but the desire to arm herself was like a physical ache. Finally, the doors opened onto a shiny black hallway. A short set of stairs led to closed double doors—the Rainbow Room's main entrance. Paul pointed to a smaller unmarked door nearby. "That leads to the musicians' green room," he whispered. "It lets out onto a balcony that looks over the ballroom."

"Paul and I will go in from the balcony," Selene said quietly to the others as she assembled her bow. "Dash, you stay here and stop anyone trying to escape. Philippe and Flint, you take the main entrance."

She opened the door to the green room with her bow at the ready. She caught sight of herself in the wide mirror. Salt caked her skin and hair, turning the black strands gray and accentuating every crease in her face. For the first time in her long life, she looked like an old woman. She gripped her bow a little harder and hurried out onto the balcony.

The room stood empty. Below them lay a gleaming circular dance floor surrounded by soft silver carpet. Chandeliers dripped from the ceiling. Ribbons of crystal prisms hung in each massive window, but they did nothing to obscure the view. Manhattan flared brilliantly on three sides—the Empire State Building to the south, the Chrysler Building to the east, Central Park to the north. Selene's gaze took it all in in a heartbeat. Only then did she look directly beneath the balcony. From the room's main entrance, Philippe cried out at the same moment.

The God of Bloodlust lay sprawled naked on a banquet table, a pair of ram's horns strapped to his head and a great gaping hole where his heart should be.

Philippe stumbled forward and stood trembling beside his father's body. Selene raced down the stairs to the dance floor, Paul at her heels. Flint just stood frozen in the doorway, staring at his brother.

Selene sprinted a circuit of the room, darted into the kitchen, and back out into the corridor, scouring every inch of the sixty-fifth floor before returning to the ballroom.

"No one here," she reported to the others. "They must have left immediately after they killed him. There's got to be evidence here that'll help us track them, but I'd need a full forensic kit to pick it all up. Which means we need to call in an anonymous tip to the cops. We can't stay."

Dash looked pointedly at Philippe, who had laid his hands on his father's chest, as if to will him back to life. He wasn't crying, Selene saw, just shaking so violently that he could barely stand. Flint hobbled into the room and took his stepson in his arms. In his strong grasp, Philippe finally stilled.

"I didn't even know him," he murmured into the Smith's broad shoulder. "What Paul said about my father finally understanding the horror of what he'd done . . . I thought maybe Love and War could finally reconcile."

Selene spoke to the others with quiet urgency. "We've got to get the hell out of here." Dash stood with his eyes glued on the body, all merriment gone, but she could tell he heard her. Paul, on the other hand, had sunk into the nearest chair, his gaze fixed on the tall window, staring at his own reflection in the glass.

"When Detective Freeman calls me about the crime, I'll get back in," Selene went on, "but I want to make sure there's no evidence that will lead back to us." Dash nodded, donned a pair of gloves from his jacket pocket, and began to pick Philippe's stray hairs off the body. Mars's eyes were open and staring. A bright, crystalline gray. *Not unlike mine,* Selene realized with a start. She wanted to close them for him, but dared not.

"We should take Mars with us," Flint said, still holding Philippe. "To give him the proper rites."

"We can't," Selene said. "We'd never get out of here without being seen if we're hauling a body. And we need the cops to run tests to help us figure out who these killers are. If they're mortals, the police are our best bet to help track them down."

Once Hansen and her team arrived, Selene wouldn't be allowed this close to the body itself. She did her own quick examination. The wound in his chest had been carved with a sharp blade—maybe Mars's own spear. Only a divine weapon would have killed him so easily. His heart had been completely removed—all the arteries neatly severed. Blood had pooled out of the wound and flowed down his muscled rib cage like a curtain to soak the covering beneath. Not a tablecloth, she saw now, but a sheepskin. The ram's horns on his head made him look more monster than man.

She turned to the rest of the scene. Seven chairs had been placed along one side of the table, facing out across the room as if to take in the view. Crystal goblets stood at each setting, filled with water. An entire bowl of honeycomb sat in the center, crystalline and gleaming in its golden puddle. And on each plate, smears of fresh blood and scraps of raw meat. She bent close to sniff at it, terrified of what she might find, but it was only lamb's flesh, not a man's. Certainly not a god's.

She turned back to the body. From the red glisten of the hole in his chest, she could tell he'd died only minutes ago—just before the outbreak of violence on the skating rink.

Flint was reading from his phone. "There were riots and brawls all over Midtown. At least a dozen killed. Ripple effects from Mars's death. But now…" His voice trailed off and he looked up, meeting Selene's eyes. "They've already stopped. As if all the bloodlust and rage were simply a nightmare to be woken from."

No one said anything, but Selene knew what they were thinking. There was something pitiful in the ease with which mankind recovered from the death of a god. His murder unleashed a brief paroxysm of power, stronger than anything he'd wielded for a thousand years, and then…he was simply gone.

If I die, Selene wondered as she brushed their prints off the balcony railing and doorknobs, *will the world remember me for even that long?*

Chapter 25

SONS OF HERA

"What do you see, Professor?" Detective Freeman stared at Theo expectantly from across the banquet table in the center of the Rainbow Room.

I see a dead god, Theo thought. *Although I don't know which one. And more importantly, I don't know if he's the only one.* He'd never heard back from Selene after his text.

"Did you contact Ms. DiSilva yet?" he asked, trying to keep the panic from his voice.

"We left her a voice mail. You haven't heard from her?" the cop asked casually, but Theo could tell by the sudden narrowing of her eyes that she was curious about their relationship.

He shook his head, not trusting himself to say more. *If she got hurt, and I was off sulking at Ruth's, I'm never going to forgive myself.* After he'd left the Earth and Space Center, he'd spent the rest of the day in his office at Columbia, poring over the limited scholarship on Bronze Age religion until five in the morning.

When he'd finally taken a break to make some tea, he checked the *New York Times* website on his phone, more out of habit than anything else, and learned about the city's strange outburst of violent crime around Rockefeller Center. He'd known then that another god had died. Terrified, he'd called Selene's cell nonstop for two hours. When Freeman finally phoned to ask him to help investigate the murder of a *male* victim, he'd felt immensely relieved. But if Selene hadn't been killed in the cult ritual—where was she?

He forced himself to put aside his fears and look down once more at the enormous man sprawled across the table with his heart cut out. He lay on a sheepskin rug amid the remains of a feast. Not exactly the usual setting for a Roman altar.

"It doesn't look like any cult ritual in particular." He struggled to find something useful to tell Freeman. "Most of the foods are all typical of a Roman feast, but the raw meat generally points to Dionysian cult ritual—although there's no wine, so that doesn't fit."

"And the chairs?" she pressed. "Why are they all along one side? It reminds me of the Last Supper. But that's the wrong religion, obviously."

"I suppose," he said with a sigh. "Although they're all syncretic, so who knows? Anything seems possible at this point."

"And the ram's horns? The sheepskin?"

"Rams and ewes were common sacrificial animals." *An allusion to the myth of Jason and the Golden Fleece? Or more zodiacal symbolism?* he wondered. So far, he hadn't found a Bronze Age cult with an emphasis on astronomy, but the pieces Minh had laid out fit too perfectly to be mere coincidence.

"Whoever did this knew their way around a security system," Freeman went on, "There's no footage of these guys entering or leaving."

"Maybe the cameras just got busted during the earthquake?" Theo offered. He'd felt the shaking all the way uptown even though the epicenter had been five miles off the southern tip of Manhattan. The tidal wave never got above the Financial District. The Upper West Side remained high and dry.

Freeman shook her head. "If it was from the earthquake, then they were extraordinarily lucky, because the only cameras that are broken are the ones in the elevators and those from here to the rooftop."

"What about the staff?"

"Nope. Our killers rented the room under a false name and asked to do all their own catering. Insisted on coming up on the service elevator from the subbasement and asked that no one be present."

"And the staff *let* them? They didn't think that sounded, oh, I don't know, just a little bit like a human sacrifice cult trying to *get away with murder?*"

Freeman raised a brow at his tone, but went on calmly, "It's amazing what a hundred thousand dollars from an untraceable shell company can buy."

"Aw, Christ. So we're looking for a murder cult of millionaires?"

The detective laughed shortly. "This is New York City. Try *billionaires*."

She sobered immediately as Captain Hansen emerged from the kitchen entrance, scrawling notes angrily on a pad. When the older woman looked up to see Theo standing beside the detective, her face settled into a grim scowl. "You need to get off my crime scene, Professor. With the tsunami and the riots, we're under intense scrutiny right now. The last thing we need is a civilian slowing down our investigation."

"*Slowing down*—"

Hansen swung up a sharp hand to cut him off. She radiated fury, and Theo couldn't understand for the life of him why it was directed at him.

"We've got another pack of serial killers on our hands," she snapped. "And once more, we're way behind. Rock Center again? This is *clearly* the work of Everett Halloran, and yet you refuse to pursue that avenue. You've told us *nothing* that could've prepared us for this, and *nothing* that will stop it from happening again." She turned from Theo's stunned expression to glare at Freeman. "Who told you to call him?"

"Professor Schultz is a consultant—"

"Then send him a description of the crime scene, if you must, but he shouldn't be here. Not with his attitude."

"My *what*?" Theo's indignation quickly subsumed his astonishment.

Hansen pursed her lips stubbornly. "You're smarter than this, Professor. I *know* you've figured out more than you're willing to tell." Theo felt his cheeks turn hot. Could she put him behind bars for suspecting he was lying?

"You're holding back, and I don't know why," she went on, taking a step closer to him; he could smell the cigarettes on her breath. "I *thought* you wanted to help us."

"I've been researching all night," he said, fighting to stay reasonable. "I've made some progress, and I'm working on an astronomical angle, but this new crime scene just doesn't jibe with any cult I know about."

The captain nodded dismissively. "Fine. Thanks for trying. Now go home. Detective Freeman wasn't supposed to call you into the *first* crime scene. She certainly shouldn't have summoned you to this one."

"Then she shouldn't have called me either?" Selene stood before them, arms crossed, looking ragged and exhausted—and thoroughly pissed off.

Theo barely heard her words. He was too glad to see her alive.

Hansen's stern face melted into something closer to disappointment. "You don't need to get involved in this, Selene."

"A little late for that. Now, are you going to let me see the crime scene?"

"The police department's been doing a piss-poor job of protecting the city recently." A shadow flitted across Hansen's face, more grief than anger. "We need to limit our exposure to more criticism. So no, Ms. DiSilva. You can't come in here."

Selene looked like she was about to snarl, and for once, Theo had no desire to hold her back. He'd thought he'd finally found an ally in Hansen. "Why the change of heart, Captain?" he asked, trying to keep his own anger under control.

"We never solved the last case, did we? Never found Everett Halloran. And you've told me *nothing* useful about this one. So I'm sorry if Detective Freeman has wasted your time, but I don't intend to waste any more of my own." With that, she turned on her heel and left.

Freeman's face was a frozen mask of professionalism. "I'm sorry she spoke to you like that," she said finally. "The captain's under a lot of pressure." Selene said nothing, only turned to leave.

"But if you think of anything...you'll let me know?" Freeman called after her.

Theo followed Selene into the hallway. He couldn't help touching her shoulder. The stormy look in her eyes warned him against doing more.

"What happened?" he asked in a low whisper. "Who's the victim? He's an Athanatos, right?"

"Mars."

Suddenly, Theo noticed the family resemblance. Selene looked more like the God of War than she did like her own twin. They had the same handsome, bold features. The same thin mouth. Even their eyes were a similar color, although his were now a flat gray, while Selene's shone with her usual silver ferocity. "So he's not the Pater. He probably had nothing to do with the cult."

She nodded solemnly. "We got here too late to stop the murder. Too late to stop the brawling in the street. They say there are eight men dead. And four women." He heard an uncharacteristic shudder in her voice. "We don't know how it works, Theo. The ripple effect from our deaths. No one of Mars's power has ever died before, so we didn't know how bad it would be. We're playing with forces we don't understand, facing an enemy we know nothing about. I wanted this to be a fight between Athan-atoi alone—I wanted to protect my city. But we're destroying it, Theo. I can feel the cracks spreading. I can feel the foundations shuddering. I wanted to protect my family too. But they're dying. They're dying just out of reach." She closed her eyes then, as if she couldn't bear to witness any further destruction. All the fierceness she'd shown to the captain dissolved into a hopelessness that Theo had never seen before. He wanted nothing more than to fold her into his embrace, to tell her it was all going to be okay. But such words were mere platitudes. Truthfully, things might never be okay again.

They walked into the empty cocktail lounge at the end of the hall and stood by the windows.

"So Mars is dead... but you're alive," Theo said.

She looked at him, confused. "Yes, of course."

He forced himself not to shout at her, but to say very calmly, "When I didn't hear from you, I wasn't sure."

"Oh, Theo." And then, she did something utterly shocking. She apologized. Her face crumpled, and she buried it in her hands. She made no audible cries, but her shoulders shook. Then very softly, she murmured, "I'm so sorry. You must have thought..."

Theo looked at the wing of raven black hair that cupped her cheek, its white streak a reminder of all she'd sacrificed for him. He relented, taking her in his arms and pressing her close to his chest. Over the top of her head, he looked around at the luxurious surroundings, the elegant flower arrangements. *The world's least romantic date at the Rainbow Room,* he thought. Maybe someday they could come for dinner and dancing and be a normal couple, although that seemed unlikely for about a dozen reasons. But he could still dream.

"About the other night..." he said finally.

"You went to Ruth's," she said, pulling away. Not roughly, but purposefully.

"Yeah. She was the only—"

"Gabriela wasn't home?"

"She'd ask too many questions," he said quickly, although in truth he'd only ever thought of going to Ruth. He didn't really want to examine that decision more closely.

Selene just nodded, as if it were all the same to her, but Theo wasn't fooled. *She obviously wishes I'd stayed with my lesbian best friend rather than someone very single and very straight.* The thought heartened him. Maybe their argument at the Four Seasons could be forgotten. Maybe they weren't so different after all.

When Theo'd arrived at the Rainbow Room, the whole of the city had spread below them, rosy in the dawn light. But now yet another snowstorm had moved in. They stood in the midst of a cloud that shrouded the windows with curtains of white. Selene gazed out anyway, as if she could read something in the pattern of snowflakes that scraped across the glass.

"I was wrong to tell you to stop searching for the culprit," she said after a moment. "I was too eager to see the worst in the men in my family. Too eager to see the worst in *all* men, for that matter." She tightened her hand briefly on his, and he knew it was her version of an apology for her comparing him to Lars two nights before. It was enough.

He threaded his fingers through hers. "I've been doing some research anyway."

She gave him a small smile. "Of course. I don't know why I worried that you'd listen to me."

"It's all pretty confused so far, but if we talk it through together, it might start to make sense."

"Good. But let me go get Flint first. Paul and the others left, but he stayed with me all night on the observation deck while I waited for Freeman's call."

"Why?" Theo tried to ignore a suspicious twinge.

She sighed. "I don't really know. He barely spoke all night. But I think he won't leave until he knows the corpse has been removed respectfully. He might've spent most of his life hating Mars—but he was the only real brother he had left." Something akin to compassion flitted across her face. A rare emotion for the Relentless One.

She turned toward the elevator bank. Then she paused and said without looking at him, "Will you wait, Theo? Can you find that much patience for me?" He knew she was speaking of much more than the next few moments.

He reached for her hand and raised it to his lips. "You once said you'd waited for me for three thousand years. I think I can handle ten more minutes."

◦

Selene emerged from the elevator onto the sixty-eighth-floor observation deck. The tall glass walls cut the wind, but did nothing to stop the bitter cold from frosting her eyelashes. She breathed into her palms to warm her face and scanned the terrace. She peeked into the empty gift shop, where they'd spent the night in the relative warmth. No sign of Flint.

She'd gotten some sleep, but every time she'd cracked open her eyes, he'd been studying her with the same look of concentration he gave to the inner workings of a broken machine.

"Flint?" she called impatiently as she walked back onto the observation deck.

"Up here," came the faint reply. She headed up the staircase to the next terrace, then up once again to the very top of the building. A narrow roof bordered by art deco crenellations and silver telescopes. No protective glass walls here; the wind whipped her hair and burned her cheeks as she crossed toward the hunched figure at the roof's edge.

Flint rested his elbows on a stone parapet, his crutches leaning against the metal railing. A dying god at the edge of the world. *His only brother is gone. Does he grieve? Rejoice? Or is he merely realizing that he's one step closer to being truly alone?*

She felt her impatience ebb. He seemed so lonely, so somber. She couldn't help wanting to ease his pain.

Together, they stared out at the view in silence. The low-hanging storm cloaked the city below. Only the tops of the tallest skyscrapers emerged like mountain peaks from the clouds. The Empire State Building loomed before them like a god itself, its blocky mass illuminated in Christmas stripes, its antenna grazing another mass of clouds high above. To the east, the Chrysler Building pierced the heavens with its graceful spire. To the west, the Time Warner Center's two towers marked the corner of Central Park. As the wind stirred the clouds, she caught glimpses of the yellow red green of traffic lights cascading down the avenues, a city alive and bustling despite the snow. Then the storm shifted and the curtain of clouds hid it all from view once more.

My city's right there and yet I can't see it. Can't even hear it. She hadn't felt so divorced from her home in centuries. "It reminds me of the view from Mount Olympus," she said quietly. For all that she'd loved and protected the lands of her birth, she'd never really been *of* them; she'd been content to be an Olympian, watching from on high, unmoved by mortal cares.

"Olympus." Flint nodded. "How much do you remember?"

"Snatches. Images. But most is a dream."

"I have two clear memories. The one the poets tell of, when your father threw me off the mountain, and the one no one else remembers, when my brother... when *Ares*... picked me back up again."

It was more than he'd said all night. "Then it must be a strong memory indeed," she replied, "if it survived so many millennia with only your own mind to hold it in place."

"My mind?" He shook his head. "No, my mind barely comprehends it. But my *heart* knows the truth. It refuses to let go."

She understood: The gods all had their own twisted relationships with the past.

"Tell me about it." It was more a request than a demand. She knew so little of the man standing beside her. And so little of the man who had once been both Ares and Mars. So little of any of her kin.

"It was a day like this," Flint said slowly, gesturing to the blanket of clouds. "A heavy rainstorm hid the earth from view. I should've known then that the Sky God was upset." He paused, as if searching for the right words to tell the tale.

I'm probably the first person he's ever told it to, she realized.

"I remember sitting outside my mother's palace, too intent on the metal in my hands to notice the storm below. I must've been young. Merely a babe. But I was already making things."

Selene smiled. "Yes, I remember that about you. They call Dash the Busy One, but you were always tinkering."

"It was a necklace for my mother, I think. Loops of gold and pearls for the white-armed queen. Then *he* walked out of her palace. The Father of the Gods—but not of me. He slammed the great door behind him, and a thunder clap cut the air. He was so tall, and his eyes flashed like lightning. He shouted at my mother, furious that she'd dared to birth a child without the help of man's seed. Without *his* help. He grabbed me by the leg, and I dropped my work. The pearls scattered like raindrops across the ground. A few rolled off the edge and out of sight. He swung me like a discus. I must have screamed and cried. I must have begged for mercy. Asked forgiveness for the sin of my birth. But I have no memories of that."

I do, Selene remembered suddenly. His tale recalled images she'd thought long forgotten. The child Hephaestus, whirling through the air, his leg turning red above Zeus's grip and blue below, wailing in agony, desperate for help. She'd been a mere child herself, sure of her parents' love and content with her place in the world. She'd made no move to stop her father. No move to assist her stepbrother. Animals, maidens, and hunters were her responsibility, not this strange quiet boy more interested in tools than arrows.

"What I do remember," he went on, "is my mother. She wrung her hands, but did nothing to stop it. And behind her stood my glorious older brother, who'd only ever looked at me with disdain. Something crossed his face, an emotion I couldn't define.

"Then, with a snap of his wrist, Zeus let go." He spoke the name defiantly. "My leg cracked with the force of his throw. I flew through the air, through the clouds, through the thunder, into a storm meant for mortal men. A stinging, cold rain that soaked my clothes and chilled my bones. And still I fell. My leg hung twisted, useless, even as my other limbs flailed in distress, trying to seize the clouds to stop myself. But still I fell. Finally, I slammed into a rocky slope." He paused, his face hard. "I shattered the other leg with the impact."

Selene wasn't sure what to say. She moved her hand an inch closer to his on the railing, but dared not touch him.

"I passed out. For days, I think. Who knows?" He shrugged. "Years, perhaps. What did I know then of the passage of time? I dreamed my mother came to find me. Or even her husband. Perhaps Zeus would relent and bring me back to my rightful place atop the mountain. But when I awoke, it was Ares who stood above me, his hand extended. It was Ares who pulled two trees from the ground and ordered me to fashion crutches for myself. He was the only one who came for me."

A look of wonder crossed his face, as if he still couldn't believe it. Ares and Hephaestus, a god of destruction and a god of creation. Two halves of the same whole. And not unlike Artemis and Apollo, they loved and hated each other in equal measure. *But my twin and I have reconciled,* Selene thought. *Flint and his brother never will.*

"I was bloody, bruised, healing too slowly from the Sky God's wounds, but Ares didn't help me as I carved the wood into crutches. He just sat there, his gilded helmet in his hands, looking at his reflection in its surface. I thought he did it for vanity's sake. But then I recognized the expression on his face. The same one he'd had when he watched his father fling me from Olympus. It wasn't pity, or anger, or even disgust. It was confusion." Flint sighed deeply, and Selene detected grief for the first time. "My brother thought he understood the world and his place in it. God of War. God of Bravery. He didn't bother protecting the innocent. Innocents always die in war. He lived for bloodlust, for the slaughter of men in glorious combat. But when he saw me in his father's grip and realized that he was about to lose his mother's only other son, I think he felt something crack open. I was one innocent he couldn't bear to see harmed. Yet his mother stood by. His father wouldn't listen to reason. I think he recognized their cruelty in his own reflection, and for once, he didn't like what he saw." He grimaced, and Selene wondered if he spoke of himself in that moment. A god without beauty, who found no solace in his own image. "Last night, when my brother cringed beneath dreams sent by a mortal man...when he faced death at the point of his own spear...he must have had that same look. The world had changed around him. The rules no longer applied. And he must not have understood what lay before his eyes."

"We will avenge him. The murder of an Olympian will not go unpunished."

She meant her words as a comfort, but Flint shook his head. "That's what he would've wanted, I know. Blood upon blood until the world overflows with red. But it's not my way."

"It is mine," she said fiercely. "I bore little love for Hades. Even less for your brother. But each time they kill us, something goes out of the world. Some control or balance over the domain we ruled." She struggled to find the right words for something she barely understood. "I thought we had no real power anymore, yet perhaps some single thread remains, connecting us to our realms. Enough so that, without us, the thread is snapped, and the world shudders, rocks, and men and women tumble off into oblivion. Without Mars, the ranks of soldiers become marauding bands, bloodlust unchecked. Without Hades, the lust for wealth and the lure of death become so powerful that those seeking riches fling themselves from buildings when they lose their money. Whoever is killing us has no care for what our deaths do to the world. Who will they come for next? My twin? Dash? Maybe even you, Smith."

He gave a small snort of disgust. "I would not fight them if they came for me. No one missed me when I fell off the world the first time. They won't miss me if it happens again."

"*I'll* miss you." She grabbed his arms and spun him to face her. "How about that? You work magic with your hands—you, who have no magic left. Don't you realize what a gift that is to mankind? You can teach them to create with purpose, to find new answers to old problems, to bring beauty to the world, despite the beauty that has so long been denied you." She hadn't known the words were true until she said them.

He teetered a little in her grip, and only her magnified strength kept him upright without the help of his crutches. He grasped her forearms to hold himself steady. He was an inch shorter than she, but only because of his hunched back and bent legs. *If not for his fall,* she realized suddenly, *he might have been glorious.* Millennia of fire and soot had lined his face; millennia of rejection had coarsened his features. She wondered if he'd grown the beard to hide himself from the world. It did a fine job of it, disguising his expressions, creating the appearance of homeliness. But his eyes shone bright beneath his bushy graying brows, and as his lips parted, she discovered a surprising softness to his mouth.

He leaned forward, and she wondered, half stunned, if he meant to kiss her.

"Selene?" She spun toward the voice just in time to catch the look of concern on Theo's face before a careful mask of indifference descended across his features. "They took Martin away. And the cops are doing another search of the whole top of the building. I figured you didn't want them to find you guys up here."

Flint, leaning once more on the parapet for support, reached for his crutches without acknowledging Theo's presence. Selene was afraid to catch his eye, unsure of what she might see there. "Come," she said to him as she headed toward the stairs. "Your brother's killers are still out there." He didn't follow her.

As hard as it was to believe, vengeance did not move this man. But now she knew what would.

"I need you at my side, Smith. Don't ask me to do this alone."

She continued down the stairs without a backward glance. A heartbeat later, the tap of crutches echoed her steps.

Chapter 26

GOD OF THE ZODIAC

Selene caught up with Theo as he got into the elevator, then held the door until Flint could limp in beside them. What followed was easily the most uncomfortable ride of her life. They stood in complete silence, eyes averted. She'd asked Theo to wait for her, and yet he found her in another man's arms. Nothing had happened, but he must've seen the tension between them. Had it not taken less than a minute to travel sixty-eight floors, she might've tried to justify herself—but even if she'd been willing to stoop to such measures, she'd never found difficult words with ease. Still, Theo's expression discomfited her: She wasn't used to seeing him keep his emotions bottled up, pretending he didn't have a million questions.

They emerged onto Fiftieth Street and came to an awkward halt on the sidewalk amid the passing crowds of morning commuters. Flint stared at the ground. Theo looked east, then west, with studied casualness, as if trying to decide whether a bus or a subway would be his fastest way to wherever he was headed. *Does he come with me?* Selene wondered suddenly. *Or should I urge him to go back to Ruth's, where he'll likely be both safer and happier?*

Then Theo's face froze. "Selene," he said very low. "Don't look, but that man is—"

Ignoring his warning, she spun around. A man dressed in a bulky black overcoat stood under an awning halfway down the block. While the other pedestrians rushed from subway to office building, eager to get out of the cold, this man just stared at them. When he caught her eye, he turned quickly aside. But not before she recognized the widow's peak above his high fore-head—this was the hawk-faced man from Governors Island. Without another word, she started running toward him, push-ing aside the commuters in her path.

She wondered belatedly if he'd draw a gun on her. Or worse, use his poppy crown to send her reeling into her own memories.

She dared not pull out her bow, not with the street full of pedestrians, but she reached into her pack and broke the head off a wooden arrow, secreting it in her palm. She knew Theo would advise caution, but there was a time to steal up on your prey and catch it unawares, and a time to run it down relentlessly until it fell before you.

The hawk-faced man immediately bolted toward the tower-ing Christmas tree in the center of the plaza. He still hadn't pro-duced a weapon—no way was he hiding Mars's spear beneath his coat, and Hades' helm would be equally hard to conceal. But that didn't mean he wasn't dangerous. Still, she dared not cry out for help—she didn't want to alert the milling cops in the plaza.

Her prey had his own ideas about drawing attention to himself. He careened down the stairs to the Rockefeller Center skating rink—empty and bloody after the night's brawl—and jumped the glass barrier wall. He stumbled on the ice, sliding headfirst toward the exit. By then, Selene had vaulted onto the rink herself. She slipped and slid like a rookie on roller skates, all her vaunted grace deserting her as she crashed to her knees on the ice.

By now, the skate rental attendant was speaking into his walkie-talkie, no doubt summoning security guards to deal with the sudden intruders.

Selene resorted to crawling toward the fallen man. As he struggled to stand, she caught a glimpse of the tattoo on the back of his neck: a circle with a dot inside. She pushed herself forward with a grunt of effort and pinned him down before he could move any farther. She twisted his head so his cheek rested against a patch of bloodstained ice.

"Do you see what you did?" she hissed in his ear as she pressed the point of her arrowhead against the small of his back. "This is your fault. Now stand up before I slice you open." She dragged him to his feet even as the rink attendant raced toward them, his face red with indignant rage.

Suddenly Theo was beside her, sliding in an out-of-control circle before coming to a wobbly halt. Before the attendant could say a word, Theo let out a cheerful yelp. "Wow, Uncle Bob, a little overexcited about skating, huh?" he exclaimed to the hawk-faced man. Selene jabbed the arrow point a little harder, warning her captive not to respond.

Theo spoke to the attendant. "Sorry, man, he's got early onset Alzheimer's, you know, and he got it in his head that he was a twelve-year-old on his first trip to the city. We'll get off the ice and out of your way, okay?"

He turned to Selene and her captive. The hawk-faced man glowered back. "Come on, Uncle Bob, let's go get you some eggnog!" He waved cheerfully for them to follow and stumbled over to the railing, pulling himself hand over hand toward the exit. He looked back for a moment, as if remembering something surprising, and Selene followed his gaze to the golden Prometheus statue towering over the rink.

Selene dragged her captive along, a forced smile plastered across her face for the benefit of the woman behind the skate rental counter, who stared after them suspiciously. She felt someone else's eyes on her and glanced upward; Flint stood at the railing on the plaza level above them, clearly about to launch himself onto the ice, crutches be damned. *Stay there,* she mouthed at him. Getting off the ice without winding up in custody would be hard enough without her stepbrother sliding around beside them.

They made it through the locker area. Theo marched ahead into Rockefeller Center's lower concourse, threading their way through the commuters rushing to and from the attached subway station. He paused before an "Employees Only" door and raised an eyebrow at Selene. She kept one arm on the captive's elbow and the other on her arrowhead.

"Front pocket," she said, gesturing with her chin toward her backpack.

Theo reached in for her lock picks, then took hold of the captive so she could open the door. The room before them was a janitorial area, full of mops, buckets, and row upon row of brass polish. As soon as the door closed behind them, she pulled a length of wire from her pack and bound the man's wrists.

Then Selene slapped him hard across the face. "Who are you? Who sent you? What are you doing to us?" Even as the skin of his cheek burned red, he didn't speak.

"Wait, Selene," Theo was saying, but she didn't listen. This man was responsible for the capture of Mars, for the tsunami and the riots that had killed innocent mortals, for the fear that stalked her twin. He would speak, or he would suffer for it.

"Answer me." She twisted the man's arms, feeling the give in his shoulder socket. He winced, even let out a sharp yelp, but said nothing. "Why are you chasing us? Are you the Pater? Talk!"

Finally, a tiny smile pulled at his lips. "I speak to the Pater, for the Pater, but never of the Pater."

———⟨◇⟩———

"Selene!" Theo shouted again, putting a hand on her shoulder to stop her from ripping the captive apart. "Stop and listen!"

Her head snapped toward him. "Listen to *what*? He's not telling me anything!"

"Listen to *me*," he replied, exasperated.

"There's no time. This man knows everything. Look at the tattoo." She pulled down the man's collar to reveal a black circle surrounding a dot.

"That's the astronomical symbol for the sun," Theo said, his excitement growing.

"Exactly. The guy in the winged cap had a tattoo of the Mercury symbol between his collarbones. I killed a man on Governors Island with Mars and Venus symbols on his wrists. So if we can just get this guy to talk—"

"You asked me to be patient," Theo interrupted. "Now return the favor. I'm almost there, I can feel it."

She took a deep breath, as if controlling her rage took a conscious act of will. The captive's eyes moved from Selene to Theo. He looked unconcerned by his predicament. He'd made no move to cry out for help. He clearly wanted to keep the police away as much as Selene did.

Theo pressed on. "I've been trying to figure out what a bull, a snake, a scorpion, a feast, and two torches have to do with each other. And why a cult would pick Rockefeller Center, of all places, as a murder site. Then, on the rink, I noticed the gold oval suspended beneath the Prometheus statue—it's engraved with symbols of the zodiac."

"So..." Selene scowled impatiently.

"Ruth and I have a theory that the objects at the crime scene are all astronomical references. And now we know all the cult members have planetary tattoos. There's a connection here." He banged a fist lightly against his forehead to shake his thoughts loose. "The sheepskin upstairs. The ram's horns. The *Charging Bull* covered in blood." He felt the pieces slot into place. "When I spoke to Minh Loi at the planetarium, she said the first murder was a reference to the Age of Taurus six thousand years ago. But if these rituals are all about sacrifice, then Hades' death may represent *killing* the bull. So what if it refers to the *end* of the Age of Taurus instead?" He couldn't restrain the grin that pulled at his lips as the solution became clear. "That would place the scene around 2000 BC, the start of the Age of Aries the Ram. Last night they kill Mars and dress him in ram's horns—aka the Greek god *Ares* becomes the constellation *Aries.* Boom. End of another age, into the next: the Age of Pisces in the first century AD. Smack-dab in the middle of the Roman era." He gave a triumphant cheer. "*That's* why I couldn't tie the killings to any Olympian cult. At that point, the Romans were already turning to new religions, Eastern cults, even Christianity."

Selene looked thoughtful. "My father mentioned the Eastern gods at the last Great Gathering. Serapis, the Magna Mater, Mithras—"

"Mithras!" Theo had visited the remains of some Mithraic temples years before on a trip to Rome. Mithraism was a short-lived Mystery Cult religion, its secret practices known only to initiates. With no written sources to consult, modern scholars knew only what could be gleaned from analyzing temple ruins. But the one thing Theo remembered was that their sanctuaries always contained the same image: a bull sacrifice. "Yes, Selene! Mithras might work!"

At the mention of the god's name, the captive's eyes widened.

"Is Theo right?" Selene demanded of him. "If *you're* not the Pater, then is *Mithras*?"

"The Pater Patrum is a man like any man," he recited, his voice even.

Selene gave him a rough shake. "But are you *worshiping* Mithras?"

"We worship the true God," he said, maintaining the same unflinching calm. "And he will reign supreme once more—when Pretenders like you are wiped from the earth. He will come to you with his armies, and you will fall beneath his might."

"Yeah? Just try me, asshole." Selene punched him in the temple. He collapsed in her arms, unconscious.

"Great!" Theo chided her.

"I didn't mean to knock him out!" she shouted back. "I'll just wake him back up—"

"*Wait.* Let me think for a second." Theo tried to dredge up his foggy memories.

"Come on, Schultz," she said. "This is your *job*. You're telling me you've never studied this Mithras cult?"

"You're the one who was *alive* back then," Theo retorted. "How come *you* don't know anything about it?"

"I was a little too busy presiding over millions of my own worshipers to worry about a new god who had nothing to do with me."

Just a little narcissistic, as always, Theo couldn't help thinking.

Selene went on. "I don't think you're on the right track anyway. How can this be about some obscure Roman deity? Who would bother worshiping him if even a classicist like you barely remembers him?"

"Oh, I see. It can't be about Mithras because it has to be about *you*." Theo instantly regretted the vitriol in his tone. Some part of him obviously was still upset about seeing Selene in Flint's arms on the roof of Rock Center. He reminded himself that he hadn't seen anything more damning than a look of desire in Flint's eyes. It wasn't Selene's fault if her stepbrother found her attractive—what man wouldn't? "Look," he went on more calmly. "I've got to get somewhere I can do some research." Now that he finally knew what to look for, the answers would be easy to find. "Let's meet back up with Paul and the others and take a second to work through all this new information. When our captive wakes up, we can try interrogating him with a little more carrot and a lot less stick. See if we learn anything new."

He reached for the knob just as the door flew toward him, nearly knocking him in the face.

Two policemen stood in the corridor.

"Whoa there!" said the first, a young black man with a shaved head and the arms of a linebacker. "Hands up, buddy. You're breaking and entering on Rock Center property."

Theo tried to find a suitably confused expression. "Am I?"

"And what's wrong with that dude?" The cop nodded toward their unconscious captive.

"Our Uncle Bob here had a bit too much nog to drink, and the stuff just knocks him flat. We were looking for a bathroom to splash some water on him, and we must have wandered into—"

The second cop, a white guy whose double chin and rosy cheeks made him appear more Pillsbury doughboy than police officer, barked at Selene in a Queens accent, "Drop the man, DiSilva. We've got you on camera picking this lock. And don't try to talk your way out of this, Schultz. We know who you are."

Theo knew without a doubt that Selene was about to throw her captive over her shoulder and take her chances outrunning the two police officers. But for once, Theo felt his role as a thanatos would serve them well. Selene had no idea how to deal with mortal authority, while he'd been navigating it his whole life. "Calm down, everybody," he said. "If you know who we are, then you know this will all be quickly resolved if we talk to Detective Freeman or Captain Hansen." Selene shot him an angry glance, clearly still intent on keeping their captive for herself, but Theo shot one right back. He reached into the pocket of his coat. "Let me just call them—"

"Keep your hands where I can see them!" The linebacker put his hand on the butt of his gun.

"Hey, no need for that! We're consultants with the police.

And the man Ms. DiSilva apprehended may be an important witness in the murder case up in the Rainbow Room."

"Don't worry, he's coming with us, too," assured the dough-boy. He grabbed Selene by the elbow. "Now, like my partner said, drop the man. You're under arrest for trespassing, breaking and entering, and assault and battery." He drew his own weapon and pointed it at her. "And any second now, we'll add resisting arrest. Now release him."

Selene snarled, but dropped her captive. His skull made a dull thud on the floor.

"Put your hands in the air." The cop waved his gun at her.

"Go on, Selene," Theo said, trying to keep his tone light. "I'll talk to Hansen and get this all straightened out. Really, it's not worth getting shot over, is it?" From her glare, he could tell she disagreed.

The policemen cuffed Selene. They took her backpack, not bothering to open it. With a divine bow about to land in police custody, Theo needed to act fast. He slipped a hand surreptitiously into his pocket, fishing for his phone, but the linebacker cop pointed his gun at him.

"You aren't under arrest *yet*, buddy, but one more move toward that pocket and I'll put you there."

Theo seethed in silence while the cops herded the goddess and the cult member into the corridor and toward the concourse exit. Then he yanked out his phone. Hansen didn't pick up. Theo left a ranting message. Then he called Freeman.

"Detective, thank God I reached you. Look, two of New York's boldest just *arrested* Selene right when she was getting an eyewitness for you." He explained the situation. "You need to call them and tell them to let her go. This is clearly all a misunderstanding."

"All right, Professor. Let me take care of this. Hold on... No one called in anything. Did you get their names or their badge numbers?"

"I was a little busy worrying about the gun pointed at my head!" He wracked his brain. "I don't think…No, I'm sure of it. They weren't wearing name tags." Theo's heart sank. "That's not normal, is it?"

The hawk-faced cult initiate slumped against Selene in the back-seat of the police cruiser.

The doughboy cop looked over his shoulder at her. "You better not have hurt the Heliodromus Primus. That's going to land you in *real* trouble."

His partner snorted. "Hard to be in more trouble than she is already." He shifted his hands on the wheel, and his coat sleeves rode up. A circle and a cross peeked out from beneath his left cuff. The sign of Venus.

The other policeman—if that's in fact what he was—followed her gaze to his partner's tattoo. He gave Selene a wink and opened the collar of his coat so she could see the Mercury symbol emblazoned at the base of his throat.

"Welcome to the Host, *Diana*."

Chapter 27

RULER OF THE COSMOS

On the walk back to the hotel, Theo felt like a shard of iron caught between two magnets, trembling with the pull of the opposing forces that nearly shredded him apart. He wanted to be pounding down the door of the police station or trolling the streets looking for the "cops" who'd stolen Selene. But Freeman had assured him that the police were doing everything they could. "The previous victims have been men," she said, clearly trying to sound comforting. "So let's hope they're not planning to use Selene for one of their sacrifices. Maybe they just wanted her off their tail." Theo couldn't very well tell the cop that gender mattered far less to the cult than divinity. "The most helpful thing you can do," Freeman went on, "is help us figure out where they've taken her."

To do that, Theo needed to give himself a crash course on Mithraic scholarship. He knew such knowledge could be useful—he'd based his entire life on the idea that problems could be solved with patient research and investigation. Yet for once, he longed to be Selene: to beat the shit out of someone until they just told him the answers.

Flint, he knew, felt the same way. Theo'd found him still waiting for Selene on the plaza. Now he lumbered along, his limp
more pronounced than ever. He wouldn't meet Theo's eyes.

"You're mad at me because I told Selene to go with the cops,"
Theo said, deciding he might as well have it out with Flint
once and for all. The Smith just grunted. "You can't be more
angry about it than I am," he went on. "So why don't you stop
sulking and help me figure out how to find her?"

Flint's head shot up. He glowered at Theo. "I should have put
a tracking device on her the minute she came to my forge."

"That's a bit—"

Flint cut him off. "I should've come to her before. I should've
never let her be alone."

Theo felt his hackles rise, sure Flint was referring to more
than the skating rink. "She wasn't *alone*."

"She was alone for thousands of years."

"She *wanted* to be that way. I don't think you had any say in
the matter."

Flint grunted again.

"Why don't you just say what you mean?" Theo demanded.

"I knew her when she was full of joy and light," he said, his
voice husky. "I knew her when stags bowed at her approach and
her skin glowed brighter than the moon."

Theo laughed shortly. "Let me get this straight. You blame
yourself for her capture, because *you* should've been with her
instead of me—because you know her better than I do... maybe
even better than she knows herself." He didn't bother to disguise
his scorn. "And you wonder why Selene just stood there while
you mooned at her on the roof of Rock Center? Why she didn't
fall into your arms as you clearly think she should? Maybe it's
because you're a pompous ass who can't trust a woman to make
up her own damn mind!"

Theo picked up his pace, not feeling a shred of guilt for leaving Flint limping far behind. He had no energy left for pity, nor

even for jealousy. Whatever feelings Flint had secretly harbored for his stepsister all these years weren't Theo's problem. And if Selene felt anything in return—well, that was something he'd deal with when he rescued her. Until then, all that mattered was that she not turn up draped across some other New York City landmark with her heart cut out.

———◁◦▷———

"So you actually *told* her to go with the cops?" Dash asked, incredulous, when Theo related the story back at the Four Seasons. "You're lucky Paul isn't here. He'd lose what's left of his mind."

"I feel bad enough about that already, thanks," Theo said as he reached for his laptop. "Now can we please concentrate on rescuing her?"

Philippe had immediately moved to his stepfather's side. "Papa, I'm so sorry." He seemed far more concerned with Flint's feelings than with Selene's imminent murder.

So he knows the Smith is in love with her, Theo realized, unsurprised. That knowledge put Philippe's Cupid and Psyche story into a whole new light. *If he thinks he's going to scare me off a relationship with an immortal so that his stepfather can have Selene for himself, he's wrong,* he decided. *I'm going to find her, with or without their help.*

But it seemed he'd have little choice in the matter. Without asking permission, Dash attached a cable from Theo's laptop to the television screen so they could all see his research, then sat beside him on the couch, peering unnecessarily over his shoulder. "So the brilliant Makarites doesn't know how to keep Selene safe, but he's going to crack the cult, is that it?" He spoke lightly, and Theo couldn't be sure if he was being sarcastic.

"That's the idea," Theo muttered, trying to stay focused.

"Goody. Maybe if you figure out how to find this Mithras, Paul will forgive you."

"Where is he anyway?"

"He said we were nuts for coming back here—thought we'd

266 Jordanna Max Brodsky

be too easy to track—but he's the one who's gone mental. Kept fading off into hallucinations, as far as I could tell. So he left—going to hole up with his thanatos girlfriend, I bet. I'm sure he'll be in touch. I, on the other hand, decided that if they're going to kill me anyway, I might as well meet my death with a Dead Sea detoxifying treatment and a flat screen facing my marble soaking tub."

"Mm-hm," Theo said distractedly while he pulled up a photo from the Vatican Museum of a "tauroctony": the bull-killing scene found in every Mithraic sanctuary.

"There he is." He gestured to the marble statue of a man standing astride a bull's back. He had one knee on the animal's neck and a foot on its back hoof. "Mithras."

Dash squinted at the photo. "How come I don't remember him? I know *everybody*."

"He was worshiped for about three hundred years or so, right around the height of the Roman Empire," Theo said, skimming through an online journal article in another window.

Dash humphed. "Well, that explains it. Three hundred years is nothing. He might've never taken corporeal form. And look at what he's wearing—" He pointed to the god's soft, conical hat. "That deeply unfashionable headgear is a Phrygian cap. No wonder I didn't know him—he must be Persian." He sounded defensive.

"Yes and no, actually," Theo said as he continued reading the article. He felt himself slipping fully into teaching mode. *At least this is something I'm good at,* he thought. But it was small comfort when he envisioned Selene as the next sacrifice. He wished his talents lay with something a bit more heroic, like knife fighting or telepathy.

"The name 'Mithras' comes from an earlier Persian god, Mithra," he explained, "so the Romans always portrayed him in a Persian costume: baggy pants and a Phrygian cap. But besides the name, he's a wholly original creation." By now, Flint and Philippe had gathered around. The slim God of Love sat cross-legged on the sofa, nervously flicking the ash from a cigarette. Flint sat beside him, bending a piece of wire into ever tighter circles as if fashioning a lasso to reel Selene back into his arms.

Philippe pointed to the photo with the lit end of his smoke. "The hat is pretty similar to the wool stocking cap Hades was wearing when they sacrificed him."

"Yeah, the whole murder scene looks like a backward version of the tauroctony," Theo agreed. "A dead man on a living bull rather than a living god on a dead animal. That might relate to the liver divination I performed—"

"You *what*?" Dash asked.

"Long story. But the omens predicted there'd be some sort of reversal. Maybe this is it." He turned his attention back to the marble tauroctony and let out a small whoop of surprise. "Oh man, I had a feeling I was on the right track. But not *this* right. Check it out."

He pulled up a photo of the *Charging Bull* crime scene next to the image of the tauroctony statue. With his trackpad, he drew a bold yellow circle around the eviscerated dog, then a line to a carven image at the base of the Vatican Museum's statue: a hound standing on its hind legs to lick the bloody slash in the bull's throat. "There's our dog." Another circle, another line. "Asp at the crime scene. And look—a serpent in the sculpture, also licking the wound." He kept drawing. "Dead crow on Wall Street. Crow perched on the marble bull's back. Dead scorpion in the remains of the sacrificial fire. Scorpion carved at the Mithras statue's base."

"*Merde,*" Philippe swore, clearly impressed. "But what do they mean?"

Theo repeated Minh Loi's description of the shift of the equinoxes, the movement of the celestial sphere, and the placement of the constellations during the Age of Taurus. Thankfully, the

Athanatoi made better listeners than your average hungover college student. As he spoke, he scrolled through other online images of tauroctonies, stopping at a Roman bas-relief now on display in the Louvre. "Look at this one. Two torchbearers on either side of the bull."

"Damn it," Dash grumbled. "I don't recognize those guys either."

"Cautes and Cautopates," Theo read. "Cautes holds his torch facing upward. The other, Cautopates, points his toward the ground. That explains the torches found on either side of the *Charging Bull*."

Flint started to laugh. Theo had never heard anything like it. A wheezing hiss like air escaping from a volcano, followed by a sharp, explosive bark. He stared, dumbfounded.

Finally, Flint regained himself enough to shout, "If it's all this obvious, why the *fuck* didn't you come up with this sooner?"

Dash jumped in. "Hey, if you and Selene hadn't been so sure that Mars was behind all this—"

Flint glared at his stepbrother, the cheeks above his beard turning ember red. "The Huntress is only trying to protect *all* of us. She's the one putting her life at risk, captured by these *maniacs*, while you just flit off to meetings and spa days—"

"Hold on!" Dash protested mildly. "Who bought the speedboat?"

Flint snapped the piece of wire in his hand in two. His voice was full of menace. "How dare you joke about this. You always were a *mercurial* little shit."

Dash's smile slipped into something twisted and dark as he rose to his feet, towering over the seated Smith. "Keep talking, Lame One, and we'll see who—"

Philippe leaped up. *"Ne menace pas mon papa!"*

"Settle down!" Theo shouted in a voice he usually reserved for rowdy freshmen on the last day of classes. "Listen to yourselves! Even while I'm *proving* to you that this cult isn't about the Olympians, you *all* keep making it about yourselves. I know you've got several thousand years of baggage to gripe over, but could we *please* stay focused on the case at hand? Unless you *want* the Mithraists to kill off some more Athanatoi so you've got fewer relatives to yell at."

After a stunned beat, Dash applauded loudly. "Well said, Professor!" He sat back down, immediately jovial once more, and rested his chin on his hand in a pose of conspicuous concentration. "Now please, continue. I for one have no intention of winding up the victim of some cut-rate god's deluded acolytes."

"Um. Thank you." Theo glanced over at Flint, whose furious expression hadn't softened.

Philippe rested a hand on his stepfather's shoulder. "Recriminations won't get Selene rescued faster, Papa," he said quietly. "We're on the right path now, and Theo led us there."

When Flint didn't respond, Theo plowed ahead. "And if we're going to find out where that path leads, we have to understand where it started."

Dash nodded. "And why a group of mortals would want to travel down it again."

"That's what I've been trying to figure out. The man on the ice skating rink insisted his Pater Patrum was a man like any other—not a god."

"If he's not a god, how can he give mortals the power to wield divine weapons?" asked Philippe.

"I have no idea, but maybe he got it through Mithras."

Dash threw up his hands. "You're assuming Mithras exists! How is that possible? How could such a weak god still be hanging around?"

"His followers certainly didn't see him as weak," Theo insisted. "If I'm right, the Roman philosophers thought Mithras brought about the shift in the Ages—the movement of the equinoxes. He'd have to be a massively powerful deity to control the motions of the heavens themselves."

He pulled up two new images of the torchbearers: marble

statues found on Rome's Palatine Hill. "Look how the upward torchbearer is shown with a rooster, so he likely symbolizes both Day and Birth. The downward guy gets an owl, symbolizing Night and Death. And here"—he opened a photo of a fresco from a sanctuary in central Italy—"we've got a tauroctony with a head of Sol the Sun in the left-hand corner and Luna the Moon in the right. Those same images appear on sarcophagi of the period."

Dash huffed. "Sounds like a lifecycle thing, for sure."

Flint finally spoke. "Plato."

They all turned and stared at him.

"You don't remember Plato?" he asked grumpily.

"I didn't know him personally," Theo said dryly. "What about him?"

"I liked the mathematicians at his Academy," Flint explained, "so I sometimes visited. And I remember Plato had a theory about celestial spheres and the afterlife."

"Damn, that's right," Theo said, quickly turning back to his computer to confirm the details of a story he only dimly remembered. "The end of Plato's *Republic* is a fable about a man who ascends through seven celestial spheres after he dies—seven spheres for the seven celestial bodies recognized by ancient astronomers. Only then can he reach heaven. A god—like Mithras—who has power over those spheres would also have power over salvation. The idea survived for centuries, so it would overlap perfectly with the rise of Mithraism."

"Salvation? Heaven?" Philippe wrinkled his nose. "Sounds Christian."

"That's probably because Mithraism was popular at the same time Christianity gained a foothold in the Roman Empire," Theo explained. "Some historians even think the Christians based a lot of their theology on it—they call Mithras a proto-Jesus. Seems like they're both part of a general trend toward religions more concerned with the fate of the human soul than with placating a pantheon of gods. Either way, the two religions have a lot in common."

The gods fell silent. Finally, Flint heaved himself to his feet, tucking a crutch under each arm. "Then we dare not underestimate this god—or his followers. Christianity has wreaked more destruction on our kind than any weapon I've ever devised. Let's make sure this Mithras doesn't do the same."

"I couldn't agree more." Theo closed his laptop.

"We will not let them get anywhere near sacrificing the Huntress," Flint continued. Theo wasn't sure exactly when the Smith had become the leader of this little band, but for all his physical fading, it was suddenly clear he was in charge. "We will find where they're keeping her and strike there."

Dash nodded in agreement, but Philippe looked worried. "Papa, I know you want to save her." He lowered his voice. "I know how you feel about her. But these men have powers we don't understand. And how will we even find them in the first place?"

Flint turned his dark, piercing eyes on Theo. "You found Orion and his cult. Time after time, they eluded you, and time after time you tracked them down. You can do it again."

"Absolutely," Theo said, although he had no idea how. With Selene's life on the line, he'd find a way.

Flint looked at each god in turn. "We chop off head after head, but another grows in its place. We've killed two of their men, yet still they keep coming. The only way to kill a hydra is to stab it through the heart. We find the Pater Patrum. We kill him. We free Selene *and* end the cult once and for all."

Dash whistled. "Sounds very bold. I assume from your tone you've got a plan to accomplish all that?"

Flint nodded.

"Et bien," said Philippe with a sigh, "I hope it's better than your last plan, where we all nearly drowned and my father *still* didn't make it."

"Oh, don't worry," Flint said. "This time, we're sending the professor in first."

Chapter 28

CHAINED ONE

Selene awoke facedown in a cold, bare cell. Cheek pressed against the concrete, she blinked in the harsh light bouncing off the white walls, trying to recall how she got there. The last thing she remembered was dying.

After she'd realized the cops who'd arrested her actually belonged to the cult, she'd cursed expletives creative enough to make Dionysus himself blush. The "cops" had pulled their cruiser into a parking garage not far from Times Square and told her to get out of the car. She'd refused, of course, but the linebacker cop pulled her last divine arrow from her pack and held its golden tip to her throat. She had no choice but to obey. He told her to turn around and get down on her knees.

They won't dare kill me here, she told herself as they forced her to the ground. She couldn't conceive that her death would be as pedestrian as a gang-style execution in a dank parking garage. Surely there'd be incense and chanting and some sort of ritualized dance at least! And then, even as death lurked a step behind her, she nearly laughed aloud at her own egotism. *Theo said I try to make it all about me. Here I go again. I'm probably not important enough to serve as their sacrifice.* She heard a gun cock. *I'm finally going to find out if a bullet to the brain can actually kill me.* She had the sinking suspicion that it might leave her permanently paralyzed instead. *Will I still crave immortality if it means an eternity as a quadriplegic?* she wondered. Then a gunshot echoed against the concrete walls, and a sharp pain pierced her back, right between her shoulder blades. Seconds later, all went black.

Now, unless she'd been sorely mistaken about the afterlife all these years, she was very much alive and still able to feel all her limbs. The cell, however, seemed its own version of hell. No toilet, no bed. A single small grate high overhead allowed a thin stream of air. Beside it, a recessed fluorescent light. The steel door had no window, no knob, no visible hinges.

She sat up gingerly, trying to reach her own back to feel the gunshot wound, and realized she wore only a thin hospital gown. On a smaller woman, it might've provided some modesty; on her it came only to mid-thigh. *They saw me naked,* she realized, rising from the ground with strength born from fury. She slammed her palm against the steel door. Once, twice, as if she could smash it apart by sheer force of will. *I will find them, I will turn them to beasts, I will rip them limb from limb for their offense.* But the wound on her back burned when she raised her arm, and the door didn't budge.

She sank back onto the cold floor, her rage dissolving into helplessness, and felt again for the bandage between her shoulder blades. It was far too small for a wound that had knocked her senseless—unless the bullet had actually been a tranquilizer dart.

A narrow food tray slot slid open near the top of the door. She sat up immediately, the movement sending a sharp pain down her spine. *Maybe at least they'll feed me,* she thought.

Her voracious appetite hadn't been sated since lunch at the hotel before the excursion to Governors Island, and her stomach growled in anticipation. *And if they stick a hand through far enough,* she decided, *I'll just grab it and drag the bastard through the slot, no matter how narrow it is.* But before she could even stand up to look through the opening, the slot slid shut with a clank. Almost immediately, another panel opened at the base of the door and a metal object slid through.

A circular bronze disk with a handle. She made no move to reach for it, worried it would start spurting poison gas or turn into some sort of attack robot. But once she decided Theo's sci-fi movies were warping her brain, she reached for it with her bare toe and dragged it closer.

The handle had been cast in the shape of a naked goddess, one knee cocked forward, her breasts tipped with golden nipples. Etched flowers, seashells, and doves adorned the disk itself. The symbolism instantly raised her suspicions; she couldn't resist flipping the object over to see if they were correct.

Aphrodite's hand mirror. Just as she'd feared. Made by the Smith as a present to his wife on their wedding night. So iconic that it became the basis for the Venus symbol that signified both the planet and all womankind—and now, somehow, it was in the hands of a cult that, according to Theo, worshiped a different god entirely.

"Is this so I can fix my hair?" she demanded of the empty room, hoping her captors could hear her. "Very thoughtful, but you must be confusing me with some other goddess who gives a shit." She picked up the mirror nonetheless and looked at her reflection in its polished bronze surface.

She nearly screamed.

The face she saw was not her own. An old man, nearly bald, his white hair floating in a wispy combover above his age-speckled scalp. Wire-rimmed glasses balanced on a pointed nose. Loose wattles of flesh hung from his neck. His lips, thin and colorless, pursed in an expression of confusion and dismay. She recognized him only when she noticed his green eyes.

"Theo?" she whispered.

The man in the mirror didn't respond. He just stared blankly ahead.

Then the image shifted. The background came into focus. A log cabin, sparsely furnished, the rugs worn with age. And a woman, tall and lean, black-haired, bent over a stove. She clattered a pan, cursed loudly, then threw a piece of crockery across the room. It smashed against the far wall; white liquid oozed down the logs. A bowl of soup, perhaps, or batter. The woman turned toward Theo.

She has my face, Selene saw with a start, *but not my name. I'll be someone else by then. Ursula maybe, for the bears. Or some other version of an old epithet. Lucinda for the moonlight.*

As the woman came toward Theo, Selene could see the fan of wrinkles around her eyes and the scowl line on her brow, more pronounced than the one she currently bore. Older, certainly, but not by much. Theo was in his eighties at least. The future version of Selene threw down a new bowl in front of Theo and stormed away, her face twisted into a furious, self-loathing sneer.

Theo moved his lips into a vague "Thank you." He had no teeth.

Selene dropped the mirror to the ground with a clatter.

——◇——

Theo sat on the couch with his head in his hands hours after Flint had finished explaining his incredibly elaborate proposal for rescuing Selene.

Philippe sat down beside him and started rubbing his back in desultory circles.

"Um..." Theo stammered. "I'm okay."

Philippe ran a hand up to the back of Theo's neck and massaged gently. "You look tense."

"Well, yeah, I'm supposed to figure out where the cult's ultra-secret hideaway is before the next sacrifice, so I guess you could say I'm tense." *And you coming on to me right now is* not *helping matters,* he wanted to say. *I'm trying to rescue my girlfriend, and you're acting like I'm already single.*

"It's okay," Philippe soothed. "It's past midnight already, and Dash and Flint have been monitoring every police scanner and TV news station in the city. No word of any strange outpourings of hunting-related emotion. So she's still alive. If they keep the same pattern of late-night murders going, then we've got at least another day to find her."

Theo nodded wearily and felt his shoulders relax in spite of himself. His mind, which had whirled with images of planets and stars and fiery gods for hours—not to mention Selene covered in blood—finally calmed and centered itself.

Philippe lifted his hands. "Better?"

"Yeah, actually."

"Where are you so far?"

Theo reached for the pad of paper where he'd scribbled his ideas. "Mithraists call the leader of each branch of the cult 'Pater,' and there are various ranks underneath him. The Pater Patrum that our captive mentioned is the 'Father of Fathers,' presiding over the entire religion. All we know about the traditional temple—a mithraeum, it's called—is that it usually looks like a cave. Sometimes they really were caves, sometimes just secret underground chambers. We already sent Dash to check on the cave in Central Park—it's empty. The city has an incalculable number of secret underground spaces, so that doesn't help either."

"There must be something more specific about where they like to put these temples of theirs."

"At the cult's height, there were upward of seven hundred mithraea in the city of Rome alone," he read from his notes, speaking quickly. Philippe might be right that they had another day to work—or he might not. "Unlike other Mystery Cults, the members were all male—and most were soldiers. So wherever the Roman legions went, the cult followed—there were even mithraea as far away as England. Then, in the fourth century, the execrable Holy Roman Emperor Theodosius destroyed them all. The Christians often built churches on top of the old sites just to prove their superiority. So I thought maybe our new Mithraists would put their temple under a church, but since there are *thousands* of churches in New York City, that's a dead end." He resisted the urge to crumple up his useless findings and toss them in the trash.

"Okay, what about finding the location of their next ritual instead and ambushing them there?"

Theo flipped to the next page on his pad. "I've been matching up what we've seen so far at the crime scenes with the archeological evidence from the mithraea. We know very little about Mithras himself, but it looks like the cult's rituals are reenacting the events of his life. The murder at the *Charging Bull*, of course, represents the tauroctony—Mithras's famous killing of the bull. The food laid out at the Rainbow Room corresponds to a ritual banquet where Mithras feasts with Sol the Sun—it's like an after-party to the original sacrifice."

"What else?" Philippe prodded.

Theo opened a photo of a statue of Mithras emerging from a large round chunk of stone. "Could be a dramatization of Mithras's birth. But we don't know whether he supposedly sprang out of a rock in a cave or an egg in a cave. Or an egg-shaped rock in a cave. See? Not that helpful."

Philippe tutted. "And lazy mythology. The egg thing sounds like Helen of Troy."

"There's another event in the god's life that's mentioned very briefly in a few Roman texts: They say Mithras participates in the 'Procession of the Heliodromus,' or the 'Sun-Runner.' Whatever that means. Maybe it's a reenactment of the sun's orbit. And I've also found some evidence for our salvation idea, because some sources claim that Mithras ascends to heaven in Sol's chariot—hence passing through the celestial spheres. But unless the cult is planning to sacrifice someone at Cape Canaveral, I'm not sure what the modern parallel would be for that."

"When you say Sol, you mean Sol Invictus?"

"Yup. The Roman 'Invincible Sun.' He had his own popular cult in the Imperial Era, remember? They based it around his birthday: December twenty-fifth, when the Romans observed that the days began to lengthen again. In Mithraism, Sol Invictus is both a secondary deity and another epithet for Mithras himself. So in a way, December twenty-fifth was Mithras's birthday as well. That's why our modern cult has chosen this week for their rituals. They're piggybacking on a date that already carries great significance. Just like the Christians did when they picked it for their own god's birthday."

Philippe sniffed. "It's just a little rude, you know? All those creepy mangers everywhere. I think the baby Jesuses look like baby *me*, honestly." He chuckled. "How great would it be if all this time the Christians thought they were worshiping their infant savior, they were actually praying to adorable little Cupid instead? But I guess that's just wishful thinking, because I'm still aging—slowly, but aging nonetheless. And don't get me started on the Christmas trees everywhere. If they wanted to pick a pagan symbol, they could've at least picked something Greek! Why should the Norse gods get all the help?"

Theo interrupted him. "None of this is helping me figure out where they've taken Selene." His visions of underground mithraea had been supplanted by those of Christmas trees. It made him think of the Rockefeller Center tree, soaring above the site of Selene's abduction. How she must have hated seeing it there—the Christian icon overshadowing the pagan statue of Prometheus that usually ruled the plaza.

I could use some help from Prometheus right now, Theo thought, reaching beneath his glasses to rub his burning eyes. Prometheus, whose name meant "Forethought," was more than just the god who'd given fire to man. He had also created humans in the first place, sculpting them from clay and then, when the other gods released a Pandora's Jar of vices and suffering to plague humanity, Prometheus added winged Hope to ease his children's hearts.

Come on, Theo prayed silently, *give me some Hope, buddy. It's about time.* Unsurprisingly, his prayer remained unanswered. *Fine. Any other gods I can call upon?*

Prometheus, he remembered, wasn't the only Athanatos represented in Rockefeller Center. *There's a famous motif of Mercury on one of the buildings. And then of course . . .* "Atlas," he said aloud.

"What about him? Long dead, I hear."

"No, not the god Atlas. The *statue* Atlas. The one in Rock Center. My students all think he lifts up the earth, but he's actually holding the heavens. A man bearing the celestial sphere. Don't you see? That's not just an ancient Greek idea—it's a *Mithraic* one."

Theo grabbed his wool coat and hat. The revelation wasn't much, but it was the best idea he'd had so far. He thumped on the bedroom door where Flint had secreted himself, then stuck his head into the hallway to shout for Dash.

He quickly explained the Atlas connection. "It might be nothing," he said, "but at least it's a possibility. If these guys know that the Athanatoi exist, then maybe they've been in the city as long as you have. Or at least long enough to plant Mithraic symbolism in some New York landmarks."

Flint reached for his leather jacket and crutches, but Dash put a restraining hand on his arm and warned, "Now hold on, we're supposed to join the fight *later*—otherwise we show our hand too early. And you, my brawny brother, are *very* recognizable. If you go with Theo now, you'll only put him in danger."

"But what if he's right?" Flint shook off Dash's grip violently. "What if this *is* the entrance to their temple, but he can't figure out how to get inside?"

"It's okay," Theo assured him, trying not to sound annoyed by Flint's obvious lack of faith. "Once I know I'm right, I'm going to call Detective Freeman and tell the police to—"

"No!" Philippe and Dash shouted at the same time.

"Bad enough you told them Selene was captured," Dash

explained breathlessly. "Now you want them there when you finally talk to these murderers? The cult will reveal our true identities!"

Theo looked from one god to the other, flabbergasted. "We know the initiates are mortal. Yet they can use divine weapons. That means we're facing a group of potentially overwhelming size and strength. We're going to need reinforcements, but you'd let Selene die because you refuse help from the police? Are you really so afraid that a bunch of hard-nosed detectives are going to suddenly believe you're all three-thousand-year-old gods? Are you insane?"

But Dash remained adamant. "We do this our way."

Theo spun to Flint. "What about you? You don't want to call the cops either? You're going to sacrifice Selene to protect a secret that doesn't need protecting? I thought you cared about her. At least that's what it looked like this morning on top of Rock Center."

Dash rounded on the Smith. Suddenly they were all talking at once.

Flint silenced them with a raised hand. "I'm not worried about the secret. But once the police are involved, they'll take all the cult's initiates into custody. We'll never get the answers we need about how they found out about us in the first place. If we don't know that, we'll never be safe again."

Theo had nothing more to say. He had no intention of following their commands, but arguing further was simply a waste of time. And Selene might not have much time left. He pulled his hat low around his ears and headed for the elevator. Philippe offered him a weak *"Bonne chance"* as the doors slid closed. Then the elevator sprang back open, and Flint stood before him, holding out his hand.

"Let me see your spectacles."

Theo grudgingly complied. Flint affixed a tiny black dot to the left temple of the wire eyeglasses. "You can't leave without a way to communicate with us. Do you remember the plan? The code?"

"Yeah. Sure." Theo took back his glasses, refusing to look impressed at yet another of the miraculous inventions the Smith had pulled from his bag of wonders. He jabbed the "Door Closed" button.

Flint stuck the edge of one crutch into the closing doors and leaned forward once more. His voice was a barely audible rumble. "We'll get Selene out no matter whose help we have to enlist. The others will never agree to it, but I know you're right. Try my plan first, Schultz, but if it doesn't work, I'll call the cops. You have my word."

<hr>

Selene closed her eyes and buried her face in her hands as if that might erase the sight of Theo's aged face from her mind. "It's not real," she murmured into her palms. Yet if she stayed with Theo, what other future could there be?

She rubbed her face, hard, and then stared up defiantly at the ceiling. "You think to scare me," she shouted. "Illusions and trickery. Aphrodite's mirror torments the holder with thoughts of love and loss, but I am the Chaste One! Such things mean nothing to me."

She tried to believe her own words, reminding herself that even if the image in the mirror were a true prophecy, it mattered little unless she escaped from the cell. If they killed her, she'd never have a chance to know just how miserable she and Theo could have made each other.

She rose to her feet and placed her palms against the walls, searching for some weakness that might allow her to break out of the chamber. She paced the perimeter, tapping for any sign of hollowness. *They called me She Who Helps One Climb Out,* she reminded herself. *Walls cannot contain me. And when I finally escape, I will come for those who chain me here. I am the Relentless One, the Punisher, the Far Shooter.*

As if summoned by her recital of epithets, a sudden hallucination overwhelmed her. This time, she recognized it for what it was: a memory of her past, brought to vivid life by Morpheus's crown. That didn't make it easier to resist. Her body registered pain as she fell heavily to her knees, but her mind was elsewhere, sucked into the past like a broken twig trapped in a whirlpool's grip.

I hear my mother crying from half a world away.

Gentle Leto, neat-ankled and veiled, sits in the halls of Olympus, her distaff unwound at her feet, her tears hidden by her hands. I arrive only moments before my twin, for neither of us can bear our mother's suffering.

"Tell us what brings you such grief," I command.

She does not speak. She is too modest to complain of her own woes. But Apollo kneels beside her, and the bright rays of his face dry her tears. He speaks in gentle tones more suited to our mother's ways, and she finally lifts her eyes to his.

"Niobe, Queen of Thebes, bans my rituals from her city," she says. "She has borne seven daughters and seven sons, and counts herself more worthy of homage than I, who gave birth to only one of each. She brags that though some children may be lost, she will never be reduced to two, while I am near to childless."

We do not wait to hear more, my twin and I, for that would but delay the punishment. Clothed in clouds, we glide swiftly down to the city upon our gleaming chariots. There we hear Niobe's words of contempt. She speaks of Artemis, girt like a man in a short tunic, and Apollo with his womanly hair. "Leto should not be proud of her sickly litter," she says, "but rather ashamed to bring two such into the world."

Aflame with rage, Apollo raises his silver bow and showers shafts upon the seven sons of Thebes. But even as the sisters rail and weep beside their brothers' biers, Niobe speaks bold.

"Feast upon my misery, cruel Leto! Satiate your relentless heart with seven deaths. More remains to me in my misery than to you in your happiness: After so many deaths I triumph still, glorying in these my seven daughters."

Hard on her words my bowstring twangs, my fury a heartless wind that hurls forth my own golden shafts.

A daughter wrenches an arrow from her vitals and swoons away with her cheek upon her brother's breast. I do not hesitate as I seek out further prey—a girl who tries to comfort poor Niobe, then falls suddenly silent, doubled by her wound. Another, vainly flying, collapses with an arrow in her heart. The fifth dies upon her sister, and the sixth trembles in concealment and prays silently to me even as I bring her swift death. The last is left.

She is little more than a child, with terror-wide eyes and thin arms clutched across her narrow ribs. Niobe shields this youngest daughter with her whole body and begs aloud for mercy, all her hubris fled. But I, stony hearted, raise my golden bow.

The cry of Leto herself, descending from the heavens to witness our wrath, comes too late to stay my hand.

The arrow slips beneath the mother's arm and into the daughter's breast. The girl screams like a small animal in a hawk's talons, pure terror ripped from her throat, echoing through the palace until the cry of one child sounds like the wails of fourteen. The sound goes on and on. I listen, unmoved, as it finally dies to a whimper. Then there is silence.

The Goddess of Motherhood kneels in horror beside the girl's limp form.

"What have you done?" she asks us. "Such vengeance offends me more than Niobe's overweening words."

We lay down our shafts, Apollo and I, but we feel regret only for our mother's pain, not for the destruction we have wrought.

Niobe grieves, rigid beside the corpses of her children. Gentle Leto, the merciful one, prays to Zeus our father that he might ease Niobe's suffering. In answer, he turns the woman's stony frame to stone itself.

Now, among the rugged crags and sky-encountering crests of mountains, sits the Rock of Niobe. The likeness of a woman bowed in the depths of anguish. A broken heart in the guise of shattered stone. Men pass with feet fear-goaded, and from the rock pour waterfalls. Weeping, weeping . . . grief-stricken . . . endless.

As Selene emerged from the memory, a swimmer fighting through a maelstrom, the weeping went on. After a moment, she knew the sobs came from her own throat. She cried for Niobe as she never had before. On Governors Island, the memory of the Great Gathering had reminded her of her impotence, leaving her hopeless and melancholy. This memory of unchecked power was far worse. She could not erase the image of the children reaching in vain for the arrows that pierced their flesh, teeth bared as they gasped their last breaths. Now she heard the prayers she'd once ignored—their pleading, their terror, their agonized questions, *"Why me? What have I done?"*

Selene clapped her hands over her ears, but the prayers pulsed inside her, an unrelenting keening punctuated by the animalistic shrieks of that last little girl. *This is merely a ploy by the cult to make me weak,* she thought desperately. But no matter the source, the memory was true. She was a monster. Her gut tightened, seized, and she doubled over, her empty stomach retching bile as if to purge herself of all the evil inside her.

When even the bile was gone, she lay beside the stinking puddle, chest heaving, cold sweat coating her arms and legs. *How long has Paul suffered from memories like this?* she wondered, finally understanding his despair. *No wonder he wants to die. No wonder mankind wants us to die. Why worship those they could not trust, could not respect, could not love?* Her tears returned, harder this time, and she grieved for Niobe's children, for her twin, and for Theo, too. For how could he love someone so cruel? The mirror's message became clear: The horror was not that Theo would grow old and die, but that she would despise him for doing so.

"Who's there?" The voice came through the grate above her head, the faintest of whispers.

Selene choked back her sobs and lay in frozen anticipation.

The voice spoke again, hoarse like that of an old man. "Who's crying?"

She held her tongue, wondering what new torment lay in store.

"Athanaton tis eis?" The voice pleaded; it did not demand.

Who else but another god would speak to her in Ancient Greek, asking if she were an immortal? Those who'd captured her already knew who and what she was.

She decided to risk it. *"Nai. Eimi he agrotera. Eimi desmios,"* she replied, slowly levering herself off the ground so she could stand closer to the grate. *Yes, I'm the Huntress. I'm a prisoner.*

He continued to speak in the ancient tongue. "It is a bitter, bitter thing that you have joined me in captivity. I can only hope your end will be swifter than my own."

"Who are you?" she begged.

"I am merely the Praenuntius."

She wondered at the Latin word. "The Harbinger?" She knew of no such god, even in the Roman pantheon.

"We all have many names, do we not, Good Maiden? Praenuntius is only the most recent of them. But it is the title by which my captors call me, and thus has it become my truest self. But I was once the Chained One. The Lofty-Minded." He laughed then, a rusty, half-formed sound. "They named me 'Forethought.' Though if I had ever seen this future before me, I would have killed myself long ago."

Chapter 29

THE TITANS

The Titan god Prometheus spoke of five hundred years of captivity and torture at the hands of his own creations.

It was hard to hear. They had chained him to a hospital bed, he said, subject to unending torment. Selene could imagine it—it was not so different from what her own father had done to him in another age. Punishment for the crime of putting mankind above the gods.

After Prometheus had created mortals from earth and water, he imbued each of them with the breath of his own spirit. He loved these mortal children of his so much that he dared steal fire from the hearth of Olympus and bring it down to them in a hollow fennel stalk. When Zeus discovered the theft, he chained Prometheus to a rock. Every day, Zeus's sacred eagle swooped down upon the prisoner and ate his liver. Each night, the organ regrew, so the eagle might feast anew the next day. And so it went for untold centuries, with the kindest and best of gods suffering at the hands of his own kin.

In all that time, the Huntress remembered seeing Prometheus in the flesh only a handful of times. In his prime, he'd been as broad-shouldered as Atlas, but while his brother's gaze was hard gray stone, Prometheus looked at the world with eyes as warm and soft as the rich soil from which he crafted mankind.

She'd seen him again when she'd happened across the mountainside where he suffered in captivity. Arms pinned above him, he hung naked from the stone. His ribs pumped like a bellows beneath his skin, riding high and swollen so that his bare stomach lay exposed to the eagle's wicked beak. *If he opens his eyes, will they still be warm and kind?* she'd wondered. Then she'd heard the shrill cry of an approaching bird and decided she wouldn't wait to find out. After all, Prometheus deserved his fate.

Once again, Selene realized, *I heard only the clarion call of vengeance, not the cries of suffering.*

"Why has the cult kept you for so long?" she asked aloud, pushing aside her own recriminations.

"I'm the Praenuntius. The Harbinger."

"Yes, you said that." He repeated himself often. *I suppose he only has a few stories to tell,* she thought, feeling guilty for her impatience. *The fact that he's kept his mind intact at all is remarkable.* "What exactly do they expect you to foretell?"

"As I decline, so do you. They have prepared all these centuries so they might be ready when the time was right."

"Right for..."

"Killing you. And all your kind."

"Yes, but *why*?" she demanded, breaking into English. "Is this really all about some cult of Mithras?"

"Mithras and more than Mithras." He spoke in English now, but with the slight Latin accent that she'd lost a thousand years before.

"Uh-huh..." She didn't understand. Not at all. But deciphering the Titan's mysterious pronouncements had at least given her a purpose. A glimmer of hope.

"They made me do it," he said after a long moment.

"Do what?"

"They needed my *pneuma*. I gave it to them. Just enough to let them wield the weapons they had stolen."

Pneuma. The breath of divinity within each Athanatos. She didn't possess the ability to transfer it to a mortal—if she did, she might have given it to Theo. But Prometheus's *pneuma* had brought the very first humans to life. Even more than the sacred coals he stole from Olympus's hearth, that divine breath was the true gift of the Fire-Bearer. *I should be angry with him for giving these madmen the use of our weapons,* Selene knew. But she didn't have the luxury of anger; she needed information. Prometheus represented her only chance of escaping before the Pater killed her.

"Do you know where we are?" she asked.

"No."

"Where did they capture you?"

"I can barely remember. But at the Diaspora, I did not stray far from our ancient home."

"Then how did you wind up in New York?"

"New York?" He pronounced the English name carefully, as if he'd never heard it before. "Is that where I am?"

"I certainly hope so. Unless I was unconscious for a lot longer than I thought."

"I'm unfamiliar with such a place."

That's because it didn't exist five hundred years ago, she realized. Even if she could keep Prometheus's mind on track, he knew nothing but what his captors allowed.

"What about the Forethought thing? Can you predict what they'll try next?"

"I have no prescience anymore, child. I live to be tortured and to live again. Such was my fate then. Such is my fate now."

Selene wanted to scream. *Prometheus has resigned himself to eternal pain. Mars resigned himself to death. But I must not do the same. I must fight to survive. Theo will help. He will come for me. As he always has. Even when I push him away. And Paul will help, too. Flint. Even Dash and Philippe will not leave me here to die.*

How strange to have so many people caring for her. A week earlier, the list would not have been half so long. Yet now she knew with a sudden certainty that they would all work to rescue her.

Whether or not they would succeed was a different story—with an ending even Prometheus could not prophesy.

◦—◦—◦

Theo stood at the base of the Atlas statue on Fifth Avenue and looked up at the art deco Titan who carried the universe above his head. Despite the dark night, a spotlight revealed every detail of the statue's bronze flesh. His brow creased with the strain, his pectorals bulged, and a skein of cloth across one hip covered his nakedness. His upraised arms held four massive rings forming the celestial spheres. One clearly depicted the zodiac, marked with the usual astronomical symbols for the constellations. Atlas bore the rings on a bronze yoke resting on his shoulders, embossed with the symbols of the planets themselves, from Neptune's trident through Mercury's caduceus. Only Jupiter was missing, obscured by Atlas's head, or perhaps left off as a sign of the Titan's eternal hatred for the Olympian who consigned him to hold up the universe in the first place.

Theo scanned the rings, trying to determine which one might represent the celestial equator. *Probably the one that intersects with the zodiacal ring,* he decided. The two rings should coincide at two constellations, indicating the locations of the spring and fall equinoxes.

He stepped to the statue's other side and followed the celestial equator's curve as it arced toward the zodiacal ring at Atlas's left shoulder. The two rings met at Aries the Ram.

A grim smile spread across Theo's face. If the statue had been meant to represent Atlas in the modern day, it would've shown the spring equinox at Pisces. The choice of Aries meant the sculptor was aware of the movement of the equinoxes and had purposely placed the statue nearly two millennia ago—when Mithraism was at its height.

So far so good. But now what? He wasn't sure what he'd expected. Maybe that there'd be a secret map on the statue's base. Or Atlas himself would be pointing toward the mithraeum's entrance. Instead, the Titan just stared straight out from blank bronze orbs.

"What d'ya say, Atlas?" he asked aloud. "Show me something. Don't just stare at me." *Well, not at me,* he realized. *He's looking across the street.* Theo turned in place and gazed across Fifth Avenue—at Saint Patrick's Cathedral.

The massive stone edifice symbolized the opposite of everything Mithraism stood for. Christian instead of pagan; lofty instead of underground; public instead of secret. Yet it was also the perfect place for a mithraeum. *There might be thousands of churches in Manhattan, but only one's the seat of the Roman Catholic Diocese of New York.* It made sense that the Mithraists would've built a pagan shrine right under the Christians' noses—the ultimate fuck you to the dogma that had displaced them.

Theo sprinted across the street. The doors to the cathedral were shut and locked. According to a posted placard, they wouldn't open until 6:30 a.m. *Who knew churches closed for the night?* he thought to himself. *What happens when I really needed to consult with God at four in the morning?* He knocked loudly, hoping for some cowled nun with a lantern to unbolt the door for him like a scene out of a BBC miniseries about medieval crime-solving monks.

"Come on!" he shouted. "What if I were being chased by an angry mob like in some Victor Hugo novel? Sanctuary! Sanctuary!"

"Hey, dipshit!"

A woman bundled in three layers of stained coats and a pom-pomed knit hat stood beside a shopping cart overflowing with cans and bottles. "God ain't gonna hear ya, but the cops sure will. Whyn't ya shut up so the rest of us can work in peace?" She lifted a plastic water bottle out of a trashcan and added it to her collection.

"Sorry." He jogged down the steps. "You usually work around here late at night?"

She shot him a suspicious glance with rheumy blue eyes. "Why? What I'm doin' is legal, buddy. It's a public service."

"Of course. I'm just wondering if you've seen anything weird happening around Saint Pat's."

"Besides you actin' like God's gonna open up the doors for you if you just holler at him?"

"Yeah, besides that."

She shrugged and reached deep into the barrel for a can. Orange Fanta. She shook it; it rattled icily.

"Is that a no?" Theo asked.

"It's a 'what's it worth to ya?'" She tilted back her head and drained the can.

"How about a night at the Four Seasons?"

She spluttered, the orange soda dribbling down her chin. "You're shittin' me."

"I'm not." He pulled his hotel key card from his pocket. "I'll call ahead and give them your name so they won't stop you in the lobby. Think of it as an early Christmas present."

She took a step back, and her mouth twisted with amusement. "Okay, buddy," she said after a moment. "I know this is some prank, but I'll tell you what I seen. I'm over here at this garbage can and there's five men groping that naked dude statue over there like he's a stripper on a pole." She pointed at Atlas. "Now, maybe it's late and dark and I'm awful tired after workin' all day and sleepin' in the cold, and my eyes ain't that good no more, but I look down at my cans and then I look up again and they're just gone. No sign of 'em nowhere. Poof."

"You see anything else?"

"No. Just snow and slush and frozen garbage."

She held out her hand. Theo passed her the key. He called the hotel, which patched him through to Dash's room, and informed the Messenger first that he'd likely found the mithraeum, and second that they'd have a guest for the evening. As she trundled away, Theo thought of warning her that the doormen might not take kindly to her cart of cans. Then he decided Dash deserved to handle that particular headache.

He crossed back to the Atlas statue and watched the snow fall on the mighty bronze shoulders. "There's something you're not telling me," he muttered to the Titan. *Either there's a secret entrance in this statue, or the homeless woman is hallucinating. One of those options is much more likely than the other.* But he didn't want to give up. Not yet.

Theo took a quick glance around the street. The homeless woman was long gone, and the block lay momentarily deserted in the wee hours of the morning. He hurried to the base of the statue and heaved himself up to stand beside Atlas. Then he clambered onto his giant bent knee, put his arms around the statue's neck, shimmied up his naked torso, and finally stood up on his spread arms. The whole thing felt completely ridiculous, mildly obscene, and definitely illegal.

He grabbed the ring of the celestial equator high above his head. He craned his neck, looking at where the massive bronze circle met the constellation Aries. It would take two thousand years for the world to move into the next age. "Let's speed it up a little, shall we?" Theo murmured. He shoved the ring with all his strength, trying to push it toward the constellation Pisces. He strained, he groaned, he felt sweat pop beneath his arms despite the winter chill. Nothing happened.

Okay, so maybe the securely welded rings of an eighty-year-old statue in plain view on Fifth Avenue aren't the secret entrance to a pagan temple. Panting heavily, he dropped his arms and rested them on the zodiacal ring.

It shifted soundlessly to the right.

Theo nearly fell off the Atlas statue in surprise. The celestial equator now passed neatly through Pisces, just as it did in the modern day. He looped an arm around Atlas's muscled neck and twisted to look back at Saint Patrick's, half expecting the cathedral doors to have magically opened. Then he dropped down to the ground and walked around the statue's base. There, on the side facing away from the street, a panel had slid away, revealing a three-foot-high opening. Theo stuck his head into the hole and switched his cell phone to flashlight mode. Metal rungs ran down the interior of the statue's base—a ladder reaching far underground. He was willing to bet it led to a tunnel that would take him straight under Saint Patrick's.

He sent a quick text message to Flint detailing the Atlas statue's secrets. But according to the plan, he needed to enter alone. *I'm heading inside,* he wrote. *I'll give it a shot your way, but if you don't hear from me, go to Plan B and call the cops. And tell Dash to be nice to the woman with the cans.*

Chapter 30

MAKARITES

Theo crawled through the entrance in the statue's base and pulled the sliding panel shut behind him. From somewhere above, he could hear a whisper of movement and knew the zodiacal ring had shifted back to its original position. With his cell phone clutched between his teeth as a flashlight, he started his descent.

He hadn't gone far when a dim light appeared below him. He turned off his phone and kept going. His palms were sweating—only his winter gloves prevented him from slipping off the rungs. Finally, his feet touched bottom. The low tunnel before him headed eastward. He had to crouch to avoid smacking his head.

He walked for about forty more yards—just far enough to cross beneath Fifth Avenue—before the tunnel ended at a large wooden door banded with iron. On either side of the entrance hung electric lighting fixtures made to look like torches—they even flickered convincingly. He figured he stood right below Saint Patrick's Cathedral.

It was hard to feel any satisfaction at having guessed the mithraeum's location correctly when the door before him looked like the entrance to a medieval dungeon. He was, without a doubt, about to walk into a metaphorical lion's den. Then he thought of how Selene had walked into a very literal grizzly bears' lair without a sign of trepidation. It was his turn to be fearless.

He tested the door handle. It didn't budge. No visible key-hole, and he had no experience picking locks anyway. Grabbing the handle, he pulled with all his strength. Nothing. He tried pushing instead. Not a creak.

Finally, he knocked tentatively on the wood, feeling only slightly less idiotic than he had on the steps of the cathedral. Of course, no one answered.

He took a step backward to examine the entrance. It had no Mithraic symbolism he could see. No signs of the zodiac engraved into the wooden door. No snakes or bulls or dogs carved on the lintel. Just two torches. Then he nearly laughed aloud. Cautes and Cautopates: the torchbearers who flanked Mithras in so many depictions of the tauroctony. Cautes, signi-fier of Day and Birth, held his torch facing up. But Cautopates, who brought Night and Death, always held his facing down.

Theo reached up, grabbed the right-hand lighting fixture, and rotated it downward. The door swung open.

He entered a bare white chamber only slightly larger than a closet, furnished with a metal desk and one chair. The ceiling paint had browned in the corners, the linoleum floor peeled at the edges. But the round steel door on the opposite wall, bolted and barred with a wheel-shaped handle like the entrance to a bank vault, made it clear this was no storage room.

Theo stood uncertainly. He scanned the ceiling, knowing there must be security cameras but seeing nothing besides the light fixture. After a long moment, he cleared his throat. "Um. Hello?" His voice sounded weak and reedy in his own ears. *Already making a great first impression, as usual.*

He tried again. "It's Theodore Schultz." All the gods had agreed there was no point in hiding his identity. The cult mem-bers had seen him at Selene's home and in the Rockefeller Center skating rink. And if they'd done any research at all, they'd find that he'd worked as a police consultant the last time a Mystery Cult stalked the city. "I've come to speak to your Pater Patrum."

Theo stood in silence for another interminable span. *I'm going to feel like a complete idiot if it turns out I'm talking to myself in an empty room.* But just then, the wheel on the far door rotated slowly of its own volition, and the door swung open. Solid steel, six inches thick.

As imposing as Theo found the door, the figure that emerged was even more so. It was not its appearance that sent a shiver of terror through Theo's gut—but its lack of one. A long, gray veil obscured the face and head; it looked like a ghost come to haunt Theo's waking nightmares. Beneath the waist-length veil it wore simple gray woolen slacks and shiny black loafers. *Looks like a very shy stockbroker,* Theo decided, trying to see the veil in a less disturbing light.

"Theodore Schultz." A man, then, with a surprisingly deep voice. Somehow, with the veil, Theo'd expected it to be light and mincing. He scolded himself for his heteronormative pre-conceptions and nodded.

"I've come to help."

The man extended his hand, and Theo clasped it in his own. *That was easier than I thought it'd be*... but the man was shaking his head as if Theo'd already done something wrong. He took a seat behind the desk. With only the veil now visible, Theo felt as if he were being interviewed by one of the ghosts from Pac-Man. Then, with a click, the door to the tunnel locked behind him, and he decided it felt more like an interrogation by the Grim Reaper.

"How did you find us?" asked the veiled man calmly.

"Atlas. Pretty obvious for anyone with an Internet connection." They didn't need to know how close he'd come to missing the clues. "Let me guess, John D. Rockefeller Jr. was a member of your cult."

"Our membership remains secret. That is the first rule."

"Right. Sorry."

"We know who you are. What makes you think we won't just kill you? You work with our enemies."

"You *think* I do," he said, trying to look the man in the eye. A difficult task when his entire face was just a gray sheet. "I've gained their trust, so I can work from within to destroy the Olympians. You know who I am. I know what *they* are. And I also know, with the utmost conviction, that they have no place in this world."

"And *you* have no place in ours. Membership is only for those sent by a syndexios, Professor."

Syndexios? A 'joining of right hands'? Theo surmised, translating the Ancient Greek. *Ah, that's where I went wrong. I didn't know the secret handshake.* Handshaking itself was an Eastern custom, not originally a Roman one. It made sense that the Mithraists, with their interest in Persia, would've incorporated it into their secret rituals. "I don't need to be initiated into the cult," he said quickly. "I just want my life back."

The veil swung back and forth as the man shook his head. "Only initiates may enter the Templo. Only initiates may know our secrets. If you want to work with us, you will have to join the cult. Surely, as a classicist, you understand that is how it works."

Somehow, Theo didn't think he could just say, "My bad," and turn to go.

"But you've intrigued me," the man went on. "You would work to destroy the very entities you've spent a life studying."

"I studied them as figments of imagination. As creations of a society long dead. I never dreamed they were real until I met Selene." That much, at least, was true. Theo mentally crossed his fingers and hoped his interpretation of Mithraism had been correct. "I believe our lives are our own," he went on. "Yet I've become a pawn, subject to a pantheon of gods who try to bend me to their will. You believe in man's ability to find salvation, right?"

The veiled man nodded slowly.

Theo considered trying to claim that he was a true believer in the power of Mithras, but he didn't think he'd be particularly convincing. Better to keep the lies modest. "I've never been a particularly spiritual man, as you know if you've been following me around all this .time. So I'm not sure what 'salvation' even means. But I do believe that if it exists, it's something transcendent, something that lifts us past the material world. Selene and her family—they reduce divinity to something pedestrian. They're like schoolyard bullies, convinced of their own mastery, turning what should be magical and mysterious into something utterly mundane."

"You believe this strongly enough that you'd risk their wrath by pretending to be their ally? You'd pollute your body by joining with the Pretender named Diana? You'd come willingly into our Templo and offer yourself up to us, without knowing what such an offer entailed?"

"There are forces at work beyond those we can comprehend." This sounded like something a Mithraist would believe. "I'm a Makarites. Did you know that?"

The veiled man didn't reply. Theo explained. "That's Greek for 'Blessed One.' It used to be that only the ancient heroes could earn such a title, but someone like me, who's spent a lifetime studying the gods' stories and—"

"There are no *gods*," snapped his interviewer. "There is only one God. That is the first thing you must understand."

"Sorry. I've picked up their language. I should say the 'Pretenders'—is that it? Okay, then I've spent a lifetime studying the Pretenders' myths. It's given me an understanding of them that borders on... well, the supernatural, although I don't want to sound pretentious. Let's just say that they're drawn to me, and I to them. I'm like Greek catnip." He tried for a charming smile, but couldn't tell if the veiled man responded in kind. *Probably not.* "Why would I be given such a power if not to use it?" he continued. "I must have a role to play. And that role is to rid the world of their pollution." It wasn't hard to imitate the Mithraist's rhetoric. It reminded Theo of the language used by fundamentalist believers of all faiths. Throw in some "moral corruption" and "false idols" and you fit right in.

"I have no reason to believe you, and every reason to distrust you."

"But if I'm right, I can tell you how to find them."

"We already know there are other Pretenders hiding in Manhattan. We don't know where they are, but it will not take us long to root them out."

Theo tried not to let his relief show—at least the cult didn't know about the Four Seasons yet. He tried for wide-eyed fervency instead. "The New York Pretenders are just the beginning, my friend."

The veiled man sat in silence for a long moment. Theo could almost feel the intensity of his regard, despite being unable to see his eyes. Finally, the man said, "I will take you to the Pater Patrum. He will decide."

Theo nodded solemnly, but inside he let out a small cheer. *Score one for the mere mortal. Ten minutes in the mithraeum and I get to meet the Big Bad.*

The man opened the massive steel door and ushered Theo into a bright, sterile hallway. None of the antechamber's dinginess here. Instead, sleek curves of stainless steel and molded fiberglass formed the walls, floor, and ceiling. Theo felt like he'd entered the Starship *Enterprise*, but without the friendly ensigns. The corridor continued for at least a hundred yards. At the very end, he could just make out another large vault door. Smaller, less imposing doors appeared every twenty feet. None of them, Theo realized, had knobs. At one of these doors, the man stopped. He didn't knock, but rather pressed his palm to a sensor on the wall.

The door swung open with a slight exhale. The veiled man gestured for him to enter, but remained in the hallway himself. Theo stepped inside, and the door hissed closed.

The only illumination came from a small fireplace at the far end of the long chamber. He took a careful step forward on what felt like thick carpet.

As his eyes adjusted to the darkness, he could make out the richly carved mahogany of the walls and the ornate plasterwork ceiling. Niches held statues and paintings, but with no lamps to illuminate them, their subject matter remained hidden. Large furniture cluttered the room with great hulking shadows.

Only when he squinted could he make out a figure sitting in an armchair beside the fire, his back to the flames and his face concealed in shadow. Theo took another step forward.

"Stay where you are." The voice was rough with age, but resonant with authority. Theo felt frozen in place like a moth pinned to a wall. "You seek to work with the Host?"

"Yes," Theo said, trying not to sound confused. *The Host? Why would they call themselves the Host?*

A small movement in the shadows beside the chair alerted Theo to another figure. The person leaned down to whisper in the Pater's ear.

"The Hyaena says I shouldn't trust you. She says your loyalty lies with the one who calls herself the Huntress."

Theo took a deep breath and prepared himself to betray the woman he loved.

———◇———

Selene tried to wedge her fingers into the nearly invisible cracks around the food slot in the top of her cell door. She tried to kick out the lower panel with her bare feet. She only managed to bruise her toes and rip her fingernails. Finally, she sat down to conserve her strength. She left the hand mirror facedown, afraid of what it might show her.

So far, she'd had no visions since the flashback to the massacre of Niobe's children, but she knew the reprieve wouldn't last. *What next?* she wondered. *The metamorphosis of Acteon, the murder of Coronis, the killing of Orion?* She had caused so many deaths in her day, could she bear to relive them all?

She tried to busy her mind with happier thoughts instead, to push away the future that Aphrodite's mirror had foretold and imagine a different one instead. *When I get out of here,* she decided, *I will take Theo to Greece.* She hadn't been to her homeland since the Diaspora, but Zeus's prohibition would no longer stop her. They would visit Knossos where the Minotaur once lurked in the Labyrinth. They would climb the steps of the Acropolis and sit in the shadow of the Parthenon's colonnade. They would hike to the summit of Mount Olympus and stand above the clouds. And all the while, she would tell him stories of her past—not the tales of bloody vengeance, but the moments of joy and peace and laughter. *Those are true too,* she reminded herself. *I helped women, I danced with my nymphs, I protected my cities. It was not all terrible.* How Theo's eyes would grow wide! He would smile and laugh, and she'd bask in a warmth far kinder than the merciless Mediterranean sun.

Then a faint humming, like a speaker turning on, broke her reverie. She stood and craned her neck toward the vent overhead. "Prometheus?" she called softly. "What is that?"

He didn't reply. Instead, a familiar voice blared through her cell.

"You are mistaken, Pater."

"Theo!" She couldn't help herself from crying out. But an instant later, as the conversation continued, she realized he couldn't hear her.

"I bear no loyalty to Diana, or Artemis, or whatever you want to call her," Theo went on, his voice stern. "At first, I didn't know what she was. And when I found out, she warned me that if I left her, she would kill me. You've heard the myths—you know how possessive the gods are. How jealous and petty. So I stayed because I had no choice, and I bided my time, waiting for allies strong enough to help me escape. By capturing her, you made my life a hell of a lot easier. But the others hold me in their thrall now. I've got the whole pantheon trying to make me their slave. I need you to help me get rid of them, so I can find my own path. My own salvation."

Selene sat back down with a thud. She could barely hear the voice of Theo's interviewer over the pounding of the blood in her ears.

"And you claim to be able to find them. All of them." *That must be the Pater speaking,* Selene decided.

"I know their aliases," Theo said. "I know what they do. Hermes is Dash Mercer, Hollywood movie producer. Apollo is Paul Solson, the musician."

"We know that."

"But do you know of the goddess Demeter, living in Peru?"

Another voice came over the speaker. "Our brethren abroad have not spoken of her," it said softly, as if murmuring to the Pater.

So there are more of them, Selene realized, her heart sinking. Even if they defeated this branch, the cult would survive.

As the Pater urged Theo to continue, Selene could hear the note of excitement in his voice.

"Aphrodite in Paris. Dionysus right here in New York." Theo kept talking, revealing all the gods' secrets, until finally, with only a breath of hesitation, he said, "Zeus in his cave in Crete."

Selene could hear the Pater's intake of breath.

This must all be part of a plan, she assured herself. *Theo didn't know where my father lives. So my brothers must have told him to reveal the location. Unless Theo's betraying them in order to save me. Does that make it any more forgivable?*

"You've taken Selene, but you won't be able to break her," Theo continued. "I know what happened to Mars at the end. He slowly went mad until he was resigned to his fate. You probably did the same thing to Hades."

"A sacrifice must go willingly," the Pater replied calmly.

"Or it doesn't carry the same power. Yeah, I know how the old cults worked. So you send the Pretenders hallucinations until they lose the will to live. But Selene thinks herself the Relentless One. She'll never submit to torture—no matter if it's nightmares or thumbscrews. But I know all her weaknesses. I can get her to crumble."

"Go on."

"She's scared."

"The all-powerful Olympian?" The Pater's voice carried the barest hint of amusement.

"She's not all-powerful anymore. She's supposed to be so fierce. The Stormy One. The Untamed. But inside she's still a little girl. Afraid of growing old. Afraid of looking weak. She's as scared of being unloved as she is of being loved. So for all the hold she has on me, she's still vulnerable."

He must be trying to infiltrate the cult, she reminded herself, *so he'll say anything.* But in her heart, she knew that if he could imagine such horrible things to say, at some point, he must have considered them. Awful, dangerous, disrespectful things. Selene searched for her old accustomed fury, but found only despair. She had said terrible things to him—should she be surprised that he could say terrible things in return? Things that, for all their viciousness, bore the ring of truth?

"She's even scared of her own body."

Selene put her hands over her ears, but the speaker's volume only increased. *They're watching me,* she realized. She put down her hands and squared her shoulders. They wanted her to grow weak and afraid—she refused to give them the satisfaction.

Theo's voice continued, merciless. "I try to touch her and she flinches away even as her flesh cries out for mine. She's the ultimate prude. Wanting to be fucked and hating to be touched all at the same time. She's completely neurotic, unfriendly, and so egotistical that she can't imagine that I would ever betray her. It makes her an easy target."

Selene wished for a vision, no matter how devastating, to take her away from this moment. But for once, she remained rooted to the present, listening to Theo rip their relationship to shreds.

———◇———

The Pater Patrum raised an arm, silhouetted in the firelight, and beckoned Theo closer. As he approached, the female *syndexios* at his side backed farther into the shadows. Theo could just make out the leather mask she wore—a hyena with a toothy grin. Beaten gold covered the Pater's entire face, like the death mask of some ancient Mycenaean king. Thick white hair hung to his shoulders and arthritis swelled his knuckles, but he sat with a king's poise.

"Theodore. You cannot progress any farther without initiation into the Host."

Theo nodded. "If that's what it takes to be free of the Pretenders, then sign me up."

"Yet you know almost nothing about us."

"I've done a fair bit of research—"

He held up a hand. "You know nothing. As such, you may only be initiated as a syndexios of the lowest rank, where you will not be privy to our secrets. We risk little by allowing you this far. *You* risk all."

All? He'd barely formed the thought before the Pater spoke again.

"If we find you false, you will be killed. No more mercy will be shown to you than was shown to the Pretenders Mars and Hades. And be assured, if they, who survived for so many millennia, could not escape the arm of our justice, then you will not either."

Theo swallowed, his mouth suddenly dry. He'd gotten this far, but he had little faith in Flint's plan. To make matters worse, he'd have to get deep enough into the cult to learn its motives and methods. The way the Pater was speaking, he doubted he'd make it that far before they saw right through him.

"Now we will see how genuine your desire to help us is." The Pater stood and moved toward the fireplace. Only then did Theo notice the metal rods hanging from the mantel. Not a shovel and poker like you might see in a cozy hearth, but a row of seven instruments, each topped by a different wrought iron design. Too late, Theo realized the planetary symbols the syndexioi bore weren't tattoos at all. He tried not to let the panic show on his face. He failed.

The Pater's laugh scraped like metal on metal. "Did you think this little talk would be the end of your initiation, not the beginning?" He picked up the leftmost branding iron, lifting it so Theo could see the symbol at the bottom: Mercury. "I told you that you knew nothing of our ways. This is only the first step— the initiation into our humblest rank: the Corvus. A way to weed out those who aren't serious. Trust me, when we are done with you, you'll think this is the easiest part."

Chapter 31

THE CORVUS

This is the moment in the movie when the villain laughs maniacally and says, "Did you really think we would brand someone as unworthy as you?" and puts down the red-hot poker. Or a messenger bursts in and distracts the Big Bad by saying, "Sir! Someone's breaking into our secret lair!" and he puts down the red-hot poker. Or the consiglieri whispers into the evil genius's ear and he turns to the hero and says, "Dominic's correct—we will wait until the time is right," and then he PUTS DOWN THE RED-HOT POKER.

But the poker just kept coming.

The pain burned so hot it felt like ice.

Worse was the sound. A sizzle like bacon. Then the smell of cooking flesh. They'd given Theo a leather strap to put between his teeth—he nearly bit through it as he stifled the screech that climbed up his throat. Then the Pater removed the iron, and the pain dissipated.

Theo looked down at the wound in the center of his bare chest. An upside-down Mercury symbol, the size of a man's hand. He'd thought it'd be red with blood, or black like charred barbecue. Instead, it gleamed pale yellow, edged with white. His flesh wasn't burned—it was just gone. Until that moment, he realized, he'd secretly held on to a child's conception of his own body, imagining somehow that *he* wasn't just muscle and tissue, but rather some glowing essence. But here lay the truth: nothing under the skin but a thin layer of yellow fat that melted and sizzled just like any other meat.

He tore his eyes away from the burn. The Hyaena removed the leather strap from his mouth. Her hands, he noticed, were veined and calloused like those of an older woman. He saw no brand on her wrist or neck. The Pater's mark, if indeed he bore one, was similarly concealed. The woman placed a gauze bandage over the brand.

"Until your ordeal is complete," the Pater explained, "the brand remains simply a wound. Only once you've finished your initiation into the rank will we color it."

"My ordeal?" Theo couldn't help asking.

"Didn't your 'research' mention the ordeal pit?"

"Pit?" He could do little more than repeat the words, hoping he'd heard wrong.

"The Host is an order of soldiers, and has been for nearly two thousand years. To become a syndexios you must prove that you can withstand whatever pain the battle brings."

The battle? Theo nearly parroted. But he kept his jaw clenched shut. Whatever happened from here on out would be beyond his control.

The door to the Pater's chambers opened behind him. A Roman legionary stood waiting to escort him out. He wore a gilded helmet, complete with an armored face mask and red horsehair crest. His leather breastplate rippled with carven muscles. Beneath a short, pleated skirt, his thick legs shone with oil. The mask bore an uncanny resemblance to the god he'd seen laid out on the banquet table at the Rainbow Room. Not in its features—the mask was an exaggerated visage with an overlarge jaw and a slash of brows—but in the eyes. They'd been painted onto the mask, steely gray, flat, and dead.

The Pater spoke. "This is our Miles Primus," he said, drawing out the first syllable—*Mee-lais*—as if savoring the Latin word for "soldier." "Someday, you may ascend to his rank. But only if you survive this one." He turned to the legionary. "Take our new Corvus to the Templo."

The Miles gestured curtly for Theo to follow him into the hallway.

"You've got quite the revealing uniform," Theo commented. He knew the only way to combat his escalating terror was to pretend he felt no fear at all. If they weren't going to give him a mask like everyone else in this place, he'd make his own out of humor. "The leather muscles were very hip in the second century AD."

The soldier didn't react. His thigh alone was as big around as Theo's waist. *Did they make him a Miles because of his physique, or did he get the physique after he became a Miles?* These were mortals—surely their ranks had no supernatural effect on their appearance—but he wasn't ruling anything out. *Maybe I'm about to start cawing and flapping my wings like Corvus the Crow. Unlikely,* he decided. *I probably won't survive long enough for any sort of interesting metamorphosis. Just plain old Theo Schultz, lanky and nearsighted and distractible, meeting his untimely end at the hands of another homicidal—or should I say deicidal?—Mystery Cult. Awesome.*

A few steps down the hallway, the Miles came to a sharp halt. He finally spoke, his voice as deep and stern as would be expected from his rank. "It's time."

"Time for dinner?" Theo said hopefully. "Time for a bath? 'Cause let me tell you—"

"Remove your clothing."

"Ah, the bath then."

"Remove it now."

"I'd rather not."

"Then fail the ordeal."

"Right." He didn't have a good comeback for that one. The Miles simply stood silently. Waiting.

Theo kicked off his shoes then peeled off the rest of his clothing. He stood naked, resisting the urge to cover his dick like some medieval Adam. This was an all-male cult, after all, with the exception of the Hyaena woman. It seemed like the kind of place where men would walk around loud and proud. "So do I get a ceremonial robe or something?" He tried not to sound too hopeful. "Maybe something in a soft terrycloth?"

The Miles just turned and continued his progress down the hall. Theo took a deep breath, squared his shoulders, and followed. Thankfully, the hallway stood empty. He tried to ignore the way his balls had retreated in the chill air—he expected them to disappear completely at any moment.

The Miles stopped at the end of the hall, where a large round portal with an iron knob in the center signaled a chamber of some import. *The mithraic sanctuary,* Theo thought, his heart picking up speed. But he refused to look scared before this lunk in a helmet.

"Very *Lord of the Rings*," he observed, nodding at the circular door. "I feel like I'm entering a hobbit hole."

At that, the Miles shot him a stare, his anger evident despite the mask. "I will inform the Pater that you make a mockery of the rite."

"No, no, just a nervous tic," Theo replied hastily. "I tend to crack jokes at the most inappropriate times. Like a teenager giggling through a drunk driving video. See, there I go again."

"You have a mouth like a leaky faucet. Drip-drip-drip-drip-drip." The words conjured an image of blood, slowly dripping from a slit throat.

That finally shut Theo up.

The Miles continued in a monotone. "Once your meditation is complete, I will return to take you inside the ordeal pit. There, we speak only Latin. We train many years to speak the holy tongue. The Pater Patrum must believe you able, or he would not allow you to enter."

310 Jordanna Max Brodsky

"I've got a Ph.D. in classical languages, so *carpe linguam Latinam*."
He spitefully tried to recall all the Latin puns he'd ever learned.

"We will see what happens in the midst of the ordeal."

"Ah. So if I start cursing in English..."

"You fail."

"And if I fail..."

"No one can be allowed to know the secrets who is not an initiate."

"In other words..."

The Miles just stared at him with his flat painted eyes.

"I see." He pushed his glasses more firmly up his nose, wishing they were held on with one of those elastic headbands like a 1970s NBA player so that when the lion jumped out at him—or whatever monster inhabited the "ordeal pit"—he'd be able to see it coming.

"For now, inside the Templo, you will sit in silence, meditating on the images that are revealed to you. Do not speak."

Theo opened his mouth—

"I said, do not speak. It seems that may be the hardest ordeal of all for you."

Theo stifled a snarky retort only because he didn't want to prove the Miles right.

The round door swung open to reveal a long, stone chamber with a low, vaulted roof. It looked very much like the mithraea Theo'd seen in his research. The Miles led him down the narrow central aisle. To either side, a wide stone ledge ran the length of the chamber, providing a place for the syndexioi to recline during the cult's feasts. Detailed frescoes covered the walls in bright hues. The ceiling above dripped with small plaster stalactites, giving it the appearance of a cave.

Like most mithraea, the chamber was fairly small. He doubted more than twenty men would fit along the room's ledges. That meant the cult's forces, though well armed, might be small enough that three Athanatoi could defeat them—especially if they had Captain Hansen's Counterterrorism task force as backup.

At the end of the aisle stood a small rectangular altar decorated with carved reliefs. Behind it sat an elevated chair for the Pater. But the central image of the temple was the tauroctony itself. A large marble statue, twice the height of a man, that glowed in a beam of artificial sun pouring through a "skylight" above.

The bull lay with his legs curled beneath him and his neck thrown back. Mithras, one foot upon the bull's back hoof and the other knee bent upon its back, held the animal's nostrils in one hand and a knife in the other. Like the statues in antiquity, this one was painted in bright colors. From the wound in the bull's throat, red blood drops streamed down its neck. A wiry brown hound and a thick green serpent each pressed their tongues to the blood. An ochre scorpion scuttled at the bull's side. A black crow perched upon its back.

It was all just as Theo had expected—except for Mithras himself. No Phrygian cap covered his head. Instead, he wore the rayed crown of Sol Invictus, made not of marble but of hammered gold. His face, too, was gilded, as were his hands. He was the Sun incarnate, glowing so brightly Theo had to squint. From the god's back hung a cloak painted cinnabar red, its brilliant blue lining spangled with stars, as if Mithras, like Atlas, bore the solar system on his shoulders.

"On your knees, initiate," the Miles ordered. "I will return when you've finished contemplating the glory of the God."

Theo found himself alone, his bare knees sore from the stone floor after only a few seconds. He folded his hands across his lap and tried to look pious. *Okay,* he decided, *this is the calm before the storm. A chance to prepare for the ordeal ahead.* He felt like an idiot college student, walking into a final exam, knowing for sure that he should've studied a damn sight harder. He wished he'd had just another few hours to review the research on Mithraism. Instead, he had only the mithraeum itself to teach him more about the cult he'd just joined.

He looked at the frescos. The figures processing down the wall must be syndexioi, ordered according to rank. On the back of the right-hand wall stood a man with a black crow's head, carrying a caduceus: the Corvus. The familiar symbol of the planet Mercury floated above his head. Before him strode a veiled man beneath the hand mirror symbol of Venus. He wore a diadem on his brow, and looked like a Roman virgin bride. *Let's hope I'm never elevated to that particular rank,* Theo thought with a shudder, imagining what duties the bride might perform for the other initiates. Next came the familiar Miles, the Soldier, walking below the symbol of Mars.

The left wall bore paintings of three other types of syndexioi—clearly the higher ranks. At the back of the procession walked a man in a lion-head mask. The thunderbolt in his hand indicated he was under the protection of Jupiter/Zeus, the Sky God.

In front of the lion-man was a figure with a Phrygian cap and a curved sword. A Persian, or Perses. His tutelary planet was not a planet at all, but the moon. *Selene would appreciate that she gets a higher rank than her father,* he thought. But she might bridle over the fact that her twin brother was even higher still.

The next man in line stood beneath the symbol of the sun. He wore red robes and a rayed crown, not unlike that adorning the head of the Mithras statue, and carried a whip in one hand. *That must be the Sun-Runner,* Theo decided. *The rank for whom the "Procession of the Heliodromus" was named.*

The Hyaena did not appear anywhere in the fresco. Six ranks depicted in all, corresponding to six of the seven heavenly bodies, and to the celestial spheres theorized by Plato. As initiates climbed from rank to rank, they likely learned more of the cult's secrets and, supposedly, moved closer to ultimate salvation. *A bit like a first-century version of Scientology,* Theo reflected.

One other figure was missing—the seventh rank, the seventh celestial body. Theo finally found his image on the altar itself, holding a sickle just like the one Saturn used to slice the balls off his father Uranus in the Roman creation myth. *Strange,* Theo thought, *that Saturn, rather than mighty Jupiter, protects the Mithraists' most revered leader.* Then again, the Romans always had a thing for Saturn, an indigenous agricultural god whom they'd syncretized with the Greek Kronos. They'd stored their treasury beneath his temple in the Roman Forum and considered the winter Saturnalia one of their most important feasts—another reason the December timing made sense for the Mithraists' rituals. Still, Theo couldn't quite make sense of any of it. *And considering scholars have been trying to figure out this cult for over a thousand years and still have no idea what went on, I probably never will either.*

Theo wasn't sure how long he knelt in the mithraeum. He only knew that he expected his knees to start bleeding at any moment. When the Miles finally returned, Theo welcomed it. Whatever ordeal awaited, it had to be better than the torture of anticipation.

He tried to school his face into a solemn mask, lest he be faulted again for not correctly revering the god. The Miles led him past the altar and the Pater's seat, through a small door behind the tauroctony.

The large circular chamber they entered dwarfed the mithraeum. Torches hung in brackets along the wall, casting flickering shadows around the room. A round pit, at least ten feet deep, dominated the center. Surrounding it stood the syndexioi, each in the garb of his rank, their faces concealed behind a variety of masks. Two members of each of the five higher ranks were present, but only one veiled man and a single crow-headed Corvus. Two men had died on Governors Island, he knew, which explained the gaps. *Glad I could help shore up the ranks,* he thought grimly.

The higher ranks stood on the far side of the pit, and Theo could only dimly make out the two figures in their lion masks and the Persae with their Phrygian caps. The two Heliodromi, however, were hard to miss in their bright red robes, matching silk masks, and rayed crowns. One held a torch upright. The other held one facing downward.

Between them stood the Pater Patrum. The firelight illuminated the old man in the gold mask so that Theo noticed his clothes for the first time. He was clad in a white, long-sleeved tunic with red piping, baggy Persian trousers like those worn by Mithras, and a long red cloak. *Sort of M.C. Hammer meets Magneto,* Theo decided with a desperate attempt at levity.

The Miles at Theo's side escorted him to the edge of the pit. Around him, the syndexioi stood in silence. As he put a foot on the first rung of the ladder, a waft of cold air circulated up from the pit to shrink his testicles still further. Then his mind momentarily went blank with terror, and he found himself standing in the center of the empty pit, the ladder pulled up to the rim, removing his only means of escape.

The slick stone walls around him reached far overhead—even Selene would've been hard pressed to scale them. At the thought of her, Theo felt a rush of adrenaline through his veins. She'd once told him that at the height of her powers, she could hear the prayers of the faithful as they entreated her for aid. *Worth a shot,* he decided.

I sing of Artemis, Protector of the Innocent.

I sing of She Who Helps One Climb Out.

Hear my prayer, Good Maiden, and lend your mighty arm in my moment of need.

It would've been better in Greek, but he was having a hard enough time getting his terrified brain to remember Latin. *And this is* before *anything enters the pit. Maybe this is all it is—ordeal by anticipation. I stand here awaiting some unknown torture for half an hour, nearly shitting myself, and then they all take off their masks and yell, "Surprise!" and buy me a drink.*

Then the flames began.

All around the circumference of the pit, a ring of fire shot six feet into the air. He could feel the waves of heat licking his skin. A voice sounded from beyond the flames. The Pater.

"Corvus per ignem intactus volat. Ita suo deo se probat."

Somehow, Theo's churning brain managed to translate the Latin: *A crow flies through fire unscathed. Thus does he prove himself before his god.*

Wait . . . did he say . . . through fire? he wondered belatedly. Only then did he notice the narrow channels in the floor running toward him from the ring of flame like the spokes of a wheel. Even as his eyes traveled their length, the fire poured down the metal paths. Instinctively, he raised his arms to shield his face. He tried to dodge out of the way, but found that the tongues of fire formed a new circle, this one only three feet across, with him at its center. He wondered how much longer he could withstand the blistering heat.

Dimly, he realized that the outer ring of fire and its spokes had vanished; only a single line of flames stood between him and safety. Now the object of the ordeal became clear. Pass through.

He peeked out from behind his arm, but had to close his eyes against the heat. *Oh shit, oh shit, oh shit,* he thought, biting back the English words. *Okay, just like passing your finger through a candle flame. The kind of thing a fifth grade boy does to impress the girls.* Theo'd always preferred to charm the ladies with an erudite joke or two, but it was never too late to regress. *Indian fakirs do this all the time, right? It's just a mental exercise. Of course, they at least have loincloths.*

He kept one arm in front of his face and decided to forgo manly pride and cover his groin with the other. He took a few heaving breaths, not unlike a woman in labor, then sprinted through the flames.

He thought he'd made it through, miraculously unscathed, until he realized his hair was on fire.

"Merda sancta!" he cursed, batting at his head ineffectually. Then water poured down on him from an overhead pipe, a

blessed, healing flood that doused the flames instantly. He patted his skull, relieved to find he wasn't bald. The hair on his arms and legs, however, had all been singed off. *But the water's a good sign,* he decided. *They don't actually want me to die.*

Except the water didn't stop. He tried to step out from underneath the deluge, but it tracked him like a follow spot on an opera singer. He could still breathe, barely, if he ducked his head and sucked air. Then he started shivering uncontrollably in the icy torrent. *Maybe I'm shaking from shock,* he hoped, *not hypothermia.* He knelt down anyway, clutching his arms around his knees for warmth. Still the water didn't cease.

He could barely hear the Pater's voice over the roar. *"Auctor luminis . . . illuminare lumine intelligentiae . . . dignus gratia Baptismi tui effectus . . . doctrinam sanctam."* Theo didn't catch every word—his teeth chattered too loudly—but he heard something about "baptism" and "enlighten him with wisdom." A pleasant liturgy for a torturous experience.

His shivering slowed. At first, he thought that was a good sign, then he realized it might mean his body had simply stopped fighting. He pushed hard against the torrent to stand up on numb feet and tried to slap some warmth back into his arms and flanks. He reached back to childhood memories of books about the high Arctic. *Keep moving,* he decided, *that's the key.* He did a few jumping jacks, head still bowed beneath the water. Then he tried to jog in place. Next, he resorted to a medley of 1980s dancercise moves, forgoing all dignity in the pursuit of survival. The water only came harder. The gauze ripped off his brand, and the water struck his raw flesh like a hammer.

Baptism, his frozen brain remembered. *It's supposed to be a baptism.* The Miles had made it clear the rite required solemnity. Theo sucked in a deep breath, then forced himself to turn his face upward into the pounding water. It slammed against his eyelids and cheeks, it streamed up his nose, but he held out his arms to welcome the cleansing of his sin and stood as still as a crucifix.

Even as his lungs screamed for air, he tried to look calm, composed, a willing supplicant. His outstretched arms began to shake with the strain, and he felt the floor beneath his feet tilt as the oxygen left his brain. In another second, he'd have to either bend his head away from the water or pass out.

The water ceased.

He found himself standing in a puddle, with only a few frigid drops falling on his skull like Chinese water torture.

The assembled crowd hadn't moved. But the Pater nodded his head slowly, as if in grudging approval. Theo tried to look calm and confident, even though he felt like begging for a cup of hot tea and one of those foil emergency blankets.

He dared not trust that the ordeal was over. *Good things always come in threes.*

Sure enough, a hidden panel in the side of the ring slid open. *Now come the lions,* Theo decided. *Very gladiatorial.* If only he had a short sword and net…

Instead, the goddess Diana stepped into the pit.

Chapter 32

DIANA

Selene entered the ordeal pit to find Theo standing naked before her. Water plastered his fair hair against his skull, the ends tipped black with char. The skin of his arms and legs flared bright pink, as if from extreme heat or cold. Just below his collarbone, a Mercury symbol, yellow and oozing, carved his flesh.

She watched his eyes travel across the clothes they'd forced upon her: a short white tunic pinned at one shoulder, sandals laced to her knees, and a crescent moon tiara in her black hair. For the first time in millennia, she dressed like a goddess, and yet she'd never felt her own mortality more acutely: They might have garbed her as Diana, but they hadn't given her the Huntress's bow. Before her stood a man she no longer felt she knew. How much of what he'd said to the Pater were his secret feelings, and how much just for show? She tried to read the truth in his eyes, but all she saw was fear.

He lifted his face to speak to someone who stood above her on the rim of the pit. The Pater, she assumed, although she dared not turn around to look. She felt safest with the wall of the pit at her back.

"*Estne Spartaci somnium quoddam depravatum est?*" he asked. *Is this some perverted Spartacus fantasy?* Selene hadn't bothered with Latin in many lifetimes, but she had no problem understanding a tongue she'd spoken daily for centuries. As always, she was both impressed and alarmed that Theo mocked those who threatened him—and in a long dead language, no less. He went on, still in Latin. "Would you have us wrestle as gladiators?"

The Pater spoke above her head. "I do not doubt that Diana is still strong enough to make short work of you. No. We have a better idea. Tomorrow is the Procession of the Heliodromus, and there must be a willing sacrifice to the God of Three Aspects. Yet Diana is still convinced that she should live. Sure that, weak as she is, she is still a goddess. She must learn her place. And you, Makarites, have promised to teach her."

Theo didn't look at Selene. "You want me to do it... right now?"

"Just tell the truth."

"About what?"

"About her."

"I told you already. You can use the information however you want."

"You told us what we wanted to hear. Now tell us the truth. We will know if you lie."

"She is cold, unfeeling—"

"You lie."

A river of icy water crashed down on Selene's head. She crouched beneath the onslaught. Then it stopped as suddenly as it had begun. She stood up shakily, dashing wet hair out of her eyes, and turned to face the men standing on the rim behind her. She knew that the white tunic clung to her skin, revealing every curve and color of her body, but she willed herself not to care. *You would see me naked again, is that it? Have you forgotten the legends of my wrath? Any mortal who dares look upon my bare flesh will be ripped to pieces.*

She tried to meet the Pater's eyes through the holes in his golden mask. *"Recte dicis,"* she said. *You speak right.* She continued in Latin: "I am not cold, nor unfeeling. I am filled with fury. And you will feel its lash."

The Pater gave a rusty laugh and motioned to the man at his side, who wore a rayed crown and held a downward torch in his hand. Despite the silk mask that covered the top half of his face, Selene recognized the hawk-faced man by the sharp jut of his jaw. He drew a sleek remote control from his robes, incongruous in the flickering torchlight.

A sudden whirring of gears sounded from the floor beneath her. She looked down to see tall walls of glass shoot up to imprison her in a narrow transparent cylinder. Instinctively, she kicked against the glass, hoping it had been made to hold mortals, not gods. But the wall didn't crack, and she only bruised her toe. She hadn't realized how much she'd appreciated the invention of close-toed boots until she'd been thrust back into Roman sandals.

"Let us try again, Makarites," the Pater intoned. "Tell us about Diana."

"She pretends she can hurt you," Theo said after a moment. "But she is weaker than you think. She brags, but inside she is weak and scared—"

"A half truth."

This time, the sheet of water didn't stop. It pounded down upon her with brutal force, bruising her scalp and her bare shoulders. She bent her head and breathed in shallow gasps, then dared open her eyes. What she saw sent a tremor of terror through her.

The water didn't drain away.

She was trapped inside a quickly filling prison. Already the water had reached her thighs. She slammed her fist futilely against the glass. *Theo wasn't lying,* she thought. *I am weak and scared.*

The water kept coming.

"Again, Makarites. You said you knew how to break her. She will drown if you don't start telling us the full truth. Now."

Selene managed to raise her head to look at Theo. His face remained stern as he watched her, but she could see the terror in his eyes. His fists clenched at his sides. Whether he truly cared for her or not, she could tell that he wanted to run to her. Good old Theo, always trying to play the hero. But what was the point? The initiates had him outnumbered, and no doubt if Theo moved toward her, another glass chamber would appear to stop him. To have any chance of escape, he would have to give them what they wanted.

"The truth." He spoke the word softly, almost wistfully. The water climbed to her ribs. She kicked off from the floor and started to tread water, but her flailing limbs knocked against the glass, and the force of the deluge kept pushing her downward. She braced her feet and hands against the walls of the chamber instead and started to shimmy her way up. As she climbed swiftly toward the top, hope sparked within her. She saw an answering gleam in Theo's eye. In a second, she'd be over the wall, leaping from the glass rim onto the stone ledge surrounding the pit and sinking her fist in the Pater's face.

Then an iron grate slammed down from the ceiling, trapping her inside the cylinder while the water continued to rise.

Feet still braced on the glass, she reached upward to push off the iron bars. Her flesh sizzled on contact with an electric shock. She screamed and fell back into the churning water, the force of the redoubled onslaught pinning her to the floor of her prison. She pressed her face against the glass, peering out at Theo. She knew she should urge him to resist: Whatever the Pater wanted him to do couldn't be good for her. And yet she couldn't control the desperation in her gaze.

Theo's face had gone ashen. Tears stood in his eyes as he shouted a single word: *"Siste!"*

Stop.

The water immediately diminished. A thick stream poured lazily into the cylinder and the water level continued to rise, but she could easily push off the bottom. With her head out of the water and her hands braced against the sides, she could hear the thrum of electricity emanating from the grate only a foot above her hair. Soon, the water lapped at the underside of her breasts, then licked her collarbone.

"Diana is only one name for her," Theo said, his eyes never leaving hers. "She is Artemis. She is the Huntress. But to me she is Selene." As he spoke, his voice grew louder, more confident. "There is rage in her. And strength beyond mortal understanding. And an uncompromising sense of justice. But above all, there is love. She does not know it. She resists it. Even resents it. But it is there in the way she looks at the people of her city. It is there in the way she would give her life for them. Or for her brother Apollo. In him are all her contradictions. She hated him once, but he is a part of her. Without him, she is nothing. She is not weak... but she is soft." His voice fell to a whisper, one meant only for her ears, though it carried throughout the chamber, a public declaration, not to be misconstrued. "And it is a softness I would bury myself in for all the days of my life."

The water slowed to a trickle. The walls retracted as swiftly as they'd arisen, sending water rushing out across the floor and Selene crashing to the ground. She fell on her hands and knees, bruising them badly, and stayed motionless, panting, wondering what new torture lay in store.

Then Theo was there.

He crouched beside her and took her shivering body in his arms. His bare flesh was as clammy and cold as her own, but she pressed her face against his neck, and the warm pulse of his blood warmed her as nothing else could.

"You're supposed to be pretending to hate me," she murmured in English.

"Seemed the gig was up," he whispered back.

No one pulled them apart. No rivers of water or walls of glass rose up to separate them. Theo clutched her a little closer and soon their combined body heat warmed them both. She felt her own shivering subside as his did.

"Diana. Makarites." The Pater stepped to the edge of the pit.

With Theo's hand in hers, she stood.

"Initia facta sunt." The initiation is over. Then the Pater continued in English. "There is no need for the sacred tongue when you profane our sacred space with your lies, Professor. Did you think we would ever believe that you would turn on the woman you so clearly love? We have watched you for many months. You have no secrets from us. But now you have given us what we want. The key to a willing sacrifice."

Theo turned toward her, questioning, but she kept her gaze firmly on the eyeholes in the beaten gold mask. She no longer doubted Theo—or herself. All the memories of her horrific past, all the visions of her uncertain future, no longer mattered beside the feeling of his grip, warm and strong, on her hand.

"You said you won't kill me if I'm not willing," she said to the Pater. "You tried to break me—but you've failed. I do not consent to be sacrificed to your Mithras. And Theo never will either. So what now, Pater? You're running out of options."

"Oh, you'll be willing." She heard a smile in his voice. "Because we must have a sacrifice for the Procession of the Sun-Runner, and what better offering than the Sun himself?"

Across the ring, another panel slid open.

A man stumbled out of the darkness, his hands on his knees. A glass cylinder immediately rose to trap him in place. When he lifted his head, she saw Apollo's divine countenance—and Paul's terrified eyes.

Selene felt as if the pit's floor rocked beneath her. She stumbled, and Theo held her tighter, but sweat slicked her palm and she slipped from his grasp.

"They were waiting for me." Paul's voice was hoarse, as if

he'd been crying or screaming for hours. He wore a slim toga draped around his hips. A laurel wreath garlanded his brows, and his golden hair sprang in perfect coils to his shoulders. His bare torso gleamed in the firelight, covered in sweat. She could smell the fear on him from across the ring. His eyes darted from her, to Theo, to the Pater standing above. "I went to Sophie's and she was lying in a pool of blood on her kitchen floor... They were already there..." His voice faded away. An instant later, his face contorted with terror as a vision overtook him, and he walked through a nightmare only he could see.

"No!" Selene took a step forward, scanning the crowd of initiates for the source of her twin's agony. The hawk-faced man had removed his rayed crown. Now he wore Morpheus's wreath in its place. The poppy buds stood upright, milky white fluid seeping through cracks in the waxy green spheres.

"Stop it! You're killing him!" she screamed.

"Indeed," the Pater continued calmly. "Apollo will choose to die rather than live as one haunted by his own past. He will be our willing sacrifice."

Selene howled and raced across the pit, flinging herself at the side of Paul's prison. She beat her fist against the glass until smears of blood blocked her twin's face from view. Theo shouted at her to stop. Paul backed away as far as his cell would allow, murmuring, "It's no use. It's no use." But she barely heard either of them.

She spun away from the unbreakable prison, sprinting to the wall of the pit, just below the hawk-faced man. *I will leap free like a wolf,* she thought, her feet ringing on the metal floor like the crash of cymbals. *I will rip the crown of poppies from his head and throttle him with it.*

She sprang into the air.

Her hands struck the wall three feet below the rim, and an electric shock sent her tumbling backward with a sharp cry of agony.

The Pater looked down impassively as Theo rushed to Selene. She lay prone, the world spinning and her vision blurred, her heart beating an irregular tattoo. Theo gathered her in his arms, his own heart racing against her cheek.

The Pater's calm voice broke the sudden silence. "There is an alternative. If we can't have the Sun, we would take the Moon."

"Take me instead," Theo shouted, pressing Selene's forehead protectively against his chest.

"*You?* You think there is power enough in your death? You mean nothing to us. For centuries, we have held one goal foremost—to find and destroy those who claim divinity, who hang on to an existence they do not deserve, who block the return of our Lord."

"And when Mithras returns, what will you do then? Move some more equinoxes? You're all fucking delusional, you know that?" Theo spat. "You're clinging to a dying religion that worships a dead god. You have *no* power, except what you *stole*."

Around them, the syndexioi murmured angrily. A few even stepped toward the edge of the pit. But the Pater's voice remained steady. "You do not understand Mithras. He is the God of Three Aspects. Your pantheon, with its petty jealousies and foibles, is nothing more than a dream, given life by man's imagination. Mithras represents the one true God. He existed before the universe. He will exist after it. He is *beyond* this world. *You* are just a product of it."

"If he's so all-powerful, why does he need a string of murders to bring him back?" Theo went on, unbowed.

Again, murmurs from the crowd. This time, more confused than angry. Theo had touched a nerve.

Selene saw the Pater turn his masked face slightly, taking in the reaction of those around him. He raised his voice and spoke over the crowd. "The Host's instructions are far older than I, but they are clear. We must destroy those who would sap power from the God. He alone rules the afterlife. He alone is the leader of soldiers. He alone guides the sun's orbit and moves the heavens on their axes. To assign such feats to false idols is the most terrible blasphemy. Now we reenact His actions at the sites most propitious. The God of Wealth dies at the seat of greed. The God of Bloodlust dies at the seat of war mongering. And tomorrow, at midnight, there must be another sacrifice. Sun or Moon. I leave it to you, Selene DiSilva."

She had no choice. Theo had spoken true. Apollo was a part of her. She pried Theo's hands from her body and levered herself to standing. "Then let the Moon set and the Sun arise."

The triumphant stomping of feet drowned out Theo's horrified protests, but she could hear Paul's keening cries above it all. Whether of grief or relief, she wasn't sure. The walls of the pit slid open, admitting two men in legionaries' armor and a third in a crow's mask. The two soldiers grabbed Selene. She barely resisted. What use was there? The crow pinned Theo in place.

As her captors dragged her toward the opening in the wall, she heard Theo's words, carrying above the crowd's roar, "The Moon may disappear from the heavens, but she always waxes again!"

Beautiful Theo, my Singer of Stitched Words, she thought as the panel slid back into place and hid him from view. *When they kill me, I will truly die. Yet the moon will rise and set as it always has. A blind, unfeeling rock that doesn't know it once had a goddess's soul.*

Chapter 33

APOLLO

Theo couldn't stop panting. His chest refused to expand, no matter how hard he willed the breath to fill his lungs. Every time he closed his eyes to the bare white ceiling of his prison cell, he saw Selene drowning.

It's my fault. His chest constricted a little tighter. *I told them about her love for her brother. I gave them the tools to make her surrender.* Who knew bringing down the Relentless One could be so easy? Just let a mortal learn the secrets of her heart, and she was done for.

Now he lay on the cold concrete floor in no more than a hospital gown, completely unable to help her. *But Flint is still free,* he remembered. This time, he didn't begrudge the Smith his attachment to Selene if it meant he would save her.

Flint had given Theo a way to communicate with him, but what information should he impart? *I've failed. They're going to kill her, and I don't even know where to tell him to go.* He doubted even the Smith's mighty hammer would be able to break through the massive vault door beneath Saint Patrick's. There must be other secret entrances to the mithraeum, but he had no idea how to find them. The plan had always been for Theo to gain the cult's trust, learn the location of the next sacrificial rite, and relay the information to Flint. Then the gods would ambush the cult, stop Selene's murder, and capture the Pater. Now, the only hope lay in Theo's ability to predict the rite's location on his own.

He closed his eyes again, forcing aside the memory of Selene's terror, and tried to recall everything the Pater and his syndex- ioi had said. Surely, somewhere, there was a clue. His brain felt as bludgeoned as the rest of his body, as if the fire and ice had destroyed decades of carefully formed synapses and left him dull and witless.

Come on, Theo, he urged himself, *think! Wall Street, the Rain- bow Room, what do they have in common? Rich people? That does NOT narrow it down.* The next ritual was…he pressed his hands against his temples, trying to force the knowledge into his sludgy mind…the Procession of the Sun-Runner, the Pater had said. But had he provided any clue to its location?

Theo stared up at the ceiling as if looking for inspiration. A sin- gle light and a small vent. A memory pierced his brain instead—he and Selene crawling through the air ducts in a building at Colum- bia as they broke into an office looking for clues to catch the Clas- sicist Cult. When he'd tumbled out of the vent, he'd bowled her over. Her shirt had ridden up, and his hands had rested on her bare abdomen. He'd felt the chill of her flesh, the planes of her muscle, her panting breaths as she demanded he get off her immediately. He'd hastened to obey, knowing even then that if he could've, he'd have stayed pressed against her forever.

At first, the music seemed to emanate from his own head. A dirge for the future he'd lost, for the goddess he'd failed. Then he recognized Paul's voice, very faint, coming through the vent. A haunting, minor key. If Theo'd had any hair left on his arms, it would've stood on end.

Sun and Moon,
Midnight or noon,

Never together.
Never together.

A quiet weeping began, a low counterpoint to Paul's song. The choked sound a person makes who's long lost the knowledge of how to cry.

Theo sat up straight. "Selene?" he whispered. Then, louder, *"Selene?"*

He was sure she could hear him. The crying stopped the moment he spoke. It did not continue. Nor did she respond. Yet the song went on.

But never say never.
When the mountains shake
And the forests quake,
They'll dance together.
Their love's forever.
Their love's forever.

The music stopped, but the tune replayed in Theo's mind, its futile optimism a ceaseless torment.

He knew Selene didn't want to hear from him. She'd made her decision, and she wouldn't want Theo to try to talk her out of it. But that had rarely ever stopped him before. "You have to forgive me," he said loudly. "I didn't know they had Paul or I never would've said anything about him."

"It's okay, Theo." Her voice was barely a whisper through the vent. "This isn't your fault. It's the way it must be."

"No. I'm going to get us out of here. You too, Paul!"

"Stop." She sounded weary, the word more a plea than command. "Don't make this any harder."

He held his tongue, but he wished she were indeed still a goddess that she might hear his silent oath. *I promise, Huntress, I will find a way.*

Selene stared up at the vent, her vision hazed with tears. She called her brother's name, but he did not respond. After his song, he'd fallen silent. Theo, too, had ceased his pleas. There had been no word from Prometheus.

She wondered if she'd ever hear Paul's voice again. She rested her forehead on her knees and waited for the next nightmare to suck her even farther into despair. But nothing came. *The Pater knows he's won,* she decided. *Why bother breaking a woman who's already broken?*

Hours had passed when a voice whispered at the very edge of her hearing. *"Moonshine..."*

"Sunbeam?" she cried, rising to her feet and looking once more toward the vent. "Are you all right?"

"You shouldn't have done it," he said. She could tell he'd been crying.

"Don't say that. How could I let them kill you if it's in my power to save you instead?"

"But I'm ready to die."

"Stop it!" she shouted. "I won't *let* you die, don't you understand?"

"The things I've seen..." He drifted into silence. Then, softly, "Do you remember Coronis?"

"Asclepius's mother. Yes, the crow told you of her betrayal. *I* killed her, not you."

"You killed her because I asked you to." He choked back a sob. "And Daphne?"

"The nymph you loved."

"She ran from me and I...I forced her to become a laurel tree."

"That was all long in the past, Paul."

"Not to me. Not anymore. The Pater sends me visions of each death. I relive every one, in all the horror of tears and blood and flame. All those women I pursued, and young men too. Some came willingly, but some did not. I had no patience for that. And so time after time, I cursed them, I killed them. You were the Protector of the Innocent, the Chaste One! Why didn't you stop me?"

Selene sank back onto the floor. "I...I loved you. I always took your side. Until..."

"Until I lied to you about Orion and made you kill the first man you'd ever kissed."

"Yes." The memory, despite the millennia, still hurt. "I couldn't forgive you for hurting me. But all those others...the nymphs and princesses, the beautiful young men...they meant nothing to a goddess."

"We are cruel, Artemis."

"No—"

"You remember Niobe."

She swallowed, the little girl's screams once more piercing her brain. "The Pater forced me to."

"Then you know we've done unforgivable things."

"We can change!" If she said it loud enough, maybe she'd actually believe it.

"I'm tired, Artemis. I've been changing for over three thousand years. When can I rest?"

"This isn't you talking. This is madness and dreams and despair." She fisted her hands and glared at the vent as if she could see her brother's golden eyes. "I will *not* give up on you. If I can just get you out of here, then you can recover. You'll come back to yourself, and you'll play your songs and write your poems and bring joy to the world. I've never done that, Apollo. *I'm* the one who brings death and vengeance. *I'm* the one who's never learned to love. Let me go in your place. Mother would want it that way."

—◇—

A voice shouted at Theo to wake up, dragging him from a coma-like sleep on the floor of the bare cell. A slot had opened in the door. He fumbled at his face for his glasses, felt a moment of terror, then found them lying on the ground a foot away. Once they were on, he could see the Miles's mask through the slot, facing him with its blank stare.

"How long have I been in here?" If it'd only been a few hours, that meant he still had plenty of time to plan how to rescue Selene. He'd tried to come up with something already, and had proven himself unable to do more than fall unconscious. Not surprising since his body was clearly in shock and he'd long ago been pushed beyond the point of exhaustion. When the Miles grunted, "Twenty hours," Theo choked.

"Surely not."

"Twenty." No inflection, just a statement of fact. He slammed the slot shut.

The sacrifice would take place in just a few more hours. If Theo didn't figure something out, and *soon*, Selene was done for.

Now that the initial shock of the ordeal was over, he found himself able to at least remember what had been said. The Pater had given some indication of why they'd targeted certain gods—they'd chosen those who competed most directly with Mithras. As a god who helped men to seek salvation in the realm beyond the stars and therefore "ruled the afterlife," his powers overlapped with those of Hades, Lord of the Underworld. As a favorite god of the Roman legions—a "leader of soldiers"—Mithras competed with Mars, God of War and Bloodlust. And as the deity associated with Sol Invictus, the Invincible Sun, he would challenge Apollo, the Bright One, who also "guided the sun in its orbit."

The Pater had also mentioned the "propitious" sites of the first two rituals. It seemed they'd been carefully chosen to reflect the victim's domain. *The God of the Underworld—and Wealth—died on Wall Street. That makes sense.* The Rainbow Room held a less obvious connection until Theo remembered that 30 Rockefeller Plaza housed all the news studios for NBC and its affiliates. Fox News was just across the street. A cynic might see that as the site of "war mongering." Another location might have a more obvious connection to soldiers—like the National Guard Armory on Lexington Avenue—but Theo suspected the sacrificial locations had another requirement: They had to be major New York landmarks. Why else would the Mithraists go to such lengths to perform secret rites in incredibly public locations? *They must be drawing some extra mojo from the power of the site itself.*

The Pater hadn't described the site for the Procession of the Heliodromus, the Sun-Runner, but he had implied that Apollo sought to "move the heavens on their axes." What landmark location would have a connection to astronomy?

It was suddenly so obvious he nearly groaned aloud. He patted his hip instinctively for his cell phone, ready to share his findings. But of course, his clothes and phone were gone, and there'd be no reception underground anyway.

Good thing Flint had foreseen exactly that.

The Miles had left Theo his glasses.

He reached up to rub his eyes beneath the lenses, then removed his frames entirely as if to get better access. He had no doubt the Mithraists had cameras in the cell. He looked down at his frames, twisting them this way and that as if examining them for damage. He peered at them myopically until he found the tiny black dot that Flint had affixed to the inside of the left temple. He placed his thumbnail on it and tapped out a message, trying to look casual. He didn't know Morse code, so he and Flint had settled on a simple cipher using the Greek alphabet. If the Mithraists happened to pick up his transmission, hopefully they'd be too obsessed with Latin to figure it out. He tapped sixteen times in a row to indicate the sixteenth letter of the alphabet, then eleven, one, thirteen: π λ α ν. So far, that only spelled out "plan."

He kept going. It took him fifteen minutes to tap out the whole phrase, and he was pretty sure he'd lost count a few times and probably sent the wrong letter entirely. Hopefully, Flint still had enough characters to transliterate it properly into English:

Plan B. Call the cops. Planetarium. Tonight.

Flint had assured him that the tiny device transmitted super low frequency waves that would pass through any walls or earth and be picked up by his own receiver. He constantly monitored seismic vibrations that traveled thousands of miles underground— something to do with his status as the Roman Vulcan, the God of Volcanoes—so hopefully he knew what he was doing.

Theo considered telling Flint about Minh Loi—she could help them secret themselves somewhere in the planetarium to make their ambush more effective. But considering how loath the astronomer had been to help Theo with his questions, he knew she'd never agree to assist in a break-in. Gabi, on the other hand, would have no such qualms. He added her name and number to his transmission, and then regretted it nearly instantly. Sure, as a Natural History employee, she knew her way around the planetarium, but if she insisted on sticking around herself (and knowing Gabi, she would), she could be in great danger. He added her to his mental picture—his best friend, black curls awry, staring wide-eyed at the Pater's blade as it curved toward her heart.

Theo buried his face in his hands, suddenly wishing the Pater would send him flashbacks of his past as he had for Selene and Paul. Anything would be better than his own visions of the future.

Chapter 34

INTERMISSIO: THE HYAENA

The Hyaena knelt on the floor of the Templo, her eyes fixed on the sacred tauroctony before her. The meditation circled like a rosary. Eyes, mind, and soul in concert.

First the Dog.

"Let me be as obedient as a hound, leaping to his master's will," she murmured. Even as she looked upon the Dog's marble form, her mind traced the trailing stars of the constellation Canis.

Then the sculpted Scorpion and Snake.

"Let me face death unafraid," she prayed, "that I might be reborn." She imagined their searing poison flooding her veins as she pictured the stars of Scorpius and Hydra.

The Crow followed, with Corvus's bright square: "Let his dark wings lift me high above this mortal world."

Next, the Bull and the starry horns of Taurus. Neck thrown back, ready and willing to accept the knife.

"Let me not fear the sacrifice, for it is through death that life begins again." This Age would end, as all Ages ended.

Finally, she gazed upon the God Himself, His golden face so

bright it brought tears to her eyes. "Mithras and not Mithras. Son and Sun. Ruler of the Cosmos, who brings the next Age into being. Let Him heal the world."

She finished the prayer and started again. Around and around, just as the heavens orbited the earth, just as the Ages spun on the wheel of time. A whirling vortex to suck her mind into emptiness that she might better contemplate the glory of the god she served.

Seven times she completed the prayer, once for each rank in the Host. Then, a final silent prayer for herself—a rank never publicly acknowledged by the ancients, created for a woman who remained an anomaly in a society of men.

Today, for the first time, another woman had stepped inside the Templo. Diana. The Hyaena had fought against the sudden sense of kinship that she felt with the Pretender. She could not allow her loyalties to waver, not now.

Yet when Schultz had held Diana in his arms, his skin singed red from the flames, hers pale as snow from the water's chill, the Hyaena had to look away. Their love burned bright and pure, like the face of Mithras himself. What sort of god would command his servants to sever such a bond?

What sort of god would let the innocents on the Staten Island Ferry die? Or those killed in the riots the night of Mars's sacrifice? Or Apollo's young lover, who'd fought off the syndexioi until her nails were bloody before they put her down with a bullet to the brain? Yet they all *must* die. The Pater had ordained it, and the Pater was never wrong.

It's my doing, the Hyaena knew. *My doing that the Praenuntius has helped us. My doing that we discovered Diana after all this time.* She'd said she was proud of her role. No other syndexios had done so much to help the Host fulfill its destiny. And yet, the same thought kept circling through her brain, more insistent than the prayer: *I bring death, not life. I bring hatred, not love. How can that be the work of the ever-merciful God?*

She pushed herself off the ground. Her knees cracked. She was not a young woman anymore, to spend hours prostrate before the tauroctony, losing herself in its glory. She looked again at Mithras, and her doubts dissolved in the warmth of His gaze.

Tonight, she reminded herself as she left the Templo, *the moon will set, and a woman will die. It is the will of the God. There can be no rebirth without destruction.* When Diana turned her face to the Pater's sickle, the Hyaena knew she would feel compelled to interfere—to save a woman she'd admired for so long, a woman who reminded her of all the best parts of herself. But she would not.

She would stand aside and do nothing—even if it meant betraying her own heart. Because that, too, was the will of the God.

Chapter 35

KHAOS

Selene had never thought much about the birth of the universe until death stared her in the face. Now, standing at the top of the Cosmic Pathway that spiraled through the Earth and Space Center, where men had so carefully explained their own understanding of creation, she closed her eyes and recited the version she knew, as if remembering her origins might help her understand her destination.

First there was Khaos. Then came Gaia the Earth and Ouranos the Sky, and from their union sprang the Titans: Kronos and Rhea, who bore Zeus and his siblings. To be king, Kronos sliced the manhood from Ouranos with his curved sickle, and Zeus usurped his father's crown in turn, ushering in the Age of Olympians.

It was a simple story. Only four generations until she herself sprang into existence. As for the science behind it, she'd never examined it too closely. She suspected she shared such willful ignorance with most mortals. To each person, the universe was only as old as his own perception of it. It would end when he did.

When the legionary at her side prodded her in the ribs, Selene opened her eyes. The sign to her left read, "13 billion years ago: The Big Bang." As the two soldiers led her down the spiral pathway, another exhibit placard caught her eye. "Each step you take," it read, "is 100 million years." *If only that were true,* she thought. *Instead, I have fewer than one hundred minutes left on earth.*

She slowed her steps; if these were her final moments, she might as well make them last.

She couldn't help feeling like the exhibition had been meant for her alone, a belated lesson in her own insignificance. She wondered if the Pater ordered her down the pathway as an essential component of his ritual, or just to further weaken her will to live. For so long, she'd stubbornly believed that man's Big Bang and the gods' creation myth could exist in conjunction. Now, she felt the two realities collide like the crashing galaxies shown on a nearby panel, exploding with a burst of light too bright to bear.

She'd taken thirty-six steps before reaching the sign that read, "Disk of Our Milky Way Galaxy Appears." It took thirty-seven more before "Microscopic Life Forms on Earth."

Does Paul feel as small as I do? she wondered. He'd already completed his procession and now stood at the ramp's base with the Pater and the two initiates in red robes and silk masks—one of them the hawk-faced man. Like his companion, he carried a whip at his side, but he also bore Paul's bow and a quiver of silver arrows slung across his back.

While the guards had given Selene back her flannel shirt and leather jacket, they'd traded Paul's modest toga and laurel wreath for his full regalia as Phoebus, the Bright One—a brilliant tunic that glowed with each successive color of the sunrise: yellow, orange, red, and purple, interwoven with strips of bright magenta like clouds illuminated by the dawning sun. On his head perched a golden seven-rayed crown. In his youth, he'd worn a similar diadem with ease; now it pressed heavily on his brow. His head hung down, his shoulders slumped beneath the draped fabric of his tunic. He wouldn't look at her.

Theo walked somewhere behind her, escorted by another pair

of men, one in a crow's mask and the other veiled. *He might understand how science and myth can coexist,* she thought. *How my old life may be a paradox, but it's still real to me.* Yet as she neared the base of the ramp, she wondered if she was fooling herself. The Age of Dinosaurs lay only a dozen feet from the end, a faded painting of a Tyrannosaurus rex battling a velociraptor that covered a mere four feet of the three-hundred-foot-long path. At first, she didn't even see where humans fit into the timeline. But there, at the very end: "History of Human Art and Creativity." All within the width of the single human hair displayed in a tiny glass case.

She knew, despite the genealogy she'd grown up with, that Artemis the goddess could not have existed until mankind dreamed her up. If the entire history of human civilization was only a hairsbreadth, what did it matter that she'd lived for three millennia? Why was her own death more important than anyone else's? In the greater scheme of the cosmos, they'd all existed for less than the blink of an eye. The thought was oddly comforting.

Her guards brought her to stand before the Pater in his robes of white silk and mask of beaten gold. "This is the Procession of the Sun-Runner," he announced in Latin. "The Sun bows before the Almighty." He turned to the hawk-faced man and his red-robed companion. "Heliodromus Primus. Heliodromus Secundo. You may begin."

They guided Paul to the base of the ramp they had just descended. Selene tensed. Then the hawk-faced man—the Heliodromus Primus—pulled a silver arrow from the quiver.

"What are you doing?" she shouted. She spoke in English, unwilling to dignify their ritual by using their sacred language. "You said he's not to be harmed."

The Pater shook his head. "He is not to be *killed.* But the Sun-Runner pursues the Sun. From the Host's beginnings, so it has been. If you try to stop us, we're happy to kill your twin, no matter what our arrangement."

Selene could do nothing as the Heliodromus Primus prodded Paul in the back with one of his own arrows.

"Run, Phoebus," he growled. Paul did not respond. The other Heliodromus cracked his whip across Paul's spine. A single line of scarlet sliced through the gleaming tunic—another cloud at sunset. As one, the twins cried out in anguish. Then Paul began to run.

The two Heliodromi chased him, but Paul could outrun any mortal. Yet the whip licked toward him, its black tongue striping his back, his calves, his arms. Up the ramp he went, rolling back time. No more humans, no dinosaurs, no primordial ooze. No earth. No Sun itself. How then could Phoebus Apollo exist? Yet still he ran. No Milky Way. No universe. No great burst of radiation and energy.

Only a singularity, smaller than the smallest atom, yet containing the energy of infinite suns.

Finally, Paul could go no further. He crouched at the top of the ramp, barely visible from where his twin stood below. The mortals who stood over him had no need to strike him further. She could hear his tears.

At the center of the spiral ramp stood the massive white sphere of the planetarium itself, representing the sun. The other planets hung in a ring around the cavernous hall, forever in orbit around the center of the solar system.

Yet the man who'd always been Selene's Sun now cowered before mortals, the center of nothing.

———◇———

From the back of the crowd, Theo could barely see what occurred on the ramp above him, but he could hear the crack of the whip and Paul's tortured weeping. He searched the darkened corners of the hall for any sign of Gabi, Flint, or Captain Hansen and her police officers. Nothing.

He raised his bound hands to his temple as if scratching an

itch and tapped out "planetarium" on the side of his glasses for the fourth time since the syndexioi had led him out of the mithraeum—blindfolded, gagged, and handcuffed—and through a series of what he assumed were abandoned subway tunnels.

The crowd parted for the two Heliodromi who descended the ramp, dragging Paul's bloody body between them. The Pater nodded his approval, then led the procession into the great orb of the planetarium.

Plush seats ringed the space. A hemispherical ceiling arched far overhead, empty and white. He watched three of the higher-ranked syndexioi take their seats in the innermost ring like students on a demented field trip. Each bore a divine item that corresponded to his tutelary planet. The Perses in his Phrygian cap carried symbols of the moon: Selene's bow and the quiver they'd stolen from her in Central Park, now holding seven gold arrows. The Heliodromus from the ice skating rink held Apollo's silver weapon in homage to the sun. The Pater stood before them with Saturn's sickle, its curved blade glinting. Only the lion-masked man—the Leo Primus, Theo had heard him called—bore a weapon that didn't correspond to his planet. Rather than Jupiter's thunderbolt, he carried Neptune's trident.

After what Selene said about the earthquake, I'd rather deal with the lightning, Theo decided.

The Hyaena stood with the lower-ranked men. If she felt any sympathy for the only other woman in the room, her grinning mask hid it well.

"*Ave, Syndexioi Secundi,*" the Pater hailed his followers. Four of the men, including one of the Milites and the unfamiliar Heliodromus, snapped to attention and saluted their leader.

"*Ave, Syndexioi Primi.*" The remaining men saluted, one of each rank, each holding a divine item.

The Corvus guarding Theo drew a gilded, snake-twined caduceus from his robe. *At least the winged cap is safe with Dash,*

Theo thought. *How dangerous can a herald's staff be?* The veiled man, who had first met Theo at the mithraeum's entrance, carried a bronze hand mirror, symbol of Venus. The others referred to him as the Nymphus, the "male bride." The burly Miles beside Selene carried Mars's golden spear, its shaft a full foot longer than the regular one held by the other legionary.

The Pater nodded in acknowledgment of his syndexioi's salute and ordered the two Milites to lead Selene to the center of the room. When the initiates laid Paul's limp body at her feet, she ripped free of her guards' grip and knelt beside her brother. Both Milites went after her, but the Pater waved them away.

Selene dragged Paul's body onto her lap, one arm under his neck, the other clasping his chest. Blood dripped from his back to pool onto the floor around them. Selene looked like the Virgin Mary—a mother cradling her crucified son. A Pietà in a temple to science, a Christian image among pagans.

A lion-masked Leo headed over to the planetarium's control booth. The ceiling dimmed to a deep twilight blue. As it darkened still further, pinpricks of light popped into view. Soon, the entire sky glittered with stars.

Music began, a minimalist tick tock between discordant notes, like the breathing of an old man, or the sound of his plodding footsteps. Theo recognized the track: the fifth movement of Holst's *The Planets*: "Saturn, Bringer of Old Age." A fitting tribute to the sickle-bearing Pater. The constellations moved across the sky with the same deliberate rhythm. Theo watched Orion rise, eternally chased by Scorpius for his sins against womankind. Then Ursa Major, the nymph metamorphosed into a bear as punishment for breaking her vows of chastity. Corvus the Crow, its feathers turned black for its crimes. All placed in the heavens by the wrath of Artemis, the Long-Cloaked Marshal of the Stars. A deity light-years away from Selene, who still huddled on the ground, holding her bleeding brother in her arms, looking as powerless as any mortal woman trapped in grief's grip.

The Pater's voice boomed out above the music. "Diana believes she created the stars themselves, but instead, the stars created her. For we are all dust, birthed at the dawn of time, forged in the furnace of the heavens, fused together by the power of the universe. There is only one God, and He kindled that first spark of energy that started it all. From Him came the planets, the sun, the galaxies themselves, the spheres spinning in perfect harmony, dancing to the celestial music."

As the symphony moved to a climax of blaring brass and pounding timpani, the stars spun in fast forward. The moon rose and set, then the sky lightened once more as the sun made its ascent. With the planetarium bathed in light, Theo could clearly see the tableau before him. Selene stood face to face with the Pater. Paul's body lay at her feet, his chest heaving.

"Let my brother go as you promised. Now," she said, her face expressionless. "Or I will not go willingly."

"Take the Pretender down to the street," the Pater told the Heliodromi. Then he looked back at Selene. "You know he won't escape us for long."

She nodded stonily. All she could give her twin now was time. Theo knew that the wounds on Paul's back would heal. But it would be too late for Selene.

As the Heliodromi dragged Paul's limp body out of sight, the sun plunged once more below the horizon, and Theo could barely make out his lover's face in the gloaming, but her voice was calm as she said, "Do it now. While I still desire it."

Theo tried to shout, but the gag in his mouth muffled his words. He stomped on one guard's foot and swung an elbow into the gut of another, but they held him fast. The Pater lifted his sickle, ready for his harvest. The Hyaena took a step forward as if she would protest, and Theo felt a moment of hope—but then she halted, her masked face unreadable.

"As the sun rises and sets, so will our God rise again," the Pater intoned, tilting his blade so its curved edge caught the starlight. "For He is the true sun."

Theo twisted in his guards' grip, nearly breaking free. The Leo Primus, a heavyset man with the hint of a double chin beneath his lion mask, rushed toward him. He pressed the tines of Poseidon's trident into the back of Theo's neck. "Keep struggling and you'll die," he said, his Queens accent identifying him as the doughboy cop who'd arrested Selene at Rockefeller Center. "You'll be no help to her then."

The Pater gestured for Selene to open her leather jacket and the flannel shirt underneath. Only a thin tank top stood between her heart and his blade. She closed her eyes and tilted her face heavenward.

The light show had cycled back to dawn. The moon set, the stars faded, and the sun rose to turn the sky from black to azure.

"Ashes to ashes," chanted the Pater. "Dust to dust. Stars to stars." He brought the sickle arcing toward her chest. Theo forced himself to keep his eyes open, to watch his love leave the world.

And then, as if to spare him the sight, the room plunged into darkness. The soaring classical music stopped abruptly. In its place, a heavy metal guitar riff blared through the speakers, drowning out the astonished cries of the syndexioi.

In the dim blue light emanating from the control booth, Theo saw Gabriela's head bent over the soundboard. Behind her, the Leo Secundo stood thrashing in Flint's grip. Philippe pierced the man's heart with a tiny dart. Suddenly, the ceiling rained stars, as if the room itself sped through space, galaxies zipping by on either side. The effect was dizzying.

In the starlight, Theo watched Flint rush forward, titanium leg braces steadying his stride and a massive hammer clutched in two hands. Philippe followed behind with his small bow raised. Theo cheered through his gag as Dash darted forward from a side entrance, a gun in each hand and the wings on his golden cap streaming behind him.

Theo had to help, but the trident in his neck promised certain death if he turned in any direction. He bent forward at the waist instead, kicking back at the pudgy Leo Primus while swinging his bound hands into the kneecaps of his other guard. Both men stumbled away from him. He lunged forward, unarmed, thinking only of Selene, when the trident's handle smacked him on the skull and sent him to his knees. He watched the battle unfold through blurred vision.

The Corvus with the caduceus stepped away to block Dash's charge. Dash fired, once from each gun, grazing the Corvus's arm and shoulder. Despite his wounds, the syndexios raised his staff, swinging it forward as if to flick holy water off an aspergillum. Instead, the snakes themselves flew from the staff—no longer gilded figurines, but living, hissing serpents. They shot toward their former owner, tongues flickering.

Dash jumped, eyes squeezed shut in concentration, as if willing his winged cap to lift him into flight—but whatever magic the syndexioi had managed to awaken lay deaf to the Messenger's call. He fell back to earth with a muted thump—right into the snakes' path. They slapped against his neck like a living noose. Eyes bulging, face flushed, he slowly sank to his knees.

Theo watched in horror as the syndexioi advanced to block Flint as well. They moved in perfect, deliberate formation, as if they'd expected his arrival. Flint swung his massive hammer to keep them at bay. The Miles thrust Mars's spear forward, but Flint knocked it aside with the head of his weapon, then struck the soldier hard in the ribs with its handle. Theo began to hope that the Smith might succeed where the Messenger had failed. But then the Perses holding Selene's bow shot three golden arrows at once, and Flint foundered beneath the onslaught, his hammer rolling free as he clutched at the shafts in his stomach.

Philippe cried out and aimed his small bow at his stepfather's attacker. Flint gasped a warning—the Miles had turned Mars's spear on the God of Love. Philippe turned to fire at the new threat, but not before the solider rammed the weapon through his side.

The gods aren't enough, Theo realized desperately. *Come on, Flint, please tell me you called Hansen like you promised you would,* he begged silently. The syndexioi might wield weapons like gods, but he doubted they could heal like them: If a SWAT team showed up with machine guns, they'd fall like any other mortal men.

Selene rushed toward her fallen kin, but a syndexios stepped in front of her. She kicked him soundly in the groin and kept running.

Then a golden arrow from her own bow sliced into her back and sent her sprawling across the floor.

Theo struggled to his feet, trying once more to throw off his captors, but the Leo jammed the trident's tines against his Adam's apple, growling to his comrades, "I know the plan is to capture the Pretenders alive, but surely I'm allowed to kill *this* prick?"

"I'll take him," a woman said from behind them. The Leo turned around, dragging Theo with him.

The Hyaena spoke again, her voice muffled by the grinning leather mask. "The Pater told me to remove the professor before he causes any more trouble."

"You?" the Leo scoffed. "He's stronger than he looks. You're just an old woman."

The Hyaena reached into her robes and pulled out a Glock. "If he tries anything, I'll shoot him."

When the other syndexioi looked at one another doubtfully, she asked, "You would disobey the Pater's instructions? Go help your comrades with the Pretenders. This man is the least of your worries." She raised the gun and pressed it against Theo's temple.

As she led him away, Theo watched the Heliodromus Primus throw a small golden net over Dash, Philippe, and Flint. The mesh expanded to cover all three Athanatoi, falling in heavy folds to the ground. They groaned and bent beneath its weight, their flesh red where it pressed against them.

Selene lay unmoving on the other side of the clearing, an inky puddle forming around the arrow shaft in her back.

"Don't even think about trying to run back to your girlfriend," the Hyaena growled, pressing the barrel of the gun more firmly against his head.

She led him out of the planetarium, down an escalator, and into the gift shop.

"It's all over for you," she said, digging in the pocket of her robe. Theo wondered what new weapon she'd produce. *Something to kill me quietly,* he decided with surprising calmness.

Gabi's curly head popped up from behind the cashier's desk.

"Oh, thank God!" She ran toward Theo. "She got you out!"

The Hyaena pulled the key to his handcuffs from her pocket.

Gabi stepped between them and ripped the gag from his mouth, talking all the while. "She dragged me out of the planetarium and told me to hide, and then I told her she had to help you get out too. Wait, where are you going?" she begged as he moved toward the escalator.

"Selene's still in there!" He turned to the Hyaena. "Unlock the cuffs."

The woman folded her fingers around the key. At the edge of her mask, her jaw clenched. "Not if you're going back in. She's not your concern."

"Then I'll go back in cuffed. I'll bash your Pater two-fisted if I have to." He took another step toward the escalator. He didn't see her swing the butt of her gun at his head, but he crumpled beneath the blow, falling against a metal shelf full of astronomy books.

"Hey!" he heard Gabi protest. Before he could regain his balance, the Hyaena had produced a pair of plastic flex cuffs and secured his metal restraints to the side of the bookshelf.

"I can't let you do that, Professor," she growled in his ear.

Then, with the smell of cigarettes on her breath, Theo finally recognized her voice.

Chapter 36

SUNBEAM

Theo's first thought was one of relief. The police had made shown up after all. "Nice disguise, but where's the SWAT team?" He could see Geraldine Hansen's eyes through the holes in her hyena mask. He wondered how he hadn't recognized her steely gaze before.

She took a step backward. "I don't know what you're talking about."

Theo wondered whether the blow to his head had messed with his brain; he couldn't believe what he was hearing. "You got Flint's message, right?"

"Whatever you're thinking, you're wrong."

He heard Gabi give an impatient grunt. "Okay, now I'm *really* lost," she said. "Who the fuck are you?"

And with that, she ripped the mask from the Hyaena's face.

"You shouldn't have done that, Ms. Jimenez." The police captain turned her gun reluctantly on Theo's best friend. Gabi's eyes widened, and she opened her mouth to scream for help, but the captain shook her head warningly. She gestured with her chin for Gabi to stand facing Theo, then used another plastic restraint to cuff her hands lower on the bookshelf.

"Oh, you are so in for it," Gabi hissed over her shoulder at the cop. "You're getting a call from the ACLU, the Lambda Legal Fund, and every goddamn lawyer I know. This is police brutality, and the people of this city won't stand for it."

Theo barely heard her. His reeling brain was finally putting the pieces together. Hansen wasn't disguised as the Hyaena—she *was* the Hyaena. There would be no rescue. And worse still, Flint's call to Hansen meant the Mithraists had known the gods would attack the planetarium. The Athanatoi never had a chance—Theo'd made sure of that.

"What are you going to do?" he demanded over Gabi's continued diatribe. "Kill us both?" He strained against the bookshelf, trying to rip free, but the restraints showed no sign of weakening. *This is my fault,* he thought desperately. *And if I don't get free, Selene and Gabi are both doomed.*

"I tried to save you." Hansen's voice sounded weary. "I wanted no more innocent blood on my hands. But I have a role to play, Schultz. And *nothing* can stand in the way of that. Now that you know who I am, I can't let you go. If I turn you over to the others, they'll surely torture you further before you die. Is that what you want? I can give you a clean death. That's the only mercy I can spare."

"Wait, wait," Gabriela interrupted, finally sounding uncertain. "I thought you were just going to rough us up. Unjustified incarceration maybe. But when you say *death*, you really mean... *death*?"

"I don't like this any more than you do, Ms. Jimenez."

"Oh, *really*. Then why don't we just switch places, huh? Give me the gun and the badge."

"And what about Selene?" Theo interjected. "You're going to stand by and let them kill her, too? You're her friend."

"She stopped being my friend the moment I realized who she really was," Hansen retorted. "Her death is needed for the resurrection. There's nothing I can do about it, even if I wanted to."

"The *resurrection*? Of *Mithras*? Why on earth would you care?"
She shook her head. "Mithras isn't who you think he is."

"Goddammit! You all keep saying that! I get it. He's more than a Persian god, he's the deity who allows you to ascend through the celestial spheres to heaven. Or at least a whole bunch of Roman soldiers two thousand years ago *thought* he did. But there *are* no celestial spheres! Let's take a tour of the museum, shall we, if you need a refresher course in heliocentrism."

"We were tasked, don't you understand? To bring Death to the Deathless Ones and return our God in their place. The Host himself visited our founder to give him the command."

"The Host?" *I thought that was the name of the cult . . . now it's a man?*

Hansen scowled at him. "I can see the wheels turning in your head, Schultz. You think you can figure this out. But this is a deeper mystery than even you can solve. You would need a lifetime to uncover our secrets. And I'm afraid yours is just about up. I have to get back in there." Her smile faded. She leveled her gun at him. "I'm sorry, Professor. This isn't how it was supposed to happen. I'll give you a moment to say good-bye to your friend."

Before he could speak, Gabi craned her head to look up at him and flashed him a tense smile. "Well, Theo-doreable, I guess this is it." He could feel her heartbeat, fast as a bird's, where his bound hands pressed against her chest. Her own hands were trapped somewhere near his belt. "If we die, at least we die in each other's arms, sort of."

"Gabi—"

"You know, this is quite the compromising position. Good thing I always carry protection, just like you told me to," she continued, her trembling voice belying her saucy wink. She slowly turned her eyes downward to her own chest.

"Glad to know that even at a moment like this, your mind's in the gutter," he said, slipping his hand beneath her jacket. Gabi's eyes widened as his fingers squeezed past her breast to brush against the plastic canister in her inside pocket.

Hansen cocked the gun.

Gabi ducked. Theo yanked the pepper spray from her chest, aimed it at the captain, and squeezed the trigger. She screamed in agony and fired at the same time, but he'd already dragged Gabi down the pole of the bookshelf and out of harm's way.

Hansen was too well trained to shoot again, not while blind. She cursed and put a hand to her streaming eyes.

Theo wished he had Selene's skills. A well-placed kick to Hansen's right hand would've had the cop's gun flying free. But before he could even think about how to manage that while bound to the bookcase, Hansen stumbled back out of his reach. She groped blindly and staggered to the opposite side of the shelves. Selene might never have taught Theo her combat skills, but he'd learned from her example to always use all the resources at hand.

"Come on, Gabi," he urged, "you said you were working out, right?" They threw their weight against the bookshelf. To his utter shock, it tipped over, dragging them with it, and crashed on top of the captain, knocking her unconscious.

Theo whooped.

"Nice work, *chico*, but now we're trapped, too," Gabi grumbled. They lay awkwardly on top of the bookcase, still cuffed to the metal rod.

"I didn't come this far to wind up lying here when the cops finally *do* show up. By then, it'll be too late. Selene will already be dead."

"You going to tell me what the hell's going on?"

"You going to help me get out of here?"

They knocked each shelf of the bookcase loose with an awkward combination of their knees and feet until they could slip the plastic restraints off the edge of the pole. They dug through

Hansen's pocket for the key to Theo's handcuffs and used a pair of scissors from the cashier's desk to cut Gabi's restraints. Throughout it all, the cop lay motionless. Gabi pressed a finger to Hansen's neck, then picked up the fallen gun, staring at it distastefully. "She's still alive. Do you think we should…I don't know, shoot her in the foot to make sure she can't come after us?"

"Leave her alone. She's just a pawn."

"Wow. You're the most naive guy ever, you know that? Do you really have to see the good in *everybody*? She just tried to kill us."

"You don't cut off the tail of the snake, you go for the head. Now give me that—I've got to go get Selene." He held out his hand for the Glock.

"I almost got killed, too," Gabi insisted, holding it out of his reach. "You owe me an explanation."

"You wouldn't believe it. And there isn't time. *Now*, Gabi."

"You don't know how to shoot it."

"And you do?" He lunged for the gun, but she took a step back, her face growing hot.

"It's embarrassing. You remember when I was doing that dig out on the Navajo reservation…"

"I do *not* have time for your stories right now."

Her words rushed out in a single breath. "Let's just say I had a brief fling with a Navajo medicine woman, and she taught me how to shoot jackrabbits, and I'm not proud of it, but I happened to be *really* good."

"Jackrabbits don't shoot back!"

"I'm coming with you."

—◇—

Selene regained consciousness with a gasp of pain. It felt like someone had just ripped her spine from her back. She twisted far enough to see the Pater standing above her holding her gold arrow in his hand. Blood dripped from its tip onto her cheek. She tried to wipe it away, but found she couldn't move her right arm.

As she tried to rise, two syndexioi hurried to grab her, and she found herself too weak to throw them off. A quick glance around the planetarium told her that the rescue had gone horribly awry. Flint and the others lay facedown on the ground beneath the golden net. The syndexioi, despite various wounds, still held their divine weapons.

Selene's only solace lay in the knowledge that the two men she cared most about had escaped. Theo was gone. *It'll be easier to die*, she thought, *without him here to watch. His very presence makes me want to live.* And by now, Paul would be out of the museum. If he could simply flee, he might escape the cult's influence long enough to recover from his despair and find the strength to fight them off when they came for him again. There was no such hope for her.

When I am gone, Apollo, she prayed to her brother, *you must take all that was mine. When women talk of Artemis or Diana, when they dream of a Huntress and her golden bow, I ask that you hear their prayers. That you help them where I have failed. And—in return—that their reverence might lend you the strength I've squandered.*

Flint, however, had not given up. Despite the arrow wounds in his stomach and the golden threads holding him down, the dam that held his rage had split open. He growled like a caged animal, his biceps bulging, the whites visible around his rolling eyes. Yet no matter how he strained, he couldn't free himself from his own net.

Dash, a red welt on his neck from the snakes' embrace, spoke rapid fire to the legionary holding the edge of the net, no doubt hoping to lie, cheat, or steal his way out of captivity. The masked man just looked away impassively.

Philippe, one hand pressed to the spear wound in his side, simply stared at his stepfather's futile battle against his own creation, his eyes filled with compassion. Then he calmly reached for the golden threads—he tore a hole in the net as easily as he might rip the tissue paper on a Valentine's gift. Selene didn't understand until she remembered what Flint had told her about the net's supernatural properties—only someone who truly loved him could escape it.

Philippe slipped out of their prison and turned to reach a hand through the hole. *"Allons-y, Papa!"*

Flint lurched toward the opening, but the gap in the net magically repaired itself, blocking his way. He roared in frustration. *He doesn't love himself,* Selene realized, *otherwise the net couldn't hold him.*

Dash began to cackle hysterically, a sound of more madness than mirth. "Oh, the irony!" he gasped. Flint kept clawing at the net, but all in vain. Philippe screamed at him to try harder, but the syndexioi dragged him away, bending him sideways to stretch his wound. He gasped in agony and then stood still in their grip, incapacitated by pain.

The Pater, his eyes bright blue behind his metal mask, looked from one god to the next. "The pantheon comes to me," he said, a smile in his voice. "Tonight's sacrifice will be powerful indeed!" He turned to the exit. "Bring the Bright One forth!"

"What?" Selene cried as the doors to the planetarium burst open, and the Heliodromi reappeared, dragging Paul between them.

"NO!" she screamed, writhing in her captors' grasp. Paul raised his head slowly, his eyes slitted. *It's all been for nothing,* she thought. *They never meant to let him go.* Still, she begged, "I won't go willingly to my death if you kill him!"

The Pater only laughed. "Who needs you when I have *them*?" He gestured toward the Athanatoi within the net. "They will all go willingly in the end, far more easily than you did." He turned to Paul, lifting his sickle high. "Ashes to ashes, dust to dust."

A crack like lightning. As if Zeus himself had sent a thunderbolt to save his favorite son. The Pater doubled over with a pained grunt. *Not lightning,* Selene realized. *A bullet.* From somewhere far overhead, Selene heard Gabriela Jimenez shout, "Next time, pray faster, *cabrón!*"

The two syndexioi holding Selene dropped her and rushed to their Pater. Then Theo was at her side, grabbing her useless right arm and dragging her toward an emergency exit.

"No, wait," Selene managed, her mind spinning as she stumbled after him. He ignored her protests, still pulling her arm with surprising strength.

Around them, bullets flew, sending the syndexioi cowering behind the seats. The wounded Pater managed to raise his head, his eyes full of fury. He clutched his stomach, and blood seeped between the fingers of his left hand, staining his white robe. His right hand still held the sickle. He staggered toward Paul.

Selene froze, barely able to process the scene before her. She knew she should rip away from Theo, but her arm was dead weight; she couldn't twist it from his grip. Pain from the arrow wound seared up her back and into her skull as she tried to break free. For the first time, Paul's eyes locked on hers.

"Artemis," he whispered, so faintly only the Huntress's ears could hear him. "I can't see the sun . . ."

Using her whole body, Selene tore from Theo's grasp just as the Pater drove Saturn's divine sickle into her brother's heart.

Around her, every mortal injured in the chaos suddenly collapsed, reaching for minor wounds that suddenly grew deeper and bruises that spread wider. The man she'd kicked in the groin keened in high-pitched torment. The Corvus grazed by Dash's bullets moaned as he tried in vain to stanch the sudden gush of blood that drenched his arms. Theo clutched at the wound peeking above the collar of his shirt, his groan of pain a stuttered hum. With Apollo's death, healing simply ceased. An atonal symphony of agony arose in its place, a discordant requiem ripped from the throats of men to proclaim the God of Music's passing.

Theo reached for Selene once more, clearly fighting through

his own suffering. "This is our chance," he gasped. He dragged her out of the planetarium, urging her to run faster.

But she heard only the dirge. She felt only the sickle as it sank into her own chest. As it sliced her twin away. As it cleaved her heart in twain.

Chapter 37

MOONSHINE

On the top of Mount Kynthos, high above the shores of Delos, I stand with my twin. His long hair catches the sunlight as the wind whips it free of its bonds. It streams forth in ribbons of gold.

Our mother sits on the rocky crest, watching her son with eyes the color of the ocean. Her gaze turns from him to me, and her pride beams as bright and fierce as the rays of the sun itself.

From the temples below, where men pay homage to the colossal statues that are mere shadows of our true glory, voices rise.

"Everywhere, O Phoebus," they sing, "the whole range of song falls to you. Over mountain peaks and high headlands of lofty hills, and rivers flowing out to the deep, and beaches sloping seaward, and havens of the sea."

Apollo lifts his lyre and begins to play. The music floats down the rocky slopes and toward the wine-dark waters that surround us. The priests below sway to its tune. The waves themselves dance to its rhythms. The music overspreads the earth and reaches Father in the heavens, who clears all clouds from the sky in deference to his glorious son, Phoebus, Bright One, whose music carries the sunlight on its wings.

Our mother's joy is a palpable thing, spurring our feet to dance upon the sun-baked ground. I twine my voice with my twin's. We sing as the

sun rises higher in the sky. We sing as it sets, knowing it will rise again.
I am perfectly happy. And I know, in the deepest reaches of my heart,
that this feeling will last forever. "O Phoebus," I sing again. "O Phoe-
bus . . . O Phoebus."

———◆———

Theo could hardly bear to look at Selene. She sat on the couch in
Ruth's apartment and stared vacantly at the wall, her lips moving in some silent prayer, just as she had for half a day. The same
words, over and over.

"Do you think she's going to be all right?" he asked again.
"Maybe we *should* take her to the hospital."

Gabriela sounded like she wanted to slap him. "*You're* the
one who told us that she *never* goes to hospitals. She's in shock,
okay? If it were up to me, we'd be in an emergency room right
now, rather than holed up in this apartment with not one but
two barely conscious women on our hands. If they die, I am *not*
responsible. I want that on the record."

Ruth was far more patient. "I checked the wound in her back.
The bleeding's stopped and the bandage is clean. I don't think it
hit a lung or she'd be breathing blood. How are *you* doing?"

"I'm fine." The brand on his chest, which had flared anew
with Apollo's death, had settled back into a dull ache as soon
as they left the museum. The bruises on his head from the syndexioi's blows were swollen but bearable. Physically, he was in
better shape than Selene. Mentally, he was a wreck. He'd made
some of the worst decisions of his life this week. Dragging Captain Hansen's unconscious body with them when they escaped
the planetarium probably counted among the worst of all, but he
knew that to protect Selene in the long term, he needed answers
only the captain could provide.

Now the unconscious policewoman lay in Ruth's bedroom,
her hands and feet securely tied to the bedposts. She had no visible wounds, but she must've cracked her skull when the book-

shelf fell on her. Theo tried to worry about her—for all he knew, she could be in a permanent coma—but all his anxiety remained focused squarely on the woman sitting beside him on the couch.

He'd never seen Selene like this. Wrath, frustration, grief, anger, even laughter—these were the emotions he knew. And on the rarest of occasions, love. But this vacancy was more terrifying than the height of her rage.

Hippo, who'd nearly fallen over with the force of her own wagging tail when Selene entered the apartment, had finally given up on getting any response from her mistress. The dog lay beside the couch, her head pillowed on Selene's feet, staring up at her mournfully.

Theo took her hand in his and tried, once more, to speak to her. "Selene?" He kept his voice gentle and calm, although he wanted desperately to shout her name. This woman who could hear a rat crawling out of a sewer half a block away now seemed deaf to his words. He wanted to call her by every one of her three hundred epithets, hoping that one would finally break through. *She has so many facets,* he thought desperately, *surely one must remain.*

He glanced at Ruth and Gabriela. His two friends stared at him, both undoubtedly burning with curiosity. He wasn't sure how he'd keep the truth from them much longer, but he owed it to Selene to try. "Could you guys give us a minute?"

Gabi rolled her eyes. "How big do you think this apartment is, *chico*? You want me to go hang out in the bedroom with the cop in the coma? Or should Ruth and I have a nice chat in the bathtub? Or maybe we should just run around the corner for some take-out except...oh that's right...there could be some masked lunatics out there waiting for us. I mean *hopefully* we lost them, but who knows, right? *I* certainly couldn't tell you what to expect, since I don't know *what is going on*." She crossed her arms over her breasts and sank back defiantly into the room's sole armchair.

Ruth, however, stood up quietly. "Come on, Gabi, I do have a kitchen, you know. Why don't we make something to eat? I'm sure we could all use it."

Gabi shot a furious glance at her, but then softened. Ruth had that effect on people. "Okay. Fine." She rose with a huff. "But when we come back, Theo, you owe us an explanation."

He nodded weakly.

He waited until Ruth closed the kitchen door. Then he waited a few moments more, knowing Gabi's penchant for eavesdropping, until he heard it close more firmly a second time.

He kissed Selene very gently on the cheek. She didn't respond.

Who do I think I am, he wondered, *that I could wake her with a kiss? Prince Charming?* Selene had never been the damsel in distress—she'd always been the hero instead. He sighed and laced her limp fingers in his. That was another thing he worried about: She hadn't moved her right arm since the planetarium. The gold arrow hadn't struck any organs, but it might've bruised her spinal cord. He'd have to trust Selene's preternatural healing powers to fix the damage. In the meantime, all he could offer was comfort.

"Selene?" he said again. Then, more softly, "Artemis? Come on, Lady of Hounds, you're freaking out Hippo." The dog lifted her head and whimpered at the sound of her name. Her tail lifted once in a halfhearted wag, then thumped back against the floor. She licked Selene's booted foot, then gave a loud sigh before lowering her head again.

"She Who Helps One Climb Out, can you help yourself?" Theo begged. "Can you escape whatever world has trapped you?" He kept talking, not knowing if it helped, but unsure what else to do. "Stormy One, Relentless One, Good Maiden. I'd rather you be angry than this. I'd rather you be cold and furious like you were when we first met. Please, anything but this, Moonshine."

And then, with the sound of the nickname only her twin had ever used, she finally turned to him.

"Theo?" Her voice was hoarse, but it was hers. Relief flooded through him. He placed his hands on her cheeks and swooped in for a kiss.

Her lips didn't move. He pulled back, afraid he'd startled her with his exuberance, and what he saw in her face made him drop his hands in shock. She was furious.

"How dare you use that name?" She nearly spat the words. And with that, she suddenly dissolved into wracking sobs. The Lady of Hounds howled. The Stormy One thundered. The Bare-Fisted pounded her chest in lamentation. Through her cries, he could just make out her slurred words. "It's my fault he's dead. It's my fault he's dead."

Hippo whined and tried unsuccessfully to crawl under the sofa. Theo reached to take Selene once more in his arms. He would weather the storm, no matter its violence. But her left arm whipped out with all her old speed, and she slammed him hard on the chest, striking his burnt flesh. He fell backward onto the ground with a gasp.

Her tears abruptly stopped. *"Do not take this pain from me."* The simple words were spoken like a curse. Never before had he seen her as Hecate, dark goddess of magic. Always, he'd found it the least likely of her incarnations. But in that moment, he could almost see the tendril of hatred that reached toward him like black smoke, and he wondered if she'd summoned some lost power in her grief, some evil spell to kill him where he sat.

He stood up hurriedly, one hand to his throbbing chest, and walked backward to the kitchen, afraid to turn his back on her. Her eyes followed him all the way, her hatred still a palpable threat. Only when he touched the knob did she turn away from him, her whole body shaking silently.

He retreated into the kitchen and turned to face his dumbfounded friends. After a stunned moment, Ruth turned purposefully toward the freezer and pulled out a handful of ice cubes. She wrapped them in a paper towel and handed them to

Theo, who unbuttoned his shirt and held them to the brand on his chest with a hiss of pain. He stared at the fish tank on the counter, where an angelfish and a blue guppy swam side by side, oblivious to the drama around them. He felt a stab of jealousy.

Gabi gave an unsympathetic snort. "*Now* who should be going to the hospital?"

Theo could only shake his head. "It's nothing."

To his surprise, it was Ruth who spoke next. Her words were firm, as if she'd known for a long time what she wanted to say and had just been waiting to find the strength to say it. "I didn't question you when you started seeing Selene, even though there was always something about her that made me... uneasy."

Gabi barked a laugh. "Understatement of the year."

"And I didn't question when you asked me to take Hippo," Ruth went on, "even though I knew you were lying to me about why... and that you'd never lied to me before. And when you showed up with nowhere to go, I took you in and didn't ask for the whole truth, even though I thought I deserved it. And I've never asked you any hard questions about Selene, even though I don't really know who or *what* she is." She lifted a meaningful brow, and he knew she spoke of the video she'd seen on his phone—Selene miraculously healing beside the stream in the Catskills. Gabi looked from her to Theo, clearly wondering what she'd missed, but Ruth plowed on. "And tonight, you show up with an unconscious cop and Selene wounded and a brand on your chest, and I let you in again. I didn't even pause. Because..."

Gabi squinted suspiciously at the hesitation, but Ruth finally pressed ahead with a deep breath. "Because you're my friend. Because despite your lies, I trust you. But if even half of what Gabi has said about what happened at the planetarium is true, you've put us both in danger. Even *that* I could forgive. I would go into danger for you. You know that. And so would she."

Gabriela rolled her eyes but didn't disagree.

"But whatever just happened in there"—Ruth's voice dropped to an angry whisper—"you have to tell us. And you can't lie. Because either you did something so terrible to that woman that she had to hit you—in which case you're not the man I thought you were, and you are no longer welcome in my house—or she is an *abuser*, Theo, and I will not stand by while you let yourself be treated like that. I will call the cops and they will drag her and her dog out of my apartment, and I don't give a shit if they discover the half-dead police captain on my bed."

Only the quiet gurgle of the fish tank's filter broke the silence. Then Gabi gave Ruth a soft, but very deliberate, round of applause.

Theo finally made a sound somewhere between a laugh and a sob and sank onto the bar stool beside the kitchen counter. "It's mostly the former and a bit of the latter. How's that for an answer?"

"Shitty academic ambivalence," Gabi said immediately. "No more circumlocutions and prevarications, Dr. Schultz. How about you *start* by explaining who you gave my phone number to." She glanced at Ruth. "Remember I told you I got a call from this dude with this incredibly low voice, like sexy-town rumbly low, and he said he was a friend of Theo's and Theo was in trouble, *again*, and could I please sneak him and his friends into the planetarium? Well, turns out he's on crutches and has these withered legs like a paraplegic or something, but otherwise he's like super-hot in this very straight, very muscly, very much needs a shave kind of way...I mean, if you're into men, which I'm not, but trust me, there's something broken about him that makes you just want to fix him."

"Gabriela, please..." Theo moaned.

"Yeah"—she held up a dismissive hand—"we're not done with you, but let me finish. So he's not alone. Sexy hairy man's with these two other guys: one chain-smoking teenager who's as gay as the day is long and one slick prick in expensive clothes who won't shut up. And they won't tell me who they are or how they know Theo." She gave her friend an accusatory glare.

He sighed. "They're Selene's family. Extended family."

She scowled dubiously.

"I swear it on all that's holy. Look, you know how private Selene is. If I told you any more, it'd be a betrayal of her trust. Her secrets aren't mine to tell. I'm sure you can understand that."

He knew Gabriela always found "keeping secrets" oxymoronic, but Ruth nodded reluctantly.

"Let's just say that Selene's family history stretches back just as far as this cult does," Theo continued. "I told you that the guys at the planetarium were members of a Mithraic cult. Well, they see her family as a threat to the resurrection of their god."

"Hold up," Gabi interrupted. "Like actual resurrection? Not like metaphorical one?"

"Yup. As far as I know, they think it's the real shebang. They wanted to kill Selene's twin brother—she was willing to die in his place. And I was willing to die for her."

"I don't see why you bothered," Gabi grumbled, "if she's the kind of girl who's going to punch you for saving her. She's got anger problems, Theo, and trust me, I know all about anger problems. She should be in therapy."

And that, finally, made Theo laugh. He envisioned Selene sitting on a leather sofa discussing three thousand years' worth of incestuous family drama while the shrink was driven slowly and inevitably insane. Then his laughter turned to a choked sob as all the pain and terror of the past few days came flooding back. For a long while, he simply sat slumped on his stool while Ruth held him around the shoulders and Gabriela clasped his waist until he could breathe again.

Gabi released him first. Ruth more reluctantly. "So now are you going to tell us why she hit you?" she asked him softly.

"I tried to make her feel better." The words sounded ridiculous as soon as he'd said them.

"Wow." Gabi crossed her arms angrily. "Honestly, *querido*, she sounds like a bitch. So it's just as well she doesn't want you around."

Theo shook his head. "She just thinks she doesn't."

He could feel Gabi and Ruth exchanging an incredulous look over his head. They thought him delusional. Odds were, they were right. But he owed it to Selene, and to himself, to give it one more try.

Chapter 38

THE HOST

From the corner of her eye, Selene saw Theo kneel before her on the rug.

"I know all the myths about goddesses who've been angered," he said gently. She didn't turn to look at him. "I know that to assuage their wrath, an offering must be made."

She didn't want to hear any of this. He might be a Makarites, yet what could his books and research tell him of the true nature of gods and goddesses? But to tell him to stop would require talking to him, and she couldn't bear it. She could just hit him again, but she found herself barely able to move. Her right arm still hung limp; her back throbbed with pain. Easier just to ignore him and hope he finished soon.

"I thought of bringing you some bacon or ham, since I know how you love pork," he said with a glimmer of his usual wit. She felt no urge to smile. "I could burn it in front of you, let you inhale the smoke. But Ruth's fridge is basically empty, and she doesn't want to set off the fire alarm." He gave her a flat, very un-Theo smile, and she realized that he joked more out of habit than anything else. He didn't find it funny either. He paused. She didn't look at his face, but she watched his body. His hands lay flat on his knees, his knuckles white. "The only offering I can make, the only offering I *want* to make, is the truth."

He dared to take her right hand in his. She let him hold it, unable to withdraw without using her left arm to do it, and unwilling to show such weakness.

"The truth is that you can never push me like that again. I told you I'd be patient—I know that violence is in your nature, and that you don't play by the same rules as a mere mortal like me. But I can't play by yours. I won't heal in a day, Selene. This is the only body I've got and I'd like it to last. So if you're angry, you can scream at me, you can throw dishes, but don't ever strike me. If you do, I'm gone, no matter how much it might tear me apart to leave you." He paused as if waiting for her to say something.

She stole a glance at his face then, noticed the red of his eyes behind his glasses and the way his shoulders hunched as if to protect his chest. She remembered the wound, then—the brand she'd seen below his collarbone in the ordeal pit—and she felt a sudden stab of horror. *Am I the wrathful goddess once more? The murderer of Niobe's children?*

"Just leave," she insisted. *For your own good.* "Stop trying to make this all right."

She saw his body tense, and knew he was on the brink of getting up and walking away. But then he took a deep breath and continued. "*I* will decide when to give up on you. On *us.* I will say my piece, Selene. Apollo is dead. But there was nothing you could do to stop that. If you're going to blame anyone, blame me. *I* told Flint to contact Hansen for help. It's my fault the cult knew that your brothers were coming—my fault that they didn't have a chance. I failed you—I failed Apollo. I failed Dash and Flint and Philippe. For that, I am truly sorry."

"You should've let them kill me, too," she whispered. "We shared a womb. We should share a grave."

"No." He sounded angry. "What I will *not* apologize for, what I will *never* regret, is saving you."

She could tell he expected her to say something. To offer him some hope for the future. But she had nothing left to give. *The piece of me that always belonged to my twin has split away, taking with it all that was civilized, or warm, or graceful. All that's left is grief so strong it will carry me into madness, and rage so hot it threatens to incinerate everything around me. To contain them both, I must turn my soul to ice.*

Theo still wouldn't give up. He pulled over the footstool so he could sit level with her. In his eyes, she saw his devotion, his intensity, his hope. "You're in shock," he said. "You're in mourning. I understand that. But I've given you all the time I could—the others are in danger, now, and we have to help them. We're the only ones who can stop the Pater."

She knew he spoke the truth, but she couldn't bring herself to care about the rest of her family's fate, not when the image of her twin's death played in an endless loop through her brain.

Hippo appeared from somewhere behind the couch and scuttled toward her mistress. Selene felt the cold nose brush against her palm. She did not respond.

"Come on, Selene!" Theo urged. "If you won't do it to save Flint or Dash or Philippe, do it to bring down the Pater."

"Justice for Apollo," she said softly. Hippo whimpered and slunk away once more.

"Yes, if that's the only thing you understand." Theo sounded exasperated, disappointed. "Do it for vengeance."

"Vengeance..." The word was bitter on her tongue. "Niobe. Coronis. Orion. I thought I could change. I thought I could find mercy in my heart. But the world needs a Punisher, doesn't it?"

"The world needs *you*," Theo replied sternly. "So get off the couch and let's rescue the others, just like they tried to rescue you."

"I don't know how," she said quietly.

"That's never stopped you before."

Theo was right. Selene took a deep breath and levered herself off the couch with her good arm. "Then we start with Hansen."

She moved into Ruth's small bedroom and stood looking down at the old woman lying spread-eagled on the coverlet.

She couldn't help remembering her as she'd been in the 1970s, when they'd worked together on the force. Geraldine Hansen had dedicated her entire life to keeping the city safe, growing careworn in its service—or so Selene had thought. How long had she actually been serving a secret master?

Theo came to stand at her side. "Trust me, I'm just as angry at her as you are. She held a gun to my head—worse, to *Gabi's* head—and threatened to kill us. But she's the only lead we've got. You have a bad habit of killing people before they can tell us anything—let's try some restraint this time."

Selene sat heavily on the edge of the mattress and placed a fingertip on the woman's temple.

"What are you doing?"

"Finding out what she knows," she said calmly.

"Not killing her?"

"Not yet."

"So you're just going to read her mind? You can do that?" He shifted uncomfortably, clearly wondering if she could do the same to him.

Selene knew what little power she might have left would never work on a man, but there was no need to spell that out for him. "Geraldine Hansen worshiped me once—as a hero, not a goddess—but it might be enough to establish a link to her," she said instead. "I've done it before, with the bodies of women who prayed to me at the moment of their death."

Selene closed her eyes and reached inside herself for the whisper of *pneuma* she still possessed. For her, the divine breath had always blown strongest in the wilderness. If she'd been outside, she could've called upon tree and moon, spring and stone, for strength. Indoors, she could only draw upon Gerry herself. The woman might be a follower of Mithras, dedicated to destroying the Athanatoi, but she had once been a Protector of the Innocent, just like Selene. As a rookie cop, she'd looked at the Huntress with adoration. If Selene could tap into that worship, however oblique, she might be able to enter the captain's memories.

She spread her awareness toward Gerry. The woman's blood pulsed slow and even against her fingertip. The skin of her temple felt wrinkled from years of squinting suspiciously at the world. Selene reached deeper, trying to recall the young woman she'd known—short red hair feathered at the temples, eyes bright and curious, a light voice and a spine of steel. What she found instead was herself.

Officer Cynthia Forrester, sleek black hair unmarred by its white streak, one or two fewer creases on her brow, but otherwise identical in appearance to Selene DiSilva. She took a deep breath, let go of her own consciousness, and tumbled into Gerry's memory.

——◇——

The smell off the lake at the top of Central Park—if you could even call it a lake—made Gerry's stomach turn. Rotting food, tires, oil barrels, all floated in the algae-coated puddle, their odors magnified by the steamy summer heat that clung to the air long after the sun went down. In these desperate hours of the morning, with the few working lampposts doing little to dispel the dark, the lake attracted criminals like clouds of mosquitoes. Their sergeant had warned that no woman could patrol such a dangerous beat. That only guaranteed that Officer Cynthia Forrester would volunteer. "If you want to learn something," she'd said to Gerry, "you'll come along."

At the moment, Cynthia was teaching her how to choke a cocaine dealer half to death.

Gerry stood dumbfounded—the man easily outweighed her mentor by two hundred pounds, and he was jacked on his own product to boot. His face had turned an alarming shade of red.

"Is that really necessary?" Gerry asked. "He wasn't exactly resisting arrest."

Cynthia grunted and moved her mouth an inch closer to the man's ear. "Tell you what, buddy. All you've got to do is escape from me, and you won't spend the rest of the 1970s in jail." He squirmed in her grasp and stomped a foot inches from her toe. Cynthia looked at Gerry. "He's resisting now, isn't he?"

"Why don't you just cuff him and get it over with?"

"Because he doesn't deserve to go easy."

"There're plenty of cocaine dealers, what do you have against—" A faint whimper drew Gerry's attention to a clump of chest-high vegetation at the water's edge.

"That's what I've got against him," Cynthia snarled, nodding toward the cattails.

Gerry swung her pistol toward the sound and approached cautiously, trying to move as silently as Cynthia always did.

"Come out of there," she said, deepening her voice. She'd never sound like a man, but it didn't hurt to try. Perps never took policewomen seriously—at least not until they met Cynthia.

The reeds parted. An emaciated child in a pair of grimy shorts and a tank top crawled through on all fours. Tears streaked her pinched face. When she stood, her knees knocked together. A large purple bruise circled her upper arm. White powder clung to her upper lip. Gerry just stared, the barrel of her pistol still pointed at the child's skinny rib cage.

Cynthia's voice was calm. "Lower your gun, Officer."

Gerry snapped back to attention, holstering her sidearm so fast she almost dropped it on the ground. She crouched down before the child. "What's your name, honey?"

The girl cast a terrified glance up at the drug dealer, just as he made a last effort to break from Cynthia's grip. Gerry turned around in time to see him fling his torso forward, hurling the policewoman over his shoulder and onto the ground. He dove toward the girl, shouting, "Don't you rat on your daddy!"

Gerry threw herself in front of the child, her heart pounding—just as a wide-heeled pump rocketed through the air and caught the dealer on the temple, sending him unconscious to the ground. Cynthia stood, brushing *grass from her uniform. The rent in her knee-length navy skirt reached all the way to her hip. She adjusted her standard-issue miniature fedora, then retrieved her shoe with a tight smile. "Damn sight more useful as a weapon than as footwear."*

It took another half an hour before the little girl let Gerry pick her up. Throughout, Cynthia stood with one foot balanced on the back of the drug dealer's neck in case he revived. He didn't.

They called in the arrest, then Gerry carried the child back to the precinct in her arms before turning her over to the Bureau of Child Welfare.

Later, in the utility closet that served as the women's locker room, Gerry took a much-needed drag on a cigarette, finally regaining her calm after the harrowing night. "My father's a great cop, but even he doesn't have instincts like yours," she said to Cynthia, tapping the ash into an empty can of Tab cola. "How did you know the girl was there?"

Cynthia shrugged as she rolled off her stockings and pulled on a pair of canvas shorts in their place. "Experience."

"Experience? You've only been on the force three years longer than I have! How old are you . . . twenty-five?"

"Then call it women's intuition," Cynthia said with her customary scowl. She slipped on a pair of sneakers and jammed a large-brimmed sun hat over her sleek black hair.

"Whatever it is, I hope some of it rubs off on me."

Halfway out the door, Cynthia turned back to Gerry. She stood silently for a moment, lips pursed as if holding back her words by force. "It's not enough, you know," she said finally. "You can help a few, but the pain goes on. We row against the tide. That child . . . she'll probably end up like her father someday." She left without another word.

Gerry watched her friend go, wishing more than ever that she could tell her the truth. It's going to be okay, Cynthia. You don't realize it, but the work we do prepares the way for the Last Age. No child will go hungry, no woman will suffer, and the sinners will finally meet their just ends.

She tossed the cigarette butt into the can, then took off her fedora with its shiny badge and placed it carefully on a shelf. Then she drew her neck-

lace from beneath the collar of her shirt and rolled the gold cross between her fingers.

"Speed the day of Your return, my Lord," she prayed, her voice no more than a whisper in the empty room. "Your children need You."

Then she reached for the round medallion that hung beside the cross. Though she knew her fellow syndexioi would never allow it, she longed to share the medallion's meaning with Cynthia. The policewoman would make a mighty soldier in the army of the Lord. But her father had made it clear long ago—the Mystery admitted only one woman at a time. That honor—that burden—fell to her alone. Still, it felt wrong withholding the truth when the knowledge could bring her friend such comfort.

"I vow to do everything in my power to bring about the Resurrection in our lifetime," she murmured, squeezing the medallion of Saint Theodosius. "So that Cynthia and I, and all the others who risk everything to bring peace to our world, might finally enjoy the fruits of our labors."

She closed her eyes and reached for her God. He didn't always respond. But today He granted her a fleeting vision: a city at rest, the sunlight warming the towers of steel, while women and men, their children at their side, all walked in the same direction. They filled the streets, eager but patient. And finally, at the water's edge, He appeared. More beatific than in any painting or crucifix. His smile as gentle as a summer breeze, His face as radiant as the sun itself. He wore no crown of thorns, for all suffering had come to an end. Instead, a seven-rayed diadem graced His brow. The wind lifted His cloak on its breath—red on the outside, star-spangled blue on the inside—and the people sighed in awe. Gerry stood at His side, and her father stood near, his face full of pride. And there, amid the crowd, walked Cynthia. The lines erased from her forehead, the frown banished from her lips. She looked up to Gerry and smiled. "Thank you," she said.

———◇———

Selene lifted her finger from the woman's temple and blinked her way back into the present, into her own consciousness. Captain Hansen's gray eyes stared into hers, wide awake.

376 Jordanna Max Brodsky

"Your heart has always been true, hasn't it, Gerry?" she asked quietly.

The captain's face remained stone, but tears pooled in her eyes.

"The Pater sent you visions, too," Selene continued. "Not memories of your past, but dreams of the future. You saw a man with a cloak of stars and a rayed crown, leading the people into an age of peace."

"Mithras," Theo said from behind her.

Selene kept her gaze fixed on Gerry and shook her head slowly. "No. Jesus."

She heard Theo's quick intake of breath. "'The God of Three Aspects,' that's what the Pater called him."

Selene nodded. *Mithras and more than Mithras,* Prometheus had said. She hadn't understood why until this moment.

"The cult's not trying to resurrect Mithras," Theo continued, his voice hushed. "Or Jesus. They're resurrecting Jesus *as* Mithras. To them, they're one and the same. Different aspects of the same god. Like a new trinity."

"An *old* trinity," Gerry snapped before turning her face aside and blinking away her tears. "Do not ask me to betray the Host. I won't do it."

Selene would not relent. "This Host killed a brother before his sister's eyes."

"We killed Pretenders."

"You killed a brother before his sister's eyes," she repeated. "You killed *my* brother, Gerry."

The policewoman's entire body began to tremble with repressed emotion. *Look how hard she fights not to weep. Not to scream. We are very alike, this warrior and I.*

Deep within herself, as deep as the old memories of working the city streets with young Gerry at her side, Selene found a sliver of empathy. Despite everything the captain had done, she couldn't help seeing Gerry as a victim of her own rectitude. If she'd been a little more compromising, a little less committed to saving her city, perhaps she would've seen how unforgivable her actions had been. *Another way we're the same,* Selene realized. *As a goddess, I killed with impunity, always convinced that my brand of justice was the only right one. How many innocents died at my hands because I was protecting the honor of the Olympians? How many have died at the hands of Gerry's cult because they were doing the same for their god?*

Selene's smooth fingers wrapped around the woman's arthritic ones. The lines across the cop's knuckles told the years like the tally marks of a prisoner in a cell.

"You wanted to share it with me—this dream of yours—but you kept your secret well," Selene said, finding a gentleness she thought had burned away with Apollo's death. "I had a secret of my own...you know that now. You probably knew it from the moment I appeared this fall, pretending to be my own daughter. Is that how the cult found me? Through you? And from me, you found my brother Dash, and from him, the others were easy to trace."

Gerry didn't respond, but her lips tightened in assent.

"Let there be no more secrets between us, Gerry." Selene took a long breath then let the truth pour forth—a cleansing stream to sweep away the dam between them. "I came into creation as Artemis. A daughter, a sister, a huntress. A woman. Others might not have seen me that way—I did not dress like a girl, I desired no children, I refused to sew or spin or bow to the pleasure of others. And in all the ages since then, for all the hundred names I've borne, I've sought to protect my people, my women, from those who would deny them those rights. Rarely have I found a companion in that quest. Once I ran beside nymphs with long black tresses and arrows soaring, and our hounds bayed in concert with our own cries—announcing the approach of justice, trumpeting the joy of the hunt. My nymphs faded away long ago...but you reminded me of them." She gripped Gerry's hand tighter. "So brave, so clear, so stubborn. The years have aged you, my friend, but your heart is still strong. Open it to me, as once you wished to. I promise that this time—I'll listen."

Gerry turned her head to Selene and held her gaze for a long moment. Then she slowly withdrew her hand, eased her way onto her elbows, and propped herself against the headboard. She winced as she moved. An old woman, with decades of cigarettes in her ragged voice. "The Holy Order of the Soldiers of Theodosius."

"What?"

"The H.O.S.T. The Host. That's what we are. But like so many things in our world, the name carries more than one meaning."

"The bread of the Eucharist," Theo interjected quietly. "The body of Christ. And the Heavenly Host, the angelic army. It's all those things to you."

Gerry nodded. "Mithras himself, whom others call Jesus—but who is both in one—visited the Emperor Theodosius and commanded him to protect the secret rituals, the *true* rituals of the original church, while his soldiers destroyed the remnants of paganism that still fouled the land. Once the Pretenders are wiped from the earth, and only then, can He rise again to walk among us and bring about the End of Days. The Last Age. We'd thought it a futile task—one that had gone unfulfilled for nearly two thousand years—until I learned Prometheus could die. His death foretold that the end of our mission was at hand—you could all be killed. Then, when I found you again this fall, and I told the Pater about the Classicist Cult's rituals, he realized we could use something similar to bring back the true God. He said that if we combined the ancient rituals of Mithras with the death of the Pretenders, we could complete both our tasks at once." She looked hopeful as she reached a plaintive hand to her friend. "Please, you of all people know the evils that haunt our world. The poverty, the violence, the chaos. When the Last Age begins, it will all stop. Is that not worth a few deaths, Diana?"

"I'm not Diana." Selene backed away. "Don't call me that. I'm no longer the leader of nymphs who haunted the forest. I'm no longer a Moon Goddess. I'm not even Cynthia Forrester anymore, full of helpless rage. I'm just Selene DiSilva. A woman whose heart has broken once already tonight." She stood up, staring down at this woman she thought she'd known. This woman she'd called friend. "I did not think you would be the one to break it all over again."

———◇———

"You sure you should leave Hansen untied?" Theo asked as Selene closed the bedroom door behind them. "She wants to kill us all—she made that clear."

"No, she doesn't. She wants her Mithras alive. We're just collateral damage."

"But why trust her not to run?"

"Because she doesn't have anywhere to run to. Her Pater knows she took you and Gabriela out of the planetarium. She might've been willing to see *me* die, but she tried to save two innocent mortals—would've succeeded, too, if you hadn't figured out who she was. They won't forgive her for that."

"And *you* won't forgive her for saying Apollo's death was justified."

"No, I won't." There was little anger in her voice—only sadness. "She's like me," Selene went on. "Broken. Twisted. She thinks she's doing the right thing. And because of that, she won't tell us anything more—not if we tortured her or begged or threatened."

"You're not *broken*," Theo began, although he wondered if the words were true.

The doorbell rang.

They both froze. Selene's right arm twitched as she tried to reach for a weapon that wasn't there with a hand that didn't work. Before Theo could look for something to defend them with, Gabriela burst out of the kitchen, Hansen's gun raised, with Ruth close on her heels.

"Who the fuck is *that*?" Gabi demanded, pointing the captain's Glock variously at Selene, the front door, and the bedroom.

Selene rounded on her. "Give me that before you get someone killed!"

"I saved your life with this gun!" Gabi shouted back. "So don't tell me what I should—"

"I know how to use it, and I'm the one they're after so—"

"You can't even lift your right arm. So unless ambidexterity is *another* one of your secrets—"

"Quiet!" Ruth's urgent hiss silenced them all. "It's probably just my super or something. Everyone *calm down*." She walked with surprising poise to the door, gesturing for the others to get out of sight.

"Wait, Ruth!" Theo whispered. Unlike Gabi, he didn't have a weapon. And unlike Selene, he couldn't knock a man unconscious with a single kick. But it was his fault Ruth had gotten herself into this. His fault a homicidal cultist with who-knew-what divine weapon and a seriously confused take on religion might be standing in her hallway. He grabbed a heavy glass vase off an end table and moved to stand just inside the door.

Ruth gave him a thankful nod and pressed an eye to the peephole. Then she turned to Gabriela, who was unsuccessfully hiding behind a narrow pole lamp, her gun still drawn. "Didn't you say something about a hot guy with skinny legs and a serious facial hair problem?"

Chapter 39

GOD OF FIRE

Selene rushed forward and opened the door. Flint stood with one hand on a bent aluminum crutch and the other pressed against his stomach. His feet were bare, his leather jacket torn, and his face twisted with agony. But when he saw Selene, he took a breath so deep it sounded like the bellows of a forge—as if it were the first deep breath he'd taken in years—and collapsed forward into her embrace.

She staggered beneath his weight, struggling to support him with her only good arm. Theo grabbed the Smith from the other side and helped her drag his limp form toward the couch. A stifled gasp from Ruth and a less restrained curse from Gabriela drew Selene's attention to the blood streaming from beneath Flint's jacket and leaving a long red trail across the carpet.

Ruth ran into the bathroom and returned with her box of bandages and antiseptic—already severely depleted from her ministrations to Selene and Theo. Flint's arms hung limp at his sides, and his jacket fell open. Selene gave a choked cry when she saw the three arrow wounds that had sliced through his thick sweater and T-shirt and into the flesh of his abdomen. They showed no sign of healing.

The ice around Selene's heart, which had cracked open with the memories of Gerry's past, now split apart with the force of a calving glacier. How could she have ever thought she didn't care about the rest of her kin? *I will not let another brother die. I WILL NOT.* Flint had said he healed no faster than a mortal. How would he ever recover from three divine arrows? Then again, if he was barely a god anymore, would gold shafts be any worse than wood?

Ruth dabbed at the slashes with gauze, but the blood soaked each pad immediately. Selene roughly pushed her aside and placed her left hand on the wide plane of muscle above Flint's heart. When her own death had loomed before her, she'd prayed that her twin would take on her attributes when she died. Perhaps he'd done the same. She could be the Healer.

She closed her eyes and dove into Flint. She could almost sense something red and glowing like the embers in a forge, fading in and out as if at the brink of extinction. She blew upon them, willing them to burst into flame, willing her own *pneuma* into Flint just as Prometheus had once breathed life into his creations of clay. But the embers remained faint, and soon she could see nothing but blackness before her.

"Bring me a candle!" she demanded.

"What are you going to—" Ruth began.

"Just do it!"

Ruth returned shortly with a thick scented pillar and a book of matches.

Selene fumbled with the matches in her left hand then pushed them toward Theo. "Light it!"

"This isn't a good idea," he warned.

"I don't know what else to do."

He handed her the lit candle. She moved the flame toward the wound. She knew that a god's attributes could speed his healing. Hephaestus was the God of Fire. The flames could help him just as the woodland streams helped her.

"Stop it!" Ruth cried, lunging forward. Theo caught her and held her back.

Selene moved the candle even closer to the wound. *Come on, Hephaestus,* she prayed. *You must still have some remnant of your power left.* As if in answer, the stream of blood slowed to a trickle as his internal injuries began to knit closed. On the edges of the wound, a millimeter of new flesh appeared, then another.

But then the wound stopped healing. She moved the candle closer, desperate, but the hair on his stomach began to sizzle and glow, and the new skin began to blister. The blood still oozed, letting off a foul burnt odor. Theo grabbed the candle from her hand and blew out the flame.

"No, no, this can't happen," Selene murmured, snatching the gauze from Ruth and trying once more to stanch the wound.

"I can help," came a raspy voice behind them. Selene turned to see Gerry standing in the doorway of the bedroom, leaning heavily against the wall.

"Hey there, Captain," Gabriela said, awkwardly sticking the Glock into the back of her waistband. "Are we over the nearly killing each other thing?"

Gerry ignored her and walked unsteadily toward the couch. She stood looking down at Flint, her face expressionless. *Does she want him dead too?* Selene wondered. *That's her whole purpose, isn't it?* As she pressed her good hand against his wounds, she tried to see him as Gerry did—as something unnatural, less than human, that should be destroyed. But all she saw was a face lined with care and a beard that hid him from the world. With his lips slightly parted and his eyes closed, he looked completely vulnerable for the first time. She'd never understood this man, but she knew she couldn't bear to lose him.

"Why would I trust you?" she demanded of Gerry.

"Because you don't have a choice. Do you really want to take him to a hospital and explain the arrow wounds?" The captain lowered herself to her knees beside the couch. "Get me a needle. Thread. Alcohol." Ruth hurried off to get the supplies.

"You won't hurt him?" Selene asked after a moment, surprised by the desperation that leaked into her voice.

Gerry looked at her coldly. "His death tonight would serve no purpose. He will not die at my hand."

Selene stood by helplessly as Gerry cleaned and sewed the wound. Ruth smeared antiseptic on the blisters. Gabriela applied bandages to cover it all. Selene knew that Theo stayed at her side, his hand brushing her own in silent comfort, but she could barely feel his touch.

Hours later, Theo finally succeeded in getting Selene to eat something. Flint remained unconscious on the couch. His bleeding had stopped, and Ruth reported that his pulse had steadied. But he didn't stir. Geraldine Hansen had gone back to the bedroom and closed the door. Theo couldn't begin to imagine the thoughts going through the captain's mind. He could barely understand his own.

He'd watched Selene tend Flint while trying to ignore a sudden needle of jealousy. The Smith was one of the only family members she had left. Of course she cared for him. Theo had urged her to rescue him, after all. But something in the way she'd pressed her hand against Flint's heart had reminded Theo of the terrace atop Rockefeller Center. Artemis and Hephaestus above the clouds, gods once more. *All night, I've been unable to break through her grief. But somehow, Flint did.*

Theo pushed another plate of fried eggs in Selene's direction. Some of the color had come back to her cheeks, and she looked less haggard. He would've liked her to sleep, but he knew it was pointless to ask—not when there was so much to do.

Three nights had passed between Hades' death and Mars's. Another three before the cult had killed Apollo. Hopefully, that meant they had some time to spare before the next sacrifice.

Theo mentally ticked off the tasks at hand. First, rescue Dash, Phlippe, and, according to Selene, Prometheus. Next, get past a small army of divinely armed men to kill the Pater. And finally, before it was too late, stop the resurrection of Jesus.

"No problem," he muttered aloud.

"What?" Selene started.

"Nothing. Just imagining what happens if Jesus really does come back. I have a feeling I'm not making it into heaven when the rapture comes. What do you think—me and the other pagans, turning to cannibalism and polygamy while all the good Christians flit around on angel wings?"

"It's not Jesus who'd come back," she said, pushing a scrap of egg white across her plate. "It's Mithras-as-Jesus. Whoever that is. Do you really think he'll be a Prince of Peace like Gerry believes? The cult that worships him is a bunch of men in an underground temple, drowning innocent bystanders, sacrificing my family, torturing people . . . does that sound very holy to you? If they manage to resurrect anyone, it will be the god they've dreamed up, the god they've created. Remember when Orion gave me back all my strength? I turned into a version of myself I barely recognized. Vengeful and all-powerful and devoid of empathy. The same thing could happen to Jesus."

Theo hadn't noticed Hansen standing in the doorway until she spoke. "Is that true?"

Selene turned around, as if she hadn't noticed the captain either. "Yes," she said shortly, before turning back to her food.

"But the Pater said . . ."

Ruth walked into the kitchen and they all fell silent. "He's awake."

Selene rose hurriedly, and Theo followed her into the living room. She knelt beside Flint and took his massive hand in her own. Theo tried to ignore how that made him feel.

"You need to leave," Selene said to Gabi and Ruth, no doubt afraid of what Flint might say.

To Theo's shock, Ruth simply crossed her arms and said, "No."

Before Selene could insist, Flint spoke.

"Huntress," he whispered. He dragged her hand to his cheek and held it there for a long moment before he opened his eyes. He looked at her for a single breath before he raised his other hand to her head and pulled her mouth down to his. He kissed her. Fierce and long and desperate.

Theo felt his hands ball into fists. Gabi snatched his elbow, holding him back.

Selene broke away. Not quickly, not angrily... but she broke away. Her face burned bright red. For all his earlier remonstrance to stop hitting people, Theo wanted desperately for her to slug Flint in the face. Instead, she just stared at him, dumbstruck, and Flint gazed back, all his surly reticence transformed to silent entreaty.

"We're all doing things we shouldn't tonight," Selene said finally.

"Only because I should've done it a long time ago," Flint replied.

Gabi laughed loudly. "I'm sure Ruth's been hoping her couch would see some action, but I doubt this is what she had in mind. How 'bout we set aside the *telenovela* for a second?" She gave Theo a look of compassion and his elbow a hard warning squeeze. *She feels bad for me,* he realized, *because even she thinks Flint is a better match for Selene than I am, and she only just met him.*

Gabi turned to Flint. "How about you start, Mr. Rumbly Sexy, by telling us how you escaped?"

Flint directed his explanation to Selene. "They let Dash and I out of the net so they could march us back to their mithraeum—figured we were too injured to run. Took my leg braces just in case... but not my phone. Must've thought it'd be useless underground. When we were passing a utility hatch, I sent a signal to the braces to explode. Then I escaped through the hatch and ran." His mouth twisted in a bitter parody of a smile. "I *crawled.*

Dash and Philippe—they were up ahead of me, near the Pater. I couldn't save them." His face tightened with self-loathing. "I found an exit into the subway and grabbed on to the back of a passing train. There was a homeless man with one leg in the station when I got off. He had a crutch."

Theo noticed Flint didn't mention how that crutch wound up in his possession. *I see kisses aren't the only thing he steals.* He couldn't hide his anger as he asked, "How did you know to come to Ruth's?"

Flint didn't bother looking at Theo when he replied; if he felt any shame at having just pawed another man's girlfriend, he didn't show it. "I had that woman's phone number. I tracked it here, hoping she'd be with you."

"Ah." *He had Gabi's phone number because I gave it to him. Great.* Selene, he noticed, hadn't looked at him since Flint's kiss.

"There's no time to waste." Flint's biceps flexed into large spheres as he struggled to raise himself from the couch. "We have to get Philippe and Dash." He fell back with a strangled groan, pressing at the long bandage across his abdomen.

"He shouldn't move," Hansen said evenly. "He strains that wound, and it opens right back up again. And this time I can't promise the intestines won't come out with it."

Selene patted the tape around the gauze, sticking it back into place. "We'll find the others, don't worry," she assured Flint. His stomach clenched into a six-pack at her touch. She turned to Hansen. "You changed your mind yet about helping us? Tell us where the next sacrifice is. And when."

The captain merely crossed her arms, every inch as stubborn as Selene. "You know I can't do that."

Theo finally dislodged Gabi's hand on his elbow and took a step toward Selene. "We can figure this out without her." *And without Flint,* he amended silently. He ran through the Mithraic rituals in his head. *Tauroctony, Feast, Procession of the Sun-Runner.* "The ascension of Mithras to heaven in the Sun's chariot," he said aloud. "That must be the final rite. It parallels the ascension of Jesus to heaven. As for timing…" Suddenly, it all made horrible, perfect sense. "What better day to honor Sol Invictus and resurrect Jesus than the birthday they share?"

Selene finally looked at him. "December twenty-fifth."

"With everything going on, I didn't even remember that today's Christmas Eve. At midnight…"

"Philippe and Dash will die."

"Unless we find them first."

"And defeat the Host once and for all."

As she spoke, Theo felt something snap back into place. They were working out the options, decoding the clues, facing unknown dangers—together. No matter what Flint meant to her, Theo was still her partner.

"But what about your injury?" he asked. "You can't fight with…." He looked pointedly at her right arm.

"Don't worry about that," she said sternly. "My only concern is their weapons. Their guns probably can't hurt me, but the other items…"

Suddenly, Gabi cleared her throat with a dramatic, "*A-hem!* What do you mean *guns can't hurt you?* Is someone going to tell me what's going on?"

Before Theo could devise some clever explanation, Ruth spoke. "Selene can't be killed by a gun. And probably our new friend can't either. Because they're not human."

"Ruth—" Theo began. "That's not—"

"They heal at a rate that defies the laws of human biology. I saw what happened to Flint with that candle, and I saw a video of Selene healing, too." She stared at the two Athanatoi defiantly. "You're aliens."

"Oh, shitballs," Gabi said, her tone hovering between incredulity and hilarity. "That explains *so* much."

Hansen loosed a croaking laugh. "*Aliens?* Oh, hon, if only it were that simple."

"Wait...what?" Ruth's face scrunched in confusion. "Mutants, then?"

Selene and Flint exchanged a glance. Theo knew he had to say something before the Athanatoi took matters into their own hands. *There's a good chance they're conspiring to knock Ruth and Gabi unconscious and give them some amnesiac drug.* For once, he didn't want to help protect the gods' identities. Ruth was right about one thing—he'd been lying for far too long. If Selene could find a way to trust the family she'd disdained for so long, she could find a way to trust his closest friends.

"She's a goddess," he said.

Gabriela snorted. "I've heard that before."

"No. Not figuratively. Literally."

Selene glowered, but didn't contradict him. Maybe she too was tired of the lies. Or maybe she was just too tired in general.

"A goddess..." Gabi repeated, with about as much conviction as she would say "unicorn" or "openly gay Republican."

Ruth's jaw hung slightly open. *Her scientific mind understands the probabilities of extraterrestrial life,* Theo realized. *But goddesses? She barely believes in God.*

He held Selene's gaze for a moment. *You owe me this,* he demanded silently. *These are my friends, and they've risked their lives for you.* As if she heard him, Selene took a deep breath and held out her left hand to Gabi. "Nice to meet you. I'm over three thousand years old. My name's Selene, but it hasn't always been. They call me the Huntress."

Gabi, eyes saucer-wide, put her hand tentatively in Selene's. "Artemis."

"Mm-hm."

"No no no no no." She dropped Selene's hand and rounded on Theo. "You *didn't* start dating a fucking *mythological immortal* and *NOT TELL ME!*"

Theo winced. Somehow, he wasn't surprised that withholding such juicy gossip was Gabi's most pressing concern.

"And that means," she went on, pointing an accusatory finger at Flint, "that the weirdly sexy guy with the amazing abs and the paralyzed legs is *Hephaestus*." She spun to the captain. "And who are *you*? Demeter? Hera?"

"Just Geraldine Hansen," the captain said calmly. "As mortal as you are."

"Gabriela…" Ruth began, still looking stunned. "Don't tell me you *believe* this."

Gabi dismissed her concerns with a wave of her hand. "Please, *chica*, you can't be an anthropologist like me and not wonder at some point if all the religions of the world are just fooling themselves or if there's really something out there. I've listened to enough Navajo shamans talk about their chats with Spider Grandmother out in the desert to at least consider they're not just deluded or stupid or lying. And if Spider Grandmother is out there, why not the Olympians, too?"

Ruth sank to the floor. Not quite a faint, but not far from it.

Selene just shrugged. "Now that we've got that out of the way, can we get back to figuring out how to find some weapons to get through the Pater's army?"

"Here." Flint patted awkwardly at his leather jacket. "The inside pocket."

Selene reached inside, hand brushing his bare chest, and withdrew a small paper envelope.

"Open it," the Smith rumbled. "It's for you."

She tipped the envelope into her hand. A cord of forged gold spilled forth, as thick around as her little finger. From where he stood, Theo could see its intricate engraving but couldn't make out the specific design.

"It's," Selene began, "a necklace?" Theo'd never seen her wear jewelry of any kind.

"It's got its hidden secrets, just like you," the Smith mumbled before falling back into unconsciousness.

Clearly confused, Selene slipped the necklace into the pocket of her pants. Theo was grateful she didn't put the gift around her throat. He wasn't sure he could bear the sight.

Hansen checked the sleeping man's pulse and proclaimed it steady. "He needs rest," she insisted. "So do we all."

"You'd like that, wouldn't you, Gerry?" Selene said, gathering her jacket. "If we all just sat this part out and no one had to get hurt. Let your comrades finish their mission. But I can't give up on what I believe in any more than you can. So if all the Smith can give me is jewelry, I'm going to need to go hunting for a better divine weapon."

"I'm coming with you," Theo said quickly.

To his surprise, Selene didn't protest. "Gabriela, you've got a gun," she said. "Don't let the captain leave, and don't let her call her friends. Tie her up again if you have to. Ruth, I'll leave Hippo here as backup in case someone from the Host shows up. And...look after Flint, okay?"

Ruth gave a vague nod of agreement, and Gabi looked liable to burst with a thousand questions—but Selene was already out the door.

Chapter 40

THE CHASTE ONE

An icy wind whipped against Selene's face as she exited the subway, but her lips still burned from Flint's kiss. Theo walked beside her down West Eighty-eighth Street as they headed toward her house. She kept an eye on the buildings and rooftops they passed, watching for possible pursuit—and conveniently avoiding his eyes. She could feel him looking at her, waiting for her to say something. They'd barely spoken since they left Ruth's apartment.

"I didn't tell him to kiss me," she finally snapped.

"That's an awesome apology." His lightness sounded forced.

"Why should I apologize? Because I didn't punch him in the face? Weren't you the one who told me to stop doing that?"

"Terrible timing on my part, as usual."

"It was just a *kiss*, for Kronos's sake!" Selene looked at him finally, not bothering to hide her anger. "He was probably half-delirious anyway. I'm sure it didn't mean anything to him."

Theo stopped in his tracks and stared at her incredulously. "Just a kiss. This from a woman who turned a man into a *stag* because he dared to spy on her naked. How many men have you kissed before today? Not including some chaste peck from a relative. Huh?"

She scowled for a full thirty seconds before answering. "Two."

"Exactly. Orion. Me. And I'd like to believe that they meant something to you. So I know Flint's kiss did, too."

She gave an exasperated huff that sounded nearly like a scream. "I don't *know* what it meant to me, okay?"

Theo's face darkened. "Why not?"

"Because you've had more experience with women in your thirty years than I've had with men in my three thousand. I just lost my twin. I didn't think I'd ever be able to feel *anything* ever again. And then Flint showed up and... I don't know what happened. And I don't want to think about it. So just let it go."

Theo nodded curtly, then started off down the sidewalk, his shoulders stiff.

Selene followed, her mind still whirring. She had far more important concerns than her feelings for Flint. Yet she couldn't forget the feel of his mouth. His beard coarse against her chin, his lips rough. He'd tasted like smoke. It hadn't been pleasant, exactly—not like the way she'd so often melted into Theo— but some spark had coursed through her body nonetheless. She could've pulled away sooner. She hadn't. *Flint barely knows me,* she reminded herself. *We've spent more time together in the last few days than we have in the last few millennia. And he's spent most of the time brooding and growling and tinkering. He's just attracted to me because I'm out of reach. I'm sure before this week, he'd barely thought of me.* She tried to ignore the tap of the heavy gold necklace in her pocket as she walked. He'd made it for her. So he'd been thinking about her before he left his forge. Maybe since their encounter in Orion's cave earlier that fall.

She caught up to Theo a few doors down from her brownstone. Yellow police tape hung across her stoop, but she didn't see any unmarked cop cars on the street. The neighbors would've reported gunshots, but hopefully they hadn't seen the flying man. Even if they had, she suspected Gerry would've buried the report. That was one advantage to having a secret Mithraist on the force.

"Hansen's cops probably searched the place," she said. "Let's hope they didn't find our last remaining divine weapon."

Theo gave a noncommittal grunt of assent.

Suddenly she was furious. "You're the one always going on about how we should tell each other the *truth*. How dare you *sulk* because I finally did!"

Theo's face flushed. "Oh, I'm sorry. You can clam up whenever you want, refuse to meet my goddamn *eyes*, but the minute I need some time to process the fact that you *liked* kissing your own *stepbrother*, you're *offended*?" He headed toward the house, muttering, "Let's just get in there and get out again."

"Don't try to force your human standards of morality on *me*. Flint and I are barely related," she called after him. When he didn't turn around, she shouted, "You didn't have to come, you know!"

He rounded on her. "No. That's where you're wrong. I did. Because I don't want you roaming the streets alone with who knows what sort of asshole chasing you with a trident or a caduceus or your own bow. Because I can't bear the idea of you trying to fight when you can only use one arm, and I'm not there to help. Because the sight of someone else kissing you feels like being punched in the gut, but the thought of someone *hurting* you feels like being *stabbed* right here"—he pounded his heart with a clenched fist—"with a goddamn butcher knife. Because I *love* you."

They stood in the middle of the sidewalk in silence. The neon icicles from the neighboring building cast a wavering blue light across Theo's face. Selene felt as if she were underwater, Theo floating beside her, his hand outstretched. All she had to do was reach for it. All she had to do was tell him she loved him, too.

I do, she realized. *I love that he's willing to do anything for me, that he can't bear to lose me, that he cares for me despite everything I've done to push him away. I love that he's stronger than he'll admit, and handsomer than he knows, and just as smart and funny as he thinks he is.* But she said none of it. She turned toward her house. She got a single step before Theo put his hand on her arm.

"Tell me what you're thinking." His voice was hard. "You owe me that at least."

"I can't," she managed.

Impulsively, she reached for his face and pulled him into a kiss. She'd intended simply to stop his further questions. Instead, she kissed him long and hard, her lips full of everything she couldn't allow herself to say. Full of the song Theo stitched across her heart, the one that Apollo had known the words to, but that she couldn't yet bear to sing aloud.

When she finally relaxed her grip, she looked Theo straight in the eye. "That's also the truth," she admitted softly. "In the only way I can tell you."

He nodded, and lifted a finger to wipe away a tear she hadn't realized she'd shed. He kissed her again, gently this time. She kissed him back, lingering over his touch just long enough to let him know she didn't want it to end. When they parted, a smile quirked his lips, bringing a dimple to his right cheek. "Then let's go break into your house."

His green eyes glowed, a reminder of spring amid the winter cold. A sudden fear drained the answering smile from her lips—the moment was too perfect. Too easy. She expected an arrow to fly through the night and take him away.

But that didn't happen.

Instead, their plan went off without a hitch. With no sign of Mithraic pursuers or police surveillance, they hopped over the yellow tape and Selene jimmied open the deadbolts on her front door. They slipped inside the darkened house and locked the door behind them. She pulled out a flashlight borrowed from Ruth—she didn't need the light, but she knew Theo did—and led the way up the stairs and into her bedroom. Her meager possessions lay strewn about—whether by the Corvus who'd attacked her or the police who'd answered the neighbors' calls, she couldn't be sure. Cotton underwear and overlarge shirts, cargo pants and flannels. A few books Theo'd left behind, along with several piles of his clothes. Splintered wooden arrows lay like kindling across the floor.

On the far wall, the only piece of art in her house hung askew. Theo had given it to her—a photo of the ancient bell-krater once stolen by Orion from the Metropolitan Museum of Art. The red-figure painting on the vessel's side showed Artemis, Apollo, and Leto. It was the closest thing she had to a photo of her mother and brother. She lifted it carefully from the wall and laid it facedown on the bed. She couldn't bear to look at it. Not yet.

The wall behind the photo showed no sign of disturbance. She picked a broken arrow from the ground and jammed its point into a nearly imperceptible divot in the plaster. The arrowhead went right through into the hollow wall behind. She twisted it like a key in a lock then wrenched it out: a large chunk of plaster came with it. She reached down into the hole—and pulled out a sword.

In the darkness of the room, the leaf-shaped bronze blade looked black. A dent marked the place she'd shot an arrow into it during her last fight with Orion. The simple, leather-wrapped grip was soft to the touch. Like other Greek swords, a small semicircle studded with rivets served as the cross guard. A practical blade. A weapon for a hunter who preferred a bow or a javelin, but carried the sword as a sign of his nobility. Only the pommel hinted at the sword's provenance and its bearer's lineage: a twisting conch shell of yellow gold, a fitting emblem for a sword given to Orion by his father, the sea god Poseidon. She'd hidden it deep, where she could forget it existed, buried behind a photo that reminded her that, even without Orion, she had still been loved. By her mother, by her twin, and now, she knew, by the man who'd given her the photo in the first place.

She moved the sword into the light of Theo's flashlight beam.

He whistled. "No oxidation, no nicks." He reached to touch the edge with his finger, leaving behind a bright drop of blood. "Could've predicted that," he said ruefully, sucking the wound.

"Divine weapons don't rust the way normal ones do," she explained. "This wasn't made by the Smith, but by Poseidon himself. Forged in the heat of an underwater volcano, or so Orion told me once."

"Awesome. But you're the Bearer of the Bow and the Hurler of Javelins. Wielder of Swords, not so much. And without Prometheus around to breathe his special divine-weapon-pixie-dust on me, I'll look like a blindfolded toddler whacking at a piñata if I try to use it. So what are we going to do with it? You going to just toss it, javelin-style?"

"You clearly know nothing about javelins... or swords," she said with a sigh. "I'm not exactly sure what we'll do. But any divine weapon is better than no divine weapon. A normal blade would never hold up in a fight against Mars's spear or Poseidon's trident."

She shoved the sword into a heavy canvas tote bag. Next, she added an old quiver and the few unbroken arrows from the cache on the floor. No gold ones left, and no bow to shoot them, but they were weapons nonetheless.

Theo watched her skeptically. "And how are you going to use the sword, or the arrows, with only one arm?"

"That, my friend, is the one problem I know how to solve."

She slung the tote bag over her shoulder and retrieved her WNBA New York Liberty cap from the floor where it'd fallen during her fight with the flying Corvus. She pulled the brim low over her eyes. It felt like a warrior's helm—far better than any crescent moon diadem. She was ready for battle.

Selene led Theo down to the bank of the Hudson. Riverside Park lay nearly empty. Most of the city's denizens were either home for a Christmas Eve meal, out-of-town visiting relatives, or lounging on a beach in Florida for the week. No one felt the need to go for a walk in the darkened park, especially on a night when the temperature hovered in the teens. The cold whipped through Selene's leather jacket, surprising her with its bite. Her exhaustion made her more susceptible to such mortal annoyances. She could only hope her ability to heal wouldn't be affected as well.

Theo'd retrieved his parka from her house to replace the borrowed wool greatcoat. She'd been keenly aware of his presence since kissing him on the sidewalk. It felt like the first week they'd met, when she noticed every step he took, every time he caught her eye. For all the uncertainty about their future, she knew now, without a doubt, that he loved her. His simple declaration—devoid of Flint's brooding or her own angst—felt like a life jacket in the midst of a storm, something that could keep her afloat even as the rest of the world roared into chaos.

They reached the water's edge, and Selene hopped down onto the boulders. Ice chunks floated in the river. *This is not going to be pleasant,* she realized. But she didn't have a choice. She dropped her bag and shrugged off her jacket. She reached to pull off her flannel shirt, but couldn't get it unbuttoned with one hand.

"Here." Theo took off his gloves. She let him unfasten the shirt, starting at the bottom and working his way to the top. His knuckles brushed against the sides of her breasts, and she knew that he felt it too, this heightened connection. Despite the cold, she could feel the heat radiating from beneath his coat. He let his fingers linger at her collarbone before he lifted the shirt free of her arms. She stood in only a sleeveless undershirt, the cold sending tremors across her flesh.

Apollo's words came back to her, so clear she wondered if he watched her now from another world, whispering memories in her ear. *I try to give her every part of myself,* he'd said of poor dead Sophie. *Body and soul.* That was the love that had kept him together before the Host had ripped him apart.

Selene glanced up and down the path—no one was coming.

"Take the undershirt off, too," she said softly.

Theo smiled. "Is this an early Christmas present?"

"This is the only way I know to get my arm healed quickly." She tried to sound stern.

Theo pulled the shirt over her head, careful not to tug at the bandage on her back. With her left hand, she reached behind for the clasp to her bra, but Theo beat her to it. Next, the zipper of her pants.

She sat down on the rock and lifted a foot so he could pull off her boots. Removing her pants presented more of a problem—she rolled onto her shoulders, wincing as her wound scraped against the rock, and Theo slipped them down her hips and over her feet. She stood once more, hooked her left thumb into the waistband of her underwear, and kept her eyes on Theo. He slipped his hand along her other hip, pushing the fabric clear until she could step free. She'd never been helpless to undress herself before—she was surprised to find she didn't mind. Lastly, she took off her baseball cap. She didn't need to—in fact, she could use the meager warmth it provided—but she wanted him to see all of her.

"Is this some new form of torture?" he asked, his voice low, his gaze roaming her body before latching on to her eyes. "Because this is more painful than a branding iron."

He took a step forward as if to fold her into his arms.

"Hold on," she said. She turned her face to the moon, which had once moved at her command. It hung in the eastern sky, a full orb of icy light. *Listen to me now,* she prayed. *I summon you, Moon and Stars. Forest and River. Lend your strength to the Goddess of the Wild, the Mistress of the Moon, the Lady of Trees.* Her body tingled in the moon's rays, and when she looked down at her bare flesh, it glowed. Still, she couldn't move her right arm more than a few centimeters.

She stepped down into the water, chunks of ice knocking against her bare shins.

Theo gave a worried hum, but she kept going, submerging herself to the shoulders. Her trembling increased until she shook like an epileptic. She closed her eyes and tried to ignore the numbing pain. *River that protects my island,* she begged silently. *Border of my realm, inexorable flow from mountain stream to broad expanse, let your pure waters heal me.* Suddenly, the shivering stopped, and a sudden flush of heat warmed the skin of her back and arms.

"Come out," Theo said with a groan. "If I have to watch this much longer, I'm going to come in there with you, and you'll feel awful when I freeze solid."

Her eyes snapped open. She spoke without thinking. "You can come join me if you want to."

"I have a better idea." He grabbed her left hand and pulled her back onto the rocks. She stood dripping like a siren. Then she raised her healed right arm and used it to grab the front of his parka. Theo crushed her against his chest, his hands running across her back, through her hair, his mouth hungry on hers.

He slid his hands lower, beneath her hips, and lifted her off her feet. Her legs wrapped around his waist, squeezing so tight he moaned with something between pain and desire.

She moved her mouth from his and whispered into his ear. "With what we're going up against…this may be our last chance." *Leave with no regrets.* Apollo's words sang though her mind. *No regrets.* She raised a hand to his lips before he could protest. "It's now or never, Theodore."

He pressed a kiss against her palm then put her down. He ripped off his parka and laid it on the frigid granite beneath them. They knelt together on the ground, and Selene fumbled off his layers of clothing, anticipation and urgency making her awkward. *But not fear,* she marveled. *Not nervousness.* She'd lost her twin. Losing her virginity seemed paltry in comparison.

When she dragged the shirt from his torso, she saw the Mercury brand on his chest, its edges red and angry. A permanent reminder of all he'd endured for her.

For now, for this one moment, she could show him how much

his sacrifices meant. She could allow him into her heart, her body—not for the sake of gratitude, but for joy. An emotion she'd thought she'd never feel again. Yet now it lay just within reach, shining in Theo's eyes.

She pulled his naked body down on top of hers, and he ran his mouth across the pulse of her throat, the slope of her breast, the plane of her stomach. With her body thrumming, he lifted her from the ground and slipped beneath her, so his own back pressed against the stone and she lay above him. "Easier for you this way," he murmured, shifting her hips into place above his.

She leaned her hands on his shoulders and stared down at him. He reached to tuck the black curtain of her hair behind her ear. His face was grave, intense, tight with need. "This is how I always imagined you," he whispered, "making love to me in a moonbeam." Then, suddenly, he was grinning. "But you know...I always thought it'd be a little warmer." She threw back her head and laughed, and at that moment, she joined herself to him. The pain was sharp, but fleeting. The bliss lasted far longer.

———◇———

Theo didn't feel the cold. At least, not at first. Then, as their body heat receded and the wind picked up, his teeth started chattering next to Selene's ear. She laughed and rolled off him. In a night of terrors and wonders, her honking laughter was perhaps the most sublime thing of all.

They struggled back into their clothes. Selene retrieved her bag with the sword and arrows, jammed her New York Liberty cap back on her head, then glanced up at the moon. "Styx," she muttered. "Only a few hours left before midnight. The sword's not going to do us much good if we don't figure out where we're going."

Theo zipped up his parka and pulled on his gloves, slapping his hands together until the feeling returned. His mind wheeled joyfully from one imagined future to another—Selene beside him as they visited the ancient sites of Rome...as they sat curled together beside the turquoise waters of the Aegean...as they walked down an aisle with their friends looking on, her hair garlanded with flowers. They hadn't used a condom, but he couldn't find it in his heart to worry. *If she gets pregnant,* he mused, *would that be so awful? A little DiSilva-Schultz hemitheos running around?*

"Theo?" she prompted.

"Hm? Oh, right, find out where we're going..." Even the reminder of the confrontation ahead couldn't wipe the grin from his face. "No problem." Tonight, he felt there was no enemy he couldn't defeat, no mystery he couldn't solve. "We need another New York landmark. One that has something to do with the ascension of Mithras in the Sun's chariot. And a place that relates to whichever god they're going to sacrifice tonight."

"The Pater won't choose Dash or Philippe for the ceremony. He'll kill them anyway—just to have them out of the way—but they can't be the real sacrifice. It would take too much time to break them, although I'm sure he's trying—I haven't had any hallucinations since we left the planetarium, so he must be using the poppy crown on his new captives. But for tonight, he'll just use the Fire-Bringer. The ultimate willing sacrifice."

"What better place to kill Prometheus than beneath his own statue in the Rock Center skating rink?" he offered as they trotted toward the park exit.

She shook her head. "Christmas Eve? The rink's open until midnight and everyone wants to skate beneath that damn tree. I don't think so. And the statue has nothing to do with the Sun."

"Maybe we need a site with a more direct Jesus connection. A church perhaps."

"Possibly, but their Jesus isn't exactly the one we're used to from the crucifixes. I saw him through Gerry's eyes when I touched her mind. He wore a cloak of stars and the seven-rayed crown of Sol Invictus."

Theo suddenly grabbed her arm and spun her toward him. He was staring above her head.

"What?" she asked.

"New York landmark. Seven-rayed crown of the Sun. The Fire-Bringer who grants hope and free will to mankind. A place closed and unguarded only one day a year—Christmas." He pulled off her hat and held it before her face. "We know where to find them, Selene." She followed his finger to stare at the logo on the cap—the Statue of Liberty stared back.

Chapter 41

PERSUADER OF
ANIMALS

On West Twenty-third Street, Hippo tumbled out of the mini-van taxicab as soon as the door slid open, ripping her leash from Ruth's hands.

Selene went down on one knee to hug the dog close, realizing how much emotion she'd always held back from those who loved her—not just tonight, but every night. Now, she buried her face in the dog's rough fur. "I love you, girl," she murmured. Words she still hadn't said to Theo, although from the glow in his eyes, it seemed he thought she had. She straightened up; the mild ache between her legs made her blush.

The scents of the city were strong in her nose, her body felt limber and strong, she could read Hippo's affection and loyalty in the dog's stance and smell. Bathing in the river had given her strength. Or perhaps renouncing her identity as the Chaste One had actually heightened the rest of her epithets rather than—as she'd always feared—diminishing them. Or maybe she was just a woman who was finally unafraid.

Gabriela followed Ruth from the cab. From the bulge in the

pocket of her jacket, Selene knew she still carried the Glock. Gerry Hansen climbed out next, her hands tied before her.

Gabriela put a hand on the captain's elbow. "You asked for her, so I brought her, but I think you're *loco*. She's too dangerous. Why not just leave her tied to Ruth's bed? No one else is using it for anything more important."

"Hey," Ruth protested mildly.

"She's a hostage," Theo explained.

Gabriela's eyes widened. "Now we're talking. How does it feel, Captain, to have *your* life in danger for a change?"

"I will be there at the turning of the Age," the policewoman replied. "That's all that matters to me."

"You're going to be disappointed." Selene felt only pity. Geraldine Hansen, so strong, so smart...so deluded. "Jesus won't rise again tonight."

The captain's chin tilted defiantly. "How do you know?"

"Because Jesus was always just a man. A mortal preacher. A rebel. Not a god. He died on that cross, Gerry. He's long gone."

"He's the son of God the Father. You of all people know that's possible."

Selene sighed. "Maybe you're right," she said, throwing up her hands. "Maybe your god came down in a beam of light like my own father did to impregnate some virgin. Maybe Jesus *was* a hemitheos. But whatever he was, or is, whether he exists or not, the version of him that could arise tonight will be something different. Something created by a cult that traffics in murder and madness. Is that the god you want? Is that the one you've worshiped? You don't really know *who* you'll be bringing back."

"You've seen the worst this city, this country, this *world* has to offer. Don't you think we should at least *try* to change it?" Despite the smoky rasp of her voice, Gerry looked like her younger self for a moment—full of hope and passion.

"Captain Hansen," Theo broke in. "How many immortals have you known? Besides Selene."

Gerry narrowed her eyes at him. "I've been tending Prometheus for decades."

"Then you know that they might have some strange powers, and their understanding of the world isn't quite the same as ours, but other than that, they're basically as human as you or I. They get exasperated, scared, tickled, depressed."

Her mouth was a thin, hard line. "Where are you going with this?"

"If you bring Mithras-as-Jesus into the world, he'll be a *person*. Just like Selene. Just like us. There's a reason, I think, that the ancient Hebrews didn't give their god a face—or even a *name*—and why *that* god went on to dominate three of the world's great religions. Because only a god with no physical being can embody all the hopes and dreams of his worshipers. Not just *three* aspects, but infinite ones. If you trap your god on earth, all that immensity becomes just a single man, shivering in the cold and wondering where his next sandwich comes from."

Gerry listened. She even seemed to hear. But she'd held on to a certain kind of faith for a very long time. "You will see. The world will see."

A sudden clatter from the back of the cab drew Selene's attention. Gabriela and Ruth struggled to unload a pile of spokes and metal poles that, somehow, metamorphosed into a wheelchair by the time they got it on the sidewalk.

"He told us how to make it," Ruth said, sounding more than a little overwhelmed. "Bicycle wheels and my kitchen chair and a pole lamp and...everything else in my apartment."

A pair of withered legs swung down from the open hatch of the minivan. Ruth hurried over, and she and Gabi helped ease Flint out of the cab and into the wheelchair.

He slumped forward in the seat, his dark eyes peering up at Selene, one arm pressed against his stomach as if to hold back the pain.

"You do *not* look ready for this," she chided him.

"You've got no one else to back you up."

Selene's tempered flared. "What do you mean, no one else?" She jerked a thumb at her lover. "Who do you think that is?"

Flint's brows lowered. "He can't understand the resurrection of a god. He can't understand *you.*"

To Selene's surprise, it was Ruth who jumped to Theo's defense. "From what *I* understand, Theo was the one who realized the connection to this Mithras character. *And* snuck into their secret hideout."

"Yeah, *pendejo,*" Gabriela interjected. "And he figured out about the Statue of Liberty. What have you done lately besides show up at the planetarium and get wounded while Theo and—let's not forget—*I* rescued Selene."

Flint looked completely flummoxed for the first time. It occurred to Selene that he'd had very little interaction with mortal women over the centuries.

"Thank you, ladies," Theo said with a grin. "Couldn't have said it better myself."

"Now," Gabriela said, waving the cab away. "How exactly are we getting across the harbor in the middle of winter?"

"Not we," Theo said quickly. "You and Ruth are *not* coming."

His friend patted the bulge in her pocket. "I'm an *amazing* shot, or have you already forgotten that?"

"Yeah, and so is Selene, trust me, even if she usually prefers a bow. I've already put you both in too much danger. This isn't your fight."

"You're risking your life, Theo," Ruth said quietly. "That makes it our fight."

"Damn straight." Gabriela crossed her arms over her breasts and glared at him.

Theo turned helplessly to Selene. "Tell them this is absurd."

"They can make their own decisions," she replied.

"Please," Theo begged, stepping closer to his friends. "I can't bear it. If you take an arrow to the back or a gunshot to the head, that's *it*. No ritual can resurrect you. And in the somewhat unlikely event that I survive tonight, I couldn't bear returning to a world without both of you in it."

Gabriela's face softened. She sighed. "Well, Theo-dorable, you do know how to sweet-talk a girl."

Ruth spoke, her voice hardly more than a whisper. "But you and Selene... you'll need help out there." She snuck a glance at Flint and Gerry, clearly sure that a man in a wheelchair would be no match for the Mithraist cop and her cohorts.

"We'll have Hippo," Selene interjected calmly.

Theo scratched the dog behind her ears. "If only we had a whole army of Hippos," he said with a rueful smile. "I mean, not *hippos*, because that would be awkward but... you know what I mean."

Selene laughed aloud. "Theo, that's the best idea you've had all week." She hoisted the bag of weapons more firmly on her shoulder. "Let's go get us some Hippos."

Theo's confusion lasted only a second before a grin spread across his face. "Good plan." He gave his friends each a quick hug. Gabriela pulled the Glock from her pocket and handed it to him. He slipped it beneath the back of his waistband.

Selene spared a moment to shake Gabriela's hand. Theo would've wanted her to. "Thank you," she said, the words awkward on her tongue. Gabriela just scowled at her.

She turned to Ruth next. "And you. Thank you." Then, as Ruth took her hand, Selene leaned in close. "If something happens to me... you'll take care of Theo."

It was a command, not a question.

———◇———

Paper cutouts of puppies and kittens in overlarge Santa hats peered down coyly from the walls of the animal shelter. *Let's hope the animals inside are slightly more intimidating,* Theo thought as he watched Selene pick the lock on the door to the holding room.

The funk of urine and antiseptic assaulted his nose the moment the door swung open, followed by a rising chorus of whines and yips. Selene walked the aisle, dispassionately appraising each animal. Hippo trotted beside Theo on her leash, tail beating the air, and snuffed each dog as they barked and pawed at the grating. Theo peered into a cage at eye level. A shih tzu puppy, a spherical ball of white and brown fluff. "This one doesn't look like he could take down a rubber ball, much less an armed man," he said, sticking his finger through the grate so the puppy could lick it.

"It's a she," Selene said distractedly, without even looking at the animal. Her gaze was far away—Theo'd seen her this way before. He knew she reached into herself for old, untapped powers. The Persuader of Animals, the Lady of Hounds, communing with the dogs around her on a level he couldn't begin to understand.

She knelt by a large cage on the floor. A hefty pit bull panted up at her. She stared into the dog's eyes. Its wagging tail rattled the sides of the cage. Selene shook her head and moved on to the next prisoner: a slim white feist—a squirrel-hunting crossbreed—with perked ears and warm brown eyes. "Leila," according to the index card taped to her cage. Her pointed head came only to Selene's knee. Selene opened the grate immediately. Leila and Hippo sniffed each other eagerly as Selene continued her quest.

Next another pit bull, this one gray and white with a torn ear. A rangy German shepherd with a kink in her tail. A black cockapoo no bigger than a large house cat. A bright snaggletooth protruded from his lower jaw, and he wouldn't stop jumping in place. His index card read, "Koko."

One by one, they joined the army until six dogs ran in frantic circles around the small corridor. Theo rocked back on his heels, trying to restrain Hippo from joining the melee. "You think we should get some leashes?" he shouted above the din.

Selene just smiled. Then she barked once, sharp and loud. The dogs instantly quieted and turned toward her. The white feist lifted a ladylike front paw, as if offering her services. Koko panted noisily, his small pink tongue flapping in counterpoint. Selene walked from one dog to the next, and each lay down in turn, like supplicants before a queen. She held out a hand for them to smell, then pressed each belly firmly with her booted foot. When she'd finished, she growled deep in her throat without showing her teeth. The dogs sprang to their feet and trotted obediently at her heels as she left the building.

Theo knelt beside Hippo and unhooked her leash. "Guess you're past the whole leash thing now," he said, ruffling the dog's fur. She panted eagerly, gave his palm a lick, then took off after the rest of the soldiers.

Ten blocks south, they rejoined Dash's speedboat at a private marina on the East River, surrounded by towering pleasure yachts. Flint lay propped on the starboard bench, wrapped against the cold in a sailcloth, while Hansen sat on the port side, her bound wrists secured to the boat's rail.

The dogs bounded onto the boat at Selene's curt gesture. Hansen raised a brow at the canine invasion but made no comment. Flint, on the other hand, cracked a rare smile that quickly turned into a glower as the German shepherd insisted on sharing his seat.

He glanced at his tablet phone. "Liberty Island is about a twelve-minute ride away. It's eleven o'clock now, and you said the ritual won't start until Christmas begins. We're going to just make it."

Theo rubbed his hands together, trying to look more optimistic than he felt. "Then let's get this show on the road. Or the water. Or whatever."

Selene stood in the middle of the boat, looking first at Flint's prone form, then out over the water. "We've got another stop first," she said finally.

"Selene—" Flint warned. "We don't have time."

"If you join the battle, you're going to get killed, Flint." He started to protest. "Think," she cut in. "You're going to slow me down—I don't care how fancy your wheelchair is. And you're too wounded to help fight. You might get *me* killed because I'm trying to help you." That shut him up. "But I know how you could help. How's your knowledge of nineteenth-century artillery?"

"I've been forging weapons for millennia. What do you think?"

"Good. Theo, you know how to drive a car. How different can a boat be? Take us to Governors Island."

"How different indeed?" Theo replied with a confidence he didn't feel. He moved to the wheel, found the key Dash had stowed in the cockpit, and started the engine. "See? Piece of cake." Then he rammed the boat ahead of them with a crunch of fiberglass. "Where are the breaks on this thing?" he muttered as the wooden yacht behind them splintered at a slightly lower pitch. But eventually, they made their way out of the marina and headed down the East River. He kept his eyes glued ahead of him, hoping Governors Island would be hard to miss. At least steering the boat kept him distracted from the upcoming battle. A battle in which his only weapons would be a gun he had no idea how to use and the brains that had gotten him this far.

The boat pulled into the deserted dock at Governors Island just after eleven fifteen. Together, Selene and Theo hauled Flint and his wheelchair ashore and hoisted him to the roof of Castle Williams using an old artillery winch. They rolled him into place beside the fifteen-foot-long Civil War Era canon. A little supernaturally strong elbow grease moved its rotating platform so the barrel pointed straight across the harbor toward Liberty Island.

On Flint's orders, Selene had lugged a hundred pounds of gunpowder from inside Fort Jay—where it was used for historical reenactments—across to Castle Williams. Just enough to fire the two cannonballs they'd found on display. Flint had disdained her offer to find him a firing pin as well. The God of Fire never traveled without his own stash of fuses.

"Try not to actually take down the statue itself," Theo said as he rolled the second cannonball within Flint's reach. "Not sure the city would forgive us for that one."

"You sure you're going to be able to handle this?" Selene asked the Smith for the fourth time.

He gave her a grim frown. "Stop treating me like a mortal. I know my limitations, and I know my strengths. I wouldn't still be around if I didn't. I just hope you know yours. Be careful, Huntress."

"Great," Theo cut in before their conversation could get any more intimate. He still didn't trust the intensity of Flint's gaze. "Let's get going. Mithras and midnight wait for no man."

They left Flint on the roof and sprinted back toward the dock. Hansen sat on her bench, staring toward Liberty Island as if lost in a dream. The dogs sprawled around her.

While Selene jumped aboard, Theo untied the mooring rope then reached for the rail before the boat could drift out of his reach. She was staring at him. He recognized the warmth in her gaze, a simmering reminder of what they'd shared on the banks of the Hudson. But he distrusted the way her lips tightened. He knew what she was going to say.

"Don't you dare." He swung aboard and moved toward the cockpit.

"Theo," she said, with far more gentleness than he was used to. "You convinced Ruth and Gabriela to stay behind because you couldn't bear to lose them. Don't you think I feel the same way?"

"Except this wasn't their fight." He turned back to her. "It *is* mine. I'm the reason Dash and Philippe are up there in the first place, remember? The Host knew they were coming because I told the Smith to call the captain."

"You couldn't have known—"

"And I thought we already had this discussion. I love you. So I'm not letting you face an entire cult of divinely armed fanatics with nothing but a sword you don't know how to use and a pack of shelter dogs."

"You don't have any weapon at all."

He patted the back of his pants. "I've got a gun."

She sighed and held out her hand. "You have to give me that. You don't know how to aim it. You'll be safe here, and I'm going to need it."

"And who's going to pilot the boat? Did you suddenly learn how to drive?"

"Gerry will do it."

"You're going to trust *her*?"

"She wants to get to that island as much as I do. And I'm not about to let her throw me overboard."

Theo refused to give up. "Fine. You take the gun." He handed it to her, then reached down into the canvas bag beneath the cockpit and withdrew Orion's bronze sword. "I'll take this."

Selene laughed. But he barely heard her. A tremor, part electric shock, part icy shiver, ran through his hand and up his arm. He'd expected the bronze weapon to be heavy. Instead, it felt like an extension of his body. He lifted it high, watching the moonlight run down the blade like water. He swung it in a wide arc. It sang.

"Did you hear that?" he whispered, swinging it again.

"Hey, watch it!"

"It's like the baying of hounds. Or the keening of a woman." He wasn't sure he liked it, but he knew he wanted to hear it again.

The captain's urgent question snapped him from his reverie. "You have *pneuma*, don't you, Professor?"

"The breath of divinity? The holy spirit? Hardly—"

"No, Theo," interrupted Selene, a look of sudden understanding crossing her face. "You do. You're a Makarites. A Blessed One. As close as a mortal can get to being a hemitheos."

Hansen raised her bound hands and laid a careful finger on the conch shell pommel of the sword. "I feel nothing. Syndexioi gain the ability to use these weapons only by a breath from Prometheus. But you . . . you're doing this all on your own."

He made a few more passes through the air, his muscles moving with a swiftness and strength he hadn't possessed a moment before. He knew exactly how he would twist a spear upon the haft of his sword and wrench it from its bearer's grasp. How to swing the blade into an arrow's path and knock it from the sky. How to slice through empty space and into a man's flesh in the same easy arc.

He tossed the sword upward, where it spun end over end, the blade a darker circle, the shining pommel a rim of fire, like a solar eclipse hovering just over their heads. It fell back into his palm, perfectly balanced. He grinned at Selene's awestruck expression. "Still want me to stay behind?"

Chapter 42

THE COLOSSUS

The first cannonball whistled overhead like a valkyrie's shriek, then struck the Host's moored yacht with a thunderous crash. The boat burst into a fireball, incinerating the Perses at the helm and destroying the Mithraists' only means of escape from Liberty Island.

They will fight us here. And they will die here, Selene thought as Theo steered them past the burning boat. The dogs around her whimpered as the heat and smoke gusted toward them, but Selene silenced them with a quick snarl.

They dropped anchor a few yards off the island's northern shore. To the south, the New Colossus stood atop her stone pedestal with her back to them. Selene only hoped the Host would be as oblivious to their arrival.

She unfastened Gerry from the boat's rail, but kept her wrists bound. A strip of life jacket canvas made a serviceable gag. "Sorry, Gerry, but I can't risk letting you warn them. And if you do anything to try to stop us, I'll just knock you unconscious—you know that, don't you? You've seen what I can do. So if you want to see your 'miracle,' then you'll do what I say." The cop nodded stiffly.

"Good," Selene said. "Then over the side we go."

Theo grimaced at the eddying black water. "You think my magic sword can keep me from freezing to death? Because otherwise this seems like a terrible way to start a battle."

In response, Selene picked up Leila, the white feist, and dumped her over the boat's rail. The small dog paddled vigorously for only a yard before gaining her footing.

Hippo followed her eagerly, splashing into the water with the grace of a large boulder and bounding ashore with a vigorous shake. Another four dogs followed her lead.

Only one dog remained. The black cockapoo lifted one hesitant paw and then another, tail tucked and ears flattened. "I'm with you, Koko." Theo patted the dog's back. "Shallow icy water is still icy water."

Selene hopped over the rail with barely a splash. She held up her arms. "You want me to carry you ashore?"

"And if I said yes? Don't answer that," he said with a sigh. "I know you could." He hoisted the cockapoo high in his arms. "At least one of us will stay dry," he muttered as he dropped over the side and waded toward the beach.

Selene watched as Hansen lowered herself awkwardly down the ladder on the back of the boat, wincing when the cold water struck her knees. *She looks old. And tired.* She quashed a sudden surge of sympathy. *She better keep up.*

Selene headed along the beach at a steady trot, the dogs at her heels, Theo keeping pace beside her, and Gerry not far behind. The air snapped with cold. The full moon lit her way as it crept toward its apex—and midnight.

She drew even with the statue and crept to the stone seawall that divided the beach from the rest of the island. Theo, panting slightly, came to stand beside her.

"I don't see any guards," he whispered. "They must've run down to the dock when Flint launched that cannonball."

"Time to flush out the rest. Send the message."

Theo pulled out the cell phone he'd borrowed from Gabriela, switched it to flashlight mode, and turned it toward the dark hulk of Governors Island across the harbor. Moments later, dim thunder echoed across the water, followed by the whistle of another cannonball. This one landed in the middle of the plaza that fronted the statue. Theo threw an arm over Selene's head to shield her from the flying shards of brick. She restrained herself from telling him he'd be better off sheltering under her. It was, after all, quite sweet.

They had only a few seconds to wait before two men burst through the door in the statue's base. The syndexioi wore their black combat gear but no helmets. The larger man bore the attributes of the Corvus—Hermes' winged cap and caduceus. Without the crow's mask he'd worn at the planetarium, Selene recognized him as the black cop with the linebacker's body who'd captured her at Rockefeller Center. The shorter man at his side was the Miles Secundo: He had a Mars tattoo on his right wrist but bore no divine weapon, only a handgun holstered at his hip.

The Corvus spoke into a headset as he walked cautiously toward the crater in the plaza. "It's a goddamn *cannonball*. No, I don't know where it's coming from!" He coughed and waved a hand through the cloud of brick dust. "But from the size of this hole, they must be offshore somewhere." He hopped into the air, his winged cap flapping, and bounced about unsteadily on the currents.

Selene crouched farther into the shadows behind the seawall and motioned for Theo and Gerry to do the same. *The Corvus has only had that cap for a day,* she realized, *since they stole it back from Dash at the planetarium.* It made sense that the cap was harder to master than the other divine items—Dash was, after all, the Trickster. She sent a silent thanks to her little brother for his perversity. The Corvus's awkwardness would give her an advantage.

His voice grew fainter as he floated northward toward the

dock. "Yes, sir, the Nymphus Primus and the Miles Primus went to the boat. We'll remain in place."

Selene grimaced. For now, only the Miles Secundo with the gun guarded the door, but the flying Corvus would return any second.

"If you start shooting," Theo said in her ear, "they'll know we're here and tell the others inside. They'll lock the doors. And I for one don't feel like scaling the exterior of the Statue of Liberty."

"Better to keep them guessing," Selene agreed.

Koko the cockapoo retrieved a driftwood branch twice his size and dropped it at her feet, waiting for her to throw it. He backed up a step and stared at her, tail wagging furiously. She looked at the other dogs. The German shepherd sat on her haunches, looking bored. Leila the feist stood frozen, her ears perked and her sharp nose pointed toward the guards. The three other shelter dogs had taken her lead and looked ready to launch themselves forward. Hippo, on the other hand, was busy sniffing the desiccated carcass of a sea bird.

Selene stood, picked up the branch, and held it high. The cockapoo reared on his hind legs, nearly falling backward in his effort to reach the prize. "Come, my *kastorides*, my hounds," she whispered to her pack. She breathed deeply, separating their scent from the salt air. They were excited, curious, fierce. She'd chosen wisely. But these dogs were not wolves; their parents had never taught them to bring down prey as a pack. And only the feist displayed any sign of being bred to hunt. But with the Lady of Hounds to lead them, anything was possible. She looked into the eyes of each of them in turn, reestablishing dominance. She let her body language, her scent, the low growl in her throat convey her desires. Hippo instantly turned away from her dead bird and stood at attention before her mistress. *Men threaten the pack,* Selene conveyed. *Men would take your food and hurt your Alpha. Bring them down,* kastorides. *Bring them down.*

She knelt beside Hippo, who looked up trustingly into her eyes.

"You be careful, my friend," she murmured to her dog. "Now go!" She slapped Hippo on the rump; the dog took a flying leap over the wall and started running toward the Secundo, a hundred pounds of lumbering, brindled fury, tail straight and teeth bared.

The syndexios, as she knew he would, cursed in disbelief and pulled his gun. Selene hurled the stick at his right hand, knocking the gun loose. The cockapoo bounced over the wall like a jumping jack and dashed forward. The little dog ignored the stick and grabbed the fallen gun instead. Its barrel dragged along the ground as he trotted happily back toward the seawall.

Hippo crashed into the bewildered guard with her jaws wide. She grabbed hold of his leg while he screamed and kicked at her ribs. Then the other dogs, Leila in the lead, rushed over the seawall like a tidal wave.

The flying Corvus returned, flapping unsteadily as he struggled to free the caduceus from his belt. "We're under attack!" he reported into his headset. "Feral dogs!"

The feist, the pit bull, and the others joined Hippo, ripping at the fallen guard's limbs and biting his nose to stifle his screams. The Corvus swung his staff. The snakes flew free, transformed from gilded metal to living monsters. Lazily, the German shepherd caught one of the serpents in her jaws, and the cockapoo—who'd already dropped the gun at Selene's feet and returned to the fray—bounded three feet into the air to snatch the other. The shepherd bit her serpent in half, then lay down with a huff, placed the head between her paws, and started gnawing at its flesh. The other snake thrashed in Koko's small jaws, its tail whipping around his neck and back, but the dog just shook his head happily, clearly enjoying the game.

The Corvus cursed and stumbled to the ground. Snakeless staff raised, he lunged toward the dogs attacking his comrade—but not before Hippo ripped the Miles Secundo's trachea from his throat. She turned to face the Corvus with blood dripping down her jaws.

Theo swore softly; Selene, her senses heightened by her connection to the dogs, could smell his fear. Whether he was scared *of* Hippo or *for* her, she couldn't tell. She felt no such emotion—she watched her pack like a proud mother, never doubting they would fulfill her commands.

Koko dropped his snake and leapt into the air, grabbing the caduceus in his jaws. The Corvus waved the staff wildly, and the dog oscillated like a child on a tire swing as he stubbornly refused to let go. Finally, with a shouted grunt, the Corvus managed to dislodge his attacker. His small black body flew through the air, landing with a sickening thud in the crater of broken bricks.

All thoughts of strategy disappeared. Selene rushed forward, gun raised, even as the other four dogs leapt on the Corvus. Before she could reach the man, he'd fallen to the ground beneath the canine onslaught, his blood flying.

He was dead by the time she got there. So was Koko. His snaggletooth still poked defiantly from his lower jaw.

Theo grabbed her arm and dragged her from the dog's small corpse. "We've got to hurry."

He smashed the last snake's skull with the heel of his shoe, then propelled her toward the pedestal's entrance. She could hear the Nymphus and the other Miles running toward them from the dock.

Hippo trotted over to join them, but Selene stopped her with a hand gesture. "You've done enough," she said quickly. "You can't help once we're on the stairs. Go back to the boat." The dog whimpered. "Go!"

Hippo finally obeyed, barking at the others and nipping at their heels until they followed.

Hansen had scaled the seawall without a word. Now she joined Selene, her face a stony mask. She barely looked at the mauled bodies of her comrades.

Theo held up his fist and ticked off one finger at a time. "One dude dead in the boat. Two killed by the dogs. Two more on our tail."

Selene nodded. With the Leo Secundo whom Philippe had killed in the planetarium, and the two she'd killed at Governors Island, that meant they faced four syndexioi ahead... and an unknown number of divine weapons.

As they neared the pedestal, she had to crane her neck to see the statue. She'd never been this close to her before—like most New Yorkers, she'd never bothered to visit. In the glare of the floodlights, she could see the seams in the massive sheets of oxidized copper. A rust stain beneath her elbow. A smattering of bird droppings across the back of her robe. *The sculptor based his New Colossus on the Roman goddess Libertas, but she's no more divine up close than any other Athanatos,* Selene thought as cold water squelched in her boots.

Over the statue's head, the moon inched ever closer to midnight.

Theo followed her stare. "They'll be in the crown," he said. "In honor of the seven-rayed Sun." He pointed to a sign above the pedestal's entrance: "354 Steps to the Top."

"So far, the magic sword has failed to keep my feet dry," he continued. "Something tells me it's not going to miraculously improve my aerobic capacity either. How about you start up, and I can deal with the guys coming from the dock. I'll keep the captain with me—that should slow them down."

She paused, torn. She didn't want to leave Theo to face two syndexioi by himself, but she couldn't afford to delay.

He drew Orion's sword from his belt. The moonlight glinted off his glasses, hiding his green eyes behind circles of brilliant white. He looked every inch a hero. "I've got this."

She placed the Secundo's gun in Theo's belt. "Might come in handy," she said. "But try not to shoot yourself by accident." She still had Gerry's Glock for herself.

He grabbed her and kissed her hard. "Now go. I'll join as soon as I can."

———◆———

Once Selene had entered the pedestal, Theo turned back to the plaza. Hansen, still bound and gagged, stood beside him looking out toward the dock. Lampposts lined the way, and Theo could just make out two figures rushing toward them in the distance.

He took the captain by the elbow and raised the tip of his sword toward her throat—not too close, since he didn't yet trust himself not to accidentally decapitate her.

"Stop where you are!" he called to the approaching syndexioi. "Or I'll kill the Hyaena!"

One man carried Mars's gleaming spear. *The Miles Primus.* He'd been the lunkish guard outside his cell in the mithraeum. The other man had Venus's mirror hanging from a strap across his chest and a shotgun in his hands. *He's the Nymphus who met me at the vault door,* Theo decided. Without his veil, he was just a forty-ish man with a slight paunch. Both syndexioi slowed to a walk, but didn't stop their approach.

"I swear it!" Theo said. "One more step and she's dead. If you try to warn the others inside, then she's dead. In fact, unless you guys sit down right now, take off your headsets, hand over your stolen weapons, and start acting like rational men instead of fanatics, she's dead."

At that, they halted. *Thank God,* Theo thought. *I'd never be able to slit Hansen's throat in cold blood.*

"Now the weapons," he called toward them. "Throw them down."

The Miles raised his spear, holding it like a javelin. "You sure you want me to throw it?"

"Not like—" Theo began, panicked.

"You think we care what you do to that traitor?" the Miles interrupted. "She helped you escape, remember? She's as good as dead to us already." He started running toward them, spear outstretched and aimed at the captain.

Theo instinctively thrust Hansen behind him and raised his sword to parry the blow. She grunted in surprise. As the Miles hurtled close, she twisted free of Theo's grasp with surprising strength, then ducked beneath the spear and rammed their attacker's solar plexus, throwing him over her shoulder with the practiced ease of a trained fighter.

The Miles rolled, still clutching his spear. Theo started after him, but the Nymphus sent a shotgun round whistling past his ribs, kicking up brick dust as it struck the ground. From the corner of his eye, he saw Hansen running toward the cover of the gift shop, abandoning him to the fray.

Then he remembered the winged cap.

Another shotgun slug sailed past as he sprinted toward the glimmer of metal beside the Corvus's corpse. He grabbed the hat and jammed it on his head with a silent prayer to all the gods that his powers as a Makarites would let him use it. *Okay, how do I…* he wondered, before the flapping of wings drowned out his own thoughts. All he had to do was wish to fly, and he did. Steering was another matter entirely. He hovered four feet off the ground, bouncing up and down with each stroke of the wings, watching with growing panic as the Nymphus reloaded his shotgun and the Miles stalked toward him with his spear. *Dash,* he remembered, *is lighter than I am.* Magic hats, it seemed, still had limitations.

Realizing he couldn't fight with his sword from this distance, he slung it through his belt and drew the gun instead. He pulled what he assumed was the safety, pointed the barrel at the Nymphus, and squeezed the trigger. The recoil sent him fluttering backward through the air, his bullet pinging harmlessly off the brick, four feet wide of his target. The Nymphus sent a slug whizzing an inch from Theo's ear in response.

"Shit, shit, shit," Theo muttered as the Nymphus pumped the shotgun for another round. He fumbled for the sword in his belt, dropping the gun in the process, and only just raised the blade in time to deflect the round from his face. The sword vibrated with the impact, and he barely managed to hold on to it.

The Miles put aside his spear to snatch up the fallen handgun, and Theo found himself swinging his blade in a whirring arc, sending bullet after bullet spinning back toward the shooters. It didn't move of its own accord like some enchanted object, it simply told his muscles what to do: All he had to do was listen. He fell into a sort of trance, all of his attention on the whizzing bullets. He barely noticed when one ricocheted back toward the Nymphus, striking him in the neck.

The Miles tried for one more shot, and the gun gave an empty click. Theo finally stilled his sword and swooped to the ground, stumbling forward a few steps and nearly falling on his face.

The Miles dropped the empty gun and raised his spear instead. It was taller than a man, its shaft covered in gold and its foot-long blade of dark iron nearly invisible against the night sky. He thrust it straight at Theo's stomach, but Orion's sword easily turned the head aside in a shower of sparks.

Theo swung for the shaft next, hoping to slice it in two, but the bronze slipped across the gold plating without a nick. *Divine weapon versus divine weapon,* he thought grimly. *This is not going to be easy.*

He instinctively turned sideways to give the Miles a smaller target. Up close, he was struck by the man's obvious youth. Surely he'd been born into the cult as Hansen had—was it his fault he believed its lies? "You don't need to do this," Theo insisted. "I don't want anyone else to die tonight." Watching the dogs devour the first two men had turned his stomach. Now he could barely stand to look at the Nymphus felled by his bullet. He would defend himself or those he loved, but he was no killer. Yet it seemed the Miles wouldn't give him a choice.

"My death doesn't matter," said the soldier calmly. "Tonight, the Last Age begins, and I will be resurrected along with the rest."

"So you're saying I *shouldn't* feel guilty when I run this sword through you?" Theo asked.

A feral grin slashed the Miles's face. He held the front of the spear's shaft loosely in his left hand and thrust the butt forward with his right. It darted like a snake's tongue. Theo had to leap back six feet to avoid its reach—a feat impossible without the winged hat.

The spear came at him again. Its length allowed the Miles to thrust high and low, left and right, without breaking a sweat. Theo parried frantically, quickly tiring. The spear's reach was simply too long, the Miles's strikes too swift. *His is the weapon of the Lord of War,* Theo remembered, *while mine was owned by a Hunter.* His only chance was to get inside the spear's reach, where his shorter blade could prove more effective.

As the Miles drew his spear backward for a stronger thrust, Theo landed a single lucky blow against his torso, but the blade didn't cut fully through his Kevlar vest. Still, the Miles staggered to the side and lost his breath for a moment. Theo took advantage of his sudden weakness to leap forward and grab the spear's shaft. He threw his whole weight against it, flinging the spear aside, then brought down his sword in a blinding crescent against the Miles's neck.

—◇—

Inside the statue's base, Selene broke into a run. Ten flights up at the top of the pedestal, it took all her willpower to continue toward the next staircase rather than duck onto the terrace to check on Theo. She had only minutes before midnight.

From here, the ascent to the crown was a double-helix staircase with protective glass walls, each pie-slice tread treacherously narrow. Around her hung the thin copper of Libertas herself, blackened with age. A branching framework of beams met a thin steel grid that held the great undulating folds of her robe in place. Selene ran as quietly as possible, but even the Huntress's silent tread made some noise in the metal echo chamber.

She sprinted around and around the central support column, growing dizzier by the second. Then she heard a pounding of footsteps above and pressed her face to the glass wall, trying to peer upward. She could see nothing but the bottom of the next curve in the staircase. She had wooden arrows in her quiver—but nothing to shoot them with. That left her Hansen's gun. During her time on the police force in the 1970s, she'd been the best shot in the city. She hadn't bothered with firearms since then. But in the life of a goddess, fifty years were nothing. She hadn't forgotten her skills.

As the syndexios rounded the bend above her, Selene flattened herself against the central column and fired up into the man's face. She would've hit him with Gerry's old Smith & Wesson Chief's Special revolver, but her Glock was a completely different animal. Selene adjusted wrong for the trigger's heavy pull weight and the bullet flew an inch wide, shattering the glass wall instead of the man's skull. Suddenly, she was looking down the shaft of a golden arrow.

Before she could shoot again, the arrow struck the gun, knocking it from her grip. It flew over the stairs, bounced off the copper walls, then plummeted ten stories, banging like a cymbal as it careered from wall to stairs and back. She stared at the man before her. "I see. You take my bow, and you think you're a Hunter now?" she snarled.

"No different from you." He aimed a second gold arrow, this one at her chest. She remembered him from the planetarium. A Perses who dared claim the moon as his protective planet. He'd shot three of her shafts into Flint's stomach and one into her own back.

"You're just a Pretender," he sneered. "Any powers you possess are either trickery or devil-spawned. You cannot defeat the true servants of the God."

He drew back the bowstring, and Selene quickly raised her hands above her head.

"I surrender, okay? Take me up to your Pater. I'm sure he'd rather use me in some ceremony than have me die here on the stairs."

The Perses didn't budge. "Sacrifices won't matter after tonight. He just wants you dead."

The instant he released the string, she ducked to the side, pulling two wooden arrows from her quiver as she fell into a crouch. The arrow flew past her ear and clanged against copper. She sprang back to her feet, an arrow in each hand, and leapt toward the Perses. She slammed her knee into his gut, launching him upward. The backs of his thighs hit the low wall of the staircase—the rest of him hung over empty air.

She thrust her arrows through either side of the Perses' neck, then stepped back.

"The difference," she whispered into his ear as he died, "is that I don't need a bow to be a Huntress."

Eyes bulging in disbelief, he toppled backward into the statue's hollow core.

Taking her gold bow and arrows with him.

Chapter 43

LIGHTNING BRINGER

Selene peered over the edge of the staircase. She could just make out the glint of her bow and arrows, over a hundred feet below. Then she heard the chanting begin from somewhere above her.

"Ego sum resurrectio et vita. Qui credit in me, et si mortuus fuerit, vivet."

I am the resurrection and the life. Whoever believes in me, though he die, yet shall he live.

There simply wasn't time to go back for her weapons. Could she launch herself at the Pater and try to throttle him with her bare hands? How would she rescue her family if she couldn't fight?

How 'bout another well-timed cannonball? she prayed to Flint uselessly; they'd found only two projectiles on Governors Island. *Still, I bet you'd come up with* some *plan. Some way to make a weapon out of shoelaces or something.* Then, for the first time since he'd handed it to her, she remembered his gift.

It's got hidden secrets, just like you, he'd said.

She pulled the necklace from her pocket. It was surprisingly heavy, even for a gold chain of its thickness. Still, it bore no magic that she could detect. Looking at it more closely, she could see intricate engravings across its surface, but no discernible pattern. Then, unsure what else to do, she unclasped it.

It immediately unfurled like a waterfall, thinning and stretching until it lay across the ground in a long coil. One end thickened to become a handle, perfectly sized for her grip. The far end narrowed to a wicked, razor-thin tip. She stared at it in wonder. *By Kronos's gullet . . . it's a . . .*

A whip cracked overhead as if in answer.

She looked up to see the Heliodromus Secundo descending the stairs, weapon in hand. He swung his leather whip, its tip licking toward her and slashing her right cheek.

"You scourged my brother with that lash," she said, raising a hand to the trickle of blood.

"Get back, Diana Pretender!" he hollered at her, cheeks aflame. The hawk-faced man had always remained calm in the face of her threats—this other Heliodromus had little control over his emotions. That would make him even easier to defeat.

"They sent a mortal with a mortal weapon to defeat me?" she asked icily.

He raised his whip again, but she flicked her hand. Flint's gift shot forward to spiral around his wrist. She yanked on the handle, pulling the man down the stairs and into the path of her booted foot. He wheezed and doubled over. She uncoiled the gold whip from his wrist and looped it around his neck instead. With the whip's grip in one hand and its tip in the other, she jerked both her arms with a sudden furious strength. His neck snapped.

Selene stepped over the body and continued on her way, no longer mindful of the sound she made. Her feet thundered on the metal treads as she entered the statue's head, announcing her approach. Before her, the face of Libertas hung in counter-relief, her enormous, heavy-lidded eyes watching impassively as a fellow goddess hurtled by.

Selene burst onto the narrow viewing platform in the crown,

expecting to see the Pater with his last two guards. Instead, she found herself nearly blinded by blazing LEDs that beamed through the crown's windows, spreading their glow for miles around. She turned her back to the glare and squinted into the small chamber before her.

Dash and Philippe lay on the ground. Alone.

They turned to her, their faces drawn and haggard as if they'd neither slept nor eaten since they'd been captured. Selene could only imagine what memories the Pater had sent to torment them.

Their bleeding lips stretched around cloth gags. Metal handcuffs and ankle fetters bound their limbs, and a thick chain secured them to a steel beam. They looked at her through eyes slitted against the light, moaning and shouting through their gags. Selene shushed them to silence.

The Pater's chanting floated through the row of windows that arched across the crown. She stuck her face against a pane and peered upward. Above her, on the round base of the torch, stood the Pater and one of his black-clad soldiers. Prometheus hung before him, chained to the torch's gold-plated flame. Little remained of the formidable Titan whom Selene remembered. In the floodlights, his naked body sagged with loose skin and atrophied muscles. His rib cage heaved, but his face looked relaxed. He wanted this.

She turned back to her family, coiling Flint's whip around her arm so she could fish her lock picks from a pocket. Dash shook his head, his eyes darting frantically around the narrow chamber.

"I'm trying!" Selene protested, jimmying the clasp on his handcuffs. Dash only shook his head more furiously. Philippe pounded his feet against the echoing metal floor. Growing more annoyed by the second, she seriously considered leaving them both to die—or at least threatening to—when a golden net descended like a colossal hand to smash her to the ground.

———◦———

At the base of the statue, Theo had no time to wonder what had become of the captain, or to worry about the fact that he'd just killed two men. His only thought was to get to Selene as quickly as possible. He took one look at the back of Liberty's head and decided there were better ways to get there than trudging up more than twenty flights of stairs. He took a running leap and lifted into the air. *Up, up, up,* he willed himself. The wind grew stronger the higher he rose, buffeting him from side to side.

He wove a spiraling path ever upward and managed to navigate around to the front of the statue without smacking into the gargantuan tablet in Liberty's left hand. Her stern Roman face rose before him—she reminded him of Selene.

Then he heard the chanting. He looked toward the torch and saw the Pater, Prometheus, and a single syndexios standing on its rim. But no Selene.

The seven rays of Liberty's diadem, the same ones that graced the head of Sol Invictus in images throughout ancient Rome, loomed overhead. He slowed his flight and approached the windows in the crown's face, checking to make sure he still had Mars's spear securely strapped to his back and Orion's sword slung at his waist. His wings folded flat as he perched on the crown's ridge to peer through a small window. Light poured out, too intense to bear, and Theo had to shield his eyes before he could see inside.

Selene lay facedown beneath Hephaestus's golden net. Dash and Philippe, chained to the wall, screamed against their gags.

Then, suddenly, the hawk-faced Heliodromus Primus—the same man who'd lured Selene into the trap at the ice skating rink, the same man who'd chased Paul at arrowpoint during the Procession of the Sun-Runner—materialized inside the chamber, removing Hades' black helm from his head. In his other hand he held Apollo's silver bow, and at his side hung Hephaestus's massive hammer. A quiver of gleaming silver arrows lay against his back. He reached to select a shaft and fitted it to his bow, just as Selene rolled over beneath the net. She strained to tear free, but the net looked heavy as lead and hard as diamonds.

Theo shouted a wordless cry of fury that turned the Heliodromus in his direction. He fumbled the spear free of his back, even as the hawk-faced man shot an arrow through the opening in the small window. Theo swung to the side just in time, pressing his back against the next window in the row. But the Heliodromus simply sent another arrow, this one grazing the side of Theo's parka and sending white feathers floating like snow.

Theo jumped from the crown, spun in midair to face his attacker, and launched Mars's spear through the window.

The Heliodromus stepped easily to the side and the shaft went sailing over the narrow viewing platform and down the stairwell beyond.

Theo wanted to hurl himself at this man who dared to threaten Selene, but even if he could break through the thick glass, the windows were too small to crawl through. He pounded a fist on the copper casements as if he could break them with brute force alone. His knuckles split. He didn't even feel the pain.

The Heliodromus stared at him impassively, knowing full well Theo could do nothing to stop him. Slowly, he turned back to Selene. She'd stopped thrashing; she lay calmly beneath the net, her eyes closed. In her hands, she clutched a strange, golden whip. The Heliodromus raised his bow once more and loosed a divine arrow at Selene's heart.

Even as Theo cried out, Selene tore apart the net as if it were spider's silk. She caught the silver arrow in the golden threads and turned it aside, bending the shaft. Then her foot struck out, slamming into the man's ankle so he toppled toward her. Still lying on the floor, she raised the gold whip in her hand—the flexible links telescoped together and suddenly she held a javelin, seven feet long. She thrust it forward.

The Heliodromus slid down its length like meat on a skewer.

After a moment, she rolled free of his body. She drew the javelin from his back in a single smooth movement, ignoring the man's dying groans as his entrails spilled onto the floor.

By that time, Theo had managed to squeeze an arm through the window opening. Selene looked not at him, but at the javelin in her hand. She rolled it slowly, staring at the engravings along its length.

"The hammer," Theo called to her. "Hand me the hammer!"

Selene looked up, surprised. The javelin melted back into a whip.

Looking dazed, she unhooked the Smith's hammer from the man's belt and passed it through the window. Theo nearly plummeted to the ground with its weight. The hat alone couldn't hold him aloft.

He managed to balance on the statue's copper brow while swinging the hammer two-handed against the window frame. It reverberated like a gong. He knew the Pater would see him, if he hadn't already. He didn't care. He struck again. And again. The safety glass shattered, the copper bent beneath the Smith's mighty hammer, and the casement ripped open into a hole big enough for Theo to tumble through.

He dropped the hammer to the floor and gathered Selene in his arms. "I saw you lying there, and I thought you were dead," he said hoarsely.

"It's okay," she murmured. "I'm all right."

He took a step back, holding her face between his hands. Besides a graze on her cheek, she appeared unharmed.

Dash started humming an impatient melody behind his gag, while Philippe tapped out a frustrated tattoo on the wall with his bound hands.

Theo let Selene go and moved to Philippe first, pulling the gag from his mouth.

"Wait until I tell Papa that you used his hammer to bust through the Statue of Liberty's forehead," he said with a weak laugh. "He's either going to be very proud or very pissed."

Selene took the handcuff key from the Heliodromus's pocket and released the Athanatoi from their shackles. Dried blood from the spear wound he'd suffered at the planetarium crusted Philippe's pale blue dress shirt. He stood awkwardly, one hand pressed against his side. Dash, who still wore the livid red welts of the snakes' embrace around his neck, stared fixedly at the winged cap on Theo's head.

"Philippe," Selene said, "you're in no shape to fight tonight. Dash, help him out of here. Take Flint's hammer and Hades' Helm of Invisibility in case you run into trouble. We left the boat moored off the northern shore. Wait for us there."

Philippe gave them a wan smile and blew Selene and Theo each a kiss.

Dash, his face as stern as Theo'd ever seen it, looked up at Selene with bleary, red-rimmed eyes. "You're going to take the Pater down. Promise me you will."

Theo wondered what visions carefree Hermes had been sent in the mithraeum's cell. Something truly awful, from the look in his eyes.

Only when she nodded her assent did Dash put on the helm, wincing a little at the press of its weight. He remained conspicuously visible. Then he picked up Flint's hammer in one hand and put the other arm beneath Philippe's shoulder. Together, they headed down the stairwell.

Theo looked from the stairs to Selene and back. "We freed them. Please tell me we're going home now."

Selene snorted. "And leave the Pater alive? Not a chance."

"I'm not interested in revenge."

"And I'm not interested in letting this cult come after us again. You want to spend the rest of our lives running?" she demanded.

Theo took a deep breath and shook his head.

She grabbed Apollo's silver bow off the ground and pulled the quiver from the dead man's back. In it lay one final divine arrow. She coiled her gold whip around her shoulders and stepped into the gaping hole in the front of the crown, staring at Theo expectantly. "Now can I get a lift, or what?"

———<o>———

Selene hadn't flown through the air since she'd guided the moon across the sky in her stag-drawn chariot. Needless to say, the stags provided a considerably smoother ride. It became clear within seconds that Dash's cap was never meant to carry so much weight. They plummeted a few feet, then rose again, only to start rotating in an awkward circle. She was painfully aware of the three hundred feet of nothingness between her and the ground. She lifted her legs and wrapped them around Theo's waist to hang on more securely.

"That's not helping." Theo's voice was strained.

"I don't want to fall." Fear made her snappish. "No moonlight would be enough to heal me from that."

"I have to concentrate to be able to steer," he said, "and I can't think straight with your..." He moved his hands a little lower on her waist.

She lowered her legs with an exasperated huff, grabbing on to his neck even more tightly.

"Better," he murmured in her ear, "but if we make it out of this, we're going back to your house and not leaving for a week. Got it?"

She could see it before her—Theo sprawled naked across her bed, the glow of a winter sun pouring through the window and dispelling the cold. Somehow, it no longer seemed impossible. Then the wind struck her face in an icy blast, whipping away all thoughts of warmth and peace.

They zigzagged heavenward, following the path of Libertas's upraised green arm. Above them, the one remaining syndexios peered over the railing of the torch's base. Selene recognized him as the doughboy cop from Rockefeller Center. He cried the alarm to the Pater.

The old man turned to look. She could see his long white hair tangling in the wind. He no longer wore his golden mask, but he turned his back before she could get a good look at his face. Prometheus, hanging limply from his chains, looked from Selene to the Pater, bewildered.

"You've got to land," Selene told Theo. "No way I can shoot a bow if I'm holding on to you for dear life."

"Stop them," the Pater said calmly to his syndexios. "I must complete the sacrifice." He began chanting again in Latin, one hand on Prometheus's bare chest and the other holding his sickle.

The pudgy syndexios bent to retrieve something from the ground. When he stood, he held Poseidon's trident in his out-stretched hand.

"Oh no, not this bastard again." Theo flapped backward a few feet.

"What're you going to do with that?" Selene shouted toward the syndexios. "Start an earthquake on the torch and bring down the whole arm—and everyone on it?"

A worried look crossed his face, but he leveled the whale-bone tines in her direction. "Stay back!" he shouted in his Queens accent.

"Hey, Leo!" Theo called, "If we're here, that means all your friends are dead. And you're going to be next, you piece of shit." As he spoke, they jigged violently from side to side, making it impossible for Selene to aim any attack.

"Hold still!" she told him. "If you're too busy yelling insults, you can't concentrate on the cap!"

"I'm trying!" he said. Sweat streamed down his temples despite the cold. "The cap doesn't like holding two people."

They swooped recklessly toward the trident's point, and Selene dared to let go with one arm and raise her whip with the other. The syndexios thrust the trident toward them, nearly impaling Selene. But she flicked the whip forward and it snaked around the trident's shaft. She jerked the weapon from his hands, the force of her movement sending Theo and herself spinning wildly in midair. The trident tumbled to the island far below.

As they lurched back toward the torch, Selene released Theo and leaped over the railing. He stumbled after her, holding one hand to his temple while he drew his sword unsteadily with the other.

The Leo lunged toward them, unarmed, but Selene slammed her foot into his kneecap, sending him sprawling. Theo stood over him. "How's it feel to have the tables turned?" he asked, the point of his sword digging into the folds of fat on the man's neck.

Selene slung her whip around her shoulders, knowing its reach would be too long for the cramped quarters, and nocked the last silver arrow to Apollo's bow instead. "Turn around!" she shouted at the Pater. "Let me look my brother's killer in the eye before I send him to his death."

"You don't want to kill me, Diana," he said, sounding like a tired father lecturing a recalcitrant child.

Selene barked out a laugh. "You have no idea how wrong you are."

The Pater slowly turned around. "No, I'm afraid you're the one who's wrong...about so much."

An old man's face, deep creases across his brow, but with none of the slack weakness of age. Blue eyes as fathomless as the spaces between stars. He showed no sign of injury from the bullet Gabriela had shot into his stomach. A faint smile played across thin lips.

"Saturn..." Selene whispered.

"Hello, granddaughter."

The bow trembled in her hand. The man she once knew as Kronos, King of Titans, held his sickle steady and relaxed at his side.

"I don't understand..." she stammered. "Why would you lead a Mithras cult? Much less a Jesus one?"

"I'm the Father of the Gods, the father of Zeus himself."

Saturn seemed to swell in size. His pale skin glowed faintly. *A divine aura,* Selene realized. *He's stronger than I am. But how is that possible?*

Beside her, Theo spoke urgently. "The Father of the Gods…God the Father. *He* is one of the Three Aspects. He's not copying Christianity, Selene—he *is* Christianity. He's stolen the Trinity itself."

"Close, Professor." Saturn barely flicked his eyes in Theo's direction. "But there's much you still don't know."

"All the deaths—" Selene snapped. "It's not about resurrecting Jesus, is it? It's about killing us all off to leave more power for yourself."

"The Ages must turn," he said simply. "From the Age of Heroes to the Age of Iron to the Age of Man. And from the Age of Taurus to Aries to Pisces. Now we shift from Pisces to Aquarius. From the Age of Man to the Age of God."

"God." Selene laughed bitterly. "Not *gods*. The sacrifices are working—you've been getting stronger every time. And after tonight, you think you'll be all-powerful. You'll be more than Kronos, God of Time, or Saturn, Ruler of the Afterlife. You'll be Mithras, God of Soldiers and the Sun and Salvation. And God the Father, the omnipotent Creator. You want it *all*, you greedy bastard."

Theo, still holding his sword to the Leo's neck, groaned. "That's the reversal the liver foretold: Zeus and the Olympians overthrew their father. Now their father seeks to overthrow them."

"I've simply taken what lay before me," Saturn said calmly. "You could've done the same, Diana. They needed a Holy Virgin. Who better to play that role than the Chaste One herself? It's not too late." He gestured to the waves, the city, the heavens above. "You could help me rule over all of this. You need only become something new, as you've done a hundred times before. With tonight's sacrifice, my power is resurrected. Then together, we can expel Zeus from this world, and the reversal will be complete. We can leave this mortal realm and ascend once more to our place in the heavens—incorporeal gods, omnipotent and omniscient."

"My father should have sliced off your head when he sliced open your gullet." She shot her arrow at his face.

The Pater didn't duck. He simply swung his sickle and sliced the shaft in two, sending the pieces sailing into the ether. "You can't defeat me, granddaughter." His aura flared, until even his robes seemed to glow. Selene had to squint to see his outline. "And as soon as Prometheus gives himself to me, no one will."

A figure emerged from the trapdoor in the floor of the torch's base. Geraldine Hansen, unarmed and unafraid, stared straight at the chained Titan hanging spread-eagled upon the torch. She'd freed herself of the gag and the bindings on her wrists. "Don't go willingly, Praenuntius," she panted, still winded from her climb.

Saturn glanced over his shoulder at the woman. "Ah, my Hyaena. You who betrayed the Host to free the professor. You come groveling back to me?"

She would not look at her Pater. "Do not speak to me of betrayal. I heard Selene. You've lied to us for a thousand years."

She stepped to Prometheus and put both hands on his sunken cheeks. His dark eyes met hers. "I promised to free you from life. Now you must free me instead. Free me from this monster by denying him your final gift."

For the first time, fear flashed across Saturn's face. He reached for the old woman, sickle raised, but Selene rushed forward and grabbed his arms, jerking him backward. He threw her off with impossible force, flinging her body through the air.

Her head snapped back to clang against the top rail with enough power to darken her vision. Her chest slammed against the lower railing, knocking the breath from her body. Apollo's bow fell from her fingers. As she lay stunned, she saw Theo kick the captive Leo aside and turn to look at her, his mouth open with a shout her rattled brain couldn't hear.

The copper floor vibrated against her cheek with a man's heavy tread. She looked up to see her grandfather striding toward her.

Theo leaped in front of him, his sword raised in both hands.

Selene reached for the railing to lever herself off the ground, but her limbs wouldn't obey her commands. She could hear the clash of metal as Theo's blade blocked the sickle's swing. As the divine weapons struck each other again and again, sparks flew like shooting stars, stinging Selene's cheeks.

Theo took a step backward, faltering beneath Saturn's ceaseless blows. He jerked to one side as the sickle swung near. Its curved blade caught him on his right wrist, sheering a long strip of flesh and tendon from the bone. Theo dropped the sword with a cry— it spun across the metal floor and slipped through the railing to tumble toward the ground. He held his bleeding wrist with his other hand and raised it overhead like a shield to defend Selene.

From the corner of her eye, she saw Gerry step to the fallen Leo, pull something long and metallic from a holster at his waist, and then return to Prometheus. She spread her arms until they mirrored the old man's outstretched limbs. She placed both her hands in his, the metal object still grasped between them. Prometheus closed his eyes. Very gently, he pursed his lips and blew a stream of air upon her upturned face.

Saturn paid them no heed. He moved toward Theo, the glow of his aura reflecting off the curve of his upraised blade.

Gerry cried out, her knees buckling. But Prometheus wrapped his fingers around hers and kept her upright, his breath a little louder now, a breeze's gentle susurrus. A new light blazed forth from their clasped hands, a white so brilliant that the golden torch, the shining god, and the full moon all seemed to dim in its glare.

Saturn turned toward his Hyaena. Selene struggled to her feet, pulling Theo upright with one arm and shielding her eyes with the other.

Gerry dropped from Prometheus's grasp and faced her Pater.

She held a shaft of blinding light gripped in her fist. "You know what happens when lightning strikes a copper statue?"

Her eyes met Selene's. A warning. A regret.

For the first time in two thousand years, Zeus's thunderbolt split the heavens.

Chapter 44

SHE WHO RIDES
THE MOON

Theo's breath left his body as Selene dragged him over the railing and into midair. They plummeted downward as the sky cracked above them—a deafening blast of sound and a blinding flare of light.

"Fly, Theo!" she screamed above the din. "Fly!"

He squeezed his eyes closed, ignored the searing pain in his wrist, and directed all his will into the winged cap, stopping their descent before they smashed into the island below. For an instant, they hung suspended.

He dared open his eyes as lightning coursed across the torch's gold-plated flame and ran in jagged tendrils down Liberty's copper arm.

As their hair rose on end and the air hummed with electricity, they clutched each other tightly. They smelled scorched flesh, but it was not their own. They heard agonized moans, but their own lips were silent.

We're safe.

Then a line of white fire shot from the torch itself, seeking them out like an accusatory finger. *You shall not live while the others die.*

It struck Selene in the chest, then leaped to Theo, blasting the coat from his body and burning the flesh beneath. The force of the strike blew them backward; they spun like a top above the swirling black waters of the harbor.

Theo fought through the pain, desperate to keep them from falling. The gold cap flared hot on his scalp, and he could hear the currents of electricity cracking across its surface. The wings beat irregularly, like a heart off rhythm, plunging them downward and jerking them up again with every stroke. Selene's body nearly slipped from his arms. His wounded right hand hung limp and useless—and she wasn't holding on.

"Selene!" Her head lolled against his shoulder before rolling backward on her neck. A charred hole in the center of her jacket revealed scorched skin. He lifted her body in his arms so he could press his ear against her neck. Her pulse had stopped beating. He tried to call her name again, as if that alone would bring her back to life, but he could manage nothing more than a strangled gasp.

Another crack of thunder split the night. He looked to the torch, where the fallen bolt continued to send rivers of electricity across the statue's copper cladding. Hansen's body was blackened gore. Prometheus's bloody frame hung from the torch like an animal's dripping carcass. He didn't see Saturn.

Electricity destroys—but it also gives life, Theo thought, willing the cap to bring them closer again to the torch. They lurched forward. The lightning sparked, dimmer this time, the thunder a growl rather than a deafening clap. *One more, one more,* he begged. He turned Selene in his arms, screaming with pain as her body scraped against his charred chest.

"Come on!" he shouted to the lightning, to the Fates, to Zeus himself. "Try it again!"

A final surge rocked the torch. A finger of electricity leaped through the air to Selene's bare breast and flung them backward once more.

The current raced through her body and into his, and Theo felt his own heart clench and stutter. His mind splintered.

Then, slowly, the shards reformed.

It felt like hours had passed, but when his consciousness returned, they were still aloft, and Selene gasped in his embrace.

She clutched his arms where they passed around her body. He could feel her heart beating beneath his grip.

He rested his cheek against the back of her head. "I've got you, I've got you."

He had no sense of direction; he knew only that they pitched through the air and that the dark harbor yawned beneath them. He wanted to slow down, to right himself. Seek land, or at least make a controlled drop into the icy waters and hope to survive until a ship came to rescue them. Instead, he had no control over the cap. It lifted them ever higher, as if supercharged by the second bolt. He tried to concentrate, to bring it back under his control, but blood poured from his right wrist, draining away the remnants of his strength.

In the distance, Manhattan glimmered like a promised land, its towers offering rest and warmth and home. And still they soared higher. The clouds appeared above them, alight with the moon's glow.

He clasped Selene with his one good arm, his muscles spasming from the aftereffects of the blast. It took every ounce of his quickly dwindling strength to hold on to her.

The wind whistled past his ears, and snatched away Selene's voice. He leaned closer and pressed his ear against her skull. He could barely hear her words. And when he did, he couldn't believe them.

"You have to let me go."

"Never." The world dimmed before him. Black sky, Selene's black hair, more blackness closing in.

"You're going to pass out. If you do, the cap stops working, and we both die. We'll never survive a fall from this height. Without me, you can control the cap, land safely."

They were passing through the clouds now, ice particles searing their skin, the thick black world dissolving into white nothingness. *Is this what death will look like?* Theo wondered, his mind spinning in slow motion.

Selene twisted in his arms to face him. They passed above the clouds. Ice formed on her lashes. Theo's body began to shake; his teeth rattled. She stared at him, her silver eyes suddenly aglow. Then she looked around at the sea of clouds spread beneath them, a glowing white world of spun moonlight.

"This is what it was like," she said, her voice hardly more than a breath. "To ride the moon across the sky." She looked back at Theo for a moment. Too short. "I love you, you know."

She pried his arm from her chest and lifted his mangled hand to her lips for a precious instant.

"What are you doing?" he gasped, clutching at her with his other hand, his legs, his heart. "You have to hold on!"

She shook her head and gave him a tiny, heartbroken smile. "It was always fated to come to this. I could never grant you immortality, Theo. But at least I won't have to live without you."

Then, with the sudden strength of a goddess, she ripped herself from his grasp.

She fell through the clouds, a needle piercing the fabric of the world, and disappeared.

Epilogus

THE NEW MOON

New Year's Day

Theo Schultz sat on a bench in Riverside Park, the winter sun weak on his upturned face. The blanket around his shoulders did little to dispel the cold. He was always cold now. Even indoors. Even sitting before a roaring fireplace in the parlor of Selene's brownstone—the brownstone Dash had told him she would've wanted him to have.

The Messenger had appeared at Theo's hospital bedside to tell him the deed to the house would be waiting for him when he got out. "Give me a call, Makarites," he'd said. "If you ever need anything." Theo had passed back into unconsciousness, as he often did those first few days after crash-landing in downtown Manhattan.

When he came to, Dash was gone. He'd thought the visit a dream until he saw the large, neatly wrapped gift box on the floor by the bed. The attached business card read, "Scooter Joveson: Cybersecurity Consultant and Venture Capital Entrepreneur." Beneath a layer of folded tissue paper lay Hades' Helm of Invisibility and Orion's sword. Theo hadn't taken them out of the box. He wasn't sure he ever would.

From his spot on the bench in Riverside Park, he watched Ruth appear at the end of the path, carrying a grocery bag in one hand and Hippo's leash in the other.

Hippo spotted Theo and began to run, dragging Ruth behind her. The dog licked his bandaged hand then settled her bulk beneath the bench.

"Brrrr!" Ruth said, sitting beside him. "You sure you didn't want to picnic *indoors?*"

"I like it here."

She peered at him through her glasses. She'd taken to wearing them, Theo noticed, rather than her contacts. Perhaps because she rarely went home anymore. She'd been staying in one of the many spare rooms in Selene's house, playing nursemaid. On the few occasions she'd left, Gabriela had come in her stead. Theo didn't have the heart to feel guilty. He didn't have the heart to feel much of anything.

"This is where you met her," she said quietly.

He nodded reluctantly, thinking, *And where we made love.* That night, he'd felt like he'd flown on rainbow wings. Now, the wings had been torn from his back, leaving only ropy scars behind.

Ruth pulled out a sandwich and handed it to him. He let it rest, untouched, in his lap. A smattering of pigeons flapped down to the path and paced in nervous circles, waiting for a crumb. Hippo sighed and ignored them. She, too, had barely eaten since Christmas.

They sat in silence, staring out at the slate gray water. A new year. A new beginning. But to Theo, it only felt like the end. After the holiday, he planned to tell the university that he'd spend the next semester on sabbatical. They'd have to get someone else to take over the department. He wasn't sure he'd ever come back. How could he spend his days speaking of Ares and Apollo, Prometheus and Hades, as if they were mere myth? As if a goddess named Artemis hadn't taught him to love and then broken his heart?

In the hospital, Dash had told him how the world mourned her death. Not through a convulsion of violence, but through an outpouring of grief. "That night, on the boat," he'd said, "the tide swelled, as if the Moon herself cried out in agony and dragged the waters to her breast. And then I knew Artemis was gone."

Theo felt a shudder that had nothing to do with the cold passing through his body. Ruth put a tentative hand on his shoulder. He wanted to shake her off.

He finally understood why Selene always wanted to be alone. His grief was too complete a thing to share. If he let someone else take even an ounce of its weight, he'd split asunder. He'd never be able to gather the pieces together again. He wasn't sure he'd want to.

Something sharp pierced the side of his arm. He swatted it away.

Ruth looked at him quizzically. "A mosquito? In January?"

"I don't know. Felt almost like an electric shock. Some left-over lightning bolt pissed that it never got a turn."

"Not sure that's scientifically possible," she said with a smile.

"I've given up on scientifically possible," he said, surprising himself with a small smile of his own. "From now on, I believe only in the supernatural."

"Oh? You're going to fly around in that winged cap and speak to the pigeons?"

"The winged cap's busted. And the pigeons probably don't have much to say besides, 'Stop wasting that sandwich, asshole, because if you don't want it, we do.'"

Ruth laughed, a delighted chortle of glee, long repressed. Theo felt a chuckle in his own throat. Not ready to emerge, not yet. But it was there.

Hippo got up suddenly, distracted by something in the distance. Theo looked over his shoulder, but saw nothing. "Here, girl," he said. He tore off the corner of the sandwich and waved it at the dog, who trundled back and wolfed it down whole before settling back beneath the bench. Then he took a bite himself, suddenly ravenous.

Ruth's hand remained on his shoulder.

After he'd finished the sandwich, he placed his own hand on top of hers and drew it down to hold it against his heart. The lightning had burst the vessels on his chest, leaving behind branching lines of red that mirrored the bolt itself, all radiating from the Mercury brand. The slowly-healing flesh felt new and raw and painful to touch. He pressed Ruth's hand against it anyway. She grounded him. Right here on this bench, on this shore, in this city.

And for the first time since he'd held Selene in his arms and then watched her slip away, he felt a glimmer of hope.

—◇—

Philippe ducked back behind the stone wall that overlooked the riverside path and lowered his bow. "And *voilà*. That should help."

He stared thoughtfully at the woman crouched against the wall beside him. "It doesn't take away his love for you, you know. It can't do that. It just opened his heart. Enough to let him feel something besides grief."

She stared down at her knees, her voice a tentative whisper. "So he'll love Ruth now."

"*Ah, non, ma chérie.* He's still too in love with you for that to happen. But perhaps, given time . . ."

She nodded quickly, wanting him to stop.

"I thought this is what you wanted," he said after a long silence.

"It is. I don't want him to suffer any more than he already has."

"What about you?" he asked gently. "What about your suffering?"

He'd tried to convince her to go to Theo. "He trusts you," he'd insisted as she lay recovering, too weak to make him stop talking. "He knows you. When I first met Theo, I thought him just a passing fancy." He didn't say he'd wanted her to be with Flint instead, but she knew he had. "But love—*true* love—is all too rare for us," he went on. "Don't throw it away." He urged her to tell Theo how she'd swum to Governors Island and found Flint, how they'd hailed the motorboat and escaped with the others back to Manhattan. How they'd dropped the dogs back at an adoption agency, then holed up in the hotel with a homeless woman and her can collection while they recovered their strength.

But she'd refused.

She'd thought when she saw Theo in his golden cap and flashing sword that maybe there could be a future for them. But then he'd almost died. *Again.* She'd saved him, but it would just be a matter of time before she couldn't.

Already, Dash—or Scooter, as he now called himself—had reported that the police had found only three bodies on the charred torch. They had to assume Saturn was still alive, and likely headed to Greece to chase down Zeus, his final target, with the help of the cult's other branches. He would have to be stopped.

Flint would come with her. She knew that for a certainty. She'd known it the moment she'd ripped free of his golden net.

When Flint's whip had transformed into a javelin, she'd finally been able to decipher the pictures etched into the gold. A single, continuous story spiraled its length. Artemis's story. Her birth on the island of Delos. Sunlit days dancing at her brother's side on the crest of Mount Kynthos with her mother's smile to lift their song. Moonlit nights running wild across the groves of Attica with her nymphs beside her. And more. Diana, presiding over her temple outside Rome, then haunting its shattered remains as her acolytes turned to other gods. Wandering through Europe in the Diaspora, finding solace in the wild places. Then Phoebe Hautman crossing an ocean to Mana-hatta. Dianne Delia, watching a country spring to life. And so many others. Cynthia Forrester protecting her city from harm. Selene DiSilva walking the riverside. Alone.

Hephaestus had claimed he couldn't invent new divine weapons. When the necklace became a whip, she'd wondered at that. But when she'd seen the engravings, she knew he'd been working on it for millennia. The necklace wasn't new—and neither was his love for her.

Flint walked toward them down the path, his stride steady on new titanium braces but his body hunched against the just-healed wound on his stomach. She would let him love her. She would accept that gift from him, just as she'd accepted the necklace now lying against her collarbone. And in return, she'd found a space in her heart for him. Not a lover's place, not yet, but something nearly as precious and rare—a friend.

That night on the riverbank, not far from where Theo now sat huddled beneath his blanket with another woman at his side, Selene had opened herself to love. She couldn't close that door, not now.

Flint stood before her and held out an arm to help her to her feet. She was still weak. She looked older than she had before, but Flint didn't seem to mind. The lightning had carved a scar upon her chest. A ragged oval, like the outline of Apollo's laurel tree. It would not heal. She didn't want it to.

"We should get going," Flint said in a gravelly rumble as she gently removed her hand from his. "Phil, your flight to Paris leaves in two hours. And Scooter said we can catch a flight to Athens that leaves later tonight." He looked meaningfully at his stepsister. "He just needs to know what name to put on your passport."

She didn't answer. Philippe packed his small bow into a satchel and slung it across his shoulder. Her own bow—recovered by Scooter, the Giver of Good Things, as he ran from the Statue of Liberty—was already packed beside Flint's hammer, ready for their flight across the ocean.

She turned to look over the wall and down to the riverside. The top of Theo's head leaned just an inch closer to Ruth's than it had before. She opened her mouth, desperate to shout his name. Wanting him to turn around so she could see his face one more time. Instead, it was Hippo who tasted the air, then leaped to her feet and turned toward her mistress, tail wagging furiously. Theo twisted around to look in the direction of Hippo's sniffing.

For an instant, she saw his face. Pointed chin, floppy hair, haunted eyes. A mouth whose taste she still remembered on her lips. She stepped out of sight before he could see her.

Good-bye, my hero, my love.

Flint was waiting for her. As they walked, she said, "Tell Scooter that Selene DiSilva is dead. Tell him Selene Aidnos is going to Athens."

Philippe frowned at her. "Aidnos? Like Greek for 'darkness'? So depressing…"

"How about Neomenia, instead?" offered Flint, his voice gentler than she'd ever heard it.

Selene Neomenia. Selene, goddess of the New Moon. Darkness that grows once more into light.

"I like it."

She couldn't smile, not yet, but she knew that someday, she would.

Author's Note

Mithraism flourished in the Roman Empire between the first and fourth centuries, around the same time that the new religion of Christianity began its ascent. An all-male Mystery Cult, Mithraism spread as far afield as England, carried there by members of the Roman legions as they conquered the world. The seven major ranks of initiates as described in *Winter of the Gods* are all depicted in numerous surviving mosaics and frescoes. Only one ancient source, however, mentions the female Hyaena. If she ever existed, she has been largely forgotten; I couldn't resist giving her a life of her own.

Scholars estimate that hundreds, perhaps thousands, of mithraea existed across the Roman Empire. Today, the remains of some of those secret temples are easily accessible to the public, such as the chamber beneath the Basilica of San Clemente in Rome or the sixteen mithraea still extant in the nearby archeological site of Ostia Antica. Others are open only one day a month by reservation, such as the spectacular remains beneath the Church of Santa Prisca. For a comprehensive database, with images included, of Mithraic artifacts and temples, check out mithraeum.eu. My website, jordannamaxbrodsky.com, contains a collection of photos from the sites I've personally visited.

The bull-killing scene, or tauroctony, exists in nearly every Mithraic temple. Scholars have debated its meaning for a very long time. Franz Cumont, the cult's first modern interpreter, theorized that Mithras was merely a reinvention of the Persian god Mithra. Current scholars see Mithraism as a primarily Roman creation instead, but their explanations of the tauroctony vary. In 1991, David Ulansey presented a compelling, comprehensive interpretation of the tauroctony in *The Origins of the Mithraic Mysteries: Cosmology and Salvation in the Ancient World*. Theo and Minh's epiphanies about the shift of the equinoxes and the astronomical significance behind the tauroctony are based almost entirely on Ulansey's groundbreaking work. Apologies to him—and to all Mithraic scholars—for the simplifications and generalizations I've used to fit their theories into my work of fiction. If you'd like a more detailed understanding of the cult, you can read Ulansey's excellent articles at mysterium.com.

The connection between Mithras and Jesus proposed in *Winter of the Gods* is inspired by actual theories. The two figures do have a number of corresponding characteristics, such as participating in a ritual feast, ascending to heaven, and an association with the sun. These similarities have led some academics over the years to theorize that early Christians may have been highly influenced by Mithraism. Some conspiracy theorists have latched on to this correlation and decided that Christianity is no more than an imitation of this "pagan" rite. However, most current scholars maintain that the religions' similarities arose because they evolved in the same era with the same influences, rather than due to any direct interaction. Since we will never know the full extent of the connection between the two religions, there remains plenty of room for a novelist's imagination.

The Piacenza liver is real, its inscriptions referring either to the Etruscan gods or to astronomical charts. Most scholars agree that its primary use was as a teaching tool for haruspicy, but don't get too excited—its secrets are so deeply buried by time that it's not about to reveal any earth-shattering omens.

While I've taken licenses with the landscape of classical scholarship, I've tried to remain as true as possible to the geography of New York. All the locations (with the exceptions of the underground mithraeum and the bootlegger's tunnel beneath Selene's house) are real. Anyone can (and should) visit the Earth Rose and Space Center, the Prometheus and Atlas statues, and the breathtaking Top of the Rock observation deck. Brunch at the Rainbow Room will cost you a small fortune, but the views are indeed spectacular—and so are the poached eggs. Although illegal to enter, an Amtrak tunnel runs down the West Side to Penn Station (as many of the city's more intrepid urban explorers can attest). Governors Island is as described—except for Mars's lair beneath Castle Williams, which is wholly fictional. North Brother Island, now an inaccessible bird sanctuary, was indeed a quarantine hospital and the site of the wreck of the *General Slocum*. Check out the fascinating RadioLab episode "Patient Zero" and photos of the island at radiolab.org. For images of the derelict hotel that houses Flint's forge, read Pablo Maurer's article, "Abandoned NY: Inside Grossinger's Crumbling Catskill Resort Hotel" on gothamist.com. And if you want to know more about the War of 1812 blockhouse, head to the northwest corner of Central Park or see photos of it on my website.

Since 9/11, you need a reservation to get into the Statue of Liberty's crown—often made months in advance. From inside, New York's Colossus seems both more intimate and more impressive: a thin sheet of copper folded into the visage of a deity. If *Winter of the Gods* has whetted your appetite for getting inside the head of a goddess, I suggest you make the trip to Liberty Island for yourself. Gazing out the windows of the crown at Lower Manhattan, towering far above the harbor, you feel divine indeed.

Jordanna Max Brodsky
New York, NY
July 2016

APPENDIX

Olympians and Other Immortals

Roman names follow the Greek, along with traditional astronomical symbols where applicable. Note that the ancients knew of only five planets, thus only their symbols have been included.

Aphrodite/Venus ♀: Goddess of Erotic Love and Beauty. One of the Twelve Olympians. Born of sea foam after Kronos castrates his father, Ouranos, and throws his genitals into the ocean. Wife of Hephaestus and lover of Ares. Called Laughter-Loving. Attributes: dove, scallop shell, mirror.

Apollo/Apollo: God of Light, Music, Healing, Prophecy, Poetry, Archery, Civilization, Plague, and the Sun. One of the Twelve Olympians. Leader of the Muses. Twin brother of Artemis. Son of Leto and Zeus. Born on the island of Delos. Called Phoebus ("Bright One"). Attributes: silver bow, laurel wreath, lyre. Modern alias: Paul Solson.

Ares/Mars ♂: God of War, Bloodlust, and Manly Courage. One of the Twelve Olympians. Son of Zeus and Hera. Lover of Aphrodite. Often considered the father of Eros. Called Man-Slayer, Battle-Insatiate. Attributes: armor, spear, poisonous serpent. Modern alias: Martin Bell.

Artemis/Diana: Goddess of the Wilderness, the Hunt, Virginity, Wild Animals, Hounds, Young Children, and the Moon. One of the Twelve Olympians. Twin sister of Apollo. Daughter of Leto and Zeus. Born on the island of Delos. Called Phoebe, Cynthia. Has many epithets including Huntress, Swiftly Bounding, Protector of the Innocent, and more. Attributes: golden bow, hounds. Modern aliases: Phoebe Hautman, Dianne Delia, Cynthia Forrester, Selene DiSilva, and more.

Asclepius/Aesculapius: Hero-God of Medicine. Son of Apollo and the mortal princess Coronis. Worshiped in the Eleusinian Mysteries and many other cults. Attribute: a snake-twined staff.

Athena/Minerva: Goddess of Wisdom, Crafts, and Justified War. One of the Twelve Olympians. Virgin. Attributes: helmet, shield, owl.

Atlas: Brother of Prometheus and leader of the Titans in the war against the Olympians. As punishment, Zeus condemned him to hold up the heavens on his shoulders for eternity. His name translates literally as "Endures." Attribute: celestial sphere.

Cybele/Magna Mater: The Great Mother, originally a primal nature deity from Asia Minor, later incorporated into the Greco-Roman pantheon. Mother of all gods, humans, and animals. Attributes: tall crown, lions.

Demeter/Ceres: Goddess of Grain and Agriculture. One of the Twelve Olympians. Daughter of Kronos and Rhea. Sister of Zeus. Mother of Persephone. Called Bountiful, Bringer of Seasons. Attributes: wheat sheaves, torch.

Dionysus/Bacchus: God of Wine, Wild Plants, Festivity, Theater. One of the Twelve Olympians. Son of Zeus and Semele, a mortal. Called Phallic, He Who Unties, He of the Wild Revels. Attributes: grape vine, thyrsus (a pinecone-tipped staff), leopard. Modern alias: Dennis Boivin.

Eris/Discordia: Goddess of Strife. Often considered a sister to Ares. She haunts battlefields, reveling in bloodshed.

Eros/Cupid: God of Love. Son of Aphrodite and Ares. Commonly portrayed as a winged infant, although sometimes as a youth. Attributes: wings, bow. Modern alias: Philippe Amata.

Gaia: Primeval Earth Divinity. Mother to all. Consort of Ouranos, the Sky.

Hades/Pluto: God of the Underworld, Death, and Wealth. Son of Kronos and Rhea. Brother of Zeus. Husband of Persephone. Called Receiver of Many, Lord of the Dead, Hidden One. Attributes: helm of invisibility, bird-tipped scepter. Modern alias: Aiden McKelvey.

Hecate: Goddess of Crossroads, Dark Magic, Night, and the Moon. Sometimes identified as an aspect of Artemis. Often portrayed as a three-faced goddess or, occasionally, as a maiden in hunting attire. Called Lady of the Underworld, Night-Wandering, Terrible One. Attributes: two torches.

Helios/Sol/Sol Invictus ☉: God and embodiment of the Sun. Also identified with Apollo, who has dominion over the sun. The Romans revered him as Sol Invictus, the "Invincible Sun," and celebrated his birthday on December 25. Attributes: seven-rayed crown.

Hephaestus/Vulcan: God of the Forge, Fire, and Volcanoes. One of the Twelve Olympians. Son of Hera, born parthenogenically. Lamed when thrown off Olympus by Zeus, walks with a crutch. Called the Smith, the Sooty God, He of Many Arts and Skills, Lame One. Attributes: hammer, tongs. Modern alias: Flint Hamernik.

Hera/Juno: Queen of the Gods. Goddess of Women, Marriage, and the Heavens. One of the Twelve Olympians. Daughter of Kronos and Rhea. Sister and jealous wife of Zeus. Mother of Ares and Hephaestus. Known as "white-armed." Attributes: crown, peacock, lotus-tipped staff.

Hermes/Mercury ☿: God of Thieves, Liars, Travel, Communication, Hospitality, Eloquence, and Athletics. One of the Twelve Olympians. Son of Zeus and a nymph, Maya. Herald to the gods. Called Messenger, Giver of Good Things, Trickster, Dissembler, Many-Turning, Busy One. Attributes: caduceus (staff twined with snakes), winged sandals, winged cap. Modern alias: Dash Mercer.

Hestia/Vesta: Goddess of the Hearth and Home. Eldest daughter of Kronos and Rhea. Sister of Zeus. Virgin. Once one of the Twelve Olympians, but gave up her throne to Dionysus.

She tended the sacred fire at the center of Mount Olympus. Called "The Eldest." Attributes: veil, kettle.

Isis: Egyptian Goddess of Motherhood, Magic, and Nature, later adopted by the Greco-Roman world. Temples to Isis were often built on the sites of earlier sanctuaries dedicated to Diana or Ceres. Attribute: throne headdress.

Khaos: Primeval embodiment of Chaos. From the same root as "chasm," the name means the void from which all other primeval divinities sprang.

Kronos/Saturn ♄: A Titan. With the help of his mother, Gaia (the Earth), he overthrew his father, Ouranos (the Sky), to become King of the Gods until overthrown in turn by Zeus, his son. Father/grandfather of the Olympians. Also identified as the God of Time. Called "the Wily." In Roman mythology, Saturn is also an ancient agricultural god who guarantees good harvests. He was thought to preside over Elysium, the home of the blessed dead. His yearly festival, Saturnalia, held from December 17 to 23, involved public feasting and revelry. Attribute: sickle.

Leto/Latona: Goddess of Motherhood and Modesty. Daughter of the Titans Phoibe and Koios. Lover of Zeus. Mother of Artemis and Apollo. Called "neat-ankled," Gentle Goddess, Mother of Twins. Attributes: veil, date palm. Modern alias: Leticia Delos.

Mithras: God worshiped by a Mystery Cult during the late Roman era, especially popular with soldiers in the Roman legion. Epithets include Sol Invictus. Attributes: Phrygian cap, Persian pants, bull.

Morpheus: God of Dreams. As a messenger of the gods, he sends prophetic dreams to mortals. Attributes: wings, poppy crown.

Orion: Son of Poseidon and a mortal woman. Artemis's only male hunting companion. Some tales describe him as blinded and exiled after raping Merope, a king's daughter. Other myths say he raped one of Artemis's nymphs and was killed either by a scorpion or by Artemis's arrows. Placed as a constellation in the sky. Called the Hunter. Modern alias: Everett Halloran.

Ouranos/Uranus: Primeval Sky Divinity. Father of the Titans. Castrated by his son Kronos/Saturn.

Persephone/Proserpina: Goddess of Spring and the Underworld. Daughter of Demeter and Zeus. Wife of Hades. Called Kore ("Maiden"), Discreet, Lovely. Attributes: wheat sheaves, torch. Modern alias: Cora McKelvey.

Poseidon/Neptune: God of the Sea, Earthquakes, and Horses. One of the Twelve Olympians. Son of Kronos and Rhea. Brother of Zeus. Father of Orion, Theseus, and other heroes. Called "blue-haired," Earth-Shaker, Horse-Tender. Attribute: trident.

Prometheus: A Titan. His name translates literally as "Forethought." After molding mankind from clay and granting them life, he gave them fire—despite Zeus's prohibition. As punishment, the Olympians chained him to a rock and sent an eagle to eat his liver every day for eternity. Later, he was freed from his torment by the hero Heracles. Called Fire-Bringer, Lofty-Minded, Chained One. Attribute: fennel stalk of fire.

Rhea/Ops: A Titan. Goddess of Female Fertility. Queen of the Gods in the Age of Titans. Helped Zeus, her youngest son, overthrow his father, Kronos.

Selene/Luna ☾: Goddess and embodiment of the Moon. While Artemis has dominion over the moon, Selene is the Moon incarnate.

Serapis: Greco-Egyptian God of Fertility and the Afterlife, later adopted by the Romans. Attribute: basket crown.

Zeus/Jupiter ♃: King and Father of the Gods. God of the Sky, Lightning, Weather, Law, and Fate. One of the Twelve Olympians. Youngest son of Kronos and Rhea. After Kronos swallowed his first five children, Rhea hid baby Zeus in the Cave of Psychro. After coming to manhood, Zeus cut his siblings from his father's gullet, defeated the Titans, and began the reign of the Olympians. He divided the world with his two brothers, taking the Sky for himself. Husband (and brother) of Hera, but lover of many. Father of untold gods, goddesses, and heroes, including Artemis, Apollo, Hermes, Ares, Dionysus, and Athena. Attributes: lightning bolt, eagle, royal scepter.

GLOSSARY OF GREEK AND LATIN TERMS

Athanatos (pl. Athanatoi): "One Who Does Not Die" (an immortal)

Caduceus: a snake-twined staff, the symbol of Hermes/Mercury

Corvus: a crow or raven

Haruspex: one who performs haruspicy, the art of reading omens in animal entrails

Heliodromus (pl. Heliodromi): Sun-Runner

Hemitheos (pl. hemitheoi): a half god, half mortal

Leo (pl. Leones): a lion

Makarites (pl. Makaritai): "Blessed One"

Miles (pl. Milites): a soldier

Mithraeum (pl. mithraea): a sanctuary dedicated to Mithras

Nymphus: a male bride

Pater Patrum: Father of Fathers

Perses (pl. Persae): a Persian

Pneuma: breath, air, or spirit

Praenuntius: harbinger, omen-bringer

Syndexios (pl. syndexioi): "joining of the right hands" (one who knows the secret handshake)

Thanatos (pl. thanatoi): "one who dies" (a mortal)

GLOSSARY OF GREEK AND LATIN TERMS

ACKNOWLEDGMENTS

When asked to write the second book of *Olympus Bound* in less than a year, I almost had a heart attack. Only through the support of so many wonderful friends and colleagues did I manage what was, to an inveterate procrastinator, a feat of Herculean proportions.

Helen Shaw, the great friend to whom this book is dedicated, first introduced me to Mithraism, and her ideas continued to shape the book until the very last draft. There is no authorial conundrum too great or too small that she can't solve it on a thirty-minute train ride from Westchester. Tegan Tigani, my role model for selflessness and dedication for the past thirty years, provided not only invaluable feedback but also much-needed enthusiasm throughout the process. Sharing my writing with her is one of the giddiest joys of my life. John Wray and Madeleine Osborn both scoured every line, sharing their advice and ideas with unstinting generosity. The brilliant Chad Mills contributed his keen eye to proofreading.

Perennial thanks to Devi Pillai at Orbit for her excellent editorial insights and for shepherding the entire *Olympus Bound* series forward with such care. To everyone else at Orbit, including Lindsey Hall, Kelly O'Connor, Ellen Wright, Kirk Benshoff, Alex Lencicki, Andy Swist, Anne Clarke, and Tim Holman, thanks as always for your talent, humor, and hard work. I owe a special debt to Tommy Harron for trusting me with the audio-book and making its recording such an unalloyed pleasure.

My career as a novelist would not be possible without the faith of my agent, Jennifer Joel, who has stuck with me for more years than I care to admit. She has my undying gratitude.

Dr. Anne Shaw and Dr. Michael Shaw once more graciously provided invaluable help with Greek and Latin usage throughout the book. Mike Shaver of the National Park Service confirmed that, yes, the nineteenth-century cannon on Governors Island could hit the Statue of Liberty (or Washington Square Park, for that matter). Eliot Schrefer and Eric Zahler kindly checked over Philippe's French, and Matthew Anderson helped out with the more prurient Latin. Any errors in the book are fully of my own making, not theirs. A heartfelt thank-you to Yvonne Rathbone, who allowed me to excerpt her beautiful translation of Calli-machus's *Hymn to Artemis*.

To my friends and family, who put up with a year's worth of authorial obsession, thank you for your patience and support. Venturing into this new world was only possible because I had the Brodskys, the Millses, Jac, Jake, Emily, Ben, Dusty, and Jim at my back. If this book gives you even the smallest fraction of the enjoyment that you have brought to my life over the years, I will consider it a success.

And to Jason Mills, my husband, who read the entire manu-script more times than any one man should have to bear (nev-er failing to offer both advice and admiration at just the right time), who scoured the museums of Rome with his camera in tow, who carried me over mountains both literal and figurative, and who patiently sweated through every mithraeum in Ostia Antica: Thank you. Yours is the song stitched across my heart.

extras

www.orbitbooks.net

about the author

Jordanna Max Brodsky hails from Virginia, where she spent four years at a science and technology high school pretending it was a theatre conservatory. She holds a degree in history and literature from Harvard University. When she's not wandering the forests of Maine, she lives in Manhattan with her husband. She often sees goddesses in Central Park and wishes she were one.

Find out more about Jordanna Max Brodsky and other Orbit authors by registering for the free monthly newsletter at www.orbitbooks.net

if you enjoyed
WINTER OF THE GODS

look out for

CHASING EMBERS

by

James Bennett

Behind every myth there is a spark of truth . . .

There's nothing special about Ben Garston. He's just a guy with an attitude in a beaten-up leather jacket, drowning his sorrows about his ex in a local bar.

Or so he'd have you believe.

What Ben Garston can't let you know is that he's also known as Red Ben. He can't let you know that the world of myth and legend isn't as make-believe as you think, and it's his job to keep that a secret. And there's no way he can let you know what's really hiding beneath his skin . . .

But not even Ben knows what kind of hell is about to break loose. Because the delicate balance between his world and ours is about to be shattered.

Something's been hiding in the heart of the city –
and it's about to be unleashed.

if you enjoyed

WINTER OF THE GODS

look out for

CHASING EMBERS

by

James Bennett

ONE

East Village, New York

Once upon a time, there was a happy-ever-after. Or at least a shot at one.

Red Ben Garston sat at the bar, cradling his JD and Coke and trying to ignore the whispers of the past. The whiskey, however, was fanning the flames. Rain wept against the window, pouring down the large square of dirty glass that looked out on the blurred and hurrying pedestrians, the tall grey buildings and sleek yellow taxicabs. The TV in the corner, balanced on a shelf over the bar's few damp customers, was only a muffled drone. Ben watched the evening news to a background of murmured chatter and soft rock music. Economic slump to the Eagles. War in Iran to the Boss. The jukebox wasn't nearly loud enough, and that was part of the problem. Ben could still hear himself think.

Once upon a time, once upon a time . . .

He took a swig and placed the tumbler on the bar before him, calling out for another. The bartender arrived, a young man in apron and glasses. The man arched an evaluating eyebrow, then sighed, poured and left the whole bottle. Ben could drink his weight in gold, but Legends had yet to see him fall down drunk, so the staff were generally tolerant. 7 East 7th Street was neither as well appointed nor as popular as some of the bars in the neighbourhood, verging on the dive side of affairs, but it was quiet on weekdays around dusk, and Red Ben drank here for that very reason. He didn't like strangers. Didn't like attention. He just wanted somewhere to sit, drink and forget about the past.

Still Rose was on his mind, just as she always was.

The TV over the bar droned on. The drought in Africa limped across the screen, some report about worsening conditions and hijacked aid trucks. Strange storms that spat lightning but never any rain. What was up with the weather these days, anyway? Then the usual tableau of sand, flies and starving children, their bellies bloated by hunger, their eyes dulled by need. Technicolor pixelated death.

Immunised by the ceaseless barrage of doom-laden media, Ben looked away, scanning the customers who shared the place with him: a man slouched further along the bar, three sat in a gloomy booth, one umming and ahhing over the jukebox at the back of the room, all of them nondescript in damp raincoats and washed-out faces. Ghosts of New York, drowning their sorrows. Ben wanted to belong among them, but he knew he would always stand out, a broad-shouldered beast of a man, the tumbler almost a thimble in his hand. His leather jacket was beaten and frayed. Red stubble covered his jaw, rising via scruffy sideburns to an unkempt pyre on his head. He liked to think there was a pinch of Josh Homme about him – Josh Homme on steroids – maybe a dash of Cagney. Who was he kidding? These days, he suspected he looked more like the other customers than he'd care to admit, let alone a rock star. Drink and despair had diluted his looks. No wonder Rose didn't want to see him. And in the end his general appearance, a man in his early thirties, was only a clever lie. His true age travelled in his eyes, caves that glimmered green in their depths and held a thousand secrets . . .

That lie had always been the problem. Since his return to New York from a six-week assignment in Spain, his former lover wouldn't answer his calls or reply to his emails. When he called round her Brooklyn apartment, only silence answered the buzzer on the ground floor. Sure, he'd hardly been the mild-mannered Englishman, leaving her high and dry, dropping everything to run off on the De Luca job.

And it wasn't as if he needed the money. He'd been around a long time. He got bored. He got restless. He *went into his cave*, as Rose would've put it. The jobs were a way of keeping in shape, and of course, his choice of clientele meant that no one was going to ask too many questions. Now he was paying the price for this diversion. A week back in the city and Rose was another ghost to him.

But once upon a time, once upon a time, when you didn't ask questions and I could pretend, we were madly in love.

Outside, the rain lashing the window, and inside, the rain lashing his heart. April in Insomniac City was a lonely place to be. Ben took another slug of Jack, swallowed another bittersweet memory.

A motorbike growled up outside the bar. The customers turned to look. Exhaust fumes mingled with the scent of liquor as the door swung wide and the rain blew in – with it, a man. The door creaked shut. The man was dressed completely in black, his riding leathers shiny and wet. His boots pounded on the floorboards, then silenced as he stopped and surveyed the bar. His helmet visor was down, obscuring his face. A plume of feathers bristled along the top of the fibreglass dome, trailing down between his bullish shoulders. The bizarre gear marked him out as a Hell's Angel or a member of some other freeway cult. The long, narrow object strapped to his back, its cross-end poking up at the cobwebbed fans, promised a pointed challenge.

As the other customers lost interest, turning back to their chatter, peanuts and music, Ben was putting down his tumbler of Jack, swivelling on his stool and groaning wearily under his breath.

The man in the helmet saw him, shooting out a leather-gloved finger.

"Ben Garston! This game of hide-and-seek is over. I have some unfinished business with you."

Ben felt the eyes in the place twist back to him, a soft, furtive pressure on his spine. He placed a hand on his chest, a faux-yielding gesture.

"What can I say, Fulk? You found me."

The newcomer removed his helmet and thumped it down on the end of the bar. It rested there like a charred turkey, loose feathers fluttering to the floor. The man called Fulk grinned, a self-satisfied leer breaking through his shaggy black beard. Coupled with the curls falling to his shoulders, his head resembled a small, savage dog, ready to pounce from a thick leather pedestal.

"London. Paris. LA." Fulk named the cities of his search, each one a wasp flying from his mouth. Like Ben, his accent was British, but where Ben's held the clipped tones of a Londoner, the man in black's was faintly Welsh, a gruff rural borderland burr. Ben would have recognised it anywhere. "Where've you been hiding, snake?"

Ben shrugged. "Seems I've been wherever you're not."

Fulk indicated the half-empty glass on the bar. "Surprised you're not drinking milk. I know you have a taste for it. Milk, maidens and malt, eh? And other people's property."

"Ah, the Fitzwarren family wit." Through the soft blur of alcohol, Ben looked up at the six-and-a-half-foot hulk before him, openly sizing him up. What Fulk lacked in brains, he made up for in brawn. Win or lose, this was going to hurt.

The whiskey softened his tongue as well. He made a half-hearted stab at diplomacy. "You shouldn't be here, you know. The Pact—"

"Fuck the Pact. What's it to me?"

"It's the Lore, Fulk. Kill me, and the Guild'll make sure you never see that pile of moss-bound rubble you and your family call home again."

But Ben wasn't so sure about that. Whittington Castle, the crumbling ruins of a keep near Oswestry in Shropshire, was in the ancestral care of a trust. The same trust set up back in 1201 by King John and later bestowed on the Guild of the Broken Lance for safe keeping. The deeds to the castle would only pass back to the Fitzwarren estate when a certain provision was met, that being the death of Red Ben Garston, the last of his troublesome kind.

The last one *awake*, anyway. Of course, the Lore superseded that ancient clause. Technically, Ben was protected like all Remnants, but he knew that didn't matter to Fulk. The same way he knew that the man in front of him was far from the first to go by that name. Like the others before him, this latest Fulk would stop at nothing to get his hands on Whittington and reclaim the family honour, whether he risked the ire of the Guild or not. Vengeance ran in Fulk's bloodline, and his parents would have readied him for it since the day he was born.

"The Lore was made to be broken," Fulk Fitzwarren CDXII said. "Besides, don't you read the news? The Pact is null and void, Garston. You're not the only one any more."

"What the hell are you talking about?"

Before he could enquire further, the man in black unzipped his jacket, reached inside and retrieved a scrunched-up newspaper. He threw it on to the bar, next to Ben's elbow.

It was a copy of *The New York Times*. Today's evening edition. Warily lowering his eyes, Ben snatched it up and read the headline.

STAR OF EEBE STOLEN

Police baffled by exhibition theft

Last night person or persons unknown broke into the Nubian Footprints exhibition at the Javits Center, the noted exhibition hall on West 34th Street. The thieves made off with priceless diamond the Star of Eebe, currently on loan from the Museum of Antiquities, Cairo. Archaeologists claim that the fist-sized uncut gem came from a meteor that struck the African continent over 3,000 years ago. Legend has it that the Star fell into the possession of a sub-Saharan queen.

According to a source in the NYPD, the thieves were almost certainly a gang using high-tech equipment, improvised explosive devices and some kind of ultra-light airborne craft, a gyrocopter or delta plane. Around midnight last night, an explosion shook the Javits Center and the thieves managed to navigate the craft into Level 3, smashing through the famous 150-foot "crystal palace" lobby, alighting in the exhibition hall and evading several alarm systems to make off with the gem. The police believe the thieves took flight by way of another controlled explosion, fleeing through the Javits Center's western façade, out over 12th Avenue and the Hudson River, where police suspect they rendezvoused with a small ship headed out into the Bay, across to Weehawken or upriver to . . .

God knows where. Ben scanned the story, plucking the meat off printed bones. The details were sketchy at best. Between the lines, he summed them up. No fingerprints. No leads. No fucking clue.

The bar held its breath as he slapped the *Times* back down. No one spoke, no one chewed peanuts, no one selected songs on the jukebox. The rain drummed against the window. Four-wheeled fish swam past outside.

"Clever," Ben said. "But what does this have to do with me?"

"More than you'd like." Fulk grinned again, yellow dominoes lost in a rug. "You're reading your own death warrant."

"If this is a joke, I don't get it."

"No, you don't, do you?" The man in black shook his head. "I've travelled halfway around the world to face my nemesis, and all I find is a washed-up worm feeling sorry for himself in a bar. Is it because of your woman? Is that why you returned? She won't take you back, you know. Your kind and hers never mix well."

"You came here to advise me on my love life?"

Fulk laughed. "You're asleep, Red Ben. You've been asleep for *centuries*. The world holds no place for you now. You're a relic. You're trash. I only came here to sweep up the pieces."

"Yeah, your glorious quest." Ben rolled his eyes at their audience, the men sat in the booth, the guy with a palm full of peanuts frozen before his mouth, the one shuffling slowly away from the jukebox. "You need to get over it. Mordiford was a very long time ago."

A storm rumbled up over Fulk's brow, his deep-set eyes sinking even further into his head. Obviously it was the wrong thing to say. The ages-long river of bad blood that ran between Ben and House Fitzwarren was clearly as fresh to the man in black as it had been to his predecessors, perhaps even to the original Fulk, way back in the Middle Ages.

Muscles tense, Ben sighed and stood up, his stool scraping the floorboards. Despite his height rivalling the slayer's, he still felt horribly slight in Fulk's shadow. The whiskey could make you feel small too.

He didn't need this. Not now. He wanted to get back to the Jack and his heartbreak.

"It was yesterday to us," Fulk said, the claim escaping through gaps in his teeth. "We want our castle back. And Pact or no Pact, when we have it, your head will hang on our dining room wall."

The bartender, cringing behind the bar, guarded by bottles and plastic cocktail sticks, chose this moment to pipe up.

"Look, fellers, nobody wants any trouble. I suggest you take your beef outside, or do I have to call the—"

The sword Fulk drew from the scabbard on his back was a guillotine on the barman's words. The youth scuttled backwards, bottles and cocktail sticks crashing to the floor, panic greasing his heels. He joined the customers in a scrambling knot as they squeezed their bellies out of the booth, tangling with the other guys pushing past the jukebox to the fire exit at the back of the bar. In a shower of peanuts and dropped glasses, they were gone, the fire exit clanking open, a drunken stampede out into the rain.

Ben watched them leave in peripheral envy. He grimaced and rubbed his neck, a habit of his that betrayed his nerves. Then his whole attention focused on Fulk. Fulk and the ancient sword in his face. There was nothing friendly about that sword. They had met before, many times. Ben was on intimate terms with all fifty-five inches of the old family claymore. Back in the Middle Ages, the Scots had favoured the two-handed weapon in their border clashes with the English, and while this one's saw-toothed edge revealed its tremendous age, the blade held an anomalous sheen, the subtle glow informing Ben that more than a whetstone had sharpened the steel.

"Who're you having lunch with these days? The CROWS? That witchy business has a nasty habit of coming back to bite you on the arse." Ben measured these words with a long step backwards, creating some distance between the end of his nose and the tip of the sword. "House Fitzwarren must be getting desperate."

"We are honour-bound to slay our Enemy."

"Yeah, yeah. You're delusional, Fulk – or Pete or Steve or whatever your real name is. Your family hasn't owned Whittington Castle since the time of the Fourth Crusade, but you dog my heels from Mayfair to Manhattan, hoping to win a big gold star where hundreds of others have only won gravestones. And as for this," Ben nodded at the gleaming blade, "tut tut. Whatever would the Guild say?"

"I told you, snake. The Lore is broken. The Guild is over. And now, so are you."

The sword swung towards him, signalling the end of the conversation. The step Ben had taken came in handy; he leaned back just in time to avoid an unplanned haircut. The blade snapped over the bar, licking up the tumbler and the bottle of Jack, whiskey and glass spraying the floorboards.

Fulk grunted, recovering his balance. The weight of the claymore showed in his face. His leathers creaked as he lunged forward for another blow, the blade biting into beer-stained wood. Only air occupied the space where Ben had stood moments before, his quick grace belying his size as he swept up his bar stool and broke it over the man in black's head.

Cracked wood made a brief halo around Fulk's shoulders. His strap-on boots did a little tango and then steadied as he regained his balance, his shaggy mane shaking off the splinters. He grimaced, his teeth clenched with dull yellow effort. The sword came up, came down, scoring a line through shadow and sawdust, the heavy blade lodging in the floorboards.

The stroke dodged, Ben rushed through his own dance steps and elbowed Fulk in the neck. As the man choked and went down on one knee, Ben leapt for the bar, grabbing the plumed helmet and swinging it around, aiming for that wheezing, brutish head.

Metal kissed fibreglass, the sword knocking the helmet from Ben's grip. Sweat ran into his eyes as Fulk came up, roaring, and smacked him with the flat of the blade. If this had been an ordinary duel, Fulk might as well have hit a bear with a toothpick. The Fitzwarrens' attempts to slay their Enemy had always remained unfairly balanced in Ben's favour, and over the years he had grown complacent, the attacks an annoyance rather than a threat. Now his complacency caught him off guard. This was no ordinary duel. Resistant to magic as he was, bewitched steel was bewitched steel, and the ground blurred under his feet moments before his spine met the jukebox. The air flew out of his lungs even as it flew into Jimi Hendrix's, a scratchy version of "Fire" stuttering into the gloomy space.

The song was one of Ben's favourites, but he found it hard to appreciate under the circumstances. He groaned, trying to pull himself up. Stilettos marched up and down his back. His buttocks ached under his jeans. He tasted blood in his mouth, along with a sour, sulphurous tang, a quiet belch that helped him to his feet, his eyes flaring.

Across the bar, Fulk's eyebrows were arcs of amusement.

"Finally waking up, are we? It's too late, Garston." The man in black stomped over to where Ben stood, swaying like a bulrush in a breeze. "Seems like my granny was wrong. She always said to let sleeping dogs lie."

Fulk shrugged, dismissing the matter. Then he brought the sword down on Ben's skull.

Or tried to. Ben raised an arm, shielding his head, and the

blade sliced into his jacket, cutting through leather, flesh and down to the bone, where it stuck like a knife in frozen butter. Blood wove a pattern across the floorboards, speckling his jeans and Doc Martens. They weren't cheap, those shoes, and Ben wasn't happy about it.

When he exhaled, a long-suffering, pained snort, the air grew a little hot, a little smoky. He met Fulk's gaze, waiting for the first glimmers of doubt to douse the man's burgeoning triumph. As Fulk's beard parted in a question, Ben reached up with his free hand and gripped the blade protruding from his flesh. The rip in his jacket grew wider, the seams straining and popping, the muscle bulging underneath. The exposed flesh rippled around the wound, shining with the hint of some tougher substance, hard, crimson and sleek, plated neatly in heart-shaped rows, one over the over. The sight lasted only a second, long enough for Ben to wrench the claymore out of his forearm.

Hendrix climaxed in a roll of drums and a whine of feedback. The blood stopped dripping random patterns on the floor. The lips of Ben's wound resealed like a kiss and his arm was just an arm again, human, healed and held before his chest.

"Your antique can hurt me, but have you got all day?" Ben forced a smile, a humourless rictus. "That's what you'll need, because I'm charmed too, remember? And as for my head, I'm kind of attached to it."

Flummoxed, Fulk opened his mouth to speak. Ben's fist forced the words down his throat before he had the chance. The slayer's face crumpled, and then he was flying backwards, over the bloody floor, past the bar with its broken bottles, out through the dirty square window that guarded Legends from the daylight.

Silvery spears flashed through the rain. Teeth and glass tinkled on asphalt. Tyres screeched. Horns honked. East 7th Street slowed to a crawl as a man dressed head to toe in black leather landed in the road.

Somewhere in the distance, sirens wailed. Ben retrieved the

newspaper from the bar, thinking now was perhaps a good time to leave. As he stepped through the shattered window, he could tell that the cops were heading this way, the bartender making good on his threat. Who could blame him? Thanks to this lump sprawled in the road, the month's takings would probably go on repairs.

Stuffing the *Times* into his jacket, the rain hissing off his cooling shoulders, Ben crunched over to where Fulk lay, a giant groaning on a bed of crystal. He bent down, rummaging in the dazed man's pockets. Then he clutched the slayer's beard and pulled his face towards his own.

"And by the way, it isn't sleeping dogs, Fulk," he told him. "It's *dragons*."

Then he took flight into the city.